PIGS

John Henry Bennett

SUNDRY DEFINITIONS

'PIG'

Definitions: Concise Oxford English Dictionary

1. Noun: an omnivorous, domesticated hoofed mammal with sparse, bristly hair and a flat snout; kept for its meat.

2. Informal (derogatory): a greedy, dirty or unpleasant person.

3. Engineering: a device which fits snugly inside an oil or gas pipeline, and is sent through it to clean or test the inside, or to act as a barrier.

Secret Intelligence Service SIS(MI6) .

Collects Britain's foreign intelligence and provides a global covert capability to protect and defend national security of the UK.

Security Service (MI5)

Britain's intelligence agency protecting the UK's national security against threats such as terrorism and espionage.

[Note: International Time: Time of the day is always local time.
Readers should remember that the Gulf countries can be 2, 3 or 4 hours ahead of UK time.]

PROLOGUE

(Source; Daily Telegraph, Monday 12th December 2005).

06.00 hrs. Sunday,11th December 2005. Buncefield, Hertfordshire.

It was unusual for Fred Mills to rise early on a Sunday, but on this particular morning he did, and was starting to make a cup of tea for himself and his wife, Elizabeth. They had lived in their rented cottage for forty years and only recently decided to sleep downstairs due to age and convenience.

As he opened the fridge door at 6 a.m. the blast destroyed the roof of the cottage.

An explosion, measuring 2.4 on the Richter scale, tore through the Buncefield depot.

A 300-foot high fireball shot into the sky and the blast was heard 100 miles away.

The oil depot could hold 16 million gallons of oil, petrol and paraffin (when full) but today, thankfully, only 7.7 million gallons of fuel were in place, representing 5% of the UK's fuel stocks.

A cloud of black, oily smoke developed, eventually some 150 miles wide, covering Southern England.

650 fire fighters struggled for 60 hours to control, what some described, as Armageddon.

The Hertfordshire Oil Storage Terminal (HOSL - Hertfordshire Oil Storage Ltd), generally known as the Buncefield complex, was the fifth largest oil-products storage depot in the UK, with a capacity of approximately 60 million Imperial gallons (273 million litres) of fuel, although it was not always filled. This was approximately 5% of UK oil storage capacity. It was a major hub on the UK's oil pipeline network (UKOP) with pipelines to Humberside and Merseyside and is an important fuel source to the British aviation industry, providing aircraft fuel for local airports including London Gatwick, London Heathrow and Luton airports. Approximately half of the complex is dedicated to the storage of aviation fuel. The remainder of the complex stores petrol and diesel fuel for petrol stations across much of the South-East of England. The terminal is owned by TOTAL UK Limited (60%) and Texaco 40%.The seat of the fire, and the worst damaged section, was 'HOSL West', used by Total and Texaco to store a variety of fuels, and the neighbouring British Pipeline Agency area.

I

Monday 12th December 2005

1000hrs. Whitehall

The Minister smashed his fist onto the desk.
'I want a blanket ban on all reporting from this department unless it has been personally approved by me. Is that clearly understood? No exceptions, not even the PM.'
'I want a situation report from the senior officers currently on site to me personally by 14.00hrs.'
'Meeting over.'
The senior civil servants and party advisers hurried out of the office well aware that in such situations questions were not what the Minister wanted. Just answers, or

alternatively, a head or heads that would roll as a result. The PM was credited as 'Teflon Tony' but this Minister had taught him practically every trick in the book. He'd survived numerous bloodlettings and purges over the years as they desperately fought for power and when it came he had been suitably rewarded.

Never once in his wildest dreams or scenarios had he imagined that such a disaster would befall the government or his department, despite repeated warnings, both official and unofficial, that the country's infrastructure was near break or meltdown, due to lack of sufficient investment both in structure and security.

The Minister's mind was racing round various reasons, outcomes and responsibilities and where he might apportion blame to minimise the impact on his own department.

As he sat at his desk he started to compile a list.

Oil Companies…Safety records…negligence…profit driven.

He would have to be careful on this. Huge tax revenues from these companies. Be careful to keep them on side. After office, comfortable Non – Executive Director appointments may be jeopardised.

Health & Safety. Yes, but too close to home.

But, Health and Safety at the plant. Maintenance and negligence. Could that be assumed or proven?

He slowly built his list, motivated by a gut survival instinct developed over many years. He would naturally express sincere public concern, horror and outrage at the event and insist that no stone would be left unturned in the pursuit of justice for the victims and where ultimate responsibility should lay. 'Lessons would be learned', 'Now we must move forward and put this behind us', 'Never again should such a tragedy occur', until the next time that is.

1400 hrs. Whitehall.

The senior Police Officer, Chief Superintendent James Bartholomew, and senior Fire Chief, Bill Masters stood with some trepidation outside the Ministers office. His fiery reputation was well known both in public and private and each knew that this was likely to be a robust encounter that could lead to early retirement or worse, if past events were any indication.

The door was opened and they entered quickly.

'Facts, gentlemen, facts. And I want them now'.

He spoke the words quietly but with the menace that they recognised.

'After the facts maybe I'll accept some brief theories.'

Police and Fire looked at each other and Fire took the lead.

'As of now we are fighting to contain the fire within the perimeter and we are increasing the number of firemen including specialists and appliances from neighbouring authorities so that we have sufficient resources. We have to identify and deal with the epicentre of the blaze, whilst at the same time cooling adjacent tanks and installations so that further explosions and fire are minimised.

The Minister shook his head vigorously.

'When is this going to be put out or properly contained?'

'I can't give you that answer right now Minister.'

'Well, when the f**k can you', he replied, allowing his northern shipyard roots to take over momentarily.

'Probably not for at least 48 hours, Minister', the Fire Chief replied, biting his tongue to stop himself suggesting that the Minister might visit the site to witness the size of the task.

Under spending had stretched the Fire Service, like so many, to the point where the ability to respond to a disaster such as this required coordinated cross regional teams in order to generate sufficient capacity and resource.

The Chief Superintendent interjected at this point in order to relieve some of the pressure on his colleague, by advising the Minister that local residents were being evacuated beyond the limit of the exclusion zone together with many of the small businesses in the industrial estates that were located around the perimeter of the depot.

The Minister was impatient and raised his voice.

'Damn all, so far, then!'

He continued,

'I'm now going to the House to make a brief holding statement, but I want some clear timescales by six o'clock this evening, as I will be giving an update on the evening news. I need as much background information, progress to date, expected time of containment, 1 day, 2 days, you know the sort of thing, and any input from the Health and safety Executive that will calm peoples fears. Got that?'

The Minister lowered his voice again. His gimlet unblinking eyes were fixed on them both.

'Now then. What happed, what caused this?'

Almost as one they responded, 'We don't know at his stage Minister.'

'Then I suggest you start investigating, pretty damn quick, otherwise I am going to have to find people who will. Do I make myself absolutely clear? 'They both nodded, looking quickly at each other, turned and left the Ministers office.The Minister slumped back in his chair, his aggression, for the present, spent.

'This is probably going to get a lot worse before it gets a lot better', he thought to himself as he poured himself a scotch. Never usually before 6 p.m., as a general rule, but today he would make an exception.

1600hrs. Hotel, Beirut, Lebanon.(local time).

'Salaam alekum, Alekum ma'salaam'

The Syrian and the Palestinian hugged and kissed and greeted each other in the fraternal way of all Arabs before sitting down at the table in the bedroom.

The Syrian poured the thick Arabic coffee and passed a cup to the Palestinian.

'My brother, God is great; we have struck a blow together for Allah!

The Palestinian smiled. 'A journey only starts with the first step. We have taken that step.'

'What next, my brother, in the fight against the American and British Kuffar?'

'We need to have a medium term strategy and more funding,' the Palestinian replied.

'The funding I can arrange but do we have the necessary experts and soldiers to carry out our plan?' questioned the Syrian.

The Palestinian then described at some length what elements had been pulled together in terms of funding, training, bribery, coercion, and murder in order 'to strike the first blow'.

In Arabic he joked about the pigs being killed by 'pigs' and the way it was done.

It had been determined by the Central Committee of Hezbollah that some major offensive should be mounted against the Americans or British in retaliation for their invasion of Iraq and Afghanistan, the killing of Muslims, seen throughout the Arab world as a direct attack on Islam.

Because of significantly tightened border security in the USA, the States was ruled out, but the UK, with highly porous borders and resident immigrants sympathetic to the cause, was considered a soft target in which to carry out the operation.

In order to have local knowledge, safe houses and a ready supply of recruits, mosques had been active in the war of words, spreading the message of 'divine mission', the Jihad, an absolute duty to create one united world of Islam.

At the same time several dummy runs were made across the Channel by low-level operatives to test the efficiency or inefficiency of so-called border controls. Light aircraft crossings from France and Holland also tested UK borders and found that illegal entry could be made at a number of small airfields with no proper checks, and carrying false EU passports bought with ease in London and major cities at about £400 each.

They laughed when thinking of the detailed checks and border controls in most Middle East countries and mocked the inability of the UK to counter their ease of entry.

They discovered that it was comparatively simple to access on the Internet the existing and proposed routes for natural gas and crude oil pipelines covering the whole of Europe, Russia, and extending down into the Middle East and Gulf.

Information is freely available concerning petrol, kerosene (jet fuel) and the distribution network throughout the UK.

Descriptions of the manufacture of explosives including 'dirty' nuclear devices were also readily available. Supply of radio-active material was difficult. However, as the Syrian commented, if Iran maintains its progress in the face of American and European threats, suitable material should be available in a few years.

The Palestinian described how one of their trained operatives had been introduced into the North East of England as a Lebanese Christian, being very western in appearance, handsome, culture and language, social activity, etc.

He had struck up a friendship with a local girl, who he had found out worked as a typist in the large, local refinery. Her brother was a plant operative involved in the batching of petrol, aviation fuel, etc, from a refinery on Humberside, down through the national pipeline grid that served various airports, docks, and distribution depots, including Buncefield.

Over the weeks and months the relationship developed, very easily, the Palestinian contemptuously describing with some graphic Arabic, descriptions of the girl involved.

The brother accepted the operative more slowly. However a few riotous weekends with friends in local pubs convinced him that the operative was thoroughly westernised.

The operative gradually obtained sufficient detail to put together a schedule of likely dates and volumes of fuel transported down the grid.

His friend, the girl friend's brother, liked to brag about his importance within the refinery, but the operative knew he was fairly low level, however, he was one of the team responsible for insertion of the 'pig' into the pipeline, to act as barrier between batches of different product.

Next, through some of the local 'jihadists', he was able to obtain the necessary explosives and timer that he would insert into the pig. He would have to calculate the speed at which the pig would travel down the pipeline so that the explosives would detonate with maximum effect within a storage depot.

Being a trained engineer, the operative was able, over a period of months, to obtain the necessary technical information from his friend as to the operation of the pig launcher.

On one dark cloudy night he carried in a rucksack the necessary plastic explosive, detonator and timer and made his way to the refinery. Enlarging an existing hole in the perimeter fence was comparatively easy and he made his way to the area of the pig launcher. He carefully placed the plastic explosive and timer within the pig so that the following morning the operatives would not see it as they dispatched a mixed batch of fuels down the line.

The calculations that the operative made were very accurate, the Palestinian explained, and the explosion at Buncefield caused maximum impact on the Kuffar Holy Day.

The Syrian smiled and indicated his respect for the operation.

'What happened to our operative?' he enquired.

'He has returned to the Bak'aa Valley and is currently training new operatives', was the response.

The Syrian suggested they work on a new operational plan for the UK, to swiftly follow up on their recent success.

The Palestinian had several ideas, some harebrained, but one in particular caught the imagination of the Syrian. He suggested that they pursue the detailed planning of that scheme in order for it to be presented to the Committee for approval and funding.

The Syrian listened carefully as the outline plan was fleshed out. Several things appealed to him.

It struck at the heart of UK democracy. It would be extremely high profile. It would garner world wide publicity. It would be a beautiful retribution to the Kuffar for their unjust Iraq and Afghanistan invasions.

It would take significant detailed planning and funding and a tight group of committed jihadists who may die in the attempt. But there was a steady stream of recruits willing to die for the cause. There would be no problem in that area.

At the end of his presentation the Palestinian asked the Syrian for his support and recommendation for funding. In his own mind the Syrian was convinced, but said he needed to consider certain elements before putting it before the council. The Palestinian demurred but hoped that 'god willing' he would be able to further God's work.

1600hrs. Hotel. Cyprus.

Harry Baxter was feeling thoroughly pissed off.

He had travelled to Cyprus to get some rest, after a combination of personal and professional frustrations, and did not require a loud mouthed and unruly family to disturb his personal battery re-charging.

He lay on his lounger by the pool and kept his eyes tight shut on the pretext of sleep, whilst mouthing mentally some obscenities that, in his opinion, summed up the family completely.

He was a middle ranking civil servant in the Secret Intelligence Service (MI6), age 47, unlikely to rise further up the greasy pole, probably due to a lack of political appreciation and a reluctance to crawl, plus a level of candour in observation that had made him some mild enemies on the promotion ladder.

The one thing he did have though was some hard won experience in the Middle East and Gulf, over a period of 25 years, and that was something they couldn't take away from him, or match.

The one advantage, he had, other than his Middle East experience, is that the powers that be couldn't pigeon hole him. He was a generalist, not a specialist.

The world was run by experts and specialists, which was probably why it was in such a god-awful mess, he thought.

He decided that what little warmth the sun gave at this time of year was spent, and as the children were continuing to be a complete pain in the arse, he gathered up his towel and went back to his room.

He switched on the television to be startled to see the dramatic pictures of the Buncefield disaster transmitted on BBC News 24.

'Jesus Christ', he exclaimed out loud. He listened carefully to the report until the information and commentary became repetitious.

He sat down, poured himself a beer, and thought carefully through what he had seen and heard.

The initial reporting was naturally highly speculative as to the cause of the disaster and reporters were not, at this stage, ruling out a terrorist attack, whilst indicating, at the same time, that there was no basis for their suggestion.

'Go on, why ruin a good story with the facts,' he thought to himself. His opinion of instant sound bite newscasters was only just below that of politicians, with their 'concerned' opinions, or policy 'on the hoof', direct to camera, on a daily basis.

1500hrs. Houses Of Parliament Westminster.

The Minister entered the House of Commons chamber and took his place immediately at the Dispatch Box.

'This House will be aware of the disaster that has occurred at Buncefield Oil Depot.

The Fire Services of several counties are presently engaged in bringing the conflagration under control. Maximum effort is being made by the Fire Services to control and prevent the spread to surrounding areas. Currently the line appears to be holding with containment within the storage depot.

I cannot give this House, at this time, the reason for this disaster but all Government Agencies will be involved in the full and thorough investigation which will commence once we have the various fires under control.

I can report that on first investigation it would appear that no fatalities have occurred although there has been widespread structural damage to many properties in the area as a result of the initial explosion.

I will report further to this House once more detailed facts are in my possession.

I cannot speculate as to the cause of the disaster and therefore will not take questions at this time in order that I may return to my office and continue with the overall co-ordination of the operation.'

He turned swiftly on his heel and left the Chamber to a cacophony of sound, representing the many questions being thrown at his departing back.

He felt quite pleased with his brief performance, including, concern, responsibility (some) and the impression of 'action man' in charge.

As he walked swiftly down the corridors in Westminster his mind was racing.

What the hell had caused this? Negligence? Terrorism? No potential threats had appeared on the weekly and sometimes daily intelligence briefings. However something could have slipped in under the radar as the SIS(MI6), at times, was working with both hands tied behind its back.

He would have to establish as soon as possible a Commission of Enquiry. Independent or HSE (Health & Safety Executive)?

The public would, quite rightly, be asking a lot of searching questions. They must be given the right sort of assurances and public panic must be avoided at all costs.

The terrorism aspect kept coming back into his mind and he wondered how they could have achieved this. That was irrelevant at present but would be a future threat and factor to consider.

As he entered his office he asked his PA to get the head of SIS(MI6) on the telephone.

His telephone rang after a few minutes. The head of SIS(MI6) sounded suitably concerned and cautious, being aware of the abrasive reputation of the Minister.

The Minister spoke quietly down the phone.

'Do we have any intelligence, however weak, that would indicate Buncefield is the result of a terrorist act? And before you answer, think carefully, because if it is proven that this was an act of terrorism, then I would suggest your tenure in your present position will not be long one.'

There followed a significant pause before the Head of SIS(MI6) responded.

'Minister, intelligence gathering, as you know is, is a slow painful process, requiring considerable analysis before credibility can be applied to a number of perceived risks.

Whilst our present resources are as limited as they are, and the penetration of various networks is hindered by the lack of suitable ethnic group recruits, I can only repeat what I said at the briefing with the PM last week. Currently we do not have confirmed intelligence information that would indicate over the last 12 months that an attack of this nature was planned.'

The Minister also paused before replying. When he did his voice rose to a soft crescendo.

'What you have just told me merely confirms my long held opinion of your organisation.'

The receiver crashed down on its rest.

The Minister then quickly left his office on his way to Number 10 to brief the Prime Minister of events to date and to prepare a statement for the evening news bulletins.

2000hrs London SW7.

The Minister's car turned into Onslow Gardens, South Kensington, and braked quickly to avoid a pedestrian who was belatedly crossing the street ahead of them. The Minister quietly cursed them in his Geordie accent, before wryly thinking that the second home allowance for MPs was a very good thing, enabling him to buy a splendid period apartment in one of the best areas of London, thereby avoiding hotels, and keeping his private life private.

After a brief conversation on his mobile with a department aide he stepped out of the car, confirming to his chauffeur his pick up time of 0630hrs the following morning for an interview at the BBC, timed for 0800hrs.

He had not noticed the nondescript VW Golf parked 50 yards up the street occupied by a man and woman who was now packing away her camera and telephoto lens.

'Did you get good ones?' the man asked. 'Of both of them', the woman replied, as the man engaged gear and moved up towards Old Brompton Road. His late street crossing earlier had enabled him to confirm the car was the Minister's.

He entered the building and took the lift to the first floor and entered his apartment without using his key.

She walked towards him, carrying a large Scotch and water.

'After today I expect you could use on of these' she said smiling up at him.

He didn't say anything but walked over to the armchair and sat down looking into middle distance. His mind was cluttered with all of the day's events and the near impossible task of determining priorities, actions, within a hugely confused scenario.

He looked up at her, a young woman of 38, who had started as a researcher for him whilst in opposition, who was now his Parliamentary PA, and lover.

His wife, in the North East, played no real part in his political life, that is, until election time, when for his safe seat purposes, she would be paraded to secure the female vote. His children were safely married and in secure local government positions in the North East, achieved by him exerting some gentle pressure, and apart from birthdays and Christmas played no part in his life

After thirty years of marriage the only real stimulus in his life was politics and the carefully constructed and protected affair that had been going on for four years with Anna Harrison.

'Opposites attract' he had thought on more than one occasion. He, quite blunt and a prickly chipper Northerner; she, Sussex born, Sussex University, attracted to power and influence, and the heady danger of an affair with a public figure.

2100 hrs SIS(MI6) London.

The digital photos were printed off and put into the file together with the action report and previous observations. The VW Golf driver went up two levels as he had been instructed to the Deputy's office.

He knocked.

'Enter' he was instructed.

The man sitting behind the desk was a 25 year veteran of the service who had reached the pinnacle of his career. There was no way he would get the top slot with his lack of political finesse or a reluctance to provide what his political masters often required to maintain their position on the rancid, greasy pole of politics.

The man handed over the file and the deputy glanced at the photos before scanning the action reports.

'How long has this observation been carried on for?'

'18 months in total.'

'Reason for initiation?'

'Possible security risk, infiltration, access to classified material and sketchy security clearance when woman was initially appointed researcher.'

'Current opinion?'

'Woman has key to apartment, relationship is certainly on a full working week basis, therefore opportunities for blackmail, classified information, etc, and obvious consequences.'

'How long is it thought she has been working for Mossad?'

'Minimum 8 years, on what evidence we have been able to find.'

'Right. Continue observation on 24/7 basis. Continue Phone taps on her apartment and mobile. Any variances, however slight, raise current code level and review.'

'Understood.'

He closed the door quietly behind him.

The Deputy read through the file again and then placed it in his secure cabinet equipped with a combination lock.

'Something useful for a rainy day if the Minister comes calling', he thought.

2300hrs.(local time) Hotel. Cyprus.

Harry Baxter woke from a fuzzy sleep and took the call on his bedroom phone, inwardly cursing the second bottle of local wine that was already making its presence felt.

'Yes, this is Harry Baxter, who's that?' he enquired.

A concerned voice at the other end identified himself as James Hertford, a similar level colleague in the Ministry.

'Harry, have you seen the news? The proverbial has hit the fan. Everybody is being recalled. You have to get back ASAP. No excuses. They want everybody to be available as they are not sure what we are really facing. I have to be brief on this open line. When can you get back?

'I've only been here three days. I've paid for ten. Who's going to pay for that?

'You'll have to argue that when you get back. When will you get back?

'As soon as I can, but you had better prep somebody re my tickets and cancelled leave. I'm not paying for myself due to this monumental cock-up.'

Tuesday 13th December 2005 0300hrs Onslow Gardens London SW.

The Minister could not sleep. Not even sex had brought that. He liked to be in control. In this situation he wasn't and he didn't like it. Get this wrong and his personal edifice would come crashing down. 'Teflon Tony' would throw him to the wolves as a carcass after he had been stripped bare. He didn't know what was coming next.

He mentally raced round the possibilities again.

A terrible accident? Terrorists? How to handle the fallout, whichever it was? If not an accident was this the first and when and where would the next occur? How to plan for that eventuality? What Intel was available and had something been overlooked? SIS(MI6) had been acting like a bunch of girls recently. Complaining about lack of funds, resources, etc. Any excuse to cover their backside.

At 0430hrs he got up to make a coffee as sleep was impossible. He started to think about the BBC interview. Those Oxbridge types posing questions whose sole intention is denigrate when nobody knows the answers yet. But it makes for 'incisive, investigative, and great TV reporting'. Anything for ratings, no matter the cost, as he recalled some of the media's actions during the Falklands campaign. 'Whose bloody side are they on?' he said at the time.

He scribbled some possible questions and answers on paper, then showered and dressed and was waiting for his driver at 0630 hrs on the morning of Monday the 13th December 2005.

0945hrs. Minister's Office Whitehall

The Minister arrived in his office spitting feathers. The BBC interview had been a disaster. He had been on the back foot all the way through and no amount of reasoned argument or excuse could counter the cynical questioning whose main thrust was that nobody knew what had really happened or why. His response that the authorities needed time to determine the cause of the accident or terrorist attack carried no weight as it was apparent that the Government and his Ministry in particular, had no real plans and resources to deal with either eventuality.

He called an immediate meeting of junior ministers and permanent civil servants.

The atmosphere could be cut with a knife.

He was at his quietest and deadliest.

'I trust I have your complete attention and make sure all your bloody mobiles are switched off.

We have a serious amount of investigation to be carried out and I don't want to hear about insufficient resources, lack of personnel, etc. Any leave is cancelled until further notice. There will be no exceptions.

We need to find out what has caused this catastrophe and why. Use your relationships across ministries to gather any intelligence that might help us nail this down.

Our collective professional lives are on the line, and metaphorically prisoners will not be taken, both externally and internally. Do I make myself clear?'

I want an agreed course of action by this ministry to be prepared, discussed, refined and presented to me by 1500hrs this afternoon. It should indicate the broad strategic approach plus at least three main areas of implementation. Any more than that and we will lose focus.

I will be giving a press conference at 1745hrs which will hit the evening TV news bulletins.

It will need to be tight, professional, credible and able to withstand scrutiny by our national media.

Any individual points can be raised by department heads to me at 1300hrs for clarification or agreement as to implementation, timescale or budget approvals.

'Have I made myself totally clear as to what is required?'

There was a subdued murmur of assent.

'Thank you gentlemen.'

This last phrase was a menacing whisper.

1130 hrs Deputy's Office SIS(MI6) London

Harry walked into the office at about 1130 hrs on December 13th to witness activity the like of which he had not seen since 9/11.

High levels of concentration (or worry, he thought) were clearly evident and he quickly made his way to his bosses' office.

Norman Spencer, the Deputy, was on his final furlong to retirement and he needed the current situation like the proverbial hole in the head.

'Sit down Harry, and listen.'

He quickly brought Harry up to speed, and then slumped back in his chair. He looked tired and spent.

Harry was silent for a minute and then the questions started to roll.

'No previous Intel indicated anything like this?'

'No.'

'No feedback of anything from ethnic group sources?'

'No.'

'Any chatter been picked up by GCHQ?'

'No.'

'Home-grown or imported?'

'No idea at present.'

'The Minister is shitting bricks then?'

'Got it in one.'

'What's the current Sitrep?'

'Meeting with Minister at 1300hrs to determine thrust of strategic response, clarify detailed response to potential media grilling, and have a pretty watertight, if not Teflon coated, package for himself to deliver to camera at 1745hrs.'

'Usual B.S. response, buy time and then get down to solid detailed investigation. Right.'

'Right.'

'Teams are working on it now then?'

'Yes.'

'I'll try and catch up and help where I can.'

'OK Harry. By The way how did you get back?'

'I conned my way on to a package holiday flight that was leaving at 0230hrs. It cost me £120 so I hope you'll sign off that and my other expenses.'

'Detail it Harry, as we've ruined your leave it's the least I can do.'

Harry went down the corridor and made himself a cup of coffee, which was not going to react too well with the airline 'breakfast', but a hefty caffeine shot was required to face what the day would undoubtedly bring.

He hooked up with Tom Denman, a unit team member, for a quick overview but did not glean any further information to add to what he had already been told.

He determined he could not add much at present to the teams preparing the media message and decided he would pick a quiet corner to reflect on what had happened and what, with his experience and intuition, could be starting points for an investigation.

At present there were no indicators, everything was cold, except for the inferno raging at Buncefield.

He racked his brains to think of anything, however small, over the last six months that would have triggered some suspicion and possible further investigation.

He was tired and that didn't help; a good nights sleep, eventually, would.

He looked in on the teams briefings, essentially a 'Why? What? From where? What if? scenario.'

The timing of the press briefing drew near and final amendments of suggestions were collated and sent across to the Minister for his 1500hrs deadline.

The Department had little hard evidence to go on so their contribution would have to rely on possible areas of investigation that were in the public domain and with oblique reference to those that weren't.

Harry wondered how the Minister would be reacting to the Department's input, extremely vague and with no initial leads or reaction to hang the hat on.

He started drawing up his own personal thoughts and used the old army acronym, SMEAC [Situation, Mission,

Execution, Administration & Logistics, Command & Communications], to cover his thinking.

Harry had started his career as a soldier in the Intelligence Corps at 18, and without the benefit of a university degree. He had worked hard over the years, serving in Northern Ireland during the IRA troubles, then a Gulf posting including Oman, Cyprus, and Turkey. He spent a short period in London, desk bound, which was followed by the UAE, Saudi Arabia, and finally, Iran, on attachment to the UK Embassy. This had brought him to the attention of the Department who offered him a position that he thought, at the time, would be both interesting and challenging, without the strictures of Army life.

As he had thought, on many occasions, 'how wrong can you be?' Political masters are twenty times worse than military ones and are often in post due to 'positioning' rather than competency or experience that the appointment demands.

He wrote SITUATION in capitals, underlined, and started compiling a basic list.

Well that was bloody obvious. Major disaster at Buncefield.

Accident or terrorism? No Intel, no group claiming responsibility.

If accident, how caused?

If terrorism, how achieved?

Objectives?

One off or follow ups?

Public reaction?

Perceptions?

Concentrate on accident to reduce public fear/panic.

Minister in deep doodoo.

Likely Minister reaction? Cover backside, shoot from hip.

Seek to transfer responsibility, assign blame to others, ASAP.

Situation normal for Minister's reaction, he thought. He glanced at his watch. 1745hrs. Switching on the television he wondered on the tack the Minister would take to try and reassure the public and also to deflect criticism away from himself as to cause and responsibility.

1730hrs Minister's Office Whitehall

In the Minister's office one could cut the atmosphere with a knife. The silence was deafening.

The Minister sat sullenly in his chair surrounded by the permanent civil servants, junior political appointees, strategy advisers, spin doctors and his PA.

He finally spoke, in a low voice, so low that some had to lean forward to hear what he was saying.

'You have had about eight hours to put together some words that I can use in about 15 minutes time to reassure the public following one of the most terrifying civilian disasters in London since World War II, and this is what you have produced.

His voice rose, 'Supposedly the best minds in the Civil Service, junior Ministers, Press Secretaries, etcetera, have produced something that I could have written in 15 minutes following my meeting this morning'.

'Absolutely pathetic', he said, his voice rising again. 'Christ knows what you cost the British taxpayer to produce this crap. Now bugger off, all of you, and let me do it myself'.

The room fell silent again as his advisers shuffled nervously through the door.

His PA walked over and laid her hand on his shoulder.

'You can wing it', she said. 'You're very good at that. Just speak from the heart.'

He looked up at her and smiled grimly. 'There's not much else I can do at this stage. I'm on camera in about 5 minutes!'

He rose and walked briskly through the door and down the corridor to the Press Room where the camera crews were waiting. She followed more slowly, allowing him to make his solo entrance to the interviewers.

1745hrs. Ministry Press Room.

The Minister walked in, his face taut and expressionless, extending a hand briefly to the three interviewers of BBC, ITV and Channel 4.

All three started to question him, so he raised his hand to silence them.

'Before we start, understand this,' he said quietly, 'I will not be answering any questions from you tonight. No ifs, buts, whatever.'

They began to protest, so he interjected, 'Any further comments from you and I will postpone any announcements to a recorded statement going out at 10 pm tonight. Understood?'

They fell silent.

'Good. Shall we begin?'

It took a few minutes for the crew to take up their final positions in order to get the non- questioning interviewers into frame, as well as the Minister, but only 5 minutes late at 1750hrs, the statement began. His PA watched from the back of the room and noticed that the Minister had not had any TV make-up applied and his forehead was glistening in the TV lights. Mistake or deliberate, she wondered.

The Minister looked straight ahead and began.

'People throughout Britain, watching their televisions this morning will have seen the massive conflagration at Buncefield which is probably without precedent since World War II.

You will have seen the continuing fight to bring this under control by our brave and valiant Fire Service whose dedication and professionalism is without parallel.

You may rest assured that we will put the Government's full resources behind the effort to contain this catastrophe within the shortest possible time.

I am aware that there have been already a number of speculative theories put forward as to what caused the explosion and the resultant fire. Let me make one thing clear immediately. They are only speculative theories with no foundation in fact.

This Ministry, working with other Government departments, will be starting its investigations immediately and I can assure the British public that no stone will left unturned in getting to the bottom of this tragedy. If culprits are found they will be punished to the full extent of the law, and I would also reassure those living within the impacted area of Buncefield that I shall be exerting pressure on all insurance companies to be flexible and sympathetic to those who have suffered loss to their homes and businesses.

This is an enormous tragedy affecting us all and our sympathy goes out to all those directly and indirectly affected. One consolation is that I believe there has been no loss of life but that is small recompense for a blighted community.

My team is working hard to find answers to your justifiable questions in the short term and I will provide a further update in 48 hours after further investigations have been concluded.

I am sure the public will join with me in extending our deep sympathy to the Buncefield community for the consequences of this terrible event'.

He stared ahead, emotionless, until he was aware that the cameras had been switched off and then strode quickly from the room. Questions were called out to him by the interviewers which he ignored.

His PA followed him back to his office to find him pouring himself a scotch and water.

'Well, what do you think?'

'Alright. Was no makeup your idea?'

'Yes. Did I look suitably concerned, drained, 24 hour days, etcetera? Do you think it was convincing enough?'

She thought briefly and replied, 'Sufficient for today. Bearing in mind it's a holding action until you have something positive to say.'

'OK. Will I see you at the flat tonight?'

'No, I have to organise some things at home, mundane things, laundry, food, etc.'

'Pity' he said. After such adrenalin flow he was often keen on 'emotional' relief. 'Never mind, see you in the morning.'

'I'll go now, if that's alright, and get an early night as well.'

'Fine. I'll have another scotch and unwind before following up with that group of idiots I call staff.'

She smiled, turned and left his office for her own, picking up her coat and bag on the way.

1930hrs PA's flat Southwark

Since the Minister had been in Government Anna had rented a small flat in Southwark, this being extremely convenient for Westminster, and if necessary she could walk to the Ministry.

She let herself in, kicked off her shoes, poured a glass of dry white wine and sat down on the sofa.

Her other mobile telephone rang. She answered with a long Hebrew number.

'What is happening?' a man asked in Hebrew.

'Early days,' she replied.

'Any leads?'

'None so far. Anything at your end?'

'One small one, but looks quite interesting.'

'Where?'

'North of Watford', he joked.' What is the general reaction?'

'Shock, horror, but no leads.'

'Don't forget we want to get some of the credit for resolving this.'

'I haven't forgotten.'

'Keep me posted.'

She ended the call and put the mobile back in her desk.

She sat down and allowed her thoughts to wander. Eight years of this. But for what, she wondered at times. Just after her 27th birthday, she remembered, she had been approached by a friend of a friend who knew her father had died in the Six Day War of 1967. She was born in the autumn of that year and never knew her father, although her mother kept his memory alive. Although a UK national he had received his training during stays in the Kibbutz. Her mother had died a few years later, Anna always thought, literally of a broken heart.

She was brought up by a close friend of her mother's, a gentile, and adopted her surname, Harrison, which had helped when applying for the researcher role.

The current situation was such that Mossad was keen to determine what had caused the Buncefield disaster, and if terrorists were involved, who they were, how and why the action had been planned and executed, and could Mossad get credit for assisting, guiding, or handing over their findings to the UK, preferably in a public forum.

Additionally, what technology were they using, so that Israel would be prepared, if a similar attack was directed at their country.

She thought back to the time she was interviewed by the opposition MP for the post of researcher.

Dressed to indicate seriousness of intent, but not to hide her femininity. The balance between positive response to questions and enough directness of gaze to interest a male. Overall, the male of the species has a certain predictability of response that a clever woman will recognise, and use to best effect, she mused.

Despite the blaze at Buncefield still raging the tempo of investigations would now increase with her Minister baying for results, if not blood. She considered some of the likely scenarios that would include other departments, including Security.

She would have access to reports coming to the Minister plus information of which teams are involved, and where.

Inter-department jealousies, point scoring, and turf wars would almost certainly arise, if only for self protection or to gain credit for interim successes. Information, in that case, would be reluctantly shared. However there will be a steady stream passing through her Minister.

This would be valuable information for her controller who may then be able to make the necessary connections with his Intel received from regional operatives.

To establish the connection between pieces of seemingly irrelevant information is often slow and laborious work, often not immediately obvious, requiring painstaking cross checking, and the use of algorithms to establish its route and veracity.

Memory sticks would be the preferred solution for carrying any information, but she would have to be very careful during any downloading. Bluetooth connection could be an alternative, but not always available. CDs were out of the question, too bulky and obvious. Laptops were now forbidden due to several having been left on trains, in cars, or restaurants, by other Departments, and which had made front page news to the acute embarrassment of various Ministers.

She glanced at the clock and decided that with the pressure that tomorrow would bring an early night was due, so after a light supper she turned in and slept fitfully, her sleep being interrupted by dreams of the Minister at his vitriolic best.

Wednesday 14th December 2005 0630-0800hrs London

She rose at 0630hrs and was at her desk in the Ministry by O800hrs, ready, she hoped, to deal with whatever the day and events would throw at her.

At 0815hrs the Minister walked briskly over to his desk and called through the open door to his PA's office, 'Come in, Anna, it's going to be a busy day!'

*

In Clapham Harry Baxter had slept well.

'Thank Christ for that', he thought. 'God knows what will happen today.'

He had watched the news reports on television and it appeared that the Fire Services were starting to get the fire under control, long distance shots mixed in with 'on the spot' interviews of local residents and their personal experiences.

He was scheduled to see the Deputy at 0830hrs so having arrived at 0745hrs spent the time reading some of the regional reports précised over the last 3-4 months.

He had just reached North East Region (Known as NUTS 1, under the EU classification of regions for statistics) when the Deputy called him in.

'Morning Harry. Sleep well?'

'Like a log. What's the plan?'

'Hard graft, Harry. We've got little to go on at present so we'll have to start digging. Balls aching, I know, but we've got to start somewhere. Have you seen any of the regional reports?'

'I've just started, but nothings leapt out so far.'

Harry, for this I'm setting up small teams of three. We can then cross link on a daily basis any major factors thrown up. Use the computer algorithms to help speed things up and shout if you need any specific help or resource. Who do you want in your team?'

Harry thought quickly, 'Tom Denman and I have worked together before; He's good, reliable, thinks outside the box. Yes Tom.

He paused again; 'What about Jane Harris for the third, she's a red hot analyst, great with computers, sparky, and isn't afraid to ask questions.'

'OK, Harry, set it up and get moving. Update me same time tomorrow, or if the proverbial hits the fan, anytime, day or night.'

Harry nodded and left the Deputy's office.

The Deputy remained sitting at his desk, thinking of the folder containing sensitive information, which was locked in his security cabinet. Depending on where the investigation went, he may well have to 'share' the information with Harry or another to ensure that a successful operation was achieved by his department.

Harry went looking for Tom Denman and found him making a cup of coffee.

'Make that two,' Harry joked.

'What's up?' said Tom.

'Let's go and find a quiet room and I'll bring you up to speed.'

Harry closed the door and they sat down.

Harry said 'Buncefield. The Deputy is setting up three man teams. I'm heading one, I've asked for you and Jane Harris. Are you happy with that?'

'Absolutely. No problem.'

'Great. I'll catch up with Jane soon, if the old man hasn't already.'

There was a knock on the door and Jane Harris walked in.

'The Deputy called me and told me I'm on your team. That's why I came looking for you.'

Fine, grab a chair,' said Harry. 'Good timing, we were just about to start updating ourselves. What have you been working on recently?'

'Analysis of regional reports, spikes, connections across areas/regions, increase in traffic, hostile website activity, recruitment to the cause, any specific jihads or jihadists, etc.'

'Good. There will be lot of analysis on this one as we have no bloody leads at present, and I gather one particular Minister is jumping up and down wondering who he can blame!

We'll use office C10, I know it's got three desks in it, so if you both move your kit across I'll get Comms to hook us up soonest. But I expect they'll need a kick up the proverbial if past performance is anything to go by! Let's meet in C10 in half an hour? OK?'

Tom and Jane murmured assent as Harry left the room to go back to the Deputy's office to get Comms backside shifted, soonest. Following the request he moved his own kit from D5 to C10 and asked Central Registry for the last three months Overview reports from the regions.

In a comparatively short time all three were sitting at their desks in C10, heads down engrossed in analysis the silence only being broken by the tapping of computer keyboards, and the rustle of turning papers.

Two and a half hours later Jane fetched repeat coffees and all three paused for a 'heads up'.

'So far, absolutely bugger all', said Harry, who immediately apologised to Jane for his description.

Jane waved it away saying 'Forget it, I'm used to much stronger stuff, so don't give it, or any other descriptions, any further thought.'

Harry said, 'We are going to have to approach this differently, so give me five and I will run some thoughts past you'.

1000hrs.Beirut Lebanon

The Syrian, Palestinian, and the Saudi were drinking coffee and eating dates as they discussed, with some jubilation, the success of the bombing at Buncefield.

The Syrian had previously discussed with the Saudi the plan presented by the Palestinian, which was both audacious and brilliant in its conception, but which would require sophisticated planning and execution to succeed. Significant funding would be required and that would require to be syndicated among the group's paymasters.

The Syrian made a valid observation when he said, 'My brothers, we can rejoice at the result we have achieved in England, but let us be aware that their security services will be at high alert to find out who the perpetrators are and to prevent a similar event happening.'

He laughed as he said, 'I am assuming that they realise it is an attack against them and not just an accident!' The others smiled and laughed with him.

Then he adopted a serious expression, and said, 'Therefore I suggest we delay the second plan to hit the Kuffar in their heart, until they have grown complacent again.'

The Palestinian expressed disappointment at this, but the Syrian quickly interjected by saying,' My brother, although I am suggesting a delay to your plan for London, I think we can use a similar method here in the Middle East to achieve certain ends.'

'There are a number of countries around us who are too close to the Western world with their non-believer customs and filthy habits. If we plan correctly we could cause them to think again of their relationships and turn again onto the true path.'

The Palestinian's interest was aroused and he asked what form this could take.

The Syrian replied, 'We can discuss in detail after our Saudi brother leaves. We need to keep such information close to us.'

The meeting broke up, and the Saudi left, after the usual Arab pleasantries and farewells.

The Syrian and Palestinian resumed their conversation with the Palestinian pushing for an explanation of the potential plan.

The Syrian spoke carefully so that the Palestinian could fully comprehend the reasons and secondary consequences of his proposal.

'You are familiar with the North Dome/South Pars Gas Condensate Field which is situated in the Arabian Gulf and shared between Qatar and Iran; roughly two thirds Qatar and one third Iran. Qatar has allowed the Americans to build a base in Qatar for the US Army, and has often acted as go-between the USA, The Kingdom of Saudi Arabia, and Iran through both formal and informal channels.

The USA and Saudi Arabia are very concerned by the nuclear energy programme being pursued by Iran, and it current plans and production of uranium enrichment. Naturally Iran is saying that their programme is for peaceful nuclear energy purposes, but nobody including the Europeans believes them, particularly bearing in mind some of the statements of the President, Mahmoud Ahmadinejad.

I was thinking of this situation, the mistrust I have indicated, and the possibility that arises.

What would be the end result if the following occurred?

A significant explosion occurs on one of the Qatari Gas Collection platforms near to the line in international waters between Qatar and Iran, which, by information carefully released, would indicate is the work of the Iranians.

Reason? Jealousy of the Qataris larger share of the gas field compared to Iran, misguided Iran National Guard rogue elements thinking this will help or please their President, etc.

Reactions? The Qataris blame Iran; USA and Europe say actions confirm their overall misgivings and suspicion over Iran's various programmes. Instability in the region is raised up another level, and our opportunity to spread the true word for a caliphate is dramatically increased.'

He paused to let the Palestinian absorb what he had said and consider the overall implications.

The Palestinian nodded his head vigorously in agreement. 'My brother this is a great plan but will be difficult to execute.'

The Syrian agreed and said, 'Yes but with sufficient funds and proper training and equipment anything is possible? Insha'Allah.'

'Insha'Allah', the Palestinian replied. 'I must think about how this can be done and what it will cost. Can we meet in three days time?'

The Syrian agreed and their meeting finished.

*

After the Palestinian had left the Syrian thought about what he had proposed, and what he would need to arrange if the project went ahead. There must be significant distance between him and the Palestinian, at least a different country, and perhaps the Palestinian should be considered expendable in any case. The second strike planned for London would require a real professional.

The call to prayer rang through the city and he turned his attention to personal ablutions and his duty.

The Palestinian hurried across the street, conscious of the call to prayer, and did not notice he was being observed from a parked Renault. The shutter clicked three times as he looked right and left as he crossed the road and turned left into the main entrance of an adjacent mosque.

He hurriedly removed his shoes which, unknown to him, produced three more clicks of the shutter, as he entered as part of a small group of similarly late worshippers.

The Renault moved quietly away from the kerb and drove south along the boulevard.

A few kilometres along the road the Renault stopped and the driver checked the photos on his Nikon camera for clarity and definition. They were excellent and hopefully would throw up something on the database. No real suspects at this stage, just observe, collect data, who's in, who's out, why, who are they talking to, why, all the boring stuff of intelligence that sometimes bears real fruit.

1200hr.Room C10 SIS(MI6) London

Harry had scribbled some notes on his pad to focus his thoughts.

He looked up and enquired, 'Can I have your comments once I've run these thoughts past you?'

Two heads nodded as one.

'1. Because we have no leads, or anyone claiming responsibility, we are going to have to start from first principles.

2. If it turns out to be an accident we will not be involved and we will be stood down pronto.

3. Therefore, until told otherwise, we must assume it is an attack of some sort.

4. Likely candidates

Real IRA? Not likely. They normally give a telephone warning, even if late!

Anarchists. Not their style, usually smashing shops, cars, laboratories, etc.

Terrorists. Overseas or home grown? If from overseas will require local

support, funding, cover, and good cover story.

If bomb planted locally, significant size. How brought into Buncefield?

Was bomb planted against tanks or pipes? Or inserted into tank or pipe.

We need some engineering advice.

Where does all the fuel for Buncefield come from?
Different types?
Distributed to where?

These are some of my initial thoughts, comments and observations please.'
Tom chipped in first.
'For this exercise we can only assume some form of terrorism. That is a given, in my opinion, until we are told otherwise. Therefore we need to start collecting some evidence on the ground at Buncefield, if possible, plus some engineering advice as you have said.'
Jane interjected. 'Why don't I start on the Buncefield operations and the engineering angles? We must be able to pull a stack off the web.'
'OK, Jane', Harry replied, 'I'll leave that to you. Brief me when you've got something substantial together. Don't forget I've got to keep number 2 up to speed on a daily basis.
Tom, why don't you see what you can get out of the Fire Service, Police, anybody who was close at the time, you know the drill.'
'Right' said Tom, 'I'm away then'.
'Call me Tom, if you pick up any nuggets,' called Harry, as Tom exited the room.
Harry composed a brief to all regional operatives on a priority 1 basis, requesting their immediate response. He asked for a review over the last three months for any unusual activity, however inconsequential, that may have been overlooked, or not considered of high enough interest to warrant further investigation.
This was emailed over the secure Government network with reports to be submitted within 48hrs.
He also called Jane, and asked her to let him have, as soon as possible, information concerning the pipelines feeding into Buncefield, and where they started. This, he thought, could provide a starting point, and a narrowing down of the regions involved.

1500hrs Ministers office Whitehall

The Minister was seething inwardly, the only indication, his eyes, boring into the man sitting across the desk.

He spoke quietly, but with the menace for which he was well known.

'Here we are, three days after the event, and all you can tell me, is sweet FA?!'

The Health and Safety Chief wriggled nervously in his chair.

'Minister, you must understand the extent of the devastation on site which is hindering our investigation. My men must follow clear H & S guidelines when examining the aftermath of such an explosion, otherwise there is the significantly higher risk of injury or fatalities.'

'I am fully aware of the devastation on site having spent two hours there on Monday. What I love about you H & S people are the weasel words you trot out linked with statements of the blindingly obvious! What I am asking you, and I think I understand what you are trying to say, is that you have, at present, no idea at all! Is that correct or not?'

'Minister, we cannot determine the cause of the explosion at present, but will report back to you once we collected solid and verifiable evidence.'

'In the meantime then, may I suggest you clear off and try and get some sense of urgency in your own actions as well as your colleagues,' the Minister said, closing the meeting, and rising from his seat.

'Additionally do not even bother contacting me until you have something more than solid. Do I make myself crystal clear?'

The Head of H & S nodded in agreement, and left the room hurriedly, glad to escape comparatively lightly, by all previous accounts.

After reflecting on the meeting for a couple of minutes the Minister called in his PA and told her to sit down.

'At present H & S is a complete waste of space; not a clue; and give me responses that mean precisely nothing.'

He paused then continued.

'If this is not just an accident, and is something with a terrorist connection, then I am going to have to talk to the Security Services, which, in that case, does not make me at all happy. They have never cooperated in the past, they cover their own backsides, they don't like sharing information, and you never know what is behind the information they give you anyway! Plus, one, rather important, consideration. The PM is on my tail and is looking for positive news to comfort a rather nervous public,'

She didn't comment, but thought of the advantage to her, if cooperation was forced by the situation.

She replied in a moderate, deliberate way, as if she was considering the matter carefully.

'If H & S are pretty useless in the short term they are not going to provide much comfort.

If the PM wants some positive news then you will have to collect it from any available source. Bearing in mind that it is still early days, all options are still wide open, as no indications, so far, point to a straight accident or a terrorist action.

Even though you are unhappy at the thought of discussions with the Security Services it is an option for you, and, dependent on eventual outcomes, will produce some shared responsibility rather than your Ministry alone.'

He had listened without interrupting, and now nodded in assent.

'Yes, dammit, you're probably right, set up an early meeting, today, if you can. Tomorrow latest.'

She rose, turning to hide the slight smile on her lips, 'I'll get straight onto it.'

She telephoned her opposite number and arranged for the meeting to take place in her Minister's office at 1100hrs the next day.

1630hrs SIS(MI6) London

The head of the SIS(MI6) called in his Deputy to discuss the planned meeting and the department's response, official or unofficial.

'Well Norman,' the Director said, 'Where are we, what do we know, what do they know or don't know, and what are we doing at present, that's shareable or not? Not forgetting he was bloody rude and insulting to me down the phone the other day.'

The Deputy gathered his thoughts.

'Right now we don't know if Buncefield is an accident or terrorism. However we are assuming the latter and I've set up three man teams on the usual basis. Harry Baxter's leading one in case this has a Middle East connection; others are Northern Ireland, Eastern Europe, or home grown derivatives with overseas connections.

No leads at all at present, one or two usual suspects but heavily discounted. The Minister clearly needs help as he has the PM leaning on him. We need a couple more days with some 24hr trawling through reports to see if there are any spikes on the radar, however small.

I cannot give you anything at present, so play a pretty straight bat to the Minister and remember to duck if he starts throwing things!'

He remembered the Minister/PA file, but thought he would keep his powder dry at present; that was something to produce on a very rainy day.

'Thanks Norman, I just wanted to get a feel as to where we are at present. He is probably expecting minor miracles, but he'll have to join the real world.'

Norman nodded, realising that the Director would be playing for time at his meeting tomorrow, and rose to leave.

'One more thing, Norman. I know the Minister is extremely volatile with a nasty temper, but does he have any emotional or other weaknesses?'

'Not that I am aware of currently', said the Deputy. 'Why?'

'Nothing specific, just wanted to be forearmed in case there are.'

Norman left, curious about the question, but putting it down to his boss's preparations.

The Director was asking himself whether his Deputy was fully up to speed, or whether there were things happening that he didn't want to discuss at the present time.

Time will reveal all, he thought.

1800hrs. Minister's office Westminster

He called in his PA and discussed the meeting scheduled for 1100hrs the following day.

'I am not sure how cooperative he's going to be bearing in mind I chewed him out the other day. I'm going to have to be diplomatic for a change. Any suggestions or observations?'

'Not really, he'll be defensive so adopt a charm offensive. He's no fool so don't treat him like one. Adopt the attitude 'we are all in this together' routine. Defence of the realm, etc.

I don't really have to tell you what to do,' she said, lowering her gaze, then looking up quickly and smiling intimately.

He smiled in response and said, 'What about dinner tonight, French, Italian, you choose?'

'Italian. Can I meet you later; I still have a few things to organise in my flat?' she replied.

'Fine, let's meet at 8.15pm at the Il Falconiere on Old Brompton Rd, you know, just up from my flat.'

She smiled, and left the Minister's office to go to her apartment.

1900hrs. PA's flat Southwark

She took out her other mobile from her locked desk and called a number. She spoke in Hebrew when it was answered. It was a short conversation giving basic details of the Minister's meeting the next day. The mobile was returned to the desk and locked.

She sat and thought for a few minutes, then changed, left her flat, and took a taxi to the restaurant, arriving about five minutes after her host.

2015hrs PA's apartment Southwark

The observer crossed the road and quickly entered the building using master keys previously obtained. He entered the flat noiselessly, and checked the most obvious places for hidden mobile phones, including the locked desk, which was easily opened with his particular skills.

He switched it on using a particular electronic device that can bypass passwords, etc, and downloaded the various call lists using Bluetooth to his own device. Switching off, cleaning and replacing the mobile in the same position in the relocked desk took less than two minutes, and he was back on the main road, task completed, in less than twelve minutes.

What he didn't see was a black Ford Mondeo about 75 yards along the road with the driver taking a number of photographs of him with a Nikon camera with telephoto lens.

After a gap of about five minutes the car started up and disappeared in a south westerly direction.

The operative who had entered the flat returned to his office and downloaded all the electronic data he had collected.

Considerable covert research would be needed on the data to determine location and ownership of numbers, etc and he sighed as he thought of the long night hours ahead retrieving it, and attempting to put it together to make some sense for the Deputy.

2045hrs Il Falconiere

The Minister had had two scotches already, as he had arrived early, principally to choose a discrete table before she arrived.

He was worried about a lot of things, and when that happened he tended to drink more, which he knew was not conducive to clear thinking or rational controlled reactions.

He rose when she arrived but avoided any public kisses on the cheek in case anyone was looking and wanted to make 2+2=5. This was just a Minister having a quiet, businesslike dinner with his PA.

Il Falconiere looked after them well. He was a regular customer, regulars deserve being looked after, and the family did a good job of that.

'Shall we go back to my flat,' he enquired quietly as they finished their coffees.

'If you like'' she said.

'What's this, 'if I like' response', he enquired testily.

'I was thinking of all the pressures you have at the moment and your meeting tomorrow morning, that's all', she replied hastily.

'Alright. I'm just a bit edgy at present and yes, you're right, I could do with a good night's sleep he said, suddenly tired and not wanting to argue at this time, particularly with her.

They walked outside, and after putting her in a taxi he walking alone down Onslow Gardens to his flat, observed by a man in a VW Golf, who after taking the photo, noted the time.

Thursday 15th December 2005 0900hrs Beirut Lebanon

The Mossad operative downloaded the enhanced images onto his laptop to send to Central for analysis and possible identification. His was generally fairly tiring and boring work but occasionally a good fish was caught.

His task was to identify strangers to the area for which he was responsible and feed back the data so that a mosaic of regular or irregular traffic would be made obvious. Computer software identity scans and matching had reached unprecedented levels in recent years, and Mossad operating on behalf of the defence of their country had a massive and sophisticated database.

The task completed he knew that any results would be flagged to him within hours together with any operational instructions as to follow up.

0930hrs SIS(MI6) London

The operative had requested an early meeting with the Deputy on 'increased risk' basis.

The Deputy looked up as the operative knocked an entered.

'Reasons for 'increased risk' status?

'Comms are now becoming more frequent between PA and Mossad. We downloaded all her contact numbers and telephone records from her mobile last night, no detection of our man. What we did discover is that her mobile is a direct satellite phone, not working on any of the usual networks, which will give her complete security during transmission. If she was on one of the normal providers it would be easy to listen in, but with this, she's fireproof'.

The Deputy was quiet while he thought through what he had been told.

'From the records is it all voice traffic or is some data?'

'From our analysis so far, it appears to be only voice, but we still have a lot more digging to do.'

'Keep at it, any major items contact me immediately, otherwise maintain observation level and monitor carefully any perceived increase in traffic. By the way, can we get a local listening post to her flat so that we can tell when she's transmitting, even if we cannot listen in to her voice traffic?'

If you sign it off Sir, I'll get it in place by tonight.'

Done, said the Deputy. 'Good luck.'

The operative left, pausing only to ask the Deputy's Senior Assistant to prepare a Tap Request for his signature, and to make sure the Deputy signed it off before 1200hrs.

1000hrs Harry's office C10 SIS(MI6) London

Harry was working his way through several region reports when Jane entered the office.

'Glad I caught you,' she said. 'I've got some leads on the fuels delivered by pipeline to Buncefield and there are probably only two sources to check, if we are lucky. In addition I've found somebody, in house, who's had a lot of oil and gas experience before being recruited. I've asked him to come and see you this afternoon at 1400hrs.'

'Good,' said Harry. 'Maybe I'll find something in these reports by then to hang a small hat on. In terms of the sources, where are they in the UK?'

'Apparently,' she replied, 'the North East, Humber, Immingham, and less likely, the North West.'

'Why is the North West less likely?'

'Distance. If something was introduced into the pipe, then much further to travel. But we'll still check it out.'

'OK. What's the engineer's name?'

'Bill Goodwright.'

'Fine. Attend the meeting please.'

Harry refocused his thinking on the reports and decided to open the one from the North East to see if there were any indicators, however small, that might show a connection.

The report was fairly general but one item caught his eye and set him thinking.

The operative had been keeping observation on any new incomers to the region based on feed back from subordinates. One had flagged an item concerning a man of Middle East appearance, very westernised, nationality considered to be Maltese, Lebanese Christian, or Egyptian, and who seemed to be fitting in well with the local population. Feedback of visits to pubs, clubs, indicate financially comfortable, but not flashy. No obvious Muslim connections, drink or food restrictions.

Harry put that on one side as something to look at again as his telephone rang, and the Deputy asked him to come to his office.

Harry entered and sat down facing the Deputy.

'I was going to give you an update later this afternoon when I have got some further information and data together.'

'Fine Harry. That's not what I want to discuss. The Director is meeting the Minister at 1100hrs today, and I was wondering if we had anything that the Director could have in hand, in case the Minister starts throwing his toys out of the pram?'

'The only thing I could say, in all honesty, is that we have got a number of interesting leads and possible connections but not yet verified or confirmed, but we hope to have something much more solid in 48 hrs'

The Deputy sighed and looked somewhat disappointed.

'Well Harry, if that's it, we'll have to live with it for now. Thanks, and crack on. Skip my briefing this afternoon, OK?'

Harry nodded and returned to his office.

1100hrs Ministers Office Whitehall

'SIS(MI6) Director,' the PA announced ushering him to the Minister's office.

The Minister rose and extended his hand which the Director grasped and shook firmly.

'Let's sit over here,' the Minister said, indicating two armchairs and a coffee table giving a splendid view of Whitehall gardens.

'Coffee?' he enquired, 'milk, sugar?'

'Let me get one thing clear before we start our discussion. The other day I was out of order; very concerned at what had happened, and made comments to you that were rude and unhelpful. Collectively we are all in this together, so I wanted to make sure that you and I start with a clean sheet. Can we do that?'

Minister, if we are going to jointly sort out this tragedy then we have to work together. From my side, of course we can.'

'Excellent', said the Minister as he reached for his coffee. 'I fully understand the confidentiality of the Service and the fact that most information cannot be released into the public domain and/or shared willy-nilly with any department, but if we are to get to the bottom of this we are going to have to put our collective cards on the table to ensure success. Do you agree?'

The Director chose his words carefully.

'Minister I am sure you understand that I wish to resolve this unfortunate incident as quickly and as speedily as our respective resources will allow.

On the question of security of my operatives there can be no risk of them being compromised, or sources of data and other information being revealed. I will personally vet and approve all information that is to be shared by us and will block anything which falls, in my opinion, into a compromise situation.

However, be rest assured that I will work with you and your department as closely as possible, to achieve a speedy resolution to our joint investigations.'

The Minister had listened closely, and felt that under the circumstances, it was about as far he would expect the Director to commit himself at this time. He was recording it, so could analyse it further after the meeting.

'Thank you Director for your offer. Let's hope we can get to the bottom of this terrible event quickly.'

The Director then broadly indicated that investigations that were underway, but cautioned the Minister that it was often slow and painstaking work, which would bring results, though not necessarily quickly.

The Director then asked the Minister if the investigations on site were giving any indications that it had been an accident or otherwise.

'No clear indications so far, there is still complete chaos with various fires still burning, and no opportunity for investigators to start a detailed examination.'

The Director indicated that the Service was assuming a terrorist attack of some sort, and their actions were predicated on this assumption.

The meeting broke up after about 45 minutes, with both men agreeing that they, or nominated representatives, would meet for exchange of ideas and information every 48hrs, until further notice.

After the Director had left the PA came into his office.

'Successful?' she queried.

'Moderately, I think. I apologised to start with and hoped we could work together, etcetera, which I think he bought. I was on my best behaviour,' he said, smiling wolfishly. 'He's got to be careful, but we've got agreement that he and I, or nominees, will meet every 48hrs to evaluate current status and share information subject to the usual Security caveats.'

She nodded in agreement and collected the files on his desk that had to go to the Registry.

1400hrs Harry's Office C10 SIS(MI6) London

Bill Goodwright had been working in the oil and gas industry for at least 15 years, UK, Europe, West Africa and the Gulf, before he was recruited as an industry analyst and specialist by the Directorate.

His reputation was as a good, solid engineer, a reliable source for matters within his field, and a man not given to hyperbole.

Harry sat him down with a coffee and Jane made longhand notes for reference.

Harry started the discussion.

'Bill, I'll outline the situation. Our brief is, to assume Buncefield was a terrorist action, not an accident. Next, (1) how the hell was this carried out, and (2) why were we not picking up any indicators whatsoever? The second part is our problem. What we need to know from you is, how do you think this was done, and is there more than one way of doing it?'

'Well,' said Bill, 'As far as I can see there could only be two ways for this to be carried out. One; a terrorist entered via the perimeter and planted a bomb against the tank. Two, if a bomb was planted and transported inside a pipe and exploded with a timer. Clearly nobody knows currently which method was adopted.

'How could they get a bomb inside a pipe?' queried Harry.

'It's possible that it could be transported via a 'pig'.

'Explain.'

Bill then went into some detail about the use of 'pigs' in pipelines, the fact that they can be of any size from, say 8' to 30' in diameter, certainly large enough to carry an explosive device.

After he had concluded a fairly lengthy technical description of all the types available, there was silence for a few moments, as Harry absorbed what had been said. Jane, meanwhile, had taken some brief notes and reminders.

'How far can they travel down a pipe?' asked Harry.

'It depends whether the pig is being used for cleaning/inspection, or whether it is a batch separator for fuels. If the latter, then over a 100 miles, no problem.'

'Bill thanks for your help; I think that will give us enough to work on at present. Can I come back to you if we need more technical help?

Bill nodded in agreement.

'Great.'

Bill left the office and Harry looked at Jane.

'That opens up some interesting possibilities, doesn't it?'

'Shall I call Tom and see when he can get back in for an update?'

'Yes, let's schedule that for 1730hrs if he can make it.'

Jane reached for her telephone to call Tom on his mobile as he walked into the office.

'Harry, it's chaos down there. I couldn't even get close to do a superficial examination and the boys in blue are paranoid about letting anybody near at present.'

'Tom, file your brief report, we are having an update meeting at 1730hrs, OK?'

Tom nodded and went to his desk to file his short and frustrating report.

Harry sat at his desk and reflected on the previous meeting. Several scenarios were now in the frame and would require some detailed investigation.

One thing that was nagging him was that no group had claimed responsibility for the conflagration, which was unusual; such actions were normally done to obtain maximum publicity for the cause. That's why an accident was still on the agenda despite Bill's briefing.

1530hrs Mossad Control London

Control was considering alternative courses of action to ensure any information obtained from the Minister's PA could be used to help, firstly themselves, and secondly the SIS(MI6), whilst, with judicious leaks, Mossad would also garner credit for such assistance.

With a world wide network of operatives, thousands of hours of computer analysis were used to find connections, links, risks and embryonic plans which could put their country at risk, or those countries with which they had a strong interest or relationship to combat terrorism in all its forms.

Control was pondering the degree of cooperation that would be established between the Minister's department and the SIS(MI6), bearing in mind the previous levels of distrust that had existed. Despite the olive branch offered by the Minister, experience indicated that any cooperation would be ignored in the event that his department could obtain maximum credit.

Perhaps a shift of emphasis to more directly assist the SIS(MI6) would yield more fruit in the short and medium term, and also generate additional good will for the longer view.

Analysis had indicated some, as yet unknown, activity in Lebanon but it was unclear what the main drivers were. Continued observation and network listening should provide more details in time.

Control continued to mull over the options in front of him.

1730hrs Harry's office C10 SIS(MI6) London

Harry brought Tom quickly up to speed on the content of Bill's meeting held previously that afternoon. Tom was not able to add further to his comments concerning Buncefield and Jane waited to see where Harry would take things now.

Harry was silent for a minute then spoke.

'We must assume from our perspective that this is a terrorist attack. On that basis we must also assume it is either home grown, imported or a combination of both. We must also deduce that due to lack of any claims of responsibility that this was a trial/test run as a precursor perhaps for bigger things. I don't know any of these things for sure, but we are going to have to find out.

We must look to see if any of the friendly security services operating in the UK have picked up anything and are happy to share. Tom, see what you can dig up in that area.

Any doubtful entries or exits through any airports to be flagged up. Check up on any robberies, break ins, vandalism at any refineries, distribution depots, etc.

See if there has been any significant increase in 'chatter' from known sources since the explosion.

That will do for starters. Jane draw up an Action Plan for me and allocate people and time. OK?'

Friday 16th December 2005 1000hrs Beirut Lebanon

The Palestinian called the Syrian to arrange the meeting for the following day, to be advised that they should meet that afternoon at 1600hrs as the Syrian had to leave Beirut that night.

No reason was given but the Palestinian thought it could be for discussions on funding.

His call had been intercepted and monitored and he would be followed and observed at that time. If they met in a public place the highly sensitive, directional microphones would be used to pick up elements, if not all, of their discussions.

The operative packed his equipment carefully in his briefcase, ensuring that all his kit was charged, tested and working.

1000hrs Harry's office C10 SIS(MI6) London

Harry realised that four days had passed since the explosion at Buncefield and that pressure was building in several Government departments to give the public at large some comfort and information.

He pursued his analysis of reports by focussing on the Humberside region, this being the shortest length of pipeline carrying the mix of fuels to Buncefield. He recalled the passing comments of the region's operative, and sent a text asking him to make contact over the secure network as soon as possible.

About 15mins later his desk telephone rang. It was the regional operative, Nils Helland, originally Swedish, now a UK citizen.

'Thanks for calling, Nils. Secure line? Good.

I want to talk to you about your report of 17th October. The item concerning the Lebanese/Maltese/Egyptian. What else do you know about him?

Is he still around, any visible means of support, why is he there, how does he earn his money, does he have many friends, who are they, what do they do, does he have a girl friend? If he's gone check airports, etc. You know the sort of thing. Plus have you got any contacts at the Humberside refineries? I want to know if they have had any break-ins recently or is their perimeter security rubbish so they wouldn't know anyway. See what you can find.'

I've only got the original feed which you've read,' replied Nils. But I can start digging and trawling straight away, if that's what you want.'

'Yes. Priority 1. Pull in some help across the region if needed. Any queries refer them to me.'

'I'll start straight away,' Nils responded.

'Keep me updated daily; secure line only. OK? Good luck.'

Harry knew these were early 'fishing' days and they had scant information to go on, but at least it was a start and may lead somewhere.

Tom, on one of the other desks, was holding a number of discrete conversations over secure lines with other 'friendly' agencies, but was not having a great deal of success or cooperation. Responses were bland or of no use.

He turned to Harry.

'Well Harry, the US were trying to determine what we needed any info for; the French were just evasive, situation normal; Saudis, at prayer, they said; Germany no ideas; Israel, nothing specific, but suggested meeting. What do you think?'

'Go and meet the Israelis' said Harry, 'you may pick up something in conversation they won't indicate on the phone.'

Tom nodded and picked up the telephone to organise a time and place.

Jane logged the exchange on her PC and carried on detailing actions and resources required.

1600hrs Beirut Lebanon

The Palestinian entered the hotel and made his way to the large public room at the rear which overlooked a garden. The weather was bright and reasonably warm for the time of year.

A window giving access to the garden had been partially opened allowing a faint breeze to enter.

He saw the Syrian sitting in an armchair in a secluded area, his back to the window, reading the Gulf News. He approached with the usual greetings, reciprocated by the Syrian, who glanced around the room to see if any other people had entered at the same time. There were none.

Whilst the two men were exchanging some general comments a man entered the room on the far side and sat down at a desk approximately 18 yards away.

He took out his laptop from his briefcase, plus some books, and started working. The Palestinian looked across at the man before asking quietly if he could present his ideas to which the Syrian readily agreed.

The man on the laptop had positioned his briefcase perfectly so that the directional microphone was clearly picking up the muted conversation. At the same time the voice recognition software was converting sound into text on his laptop as they spoke.

The Palestinian reiterated his thoughts as to the next potential target and the logic of relocating it to the Gulf; the involvement of two states where the resulting attack would confuse observers, but at the same provide fertile ground for accusations and recriminations.

The Palestinian went into some detail of the operation, finishing by saying that he could organise it within the next thirty days, subject to the provision of funding.

The Syrian congratulated him on his plan, gave assurances of his support, and said it would carry his recommendation for funding. He told him to start planning immediately and that he would contact him within five days.

They rose and left, whilst the man at the desk continued working studiously with his laptop and books. He glanced at them as they left, and then carefully closed down his laptop, which on the text programme gave an indication of what was planned in the next thirty days. His control would be reading that in less than four hours, sent by secure satellite transmission.

The Syrian and the Palestinian went their separate ways, the Syrian by car to Damascus, the Palestinian to arrange his flight to the Gulf to start his detailed planning of the operation.

She opened her desk and retrieved her other mobile, dialling as she crossed the room to sit down in an armchair.

The Hebrew request and response was confirmed and Control then explained that they had observed, they thought, an operative from a Security Service entering her flat on the 14th, and leaving about 15 minutes later.

She replied that there were no apparent signs of entry or any disturbance internally and thought it might just be routine check due to her sensitive position.

Control advised her to keep a watchful eye for any apparent increase in security checks and report accordingly.

Additionally, Control indicated that, wherever possible, they wished to assist, in a covert way, the UK Security Services in their investigations and that a meeting had been arranged between a local operative and a man called Tom Denman. The name should be remembered for future reference and discrete enquiries should be made as to his reporting line.

The conversation finished and Anna sat and thought through what had been said, and any implications that could result in either direct or indirect consequences.

*

A few miles South West of Southwark Harry Baxter let himself in to his cold flat in Clapham.

He switched on the central heating and poured himself a strong gin and tonic. He was tired with his head buzzing with unlinked information and half-thought through ideas. He slumped in the chair and took a deep drink from the glass, the gin hitting the back of his throat and causing his eyes to blink. 'The first this week,' he thought, 'and what a bloody week!'

'Lonely job, lonely life,' he thought. 'For Christ's sake stop feeling sorry for yourself,' he mentally remonstrated himself. He thought back to when he had been married, but the job was too demanding a mistress. His wife was a teacher and they had gradually drifted apart, resulting eventually in an amicable divorce with no recriminations. But sad.

He got up, angry with himself, in allowing, so he thought, some self indulgent sentimentality to creep in.

He went into the kitchen and looked to see what was in the fridge. Not a lot. Milk, eggs, butter, bacon, and a very old piece of pizza that was developing some very interesting looking greenery on one edge. He threw it in the bin.

He sighed, turned, and thought, 'Indian takeaway, it is. Great start to the weekend!'

Just then his mobile rang. It was the Deputy.

'Harry, I won't wreck your weekend, but something interesting appears to be developing. Can we meet 0900hrs Monday? Good, see you then.'

Harry wondered what Monday would bring. Good, bad or indifferent. Anyway the Deputy sounded quite positive. A good sign.

Sunday would be a week since the explosion, and progress was slow, if it was terrorism. The pace would have to be raised a notch or two starting Monday. If the Department didn't ratchet things up one could always rely on the politicians. Self preservation is a great driver in our political classes.

He left his flat for the short walk to his favourite Indian takeaway. The high street was lined with parked cars, it being Friday evening and the various ethnic restaurants were doing a brisk trade. Immersed in thought he didn't notice he was being observed, discretely photographed, and timed, as part of a routine observation by Mossad.

He bought some lagers at the small supermarket on the way back to his flat and settled down to his Indian and mind-numbing TV, anything to think of something different for a while.

His Sunday was a late rise, a long walk over Clapham Common to clear the cobwebs, and a film at the local cinema, which unfortunately turned out to be lacking in the basic ingredient, namely comedy, and therefore a complete waste of money. But, he thought, any alternative can be viewed as therapeutic.

He slept well on Sunday night, rising early on Monday morning in order to be in the office no later than 0745hrs. All had been logged by the observer and his alternate during the two days.

***

II

Monday 19th December 2005

0900 hrs Deputy's Office SIS(MI6) London

Harry knocked and entered the Deputy's office.

'Good morning, Harry. Sit down and grab a cup of coffee.'

Harry pulled a cup towards him, poured it, black, and sat down wondering what was going to be discussed.

'Alright Harry, I know you'll be curious following my call on Friday evening, so let me explain. As you can imagine we've got a number of teams working on this, unavoidably in silos, but sometimes it is necessary, and sometimes we get a break.

As you know in the normal work of security checking and vetting we include all the potential suspects plus researchers and PAs to our political masters. Generally not a problem, but occasionally we turn up something that has a bearing on one of our other investigations. I think we have one now.'

He drank from his coffee before continuing.

'What I am now going to tell you must remain Code 1 between us, and is not to be shared within your or any other team. Clear?'

Harry nodded and the Deputy continued.

'You are aware of the Government department which is responsible for determining the cause of the Buncefield disaster?'

Harry nodded.

'As you know the Minister has been looking at the possible causes, namely Accident or Terrorism. We have started our operations and your team is part of the matrix investigating the latter.

Prior to the disaster, in fact for over a year now, we had been running a separate operation concerning the Minister and his PA.

During some routine checking and updating on security clearances and positive vetting on the PA we found one or two gaps and question marks, bearing in mind her access to sensitive information. We found that when she moved from being his researcher to becoming his PA following the Election there were certain gaps; in fact the initial clearance had been quite cursory. From our covert operations we know that she is a Mossad agent, and has been, probably for the last year. We think she was recruited quite some time ago, and has been a sleeper, until activated very early last year.'

Harry looked suitably surprised, but made no comment, as the Deputy continued.

'Additionally, and this is an extremely sensitive point, we believe she has been conducting an affair with the Minister for at least three or four years. This fact, to the best of our knowledge, is not known by his wife; apparently they live pretty separate lives, except at elections!

Harry opened his mouth to speak, but the Deputy held up his hand and continued.

'We have dates, times, overnighters; in his flat, and most critically evidence of satellite telephone conversations, we believe with Mossad control. Analysis of telephone data is currently being carried out, all in all, pretty irrefutable.'

Harry was silent for a minute as the information sank in.

'OK, so let's assume all the intelligence on her is genuine, how can we use it to help us in the current investigation? It actually raises a lot more questions than answers, and, if I may say so, we don't really need the waters any more muddy than they are at present.'

The Deputy started to say, 'Har...' when he was interrupted.

'One thing I've just remembered, perhaps no connection, but who knows.'

'What?' said the Deputy, faintly irritated at the interruption.

'I had asked Tom to check with 'friendly' agencies as to any gossip or trades that might interest us. No joy at all with any of them, but the Israelis suggested a meeting. Could just be co-incidental, but who knows.'

'Follow it up and if there is a connection, I want to know.'

'What do think the Mossad connection, through the PA, indicates?' asked Harry.

'At present, no idea, other than the fact that Mossad likes to be in on everything; or at least in the know. They are obsessive about intelligence gathering, in case they miss something. Bearing in mind what some of Israel's neighbours say they would like to do to the country, I'm not surprised.'

'One further thing, Harry. Because this particular trail is not yet fully detailed and complete, in other words, work in progress, I have not, as yet, briefed the Director. I do not intend to do so, at the present time, as this may handicap or hinder his relationship with the Minister. If some of the details were known to the Director, it would be extremely embarrassing during their one to ones, especially if the PA was present. I do not wish any indications to be given at present which would harm our further investigations. That also includes members of your team. Right?'

'Understood', said Harry, thinking that, perhaps, there was more to this than was immediately apparent.

I'd like to get Tom at his Israeli meeting soonest, if that's all for now?'

'Fine, Harry, keep me posted if anything significant surfaces.'

1015hrs Harry's office C10 SIS(MI6) London

Harry walked into their shared office and saw Jane at her desk.

'Where's Tom?'

'Just about to go and see the Israelis.'

'I need to see him before he leaves, OK? Can you track him down?

Jane rose from her desk and hurried from the room, pretty sure Tom was stealing a quick cigarette outside. She caught him coming in to the building.

'Harry needs to see you before you go. He's in the office.'

Tom and Jane grabbed the lift and entered the office together.

'Jane, I need to brief Tom on his own, so can you give us ten? Sorry about that,' he said as Jane looked a little perplexed. 'All will be clear eventually, I think and hope', he joked.

Jane left and the two of them sat down.

Tom enquired, 'What gives?'

'Well,' said Harry, You need to be diplomatic and clever this morning. Who are you seeing, and do I know him?'

'I don't think so. His name is David Hadar. He is filling the role of Commercial Attaché as usual. He says he has only been in London about a year. I've arranged to meet him at 1230hrs. We'll go for a walk and a pint, if he wants one!'

'OK. See if you can determine whether he is from military intelligence or Mossad. That could determine the quality of any information they are prepared to give us and the type of co-operation we can expect. At this stage he'll keep his cards close to his chest, but clearly he will have seen all the media about the explosion. Indicate that our response is a normal investigation by us to rule out any possibility of terrorist involvement.

But, this is the crux, do they have any reports from their network, UK or overseas, that there may be foreign activity, of one sort or another, that could have some linkage, however slight, with this particular event?

The main thing is, Tom, is he likely to be good asset in the short to medium term, or do we have to think again? Think of potential nurturing.

It may be they are just fishing, and there is no value, but play him gently and see what comes. Good luck.'

'Thanks. See you later today.'

Tom left the office and Jane entered.

Harry looked up from his desk.

'Jane, sorry about that, but the old man put his own 'D' notice on a couple of pieces of information. No doubt they'll be released soon and I can bring you up to speed. OK?'

'No problem Harry, tell me when you can.'

1230hrs Tom Denman Meeting High Street Kensington

Tom had agreed meet David Hadar at Kensington High St Tube Station, it being a short walk from the Israeli Embassy. Identification had been prearranged, so they met each other cordially. They decided to walk westward along Kensington High Street towards Earls Court Road, turning into Allen Street and entering the Britannia pub and restaurant.

As it was lunchtime it was starting to fill up so they picked a quiet corner at the back, where hopefully they would not be overheard. They chose their drinks and food and sat down.

Tom explained, in much the manner, as Harry had suggested, that following the explosion at Buncefield, it was very much a case of exploring all avenues as to cause. Hence his call.

David Hadar expressed sympathy for the catastrophe, and enquired how they might be of assistance.

'Well,' said Tom, 'We are looking at this from several angles. If it is not an accident, then 1. How caused? 2. If so, is this home grown or imported? 3. Do our friends, like you, have any indication/information that could help us in this connection? 4. If so can this information be shared with us and are there any implications from such sharing?'

David paused before responding.

'To be frank Tom, I don't know. I will have to report back and see if there is any background from our side, and whether there is an appetite, or otherwise, for sharing, assuming such information might exist. Being the new boy on the block I am not completely up to speed as to any conventions that may exist between us so must take advice on this. You understand, I'm sure?'

Tom nodded, fully aware that David was buying time, in order to fully discuss the matter with his Control.

'Fully understood. By the way, changing the subject, I was thinking as you spoke, how our respective careers brought us to be discussing such matters in a London pub! I came the university route, was yours the same or military?'

'Half and half,' he replied hesitantly.

Military route definitely, thought Tom

'Shall we walk now,' suggested Tom.

They left and walked back up to the High Street crossing the road and continued up Argyll Rd.

'David, do you think, hypothetically, that there could be a Middle East connection? Nobody has claimed responsibility but that doesn't always happen. What I'm asking is, would your own network pick up random information that would be run through your own algorithms, against potential scenarios?'

David smiled, 'Sounds a bit too technical for me. As I said I'll have to report and then get back to you, OK?

David thought to himself that Tom was indicating what the UK ran through their programmes on a regular basis, and was checking to see if similar software was employed by them. With a close working relationship with the CIA, Israel had access to some of the most sophisticated analytical systems available to anybody. Some which would probably make the UK green with envy.

They turned right at the top of Argyll Rd into Upper Phillimore Gardens which led into Holland St, finishing at a T junction with Kensington Church St. They had exchanged a few thoughts along the way, but Tom wanted to leave David in no doubt as to UK intentions.

As they stood on the corner, he said, 'David, I would appreciate it if you could get back to me as soon as you can with respect to possible cooperation. My boss is keen to work with our friends, and, as I'm sure you can appreciate, there may be joint security interests that could arise from this.'

'Tom, I understand your request and will revert as soon as I can, subject to necessary higher approvals and the possible sharing of appropriate material.'

Having made their farewells, David continued his short walk to the embassy in Palace Green, Tom continuing down to the Underground on Kensington High St.

Tom sat on the Tube reflecting on what had been said. Yes, David had kept his cards close to his chest, but there was an indication of cooperation, subject to higher approval. What was David's level? Almost certainly Mossad, not just military attaché, London is too important a capital, bearing in mind it is often referred to as Londonistan by several critical western agencies.

1500hrs Harry's office C10 SIS(MI6) London

Tom walked into the office, as the occupants heard Big Ben chime the hour.

Harry looked up.

'How did it go Tom? Fill me in.'

Tom then explained in careful detail the discussions that had taken place; David's limited responses, and his own analysis.

Harry listened attentively, and sat silently when Tom had finished.

'When's he getting back to you?'

'He didn't give a precise date but said soon. Besides approval, I think he is going to do some digging to see if there is a real basis for cooperation or not.'

'Friendly, cooperative, cautious?'

'Yes, all of those things, but I think he would be happy to work with us.'

'Even if his boss said No?'

'I don't know about that. I don't think, at this stage, he's for turning.'

'You never know, Tom, just keep that in the back of your mind. Let me know as soon as he gets back to you.'

'Will do.'

1630hrs Israeli Embassy London

David knocked on Control's door and entered.

Control was on the telephone and waved David to sit down whilst he finished his conversation.

'...get detailed reports and photographs sent to me, securely, as soon as possible. OK?

The call finished he turned to David.

'Well, what do they want, and is there benefit for us?'

David explained the background of the Buncefield disaster and that it was clear the UK Security Services were spreading the net through 'friendly' agencies to see whether there were any indications of Middle East involvement. No claim for responsibility had been made which was not helping identification.

Control listened to the end without interrupting, but had been wondering during the presentation whether any indication had been given to David by Tom concerning the Minister and his PA. Obviously not. This information was known to Control and the specific team but not to David. Silo security was essential in certain areas and ensured 'a need to know' basis was operating.

David had emphasised Tom's request and expressed his thoughts that there could be mutual benefits to be accrued, subject, of course, to relevant authorisations and careful dissemination of approved information and data. Their own Israeli agenda must be paramount, but, by working with the UK in a particular way, could improve their own database, and at a time, of their choosing, suitable leaks could enhance public kudos.

Control reflected for a minute and then told David he would consider what he had said, whether they would cooperate with the UK, and if so what form that would take.

He emphasised to David that invariably he had to consider the bigger picture and not just be focussed on one specific challenge.

However, to soften the comment, he said that he hoped to establish a strategy which would be to mutual benefit to both Israel and the UK. He would revert to David within 48hrs so that he could relay the decision to his UK opposite number.

After David had left, Control ran through, in his mind and in his notes, some of the data and reports only available to him and the options he might consider.

He scribbled them down.

* Apply pressure on UK Minister. Not sensible. Risk to PA. Long term asset.

* Use new contact for further penetration of UK Security Services

* If terror threat, then cooperation yields dividends to both.

*How far to include David Hadar. Probably necessary

* Review recent data, connections, however weak

*Network wide Amber notice, prime focus Middle East & Gulf

He was deep in thought when his PC pinged. He glanced at the screen to see what was coming in over the secure network. Usual daily reports from various overseas stations.

He returned to his current task, thinking that he would review Gulf and Middle East reports next, as a matter of priority.

Later having determined how he would proceed with the request for cooperation he turned to his PC and started to scroll through the most recent reports, paying particular attention to Middle East and Gulf countries. The system also showed at the bottom of each report a précis link that referred to previous submissions.

Within the Lebanon section he noticed a station report concerning 'observation and eavesdropping' where the operative had submitted full details of a discussion between a Syrian and a Palestinian.

This had been picked up in a hotel using the latest directional microphones, whilst under observation. This was the second or third observed meeting between the two men and the content of their discussion caught Control's interest.

Essentially they had referred to high security levels in the UK and Europe, and were planning some sort of bombing operation between Qatar and Iran.

What Control could not understand was, why Qatar and Iran because of high security in Europe? The connection from the dialogue was not clear, but worthy of some investigation and follow up.

He telephoned one of Control's operatives, who had specific responsibility for close liaison with overseas stations and who had specific access to secure networks.

'Avner, I've been reading the regional reports, and I need some more digging on a particular matter. Can you come to my office so I can explain what I want?'

Avner said he could be there in 10 minutes.

When he arrived Control took him through the reports and pointed out the item that had caught his interest. He further explained that he wanted as much background on both men, their current locations, activities, where, what, why, etc?

Avner got a clear picture of what was required, but believed, from links to the report, that both had now left Lebanon. He suggested that the local operative would have connections at Beirut Airport to check if either had passed through.

Control asked him to follow up as quickly as possible and report back with any relevant information.

Control thought long and hard as to how best use this information and decided that if they were to cooperate with the UK as suggested it would be a good ploy to provide some 'soft' intelligence initially. Without direct linkage to Buncefield, it would be interesting to see how they used it. Plus Mossad operatives could monitor any increase in activity or different patterns by Security Service personnel they already had under observation.

One factor that would have to be built in at some time was the Minister's PA. She was not party to this current intelligence, but if cooperation developed satisfactorily she should be included in the loop, in order to maximise cause and effect.

Control decided that at an early date he would update her as to current status, and ensure that she was then able to determine the significant players on the UK side. With such knowledge she would be able to see if the authority levels had been raised and what priorities were being applied.

One thing he would like to do is to move the level of contact up the UK control tree; now that would be useful.

Control decided to reflect on things overnight, but, in principle, he would approve the cooperation request and brief David Hadar accordingly.

Tuesday 20th December 2005 0930hrs Minister's office Whitehall London

The Minister was not in a good mood.

The previous evening meeting with the PM had been humiliating. The Minister had had to bite his tongue on more than one occasion, as a number of Cabinet colleagues had been present.

The loaded sarcasm, dripping from the PM's lips, had infuriated him.

Taking this crap from the little bastard I supported against his nemesis, he thought, keeping silent, whilst the perceived ineptitude of his Ministry was described by the PM.

Never mind, he thought, through mentally gritted teeth, revenge is a dish best served cold.

He sat at his desk reviewing the problem, and wondering which direction to take in the absence of any solid information.

His PA entered carrying his coffee and sat down to await his comments or instructions.

She recognised the mood, she had seen it on many occasions before, and it normally spelt trouble.

'Any reports from Health & Safety?' he enquired.

'No, just a comment that they are still hindered by the conflagration and inspectors cannot get near until it is considered to be of no risk to the investigators.'

'Bloody typical, the damn thing will have rusted and gone to hell before those idiots can tell us anything.'

She did not respond, as at times like this it was completely pointless.

'I've heard damn all from the Security Service so far. What the hell are they doing? Either sitting on their arses, or playing cops and robbers!!'

She remained silent.

'I was completely stuffed by the PM yesterday evening.'

This was the reason for his mood, she quickly concluded.

'In what way,' she enquired.

'He had some of his sycophants round and decided that it would be amusing to take the piss out of me because of lack of any information so far about Buncefield. There was damn all I could say because I've had damn all from anybody! The little creeps thought it was frightfully funny, but I've got their number. I'll give them a bloody good kick up the arse, mark my word!'

His neck had reddened, she noticed, in the usual way when he was angry.

She spoke quickly, in order to try and defuse the situation.

'Forget it. Most of them are political pygmies anyway, and the PM should remember where the bulk of his support comes from. Do you want to meet this evening, as you suggested yesterday? I can organise things if you like.'

He sulkily agreed and asked her to get SIS(MI6) on the telephone.

She left his office and a few minutes later his telephone rang. It was the Head of the SIS(MI6).

'Minister, good morning.'

'Good morning, Director.' The tone was icy.

'Is there any news that I could find encouraging?

'Well Minister, it is fairly early days but I believe we are making some progress. I don't want to pre-empt anything at this stage, particularly over this open line, but there are certain facts and agency information that are helping us form a view. I would hope to have something more solid in a few days, say after Christmas.'

The Minister was quiet for a few seconds and then exploded. A stream of invective poured down the phone for at least a minute, finishing with a question as to whether the Director had anything sensible or constructive to say at all.

A short pause from the Director was followed by the polite reply, that as a new style of working was operating between them, he hoped that he would be able to provide further information to the Minister in the next few days. At this point the line went dead.

The Minister smashed his handset down cursing everybody and everything, the veins on his neck reddened and pulsing.

He rose and walked quickly out of his office, advising his PA that he was going for a walk, slamming the door behind his retreating body.

She thought to herself that the proposed meeting that evening would be fractious, at least; perhaps to call in sick after lunch might be more politic and diplomatic.

In any case she needed to call Control.

1145hrs Control's office Israeli Embassy London

David Hadar hurried up to Control's office, from where he had been called a few minutes earlier.

He knocked and entered following the invitation, and sat down facing the Director.

'David, I have considered all matters relating to the request by your contact in UK Security to cooperate with them on this particular operation, and believe it will be in our country's best interest to do so.

Let us be quite clear there are integral risks within any such operation, and we need to be cautious, initially, until some precise operating parameters have been agreed, and are clearly working well.

Whilst wishing to help our friends we must be very circumspect in not jeopardising our own position or security. We do want to find ourselves as the focus of a public incident that could, in any way, affect our other international relationships, and undo years of painstakingly built diplomatic cooperation.

There are other factors that will come into play, some of which you have no knowledge of at present, but which will be critical elements over the ensuing months.

Whilst active on this operation you will report solely to me, and all communications will be routed through me, unless otherwise authorised. This may appear cumbersome at present, but in order to maintain complete security for persons involved, it must be enforced.

Do you understand and have I made matters completely clear?'

David concurred and Control then went on to describe some of the main elements that should be of interest to David in his relations with Tom Denman.

Control wanted to determine the command and control structure within the unit above Tom, and any indications as to the type of working relationships that existed between the Service and the Ministries.

Were there any obvious sensitivities or sensibilities that were in play, was contention a problem? Were Departments working well together, or were there 'turf wars', or outright competition due to Ministerial vanities? Anything of this nature must be reported, as directly or indirectly it could have a significant impact on how situations would play out, and not necessarily in their best mutual interest.

Without divulging the exact name or position Control indicated that they had a person 'in post' in one of the Ministries who was able to contribute, and confirm or otherwise, their readings on internal policy debate and execution. This source would also be made aware of the key relationship that was about to commence and would report back any comments, observations, true or false fed intelligence, Ministerial relationships, etc that could be used to exploit or improve Mossad's own position within the operation.

Control then authorised David to have access to current station reports and to be briefed on current activity and research by Avner. Following this David would have a further joint briefing by Control and Avner before making contact with Tom Denman.

1530hrs PA's flat Southwark London

She'd called in sick. The Minister was not pleased, and with poor grace accepted her excuse.

She caught up with her flat, then bathed and read for a while. At 1740hrs she called Control on her other mobile.

With little to report she then listened, at length, to a guarded explanation of the pending cooperation exercise between UK Security and Mossad. At this stage only outline was given, no names at all. The reason for this was to ensure that she would express genuine surprise when a name finally surfaced and not to be looking for connections before events occurred.

She was instructed to take a passive role, observing and reporting on anything she thought showed a link to the operation and the joint working, including exchange of intelligence.

After the briefing she sat and wondered which direction this cooperation would take bearing in mind the previous discussions between her Minister and the Director of SIS(MI6). For both the SIS(MI6) and Mossad there were some considerable risks, a 'thin ice' scenario which would have to be carefully managed. On a 'need to know' basis she would keep a low profile and listen only.

The Minister called, with a conciliatory tone, at about 2100hrs, to enquire as to her health. She responded in a low key voice, ensuring that she sounded sick, but also reassuring him that she would be in the office tomorrow.

She was aware that Control must ensure secure lines between operatives, particularly when playing a double game, but if the theatre of operation expanded to include the Middle East and Gulf then it became doubly dangerous, if not more, with many other vested interests, and conflicting agendas becoming part of the muddied mix.

She was totally committed to the defence of her country and the defeat of its enemies, but the stakes were becoming higher by the minute, and nobody really knew where this was leading.

She prayed that Mossad had picked the right partners for the immediate future.

Wednesday 21st December 2005 0915hrs Hotel Al Manama Bahrain

The Palestinian, Fayez Al-Hourani, walked across the hotel lobby to a table in the corner by the window overlooking the Corniche.

Salutations were given and received as he sat down opposite the Iranian.

Arabic coffee was brought and served before they started talking.

The Palestinian outlined the plan to the Iranian, Atash Akbari, and what would be required in terms of both equipment and personnel. They discussed the funding required and a likely timescale for all the project's elements.

He then went into some detail of the reason for this particular Jihad, saying it was one of a series of actions against the Kaffur and which would bring great joy to the Muslim world, and significant publicity to their cause.

The Iranian listened politely, and murmured agreement at appropriate points, but inwardly was only interested in the financial return for himself, and the profit he could make on any commercial deal.

Fayez finally finished his address, and they agreed to meet in the next 72 hours to confirm funding, planning and timescale.

As the Iranian left, the man standing behind the check-in desk pressed the button in his coat pocket that activated by radio the miniature camera located at the top of one of the columns that was covering the lobby. Simultaneously, the digital image was sent to a laptop sitting in a secure compartment of a locked car in the hotel car park.

Fayez went to his room to review the project and to see if there were any weaknesses in what was being planned. He needed to be sure of all his facts before his next discussions with the Syrian representative of the Committee.

1200hrs Hezbollah Majlis Damascus Syria

The Syrian, Karim Al Halbi, sat facing the committee and outlined the plan he had discussed with the Palestinian. The faces opposite him were mostly inscrutable, so he described in some detail the success of the Buncefield operation, the choice of the Gulf for the second, and gave a tantalising glimpse of the major attack planned for London the following year.

He took his time, giving significant detail, which would indicate a thorough research and costing of what was planned. Risks were identified, costs of delay, potential casualties both to their own 'soldiers' and indicated targets.

After his full presentation the Majlis opened up for questions.

The first one was concerning potential casualties in the Gulf proposal.

Karim covered this by saying that the explosion was planned to disrupt gas flow for a time, but not to destroy the installation with loss of life. This seemed to satisfy the questioner, but as Atash knew himself, the consequence of the planned explosion could be a chain reaction, culminating in complete destruction of the platform.

Following a number of general questions, which he handled with ease, Karim was advised that approval, both for the operation and funding, was granted. He was to liaise with their Finance chief to organise the pick up of cash for the project in Bahrain, Qatar and Al Khubar, Saudi Arabia.

He left the building and made his way to the airport to start his journey to Bahrain. He was taking a circuitous route over three legs to avoid any suspicion when he arrived in Bahrain. His flight plan, of separate single flights, was Damascus to Jeddah, Jeddah to Abu Dhabi, and Abu Dhabi to Bahrain, staying at least one night in each city.

When in Bahrain he could take the causeway for his meeting in Al Khubar in Saudi Arabia, and after his return to Bahrain, he could then take a 40 minute flight to Qatar.

He planned to arrive in Bahrain on either the 26th or 27th December 2005.

1600hrs Mossad Bureau Beirut Lebanon

The bureau was operated under the guise of a Lebanese trading company with a legitimate front, but covert back office.

It had received requests under 'Very Urgent' category concerning observation of the Palestinian and Syrian and the interpretation of their discussion picked up by the directional mikes.

Subsequent analysis of airport departures had shown the Palestinian had flown to Bahrain. Trail had been lost of the Syrian, last seen leaving the city by car.

All stations had been advised by photo and description to check for any likely sightings in airports, hotels, etc and to report to the centre accordingly. This in turn would be redistributed to all stations.

Avnar Mazar, Head of Station, was sitting at his desk at the rear of the building, situated behind an apparently solid wall, which however, with the correct radio key, would slide back to gain access.

He was reviewing a number of reports, including the detail of the overheard discussion, when one point caught his attention.

It was a reference to tight European security, because of something unspecified, which was redirecting their efforts to planning an attack in the Gulf. He recalled the request from Central that wanted input on anything that may indicate a connection with Europe. He compiled a brief report highlighting the specific reference and sent it over the secure satellite link.

It was clear that the planned attack would create some initial instability in the region, not something that Mossad was averse to, if Arab was blaming Arab, but of no strategic value, if enmity was further directed against Israel.

What he wanted was clearance to pursue this lead as a priority. With limited resources and manpower he needed approval, but what was clear, was that something specific was planned, and which was moving steadily towards an operational status, date as yet unspecified.

The following morning, 22nd December 2005, his telephone rang and he took the call, over his secure line, from an operative in Bahrain.

Covert photos had been taken of new arrivals and a match had been made with the Palestinian, Fayez Al-Hourani.

Their previous observations and photographs taken in Beirut had been downloaded onto the central database which ensured rapid matching and dissemination to stations. The photograph had been taken following discussions Al-Hourani had held, it was believed, with an Iranian, but there was no information as to content.

The next day, the 23rd, a further call came in advising that an agent, believed to be the Syrian, had landed in Jeddah, and was staying at the Inter Continental Hotel. On the basis of flight arrivals his flight had started in Damascus.

Avnar logged the call and information and wondered why the Syrian had not gone directly to Bahrain to meet up with the Palestinian. He circulated appropriate agents to maintain observation and report on a Priority 1 basis.

Friday 23rd December 2005 1500hrs Central London

Late Christmas shoppers scurried along the Strand, heads bowed against a breeze and flecks of rain. Tom Denman, turning right at the top of Northumberland Avenue into the Strand, weaved a path through people hurrying for trains in Charing Cross carrying them into the suburbs, Kent and Sussex.

A few office party revellers made their way raucously across the forecourt of the station as Tom entered the hotel and made his way to the first floor lounge.

He spotted David Hadar sitting at a table in the corner with a tea setting already placed in front of him.

'David, hullo. I see you're well organised,' he said nodding at the tea set.

David smiled and stood up to shake hands.

'Well Tom, how's it going?'

'Forward one, back two, I'm not sure. Any joy from your side.'

'There might be something that I'll tell you about in a minute. First let me tell you of a discussion I had with my boss. By the way is your head man in the loop?'

'Absolutely. He dotted the Is and crossed the Ts and is updated on a very regular basis. Why?'

David ignored the direct question and went into a well prepared presentation of why Israel wanted to work closely with the UK on this particular problem. It was to be hoped that this would create the sort of environment for all levels within the respective services to cooperate together on similar 'projects'.

Tom listened, thinking that David had been briefed to expand on the project, and to glean as much as possible as to their current methods and style of operation. Additionally, to fill in the gaps concerning their understanding as to overall resources, and manning levels.

Tom did not comment directly, but asked, 'What was the 'something' you referred to?'

'We are getting some feedback from one of our stations, not in the UK, that might, I am saying might, indicate some connection with the matter that interests you. As yet it is not firm, and clearly needs further analysis and corroboration.'

'If that was the case, then there could be some offshore connection, not just home-grown. Interesting. When do you think you will have some positive information or something for us to work on?'

'Possibly in the next week, dependent on what we pick up. The info is related to two sources and there is some distance between them at present. Once things are stationary for a period we ought to be able to confirm or otherwise our initial intelligence.' 'Fine,' said Tom. 'One small step...! Keep me posted as soon as anything is available.'

'Any trade off?' David asked smiling.

'When there's something solid, who knows?' Tom responded, also smiling.

'Seriously call me as soon as you have anything. OK.'

They shook hands and Tom sat and drank his tea as David disappeared down the stairs to the lobby. He waited about ten minutes and then left.

He decide to walk down the Mall as a different route to the office, wondering, as he walked, if what David had told him was solid, or was it a fly on the water to wet the appetite, a teaser, testing the boundaries, in an attempt to gain entry to the Service?

If it was solid it would certainly open up a whole new perspective on the investigation. Where would this take them? David had referred to somewhere other than UK. European connection? Middle East, Gulf, who knows? Whatever comes out we will have new dynamics at play. That's a certainty!

*

Harry was catching up, no, tidying up his desk, and filing reports. He had told Jane to go early; Christmas only comes once a year.

He thought about the next few days. Without family, Christmas can be the loneliest time of the year, so on the spur of the moment he decided to ring a small pub in Sussex where he knew the owners, and that had a few rooms and did Christmas lunch.

His luck was in, as there had been a cancellation, so at least he would get a well cooked meal for a change.

*

He updated the Deputy as to the conversation Tom had held with David, emphasising that further corroboration would not be available for a week, but promising to make contact if information became available sooner.

*

The Deputy decided he would not, at this time, brief the Minister on the latest possibility, as knowing his predilection for shooting from the hip, he would then want chapter and verse to report to the PM. It was too light and sketchy and no confirmation was available at present. Let the bastard wait, he thought!

*

The Minister was leaving for his home in the North; family duty, ten boring days with his wife and family, going through the pretence, all for the sake of the odd constituent that might see him.

His PA was staying with some friends in Surrey, which faintly irritated him because he knew she would have a good time, without pretence.

His diffident, truculent manner did not bother her as he left his office.

She was well aware all would be sweetness and light after his return to Westminster in the New Year.

The Director of the SIS(MI6) had a brief update with his Deputy which provided little additional Intel as to progress, but indicated that certain, as yet unspecified, sources would be contributing to the mix in the New Year.

***

III

Tuesday 27th December 2005 1030hrs Sheraton Hotel Al Manama Bahrain

The Syrian walked into the hotel lobby at the same time as a Mossad operative was calling his Control by secure satellite line, to advise him that Karim Al Halbi had been observed at Bahrain International Airport, arriving on a Gulf Air flight from Abu Dhabi.

The Syrian checked in, and from his room called the Palestinian at the Gulf Hotel to arrange a meeting for later in the day.

He spent some time checking the flights to and from Doha, Qatar, and also the taxi costs and schedule across the causeway from Bahrain to Al Khubar, Saudi Arabia. He had the necessary contact points for the fund providers in the three locations and the confidential passwords to secure entry and acceptance. His passport details had been emailed in advance to assist recognition.

The Syrian went to the Gulf Hotel to meet the Palestinian and to discuss funding and timing of their planned operation. This was carried out on the balcony of the Palestinian's room to prevent any eavesdropping.

As they ran through the main elements, the Palestinian almost immediately indicated that that the original estimate was too low, and would have to be increased by at least 20%.

The Syrian responded angrily and demanded to know why this had not been accounted for in the original planning, as this would require an increase in funding, which was already under close scrutiny.

The Palestinian explained that since the Syrian had proposed the initial operation, general security on both sides of the international border between Qatar and Iran in the Gulf had been tightened. This meant that there was a heightened risk of discovery by either country, and therefore the group carrying out the operation felt there should be a premium paid to reflect this.

The Palestinian explained, in some detail, exactly how the operation would be handled, and the consequences arising from failure, which served additionally to reinforce the increase in costs. He further explained that it would take at least two weeks to get the team together, plus a further 2-3 weeks to train and equip, with a target date of say five weeks from now in early February 2006.

The Syrian reluctantly had to accept the various arguments and said he would be following up on the funding over the next few days, but due to what had been presented by way of extra costs, some delay would be inevitable.

They parted with the Syrian saying he would make contact within a few days, meanwhile asking the Palestinian start his preparations, so as to ensure no additional slippage.

1130hrs 'The George' Pub SE of Lewes Sussex

Harry had had a great Christmas with his friends, the owners of the George, eaten too much, perhaps drunk a little too much, but what the hell, once a year.

He was staying now until the New Year, bearing in mind his interrupted holiday in Cyprus, and was confident the Deputy would not begrudge him that. He telephoned the Duty Officer advising him of his location, and 24hr availability by mobile.

His hosts had suggested he accompany them to a 'drinks and nibbles' do at a friend's house just south of Dorking, so he was sitting in the back of their car, happy to be driven for a change.

They turned off the A24 towards Strood Green and then turned into a gravel drive leading to a mock Tudor house standing in grounds of about two acres.

The drive had already started to fill up with parked cars as they made their way to the already opened front door.

They rang the bell and entered to be greeted warmly by the host and his wife. Harry's friends introduced him with a short explanation as to why he was with them, at which point the host put a glass of hot punch in their hand, and pulled them all through to meet some of the other guests.

Harry did not make any attempt to remember anybody's name or face, as he was unlikely to see them again, but contributed to the small talk and general conversation.

His friends from the 'George' had always been told that he was middle ranking civil servant at the M.O.D., involved in procurement. Boring, but steady, was his usual response, and people's eyes would normally glaze over if he started recounting some of the procurement issues already in the public domain.

Harry was joining another small gaggle as the host came over with a refill for his glass. He also introduced Harry to the four people standing in the corner by the French windows as,

'Friend of a friend, does something in the MOD, spending all our taxes on boys toys, I'll be bound,' at which point he left, laughing.

Harry grimaced, and said, 'If only that were true, Our political masters can't seem to make up their minds, so a lot of things are running late and over budget, as you've probably read in the papers.'

A woman standing on his left said quietly, 'I don't think it's just confined to the MOD. I think in many ways it's endemic.'

'I'm glad you said that and not me, but I agree with you. Do you have connections with the Civil Service?'

Not the Civil Service per se, but I work as a PA to a Minister.'

'Which Ministry is that, if I may ask? Unless it falls under the Secrets Act.' He said jokingly.

She readily advised which Ministry it was, and in the absence of having seen any photographs, Harry immediately made two plus two equal four. It certainly made the adrenalin flow more quickly, and he lowered his eyes to avoid giving any signs of recognition of her position.

Harry decided to play the long game and enquired where she lived, town or country; all the usual small talk questions that then moved on to music, theatre, film, etc.

She was an attractive woman and Harry did not find the task difficult, in fact quite the reverse. He wondered what the Deputy would say when he briefed him in the New Year, and what he would think as to a course of action.

Harry then excused himself to continue circulating among the guests, but determined to have a final word before departure.

At about 3.30pm guests started to drift away and Harry approached Anna to say goodbye.

'Nice to have met. I was thinking, you live in Southwark, I live in Clapham, we both like the theatre. What about seeing something at the Old Vic or Young Vic?

She paused before replying. She had liked the conversation with Harry. There was something of the realist about him, a bit craggy round the edges, but a certain charm; why not?

'Why not,' she replied. 'I would like that.'

'Have you got a mobile or home number I can call you on?'

She gave Harry her mobile number and he promised to call in the New Year with some suggestions as to plays and dates.

Driving back to Sussex with his hosts they pulled his leg affectionately about his prospective date, but were quite glad to see what had occurred, bearing in mind Harry had been on his own for some years. He reacted in the way he hoped they expected, a little embarrassment, but that was all.

Harry had plenty to think about over the next few days prior to seeing the Deputy in the New Year.

Anna, in turn, wondered what Harry's choice might be at the theatre. Always a good indication of mindset. Well, let's see, she thought. In any case, a contact within procurement at the MOD could always be useful.

Saturday 31st December 2005 1130hrs Hotel Al Manama Bahrain

The Syrian concluded the conversation on his mobile and sat back in his chair. He had just finished a long and guarded conversation with Damascus concerning extra funding.

There had been a similar reaction to his own, but by describing a number of obvious examples where costs had clearly increased, he had secured what was required.

He decided to stay in Bahrain for the next few days as the expatriates would be celebrating their New Year in various cities in the Gulf, including Doha, Abu Dhabi and Dubai.

He thought long and hard about the planning of the pending operation and felt some concern on the limited strength of security both within his own circle of operatives, and that surrounding the likely target.

He considered the amount he would deposit in his own bank account in Beirut and the further option of moving a substantial amount into another bank account under an assumed name. If any investigation was carried out in the future by his masters he wanted to ensure that the paper trail was convincing.

***

IV

Tuesday 3rd January 2006

0845hrs Harry's office, C10, SIS(MI6) London

Harry walked into his office, C10, noting a rather stale smell of coffee.

He had spent New Year with his friends in Sussex, a good time being had by all, and his dull throbbing head merely a memory by the 3rd of January.

As New Year's Eve had fallen on a Saturday, therefore New Years Day being Sunday, Monday had been made a public holiday, with everybody back to work on Tuesday the 3rd.

He smiled to himself, thinking of his service days, when nothing like that ever interfered with operations.

He poured himself a coffee and sat down, reflecting on his meeting with Anna, and what the Deputy might think, say, or suggest.

Whilst he was lost in thought, Tom and Jane entered, both wishing him a Happy New Year in chorus, which gave rise to some shared laughter, on the basis that more rehearsal time was needed!

Harry decided he would keep thoughts to himself until after the meeting with the Deputy and instead asked Tom if there had been any further contact from his Mossad contact, David Hadar.

'Nothing over the holiday period,' said Tom, 'But I'm going to contact him anyway to keep the line warm. Don't forget he hinted at something in our last meeting, so I have a good reason to follow up with him.'

'OK, but try to determine if this was just a fly on the water to pull us in, or is there really something solid we can work on. Tell him that, even if the information is slight, let us have it, because we may be able to link it with some of our data and make some sense of it. At least we can see whether there is any real credibility in what they are saying or whether it really is just a fishing trip.'

'Understood, but can I dangle something in front of him?' Harry thought for a minute.

'Tell him we have identified, we think, a Lebanese, who was operating in the North East, without visible means of financial support. Not absolutely sure what he was up to. Did they have any leads from their operatives? Usual stuff. Alright?'

'I'll see what I can dig out. David is fairly cagey though. However it's worth a try.'

Jane cut in and said, 'I'm chasing Nils Helland to see if he's dug up anything. If so, then perhaps we can add something to make it more tempting to David.'

'Good,' said Harry. 'Hold back Tom, until Jane has done that. Let's think carefully of what we say if Nils has got something solid. I need to see the Deputy soonest so can we meet for update, say, 1130hrs?'

With a murmur of agreement the meeting broke up and Harry called the Deputy's office to ask for an early meeting which was confirmed for 45 minutes time.

0915hrs Minister's Office Whitehall

Anna was sorting through a pile of internal memos and minutes as the Minister walked into his office, voicing his New Year's greeting.

'Good holiday?' he enquired.

'Fairly quiet', she replied, reflecting that anything higher up the scale of enjoyment would produce some loaded sarcasm at some future date.

'VERY quiet, and VERY boring', he retorted, covering his own experience.

They spent the next hour dealing with some fairly mundane administration matters, ensuring that his diary was up to date, and that he was fully aware of his schedule over the rest of the week.

He then sat back and enquired when they could meet for dinner. Anna, conscious of his schedule, pointed out, that realistically, Friday would be the first sensible time, assuming he did not have to travel back to his constituency.

The Minister reluctantly agreed and then left for his first meeting with his junior Ministers and permanent civil servants.

Anna busied herself with various papers and wondered if Harry Baxter would ring, or whether he had changed his mind when the euphoria of the drinks party had worn off.

1000hrs Deputy's office SIS(MI6) London

Harry entered the Deputy's office just before ten and wished his boss a Happy New Year.

'Similar good wishes', the Deputy responded. 'Any progress?'

'Slow, but there is one item I wanted to discuss with you. It may have some benefit, but I'm not really sure at this stage what's the best way to handle it. If you think it's worth pursuing then I would like your comments and advice.'

'Fire away.'

'I stayed with some friends in Sussex over Christmas and the New Year and on one occasion they took me to a drinks party at one of their friends. About 20-25 people there and I chatted to one woman who turned out to be the Minister's PA.'

The Deputy looked questioningly at him.

'Yes, that Minister. My cover, to my friends and everybody else, is that I am a middle ranking civil servant in MOD procurement, and that's what I told her. We got on quite well; and yes, she's quite attractive. I suggested that we might go to the theatre some time. She lives in Southwark and as you know, I live in Clapham, so it seemed quite natural. The question is or rather there are several questions that come out of this.'

'What are your thoughts Harry?' the Deputy enquired.

'Well, is such a connection worth developing? If so what do we want to get from it? I am aware of the Minister's character and temper, and his attitude to us at present. Question, will such a contact help or hinder? You see my thinking before I ask her out on a harmless theatre date?'

The Deputy paused before replying. He had been thinking of the background information concerning the PA, the Mossad connection, the months of surveillance and reports of her relationship with the Minister; some of which was known to Harry.

'Harry, I'm going to have to give this some thought. There are obvious implications both good and bad, and if this connection is to be developed it must be very carefully handled. The last thing we want is for something like this to blow up in our face, but there could be considerable mileage if properly handled. Give me a couple of days and we will meet on Thursday, same time, and I will give you my thoughts, etc.'

Harry started to speak but the Deputy interrupted him.

'By the way. When are you contacting her about the theatre?'

'No specific date. I said I'd contact her in the New Year after I've had a look to see what was on at the Old or Young Vics.

'Fine, Harry, see you Thursday then?'

Harry concurred, rose and left.

The Deputy sat for a while thinking about what Harry had said and the implications if such a connection was developed.

Harry did know of the PA's long Mossad connection and her relationship with the Minister. That relationship had not been passed up to the Director. The Deputy was saving that for a rainy day.

Harry was obviously attracted to her; otherwise why bother with the invitation. However, Harry was very professional and could see some benefit in developing the relationship, if only for further input into the overall mix.

What would be the best course of action? Slowly, slowly.

He decided to think on this and prepare in his own mind a scenario that Harry could work with without compromising his position. There was no requirement for disclosure, at this time, of the Mossad or Minister relationships, and which if nurtured carefully could perhaps produce some information as to the Minister's private thoughts, compared to his public utterances.

On the other side of the coin, knowing of the PA's Mossad role, she could be thinking that any information as to MOD procurement (Harry's cover), would be useful to her Control, and their wider interest in all things geopolitical.

The Deputy thought around these implications for some time before reading the latest surveillance reports covering indigenous groups in the UK being groomed via the internet for possible terrorist activities.

The numbers were increasing almost exponentially, and his and other government resources were being heavily stretched. Link that with the EU and Human Rights legislation, and at times he wondered which side the law was on.

Harry went back to his office thinking of the Deputy's reaction. He prided himself on being a good reader of body language and the Deputy's initial response had surprised him. He had expected quite a robust answer, perhaps suggesting that it was far too sensitive and political to pursue, particularly bearing in mind the Ministers reputation.

No, the Deputy clearly had additional information, not in Harry's possession, which was causing him to consider how such a relationship could be handled.

Thursday's meeting could be interesting.

Tom and Jane were in the office and both looked up enquiringly as he entered.

'Any Intel?' Tom enquired.

'No, just post holiday catch up,' Harry lied cheerfully, not convincing Tom or Jane one bit. However they knew they would be brought into the loop at the appropriate time.

Jane had left a message for Nils and at that moment the telephone rang. It was Nils.

Before she was able to ask him any specifics Nils told her he was sending an interesting report over the secure network for Harry's attention. At that moment the printer started humming.

1035hrs Doha International Airport, Qatar.

The Gulf Air flight turned gently to starboard to line up on Runway 16 for its final approach.
The Syrian looked out of a right hand window at Doha as the plane steadily approached touchdown over the shimmering sea. He could see the West Bay development and Corniche before the sand and heat haze close to the ground obscured his view.
Clearing customs and immigration he took a taxi to the Doha Marriott Hotel and checked in, telephoning his contact from his room. A meeting was arranged for that evening at 1900hrs.

1115hrs Harry's Office C10 SIS(MI6) London

Harry was reading Nils report. It was interesting but not conclusive.
Nils had pulled in some additional resource across the region to dig further into the activities of the Lebanese, of which now, there was no trace.
What was clear was that there was a clear connection between the girl friend, her brother, his place of work, the refinery and evidence of further break-ins in the perimeter fence.
However, motive, funding, organisation, etc were the areas where no facts had arisen. No organisation had claimed responsibility, so was this a one-off, or a test run for a subsequent attack?
Harry felt that they were fumbling in the dark and not making real progress, but it was all they had, and was something that they could use in discussions with Mossad.
Tom walked into the office as Harry looked up.

'Tom, let's cover what you are going to discuss with David Hadar. Nils report goes some way to explain what is going on but it's thin. As we've said there is no one claiming responsibility. Why not? Is this a fore runner of something much bigger? We don't know.

What I want you to do in your discussions with David is to try and see if they are getting any feeds from outside the UK that might have a bearing on this. Say that we think this Lebanese Christian could just be a front, and why is there no trace of him at all. Indicate that we are very keen to work with them and this assumed attack would serve as a very good proving ground for our joint investigation. Incidentally, indicate that if the man is posing as Lebanese then a number of nationalities could fall under that alias, Syrian, Palestinian, Iranian, Egyptian, whatever. Are you happy going down that path Tom? '

'Not a problem at this stage, but if they start looking for trade-offs then we have to be sure they are kosher in both directions, if you'll excuse the pun! I'm happy sharing as much information as you see fit, but I think both he and I will be skating on thin ice from time to time. As long as you support me with the big chiefs if things hit the fan, then yes.'

'Fine. You have my support. When have you arranged to meet him?'

Tomorrow 1000hrs outside the Albert Hall. We'll go for a walk in Hyde Park.'

'OK. Give me an update by close of play tomorrow as I'm seeing the Deputy at 1000hrs Thursday morning. Anything positive will be a help for me and him!'

1900hrs Doha Marriott Hotel Qatar

The Syrian, Karim Al Halbi, crossed the vestibule on his way to one of the lounges, looking for his contact, Haji Massri, an Egyptian.

Haji Massri used to be a member of the Muslim Brotherhood but was expelled under a cloud of terrorist rumours, which had lifted his profile within extremist groups committed to acts of violence against all things Western.

Massri rose as he saw Al Halbi, exchanged fraternal greetings and kisses and sat down at the table already occupied by Massri and coffee cups.

Their discussions, in Arabic, were carried out in low voices and covered the main details of the cash to be given to Al Halbi to cover the project expenses. This would be provided in two tranches, one in Doha, and the other in Manama when Karim returned to Bahrain.

The first tranche would be delivered to the hotel the following day at 1500hrs prior to Karim taking a Gulf Air flight to Bahrain at 1800hrs.

Al Halbi urged Massri to make sure that the delivery was on time as he had no wish to miss his flight and stay a further day. Massri reassured him and gave him details of the courier who would meet him in Bahrain with the second tranche on Thursday the 5th January. He provided the name and an unusual Arabic phrase and answer to confirm their respective identities.

Al Halbi did not discuss the operation with Massri, it being understood between them that within their organisation information was only shared on a 'need to know' basis. Any loose talk or leaks discovered were dealt with summary justice, and swiftly.

After finishing their coffee they went their separate ways.

Wednesday 4th January 2006 1000hrs Albert Hall, Kensington, London

Tom Denman and David Hadar met outside the Albert Hall on a cold but dry day, and crossed Kensington Gore to enter Hyde Park by Queen's Gate next to the Albert Memorial.

They had exchanged the usual pleasantries during the first few minutes before Tom brought the conversation round to the reason they were there.

'David, let me be frank. This 'incident', and I am choosing my words carefully, is odd. It is not following the usual patterns and unusually, nobody, even in a covert way, is claiming responsibility. My boss has given me considerable licence in what I can share with you, obviously on a non-attributable basis, but if we are going to crack this one, then we need some solid input from your side.'

David was initially surprised at Tom's comments but decided he would take them at face value to see how the dialogue would develop. In any case there was nothing he would be sharing today. That would only occur if Control sanctioned it, and the extent to which he would be allowed to share and co-operate.

Tom then raised the question of the Lebanese, and explained in general detail what they had found out and which had been contained in Nils Helland report. The question of his true nationality was raised and this was where Tom surprised David by widening the investigation significantly.

Tom said, 'Look, we are casting the net a lot wider and it is thought this could be an area where you could help us. Let's make an assumption that this has obviously got a Middle East or Gulf connection. If that is the case then do any of your stations have anything that could indicate a possible connection to our 'incident' however slight? If the original suspect is Lebanese, then have you got any Intel that could narrow down our search? If Lebanese nationality is a front, could he be Syrian, Palestinian, or Egyptian? As you can see David, we need anything from the region that is going to help us identify the man; once we've done that it's going to make life a lot easier to determine the Who, Why, and how much?'

'I can see where you're going with this, but I obviously haven't got the answers today. I'm going to need additional clearance from my boss, plus a lot of analysis from our stations, if approval is given.'

'Fair enough, but I cannot stress enough how committed we are to get the show on the road. Will you recommend it, and push your boss. We think time is of the essence, and we need to get the additional horsepower onboard.'

Obviously Tom, I'll do what I can and get back to you ASAP. I'll try and get approval first and let you know, the analysis will follow as a consequence.'

They bade each other farewell at the edge of the park and Tom crossed the road to take the tube from Knightsbridge Station. He thought the discussion had gone well but everything would depend on David's Control and where they went from here.

He would brief Harry this afternoon so at least he would have something when talking to the Deputy tomorrow morning.

As Tom sat on the tube he wondered what the current discussions were between Harry and the Deputy bearing in mind Harry's obvious lie yesterday.

No doubt I'll find out in due course, he thought.

David Hadar went back to his embassy and compiled a short report for Control and requested an early meeting. This was agreed for1400hours.

Control would have had a chance to read the report before the meeting and David was hoping that approval, if it was granted, would not take too long, as he could see substantial gains to be made by working with Tom Denman.

Control read the brief report, smiling and nodding at certain points made. Things were going in the right direction, he thought. With careful and measured handling most of what he had previously outlined could be achieved. He looked forward to the meeting at 1400hrs.

1300hrs Meeting Harry's Office C10 SIS(MI6) London

Harry bumped into Tom as he left the building to get a sandwich and some fresh air.

'How did it go Tom?' Harry asked. 'I'm just grabbing a sandwich; do you want to join me?'

Tom fell into step beside him as they walked down the street towards the café.

They chose a corner table at the back after buying their lunch, and Tom briefed Harry on his earlier meeting.

'I took the line exactly as you suggested and, I think, he is supportive of what we want and where we want them to look. David is going to recommend it to his boss who, obviously, has the final word.

He said he would get back to me on the approval or otherwise soonest, but, clearly, it will take some time following that, to get any feedback as to intel/connections etc.'

'Good' said Harry. 'Let's hope you get confirmation soon, go or no-go. If it's on then at least we are beefing up our resources and able to factor in their contribution.

I'll include this in my discussions with the Deputy when I see him. At least we've got some traction in that direction.'

They walked back to the office, posing each other questions, some of which might be answered by the cooperative effort through David Hadar.

1400hrs Meeting Mossad Control London

David had verbally repeated all that had been covered in his conversation with Tom and which had been included as bullet points in his report to Control.

Control had insisted on a verbal briefing to ensure that nothing essential had been missed in the report and also to ensure he understood the full nuance of the discussions between David and Tom.

Control listened intently, without interruption, during David's briefing and allowed a few minutes silence to elapse before commenting.

'David, Firstly, you have my authority to continue and develop this cooperative relationship, so you can advise your contact Tom of this after twenty four hours. This will show them that we have considered it properly and have followed our own approval channels.

With respect to any intelligence information that may be passed to them, then I alone, will authorise any such release. We will, of course, be looking at what we may find of interest to them, balanced against any information they may give, or share with us.

It is quite possible that they may obtain information that has no connection with this particular activity, but could be extremely valuable to us in protecting our country and its interests against commercial, political or terrorist attacks.'

David nodded his head in agreement, and said, 'Yes, I understand completely. The prime question I have at the moment is whether you think that any of our current intelligence gathered from the region impacts on the current situation?'

Control replied, 'I believe that there could be from some summaries I have seen but this will take a little time in analysis and for the summaries to be run through our software. Once we have got some detail attributed to this we can then decide the form in which this intelligence should be given to our new partners.

I do not want our operational methods to be transparently clear to UK Security, nor do I want any of our operatives, surveillance or otherwise, to be put in jeopardy.

David, in the game we play, events can sometimes overtake us. The trick is to spot the event before it happens!'

'I'll contact Tom in a couple of days and keep you posted. I appreciate your comments.'

David left Control to his thoughts as to how this relationship would develop and to what extent they might be able penetrate UK Security. He wondered if, in time, they might be able to turn or convince someone to act in the same way as the Minister's PA.

Thursday 5th January 2006 0730hrs Dubai Creek United Arab Emirates

For hundreds of years the Arab dhows, whether for trade or fishing, have been passing up and down the Gulf and across it from Bahrain, Qatar, Abu Dhabi and Dubai to Iran, Pakistan and India.

The illegal gold running and pearl smuggling still lived on in minds of many, a romantic connection with the past. Nowadays the dhows were stuffed with electronic goods, car spares, and even cars. There was also a sizeable fishing fleet that served the Dubai Fish Market well, with a large variety of fish and shrimp. It used to be said that a good indicator of the local economy was the number of dhows sitting in Dubai Creek.

The Palestinian, Fayez Al-Hourani sat in the rear of the dhow as it cast off from the quay in Dubai and chugged slowly out to sea, its fishing nets and tarpaulins covering the foredeck and four unidentifiable bundles.

This was a dry run. He wanted to see how his men and the crew handled themselves and the dhow, bearing in mind that it would be a dark night, with no moon when the operation would be carried out. Rehearsals were vital and for very good reason.

What he wanted to do was sail in a westerly direction for about 145 miles to Das Island. This would take about 21hrs if they could manage 7 knots under sail and engine, and from there he would head to Doha, Qatar, a distance of 80 miles, and 10hrs.

By the time he reached Doha he expected to hear from the Syrian with confirmation that the operation would proceed. With payment made and most deposited in a co-operative Qatari bank, he would have the necessary cash to pay the crew and skilled operatives.

He settled back under the awning on the after deck protecting him from the rising sun and watched the crew go about their business with a practised air.

1000hrs Deputy's Office SIS(MI6) London

'Come in Harry,' was the Deputy's response to a knock on his door.

Harry entered, greeted the Deputy, and sat down across the desk from him.

'Tom met with David Hadar yesterday and I think we have the basis of some significant cooperation, if David gets the necessary approval. We have floated some fairly important questions to them concerning our current investigation and our need to widen the net and see if there is a Middle East/Gulf connection. We've asked if any of their regional Intel can provide a hook to what we're working on.

They seem to have bought into the idea, and we will know shortly if that is to be sanctioned. If so Intel will follow after that.

It does mean that we are adding some quality horsepower which might shorten the timescale.'

'Good. Keep me up to speed with what is happening, but, if we are looking to exchange information I want notice of what information and for what reason.

They will want something as much; if not more than we do, so let's just watch that Intel levels are not breached. Final approval is mine. OK?'

Tom nodded and said, 'Absolutely, we are playing a long game, not rushing it. Changing the subject. What do want me to do about my prospective theatre date?'

The Deputy rose from his desk and started slowly walking up and down his office, before he started to speak.

'Tom, there are elements contained within what I am going to discuss with you that are to remain solely between us, and which must not, at this stage, be shared with your colleagues. Clear?'

'Understood.'

'Your chance meeting with Anna Harrison over Christmas was quite timely.

First fact; she has been having an affair with the Minister for the last few years. How do we know? Routine surveillance of Ministers holding sensitive briefs. How they think it will remain undiscovered beats me, but there it is. His wife and family, to the best of our knowledge, are unaware of his affair, but I think there is a sort of accommodation between him and his wife anyway.

Second fact, as you are aware, she is a Mossad agent. Access to Minister's confidential matters. Passes on Intel to London Mossad Control. Israel loves collecting any bits of the jigsaw. Not Highly Confidential but High enough.

We're not sure of Anna's end game, but decided to let her run anyway. His Ministry is not critical, and we've had her under observation for some time. Although she continues to see him the frequency seems to have decreased a little. (The Deputy introduced this point to ensure that Harry's interest was still maintained).

I've obviously been thinking of what benefit we can get out of this, and I think Harry, we should adopt a 'slowly, slowly, catchee monkey' approach.'

The Deputy then spoke slowly, with heavy sarcasm.

'If the Minister, with his well known, urbane, fair and reasonable approach to most things, decides he wants to sacrifice us to save his skin over Buncefield, then we need to have something with which to respond.

His affair would be starters, but any other unreasonable facts would be useful.

Therefore, proceed with your invitation to the theatre, and see how things develop. She may like your rustic charm Harry, or it might not work. We'll just have to see,' he said smiling at Harry.

'Any other background issues I should be aware of?

'Like what?' the Deputy responded quickly.

'Do we have much background on Anna?'

'Not really, she was adopted as a child, brought up by a family friend, who has since died. No other family to our knowledge.'

'Just interested, in case something comes up in conversation. I like to be prepared.'

'As and when the theatre date occurs keep me posted. I will be interested to see if you convince her to see you a second time!'

'In the line of duty I shall do my best,' Harry said smiling at the Deputy.

'Best of luck' said the Deputy as the meeting was concluded.

Harry walked down the corridor convinced he had not been told the full story.

The Deputy could have dealt with the situation in this manner at the time of their last meeting. He didn't need 48 hours to consider what had been decided. What additional detail was contained in the existing relationship between Anna and the Minister he could not guess at this stage, but events may play out and provide an answer in due course, assuming he was able to dig further over a period of time.

He entered his office to be greeted by Tom and Jane, who enquired how the meeting had gone.

'Usual update, why no real intel, too many problem areas, caseload numbers too high, no further resources and funding, Ministers wanting instant action and sound bites, shall I go on?

Incidentally, Tom, I did bring him up to date on your meeting with David. He likes the drift but doesn't want things rushed. I told him we were playing a long game, but he is keen that any Intel exchanged is good value and also wants final approval as to release. Understood?'

'No problem,' said Tom, 'let's keep our fingers crossed for David's approval.'

1200hrs Ministers Office Whitehall London

The Minister was not in a good mood, again, thought Anna.

He had attended a Cabinet meeting that morning and had been made to look foolish, again, by the PM. The immediate sycophants had joined in the ribbing with glee as his short fuse was well known, and they were hoping for some rude, petulant behaviour. They were not disappointed. A sullen response with an ever reddening face told them all they wanted to hear, and the subdued laughter continued through his response.

'I shall bloody have him, mark my word', he said, as he slumped in his chair.

'He really is a condescending shit, and those arse lickers are no better. How the hell am I supposed to come up with answers when the investigation has only just started? He only wants something so he can go on TV and ponce around being the big I am, and how I save the nation! He couldn't give a

bugger for anything, or anybody else. And as for those loyal Cabinet members tittering away, most would stab him in the back if it suited them!

His PA sat silently in her chair, knowing it was futile at times like this to interrupt. Best to let the head of steam subside, then apply a few soothing words.

He looked at her with annoyance.

'Well, aren't you going to say anything?'

'There's nothing I can say at the moment that is going to help, other than your time, I am sure, will come,' she replied diplomatically.

'Yes, I'm sure too,' he said sarcastically and stomped out of the room slamming the door behind him.

She quickly checked his diary and saw that he was visiting Buncefield later that day, and breathed a small sigh of relief that she would be free of his petulant mood for the rest of the day.

She had been reflecting on the relationship, both public and private, the pressures exerted on Ministers in office, the demanding, rolling 24 hour news animal that required to be fed, the backbiting and backstabbing that was continuous in the fight between Cabinet members, their position on the greasy pole, and the envy and jealousy that drove men to be part of the inner cabal, close to the PM.

She idly wondered if Harry, it was Harry, wasn't it, would call. He seemed fairly grounded compared to most of the men she was used to. Well, we'll have to wait and see, she thought.

1800hrs The Gulf approximately 80 miles West of Dubai

Fayez had just finished his evening prayers and was starting to eat some food when he noticed a fast patrol boat heading towards them from the direction of the coast. It was clearly not a large pleasure power boat, frequently bought as a weekend plaything by wealthy Arabs, but an armed forces vessel, judging by size and paintwork.

He barked instructions to the crew to make sure that the objects forward were properly covered and then sat down near the skipper to await the patrol boat's arrival.

About 100 metres from the dhow the patrol boat throttled back it two engines, turned and drifted towards it. The only sound was the wash slapping up against the dhow, interrupted by the patrol boat commander calling out as to their business.

The dhow's skipper responded in a jocular fashion, advising that they would be fishing soon and afterwards possibly taking their catch to Abu Dhabi as they could get better prices than Dubai. This brought laughter from the patrol boat's crew who were based in Abu Dhabi, and after salutations the patrol boat gunned its engines, turned and accelerated away in an easterly direction.

Fayez exhaled and smiled at the skipper, 'Well done, my brother, the problem has gone away, Shukran.'

'Afwan,' he replied.

'We need to make more speed; can we use the engine through the night?'

The skipper nodded, 'when the sun has gone down in about half an hour.'

'Good,' Fayez replied, 'I want to test our equipment off Das Island tomorrow night.'

The skipper agreed that with sail and engine that would be possible, Insha'Allah.

Fayez settled down for a long night at sea, continually going over in his mind the 'dry run' to be carried out the next night and the likely problems that may occur.

He slept fitfully during the night, conscious of a change in the strengthening wind, that avoided running the engine all the time, and which gave some respite from the vibrating hull.

He rose at 0500hrs, as the sun rose over the horizon, completing his morning ablutions and prayers before eating breakfast.

He was clear in his own mind of what he wanted to happen that night and spent some time discussing his ideas with his four men, repeating the scenario so that it was clearly understood and embedded in their minds.

The sun rose higher and the wind eased, requiring the engine to be started again. The deck vibration continued relentlessly, as the dhow pushed westwards through a leaden swell, and the broiling sun in a cloudless sky beat down on a lethargic crew.

A few tankers and cargo ships were seen from time to time heading north west and south east up and down the Gulf, but there was no further evidence of patrol boats.

The hours passed slowly until at about 1700hrs the skipper pointed out to Fayez the low outline of Das Island in the distance, at which point they hove to, draping some fishing nets over the side to indicate activity.

After the crew had completed evening prayers and eaten, Fayez instructed the skipper to head slowly towards Das Island, planning to arrive approximately 3 kilometres offshore, on the eastern side of the island by 0100hrs.

By the time the dhow threw over a sea anchor it was 0120hrs, and the four man team quickly uncovered the packages on the foredeck.

The two inflatables were readied with compressed air bottles and the electric outboards checked and placed on board ready for launching over the side.

The other container was emptied of its grey plastic wrapped packages, each weighing about 3 kilograms, plus assorted wiring, timers, detonators, etc.

Das Island is almost rectangular in shape, north to south, and on its eastern flank, two long jetties about 900 metres apart, extend about 750 metres into the Gulf, used for loading oil and gas onto tankers.

Through his night vision binoculars Fayez could see that that the southern jetty was currently not being used for loading so instructed the leader of his group accordingly. All activity was on the northern jetty, 800 metres away, where floodlights could be seen illuminating a tanker currently being charged.

As far as he could see there was no activity on the southern jetty, in fact there was nobody on it at all. Minimum illumination was evident but this would be no hindrance to the team.

Clouds had gathered and the moon was currently hidden, further assisting his team; the morning forecast being sea mist/fog allowing for easy withdrawal.

The inflatables were lowered gently into the water, and the electric outboards mounted and connected. The grey plastic wrapped packages, wiring, timers, etc were carefully stowed. The four man team reappeared on deck in their wetsuits, plus masks and fins, and slid silently over the gunwales into their craft.

Almost silently the two inflatables pulled away from the dhow, turned around its stern, and headed towards Das Island's southern jetty.

The team leader, communicating by hand signals, kept the companion boat close as they headed westward keeping to a steady 3-4 knots.

As they approached the jetty they separated and approached in an arc from the north and south, switching off their electric outboards about 400 metres from the end of the jetty, covering the remaining distance by careful paddling.

With the night being dark, no moon, and relatively calm sea, fluorescence by paddling was kept to a minimum as they tied up on either side of the end of the jetty.

They waited in silence for 15minutes to see whether they had been seen or heard, but it was clear that there was no security on the southern jetty, and that they had arrived undetected.

The two teams put on their masks and fins and dropped over the sides of their inflatables with their packages. It took about 45 minutes to complete the installation on both sides of the jetty, and with no tide to concern them, the packages were mounted about two metres below the water. The timers were set for 24hrs ahead, giving the dhow ample time to be well away from the area.

The four men then took their place in one inflatable. The other was then partially deflated, the air valve restored and the sides thoroughly knifed to give the appearance of severe damage. A long line attached it to the jetty.

This inflatable carried markings of the Iranian Navy.

The four man team paddled away and started the electric outboard when they were at least half a kilometre away from the jetty. They boarded the dhow at about 0400hrs; the inflatable was pulled onto the deck as the skipper pulled in the sea anchor and turned the dhow westward to start the journey to Doha, Qatar.

After the inflatable had been packed away, the team leader briefed Fayez in quiet tones that all had gone to plan and that it could be considered a successful operation. 0400hrs tomorrow would confirm that, he joked wryly.

Fayez clapped him on the back and congratulated him, but cautioned that the main operation scheduled for some time in the future would be much more difficult, but good progress was being made.

As the sky lightened on the morning of the 7th January 2006, the dhow made steady progress under sail and power towards Doha.

***

V

Monday 9th January 2006

0900hrs SIS(MI6) London

Harry dialled the mobile number which was not answered, but which switched him over to the message service. He left a message.

'Hullo Anna, this is Harry Baxter. You may remember we met at our mutual friends' drinks party over Christmas down in Sussex. You gave me your mobile number when I suggested we might go to the theatre some evening. Hence the phone call. Give me call on this mobile number when you can. By the way, a belated Happy New Year! Bye.'

Harry wondered if he had been a bit short but almost immediately his mobile rang. It was Anna.

She apologised for not picking up his call, but had been tied up at her desk when he rang.

Yes, she would like to go to the theatre; when?, what was on?, what did she like?; they chatted for a few minutes exchanging the hesitant pleasantries of two people who don't know each other, but are interested in exploring further.

Harry promised to get back to her with some suggestions in the next 48hrs, and they ended their conversation mutually agreeing they were looking forward to the event.

Harry was pleased with the way the conversation had gone and decided to look up the theatre listings that night and come up with a choice of three, as varied as possible.

Harry called the Deputy's office to advise him of the conversation and was asked to attend a meeting with him at 1000hrs. He caught up on some admin, and following a quick update with Tom and Jane, Tom hurried to the meeting.

Harry quickly told the Deputy that a theatre date had been agreed with Anna and he would keep the Deputy posted as to reaction, comments and observations.

Deputy nodded in agreement and said, 'Fine Harry, the reason I wanted to see you is that we have had a report from the UAE station advising that there had been an explosion on Das Island yesterday morning at about 0400hrs.

It appears several small packages of explosives were planted at the extremity of a jetty. Gas or oil explosion has been ruled out following initial examination. What is strange is that a large tanker had been loading on the other jetty which is about 6-700 metres away, and would I think, have been a more likely target.

No group has claimed responsibility. Information is still sketchy, but there were no casualties. However remains of an inflatable were found, with what would appear to be Iranian Navy markings. Why Iran? Or is that a smokescreen? Could just be some small group trying to get a message across or perhaps a disgruntled employee group. Who knows?'

Harry was churning over in his mind what the Deputy had said, but could not see what the possible connection could be to their present investigations.

Before he responded, the Deputy spoke again.

'See if Tom can glean anything from his contact. David?'

Harry nodded.

'Perhaps their network will have picked up something extra that we haven't got. Mildly trade our Intel to pull it out if it exists. Ok?'

'I'll get Tom on it straight away. If you get anything else in the meantime please let me know.'

'Naturally,' the Deputy replied.

Tom returned to his office and briefed Tom, who telephoned David to arrange a meeting. It was scheduled for 1600hrs that afternoon.

Harry reflected on what the Deputy had said, and was still at a loss to see any real connection with their current activity. However, he was long enough in the tooth, to recognise that in this game not everything has a direct relevance, and that connections could be both obtuse and opaque.

Tom met David that afternoon as planned and reported back to Harry at 1730hrs.

'I put a few flies on the water as you suggested Harry, but I think they are as much in the dark as we are. They have the same Intel but nothing further. I think he was genuine, and said if they got anything they would share with us. His one comment was that with so many disparate groups operating in the region with independent objectives, it is almost impossible to keep tabs on them all, and they were relying on trying to turn people in order to get decent Intel.'

Just make sure he doesn't try and turn you,' Harry joked, whilst noting the point for future review.

'No chance,' responded Tom in the same vein, 'I want to collect my pension!'

Harry left the office at about 1815hrs, picking up the evening paper at the station, and scanned the theatre columns whilst the tube train rattled its way to Clapham.

He had decided on the options by the time the Northern line train reached its destination, and he walked with a little more spring in his step to his flat.

About the same time Anna had reached her flat in Stockwell and had called Control on her secure mobile. She quickly briefed him as to what had been discussed and arranged between her and Harry. Control repeated the basic outline of what he wanted, and agreed that she would contact him further after the theatre date.

Anna sat and thought about what implications there would be, if Harry, on the procurement side of the Ministry of Defence, became aware of her real interest, and any possible consequences that could arise. She determined that she would play the long game.

Tuesday 10th January 2006 0700hrs Al Wakrah Qatar

The dhow slid gently into Al Wakrah, a little fishing village south of Doha, Qatar, and tied up at the quiet end of the quay.

The voyage from Das Island had taken longer than anticipated due to sudden dropping of the wind, which had meant longer periods under power at reduced speed to conserve fuel. It had been necessary to have a catch of fish to avoid suspicion, and which was now being unloaded in large baskets onto the quay.

Fayez bade the skipper goodbye and walked a little unsteadily through the village as he regained his 'land legs' after the long sail from Dubai.

He located a coffee house from where he booked a taxi to take him to the Marriot Hotel in Doha.

About an hour later he walked into the reception area of the hotel and booked a room.

A member of the hotel staff at the end of the Concierge desk looked up with interest when he heard Fayez making the booking. Most reservations are made in advance. A 'walk-in' is the exception. He listened carefully to the accent, hoping to place the man; possibly Palestinian, he thought judging from the inflection and appearance.

Fayez went to his room, drew the curtains and slept until 1800hrs. After showering and dressing he called a mobile number and arranged to meet the man in the hotel car park at 2100hrs. The registration number of a hire car was given to him to confirm identification. He passed the time by watching various news channels to see if there was any indication of what had happened at Das Island, but apparently there was a news blackout.

At 2100hrs he walked out of the hotel into the car park, his movements being watched covertly by the man on the Concierge desk. He walked down the first row of cars, just as the car with the nominated registration turned into Row three, and proceeded slowly to the end, parking near a dusty group of palm trees. The driver emerged, leaving the engine running, and walked over to Fayez.

Greetings were exchanged and an Arabic saying expressed and responded to. Haji Masri handed Fayez a holdall, turned, walked to his car and drove away. The whole exchange had taken no more than two minutes.

Fayez walked back to the hotel, crossed the lobby, taking the lift to the third floor and his room. He was observed as he crossed the lobby; the man on the Concierge desk noting the addition of the holdall after only about five or six minutes in the car park. The observer was also aware that he had arrived by taxi, not car, so the holdall had not been retrieved from his vehicle.

Fayez entered his room and rang Room Service for his meal, to be delivered in 45 minutes. He opened the holdall and counted its contents, all in $100 bills. He then padlocked the holdall with a combination lock and placed it in the back of his wardrobe, next to his suitcase. He would fly to Bahrain the next day.

The man from the Concierge desk was standing in the car park talking softly into his mobile telephone. He was advising his Control that it was now the second time he had seen this individual, his concerns as to his actions, his movements in and out of Doha, and whether their 'friends' at the airport could

check on his suitcase and holdall contents tomorrow.

Control indicated some attempt would be made but time may work against them.

Fayez woke at 0700hrs on the Wednesday morning and left for the airport at 0930hrs, his departure logged by the man at the Concierge desk who quickly sent a text of three letters on his mobile telephone.

Wenesday 11th January 2006 1300hrs Manama Bahrain

Fayez cleared immigration quickly, took a taxi to the Sheraton Hotel in Manama and called the Syrian, Karim Al Halbi on his mobile. There was a delayed response on the network before Fayez was connected to Karim and they arranged to meet for dinner that evening at 2000hrs.
The operative who had hacked into their transmission turned to his Control and passed on the information he had heard. Control instructed him to observe and overhear if possible, using their sophisticated directional microphones, otherwise a bug in the room may throw up additional facts.

Fayez had been observed at the airport in Bahrain, operatives being forewarned as investigation of bags had not been possible due to time constraints. Specifics were not, at this point, known, but both Al Halbi and Al-Hourani had been under surveillance for some time. The difficulty was in joining up the dots.

Fayez and Karim met in the lobby and walked through to the restaurant, observed by the operative, who, after a discrete pause, followed them, taking a table about twenty feet away. He placed his attaché case on an adjacent chair which focussed the directional microphone on the two men. He noticed that Karim had brought a small trolley bag with him, which he placed adjacent to Fayez' chair.

They discussed generalities during the meal, the only difference at the end of the meal being Fayez taking the trolley bag as he bade Karim goodnight.

Fayez went into the lift alone in order to go to his room, the operative noting the floor on which it stopped by the illuminated indicator over the lift door.

Leaving a gap of about half an hour the operative then approached the Check In desk to book a room, and through conversation determined that his 'colleague' would be checking out at 0800hrs. After getting to his room the operative checked the recording of the directional microphone, but no additional information was provided by the desultory conversation between the two men.

Fayez entered his room and opened the trolley bag to count the significant amount of US dollars in packs of fifty, $100 bills. He noted with satisfaction that the total included the additional amount he had requested and mentally noted his first stop on the way to the airport would be to his 'friendly' bank.

He telephoned reception for an alarm call and confirmed the taxi to take him to the airport. He also telephoned Gulf Air and Iran Air to confirm his flight connections and faxed the taxi firm in Iran confirming flight details and pick up time.

Thursday 12th January 2006 Manama Bahrain & Tehran
Iran

The operative slept fitfully until 0600hrs, dressed and
made his way to breakfast, keeping the lobby in view. At
about 0745hrs he saw Fayez exit the lift, cross to Check
Out, complete formalities, and leave by the main door to
a taxi, with one suitcase and a trolley bag.
He followed about 15 minutes later, checking out, and
joking that his colleague had not called to wake him, and
that he hoped they would meet at the airport. This was
confirmed by Check Out who had ordered the taxi for
Fayez, but who had said he also wanted to do some
shopping on the way to the airport.
The operative took a taxi to the airport and positioned
himself near the main entrance to observe when Fayez
arrived.
Fayez had taken the taxi to his 'friendly' bank, instructing
the driver to wait for him. He deposited a significant sum
in a specific account and gave an instruction for a transfer
of funds to be made within 24 hrs. Proceeding to the
airport he went straight to the Gulf Air desk to check in
for his flight to Tehran leaving later that day.
The operative, having observed flight and timing, called
Control on his mobile to update the situation. Control
without hesitation instructed him to follow on the same
flight, if possible, and continue surveillance as far as he
could, reporting back on a 12 hour basis. He was able to
join the same flight which left on time. The journey was
uneventful and the Gulf Air flight landed on schedule at
the Iman Khomeini International Airport, Tehran. He
followed Fayez to Transit where he was able to overhear
that he was taking an Iran Air flight to Shiraz early that
evening. After Fayez had gone to the Departure Lounge
he asked if could take the same flight but was advised it
was full, however another flight leaving 90 minutes later
had some spare seats, so he booked accordingly.

About 40 minutes later he saw Fayez pass through the Departure gate for the Shiraz flight and resigned himself to another 90 minutes of boredom.

Fortunately his Shiraz flight was on time and he passed through Arrivals quickly, due to the fact his flight was the last one from Tehran. He went out to the taxi rank and using his 'colleague' story found out that Fayez had been taken to the Pars Hotel located about 30 minutes from the airport. He took a taxi and checked into the hotel, weaving another 'colleague' story about 'not wishing to wake him, had he made a car booking for tomorrow? Etc.'

Having determined that Fayez was leaving at about 0900hrs he booked a self drive car, completing details and taking possession of the keys, with the explanation that he was leaving very early in the morning.

Friday 13th January 2006 Shiraz Iran

He slept until 0530hrs and readied himself in his car by 0815hrs, in front of the hotel, from where he could observe when Fayez left with his car and driver.

At 0845hrs a car drove into one of the few bays in front of the hotel and the driver walked through the main entrance, reappearing a few minutes later with Fayez. The driver placed the suitcase in the boot; Fayez sat in the rear of the car with his trolley bag.

As the hire car left the hotel the operative followed at a discrete distance, maintaining observation, which was not difficult despite early morning traffic. Leaving the centre of Shiraz, Fayez' hire car headed in a south east direction travelling towards Route 67.

Route 67 from Shiraz tracks initially in a south easterly direction, before turning South, and both cars were able to maintain a comfortable cruising speed.

The operative had no idea where they were headed, so deliberated what he would do, as, and when Fayez stopped to refuel and eat. As the traffic had thinned out considerably he was able to hold a reasonable average speed with good fuel consumption. If Fayez were to stop he would pass, and then about 2 kilometres down the road return, passing again and then returning to refuel his own car. If Fayez had left he could certainly drive quickly enough to catch up and judging by the general direction was heading towards the coast.

If that was the case, then they had about 300 kilometres of driving which would take about six hours.

After about two and a half hours Fayez' car pulled off the road beside a mosque in the small town of Firuzabad. Fayez and his driver entered the mosque. The operative had slowed, and pulled into the shadow of a run down building, which provided him with cover.

After about an hour men started to drift out of the mosque and he saw Fayez and his driver get into their car and start off down the road. He followed, wondering where the final destination was, and what was the plan. Fortunately he was able to communicate with Control on his satellite telephone, but unfortunately could not give him any real indication as to final destination or likely outcome.

The time passed slowly and monotonously, except for the occasion when the hire car pulled suddenly into a garage to refuel, causing the operative to momentarily brake before resuming speed. Passing the garage and travelling for a further 2kms, he then returned to refuel his own car.

The road was hilly, the country wild, large container lorries ground along in convoy, sometimes making overtaking difficult and also giving rise to shortening or lengthening gaps between Fayez' car and the operative's.

Fayez finally turned off Route 65 onto Route 96, and the operative saw the sign for Bandar-e Kangan. Was this the destination, he thought.

Arriving in the middle of the town at about 1730hrs Fayez' car turned off the main street and pulled up outside a small guest house. The operative had stopped on the corner and seen Fayez alight from the car, the driver taking his suitcase into the guest house. Fayez followed with his trolley bag. After shaking hands the driver got back into the car and reversed back down the down the street.

The operative busied himself with something on the passenger seat as the hire car drove away. He saw that there was another guest house on the corner of the main street and decided that it would be his base to continue surveillance.

Entering the guest house he agreed terms for two days and paid in advance.

He doubted there would be any activity now as it was nearly dark, and Fayez would be tired after such a long drive.

He would rise at 0600hrs and maintain observation from a coffee shop across from Fayez' guest house.

Saturday 14th January 2006 Bandar-e Kangan Iran

He slept soundly and rose at 0600hrs, sending a brief coded update report to Control as to where he was located and that surveillance was continuing. Automatic acknowledgement was received, and he walked slowly up to the coffee shop.

He sat down listening to both Farsi and Arabic languages being spoken and ordered his choices in Arabic, this not raising any particular interest with the other groups of men already seated at tables.

At about 0815hrs he saw Fayez walk out of the guest house and cross the street to the coffee shop, choosing a table close to the door. He also ordered his selection in Arabic.

The operative carefully studied a day old Arabic newspaper, not lifting his eyes, avoiding any eye contact whatsoever.

After about half an hour Fayez rose and returned to his guest house quickly reappearing with suitcase and trolley bag as a local taxi pulled up outside.

Fayez got into the taxi whilst the operative exited from the coffee shop side door, getting into his car and driving slowly round the corner to see the taxi about 200 metres ahead, travelling in the direction of the harbour.

He tailed the taxi down to the harbour edge, where a large man-made curving breakwater pier extended some 300 metres into the Arabian Gulf, curving like a crescent at least 600 metres long, providing protection to the various fishing boats and dhows anchored there.

The operative watched from a distance as the taxi drove slowly along the pier and stopped by a large dhow. He saw the suitcase being lifted onto the boat, and Fayez carrying his trolley bag, pausing to embrace a man, presumably the captain, before descending below decks.

The operative maintained observation for over an hour as the crew of the dhow went about their business of preparing the boat for an obvious departure.

At about 1100hrs a large closed van appeared on the pier, and drove slowly along it until it stopped abreast of the dhow.

Three members of the crew assisted the driver and his companion in loading a number of large packages and boxes onto the dhow which was repeated with an old flat bed lorry about an hour later.

The various packages and large boxes took some organising both on and below decks before the captain was happy with the distributed load.

Some two hours later a car pulled up at the dhow and four men quickly boarded as the captain called the crew to cast off. The engine was started and the dhow pulled away from the pier and chugged slowly towards open water as the crew raised its lateen sail.

The operative then sent a coded update to Control indicating that he could continue observation no further and suggested his return to Bahrain via Shiraz and Tehran the following day. This was agreed and he returned to the guest house, disappointed that the trail had effectively gone cold.

0630hrs Clapham Common London

Harry rose early, threw on his tracksuit, and went for a gentle and medium length jog on the Common.

He was looking forward to the evening, not only because it was a theatre and dinner with an attractive woman, but with the added interest of what he knew about her, and her ongoing relationship with the Minister.

The Deputy had hinted that perhaps the affair was cooling, but it could just be a temporary blip. Softly, softly, he had said himself, play the long game, don't rush it.

Tonight may be a one off, who knows, we'll just have to see, he thought.

He caught up on the inevitable household chores, read the paper, had a quick power nap, then showered and dressed for the evening. Not too formal, not too casual, but obviously made a bit of an effort. He smiled wryly to himself. It had been a long time since he'd thought about his appearance.

He had arranged to pick Anna up by cab at 1815hrs, giving them plenty of time to get to the theatre and have a drink before the performance.

The local cab company had a mixed bag of cars, and to be honest, pretty scruffy on occasions, so he called up a black cab, definitely a clean car.

Arriving 5-6minutes early he had the inevitable wait before she came down and climbed into the cab.

He had to admit she looked stunning, wearing a simple LBD (Little Black Dress) that highlighted her soft olive skin and subtle makeup.

She smiled at him and he smiled back.

'Bit of a first for me', he said.

'Why?' she replied.

'Got out of the habit over the past few years, I suppose. Being single, unattached and wedded to the job is perhaps, not the best recipe for entertaining a good looking woman to theatre and dinner.'

'Is that your opening line with all the girls?' she said smiling at him with a direct gaze.

'Not at all', he said, somewhat sharply, reddening as he said it.

She realised a slight offence had been given, and laid a hand on his arm, leaving it there slightly longer than was necessary.

'My apologies,' she said, 'Dealing with politicians makes one naturally suspicious!'

They both relaxed and indulged in gentle verbal sparring on the way to the theatre.

Arriving in good time they had a couple of drinks in the bar, which further relaxed them, before taking their seats in the middle stalls, Harry having baulked at the increased price of the front stalls since last visiting the theatre.

They both enjoyed the play, losing themselves in the plot and the effortless professionalism of the award winning cast.

As they walked out of the theatre they found, that although it was cold, it was a rain free night, so walked quickly across the road to the Italian restaurant, La Barca.

Harry had been several times over the years and loved their style, their cooking, and how welcome you were made to feel.

He had booked a table and was greeted like a long lost friend, slightly over the top, but as he reminded himself, he was competing with a Minister.

The meal, as usual, was excellent, the wine was enjoyed, and the conversation flowed.

Harry reflected on the ebb and flow of the variety of subjects covered in their conversation and decided that his pragmatism and objectivity developed over the years was an interesting mix with Anna's more academic and theoretical background, leavened with a developed sense of ironic humour. She had many amusing observations on a number of unnamed politicians, and he found her company rewarding and comfortable.

At the end of the meal he ordered a cab which arrived within ten minutes and took them back to Anna's apartment in Southwark. She invited Harry in for a coffee, which was added to with a good cognac. Harry wondered whether it had been a gift or bought by the Minister for his own consumption, no matter, he thought.

There was a pause in the conversation whilst Anna had prepared coffee and Harry decided to be a little more inquisitive.

'How long have you been working for the Minister?'

'A few years now, both in Government and Opposition.'

'How did that come about?'

'Following university I got a job as a researcher. Through a friend of a friend.'

'Quite interesting or is it fairly mundane?'

'Not terribly exciting, but how did you get your position in The Ministry of Defence?'

'Been in the Army a number of years, nearing my first option for leaving, the job was advertised internally and I got it. Not terribly exciting but comfortable with a reasonable pension at the end,' he joked. 'How are things shaping up on the Buncefield disaster?'

'Very slowly. I understand the investigation hasn't really started due to Health and Safety issues. They can't get the Inspectors properly on site yet with the engineers. It will be some time yet.'

Harry felt that due to the lateness of the hour it would not be sensible to continue this line of questioning without raising suspicions so he changed the subject quickly.

'Well Anna, let me tell you this has been one of the best evenings I have had for a long time. Most enjoyable. If it's not a rude question, and if there is no one permanent in your life at present, can we agree that we will repeat tonight in the near future?'

Anna looked at him, half smiling,

'You wouldn't be fishing would you Harry?'

'Fishing? Certainly not. I've really enjoyed myself tonight and if you feel the same then let's do it again and soon. Perhaps next time you would like to take in a concert, classical or jazz, or maybe opera. Your choice.'

She was silent momentarily.

I've really enjoyed it too, Harry. Yes, let's do something in about two weeks time. I know I'm going to be rushed off my feet the next ten days as the department is starting its budget review for next year, loads of meetings, minutes to be taken, etc. Plus continuing activity on

Buncefield. You know the sort of thing. It will give me something to look forward to.'

'Great,' said Harry, although a little disappointed in the two week delay, but understanding of departmental pressures.

'I'll call you in ten days so you can have a think as to what you would like to do.'

'Agreed' she said, smiling at him.

Harry stood up looking at his watch. '12.15 already, I'd better be off.'

'Thanks for a lovely evening Harry, I really enjoyed that, no pressure.'

She put a hand on his shoulder and kissed his cheek which was reciprocated by Harry.

Harry walked out of the apartment and onto the main road in Southwark, easily picking up a black cab, which was happy to take him to Clapham as the driver was going off duty and home to Tooting.

In the short cab ride home Harry thought that the evening had been a success, and yes, the Deputy would be pleased another date had been agreed. Nothing of any consequence had been revealed, but early days yet.

He had enjoyed her company, she was an attractive woman, who made the assignment very bearable, but there were clearly going to be some very sensitive areas to be dealt with at some time in the future.

Anna sat drinking more coffee and thought about Harry and the evening. She wondered what she would tell Control and the Minister when he found out. Control would want her to maintain contact with Harry for any information she may obtain concerning the Ministry of Defence, whereas the Minister's reaction could probably be measured in jealous decibels.

She had to admit to herself that she had enjoyed Harry's company and felt that it made a welcome change to the peak and trough relationship with the Minister. However the Minister was her assignment and somehow, if she wanted to see Harry again, then she would have to juggle the issue carefully. Very carefully.

Harry entered his flat in Clapham, kicked off his shoes, poured himself a lager, and sat in an armchair thinking over the evening and the very general conversations.

He had to admit he found Anna attractive and found her company enjoyable, clearly hoping that the event would be repeated again before long. Against that his professionalism cautioned him to remember the current assignment and not to jeopardise or compromise that for the sake of, perhaps, a passing relationship. His thinking effectively placed the potential hazard in its own compartment, whilst pursuing something on a professional level.

He would report to the Deputy on Monday; progress had been made and there was the opportunity of a repeat in about two weeks time.

Sunday 15th January 2006

0700hrs 15 miles SE of Bandar-e Kangar Iran

The dhow had anchored in a cove overnight and the cook was now preparing breakfast for the crew and guests. The men that had joined the dhow the previous afternoon were now sitting in a small group in the stern under a tarpaulin shading them from the sun.

Fayez, speaking in a low tone was outlining the proposed plan, which would involve several days of training, initially in daylight, then at night, and the voyage which would take them by a circuitous route to their ultimate objective.

None of the four men who had joined the day before were aware of the final destination and required action, but were said to be experienced scuba divers trained in the use of explosives, both on land and sea.

Half of the fee had been paid in advance in cash; the remainder was to be paid after satisfactory completion of the assignment, also in cash.

After breakfast, the dhow pulled up anchor and continued its course, under sail, in an ESE direction along the coast, maintaining a position about a mile offshore.

The men took this opportunity to unpack a number of the packages and boxes, revealing wet suits, masks, fins, and compressed air cylinders. They spent several hours checking fit, working valves, capacities, etc, before stowing them carefully below deck. The dhow moved slowly down the coast giving the impression of slow fishing, aided by a couple of lines trailing over the stern.

After about forty miles and ten hours sailing, the dhow was offshore of Siraf, and, as dusk fell, made its way to a sheltered cove. There the men ate, prayed and slept, for tomorrow would be the first training day.

Fayez had prepared a schedule for the training tomorrow which included 'blind' practice with dummy charges and timers, this to be carried out initially by day and then at night.

He did not know the men before this operation but had been assured by Central Command in Damascus they were committed, well trained and dedicated Muslims who hated the West and those in Arab countries who dealt with and accommodated Western ways, considered totally abhorrent by typical jihadists.

He knew they were not aware of the detail of the operation, or the way it would be perceived by both the West and various Arab states.

1100hrs Southwark London

Anna, using her secure mobile, phoned Control to provide an update of the situation with Harry. She described the evening, being careful to maintain an objective attitude, describing the general conversations and indicating that Harry would be telephoning her in about ten days to arrange another meeting.

Control made no comments on the evening, agreed that further meetings could be beneficial, but cautioned on the risk of upsetting the Minister if her developing friendship was uncovered. She responded by saying that she was already aware of the risk, but had prepared contingency plans to take care of that. Following those comments she signed off.

Anna sat, drinking her coffee, thinking of a number of scenarios if the Minister became aware of Harry, and possible reasons for the relationship.

Be prepared; forewarned; forearmed.

1500hrs 30 miles SE of Bandar-e Kangar

Following the morning dive practice the dhow had sailed further along the coast, maintaining its pretence of fishing. This also gave the divers an opportunity to rest, pray, and eat before starting an evening dive in semi-darkness.

Fayez took the opportunity over the meal to start providing a general idea of

the plan, describing it as a blow against the West, and the repercussions that would follow. He indicated that it could create further instability in the region, leading, Insha'Allah, to the establishment of a wider Caliphate under strict Sharia Law.

The divers nodded their heads vigorously in agreement, repeating 'Insha'Allah' or 'Allahu Akbar'.

There had been several technical mistakes during the morning dive. Dummy explosives and timers had been dropped and not recovered, fitness levels were clearly not high enough yet, and some of the compressed air tanks had leaking valves. The valves were soon repaired, but fitness levels would have to be raised over the next few days before the operation.

Fayez outlined a programme to achieve what he wanted in all areas before the evening dive, which he shortened in order to encourage the divers to work hard on their fitness over the next few days.

The night dive showed poor coordination between divers in semi-darkness, which would be worse at night with no moon.

Fayez realised a number of drills would need to be heavily practiced over the next week or two, in order for the operation to be successful. There could be no let up in the training, and failure was not an option, as he repeatedly told them.

Before they went to sleep he could hear one or two grumbles between divers and smiled grimly to himself, thinking, 'whilst they continue to grumble that's alright; when they stop grumbling, be prepared!'

1700hrs Minister's home NE England and London

He had gone for a walk on Saturday evening; the excuse being a heavy meal, the reality to telephone Anna on his mobile, and had been irritated when there was no reply or even an answering machine.

He remained sullen for the rest of the evening, giving indigestion as a reason, and leaving early for London the next day, on this occasion citing pressure of work and early meetings on the Monday.

On reaching London on the Sunday he had telephoned Anna without success, this adding to his irritability, and certainly not helping his existing high blood pressure.

Anna had not been aware the Minister had telephoned on the Saturday evening as she had deliberately switched off her answering machine. Sunday was different. She heard his call but did not answer it, leaving it to switch through to the answering machine. Monday would be soon enough, she thought. Unusually she found herself thinking of Harry at the same time.

VI

Monday 16th January 2006 0900hrs Deputy's Office SIS(MI6) London

Harry knocked and entered the Deputy's office on the hour.

The Deputy, who was talking to the Minister, waved Harry to a chair.

'Minister, with respect, we are all somewhat in the dark for leads. May I pose certain questions which in the normal scheme of things would help us in our investigation?

Has any organisation claimed responsibility for Buncefield? No. This in itself is often the starting point, but on this occasion absolute silence.

Have we any solid confirmed Intel that would indicate the one slender lead we have was actually involved in the operation to blow up Buncefield? No.

Have our intelligence allies provided us with any Intel that might indicate any group that has a connection with the disaster? Nothing as yet.

And finally, have the police or H&S found anything, either on the site, or in the immediate neighbourhood, that can provide any indication that this was a terrorist action? No.

Therefore Minister, with my resources already overstretched, I am doing the best I can with precious little information so far. Rest assured that when I have something positive you will be the first to be informed.'

The Minister who, uncharacteristically, had not interrupted the Deputy during his comments, truculently and sullenly ended the conversation by responding,

'Bloody well make sure I am the first to be informed, and not Number 10!'

The Deputy replaced the telephone, got out of his chair and started to pace up and down.

'Excuse me Harry, just my way of venting my spleen after being talked at by the Minister!'

Harry smiled.

'No prizes for guessing what he was banging on about then?'

'Not one, I can assure you', replied the Deputy grimly.

'Harry, we don't appear to be making much progress. By that I mean we do not appear to have much of a clue whether this was an accident or deliberate. How is our relationship developing with Mossad? Is it developing or are they stringing us along to see what they can pick up? Have they given any hint of any connection, however weak, with any active groups in the Middle East or Gulf? I appreciate it's early days but what do you think? Shall we nurture it, or give it a time frame to see if it develops and if not cut it off?

I think you can see what I'm driving at Harry. Let us both do a review, meet again and decide on a slightly more structured approach if needs be. OK?'

Harry paused before replying, gathering his thoughts and trying to get some semblance of order in what he was about to say.

'Before I reply to your questions can I bring you up to speed with my date last Saturday?'

He continued without waiting for a response.

'We went to the theatre and dinner afterwards. Great evening, got on well, probably meeting up again in about two weeks. Kept the conversation general, no secrets given or taken. Think and hope it might develop quite well.'

'Alright Harry, keep the connection going. See if you can find out anything about her family, other connections, friends, etc; eventually I hope to hear of some indiscretions by the Minister, but those will be a long time coming, I think!'

Harry smiled.

'One important point Harry. At some time if this relationship develops she might make suggestions about you working with a 'just cause'. She knows you're MOD procurement. That could be useful to them, and they would probably play on moral and financial issues if it was ever raised. Keep your eyes and ears open to signals.'

Harry nodded. 'Understood. Can I give you some thoughts on where I think we should go on the investigation?

We have established, through Tom, I think, a reasonable relationship with David Haddar at the Israeli Embassy. Now's the time to move it up a notch or two, so I'll be telling Tom to arrange a meeting which I will attend. The purpose will be to push for a face to face with their Control in the Embassy so that we will be communicating at a higher level. This will indicate our seriousness, plus I can see if they're really willing to 'trade'. At the same time I will be pushing hard to see if they have any real feedback Intel from the region and whether there are any positive connections. With your agreement I will suggest I go to wherever they've got significant leads, to check it on the ground, or confirm or otherwise whether this is just something from the operatives to their bosses to keep them sweet.'

'Harry, you and I have been round the block a few times. Yes, crack on as you've said. Just keep me posted, direct line reporting; satellite comms in the field. OK?'

Harry agreed, got up from the chair and turned to leave the Deputy's office.

He paused and then said,

'If Buncefield had been a trial run and it was successful, what is likely to be the real target? Whoever they are, they will leave it a long time before attempting a hit, knowing heightened security levels all round. But they'll want to keep essential team members together and keep the stress levels up otherwise the enthusiasm will disappear. Excuse me, I'm just thinking aloud, as we've got no hook into anything yet.'

You're right Harry, just start pushing all the buttons, one's got to show a red light sooner or later!'

Harry walked down to the lift still thinking about what the Deputy had said and his reply. Did he really want to get involved again, on the ground, overseas? What connections, if any, with Anna and the Minister, would develop from discussions with Mossad London Control? Was Anna aware of the discussions between Tom and David Hadar? His meeting with Mossad Control, assuming it took place, would have to be carefully handled under pseudonyms, in order for there to be no connection with Anna around the Israelis internal loop.

Arriving back in his office Harry called Tom on his mobile to come in for an early meeting. This was arranged for 1200hrs. He updated Jane on his meeting with the Deputy in a very general way, but left out many of the details concerning Mossad Control. He wanted to discuss this in detail with Tom, before involving everybody on the team.

1030hrs Ministers Office

The Minister swept into his office, a truculent expression fixed on his florid face, following the early morning Cabinet meeting at Number 10.

'Come in', he mouthed to Anna as he passed her desk.

He sat down heavily in his chair, his hands palm down on the desk in front of him.

'Close the door.'

Anna sat down in the chair facing the desk waiting for the anticipated remonstration.

'I tried to phone you yesterday evening, but couldn't even leave a message. Why was your answer machine off?'

His tone was sullen and Anna recognised the quiet before the possible storm.

She adopted a conciliatory manner.

'I had been getting quite a few wrong number calls, got totally fed up and switched off the machine. I forgot to put it back on. Sorry. I didn't know you would be trying to call me as you were at home. However, how did this morning's meeting go?'

'About even I would guess. Nobody has any real clue what happened at Buncefield yet; police, security, health and safety, you name them, no information, just speculation. At least himself won't be poncing onto TV tonight, trying to look caring and saving the world!' he laughed cynically, referring to the PM.

'What about dinner tonight?' he enquired.

She couldn't think of a reason to reject his request on the spur of the moment, and agreed to meet at Brinkley's, just off the Fulham Road, where seating was quite discrete.

The day was then occupied with several meetings, a stream of civil servants with their respective axes to grind, achieving no useful purpose other than to fill their day. 'Value added' is not a phrase that springs to mind when viewing such animals, she thought.

She left the Ministry at 1800hrs and went back to her flat to change prior to catching a cab to the restaurant at about 2000hrs.

1210hrs Harry's office C10 SIS(MI6) London

Tom entered apologising for his late arrival. The underground train had been stuck at Earls Court due to a signal failure; Tom had then grabbed a cab and completing his trip over ground.

Harry then took Tom to a separate meeting room where they could speak confidentially. Harry outlined, briefly, what he wanted.

'Tom, I have had a series of discussions with the Deputy and what we have decided to do is this.

We don't seem to be getting any real feedback from anywhere and the only lead we seem to have is a tenuous Middle East/Gulf connection.

Because of certain intelligence information that the Deputy has, we need to crank up our relationship with Mossad to see if any of their stations in the Gulf and Middle East have any indicators or assets that might assist us in our investigation.

Therefore the plan is for you to speak to David, advise him that we are raising the level of involvement, and that we wish to have a meeting with their Control.

The senior officer at that meeting will be me, operating under a pseudonym, at this stage don't ask me why, and the meeting would take place in one of our safe houses in North London.

If such a meeting were to be positive with clear co-operation, then it is planned that I would go out to the region and continue investigations with their assistance. Incidentally, you would then be running the op here in my absence, reporting to the Deputy with comms liaison with myself.

Therefore, the first task is to see David Hadar, stress the need for such a meeting, also pitch in that there is no obligation on either side at this stage, but we do need to talk, and talk soon.

It is critical to what we need to do, as too much time is passing with damn all results. I can expand on various elements once you've nailed the meeting with Control.

Do you think you can do it, and convince David we're bloody serious and in this situation two heads are definitely better than one?

Tom was silent for a moment.

'Harry, I'll give it a damn good try.'

OK, get onto it straight away, and let me know as soon as you get a response, yea or nay.'

Tom left, and went back to the office, wondering what additional information he had not been told, but recognising that the situation was definitely moving up a gear and he was definitely involved, so get on with it!

He telephoned David Hadar, stressing the urgency of a meeting which was arranged for later that afternoon at 1630hrs.

Harry remained in the meeting room to think through his role and pseudonym in the event that Mossad agreed to their request.

The Deputy would have to approve any such actions with all necessary back up and detail to cover the trail if he was investigated by Mossad. It was not an easy option at any time, but the connection with Anna would not make it any easier.

He decided on his name, Harry Spencer. Harry would remain as his forename. If Mossad was tracking then Spencer would not show up. By keeping his forename he removed any risk of not reacting spontaneously if it was used by friendly or unfriendly connections.

If the discussions took place he could be direct and specific with Mossad as to what help and assistance they required. He would promise to share any Intel that he gathered during the operation and any peripheral items that could be of mutual benefit. From the outset he must establish trust and co-operation and ensure that local

Mossad bureaux in the Middle East and Gulf were aware of his presence and operation.

After returning to his office he prepared a brief Sitrep for the Deputy with his proposals, to ensure speedy approval or amendment if agreement was reached with London Mossad. This was sent over the internal secure message system, Deputy's eyes only.

Harry advised Jane that a full briefing would be held in the next few days subject to certain meetings being agreed, and thanked her for her patience despite her obvious and increasing curiosity of current events.

1630hrs Duke of York Steps, The Mall

Tom Denman and David Hadar met at the bottom of the Duke of York Steps on The Mall, crossed the road, and started their walk down Horse Guards at the eastern end of St James's Park.

Tom quickly came to the point.

'David, you are obviously fully aware of our current investigation which you and I have discussed previously.'

'Of course.'

'Frankly, and I don't really like to admit this, we have drawn a blank so far in establishing a reason for the catastrophe. We have only one tenuous Middle East connection, but, it's all we have to go on.

I have been instructed to ask if a meeting can be arranged between one of our very senior officers and your Head of Station in order to discuss a proposed plan of action which would require close co-operation between us and your regional stations in the Middle East and Gulf. There could be considerable mutual benefits in the sharing of Intel arising from this operation, and additionally, if the group is identified who are carrying out these operations, then that, in itself, will be highly beneficial to our joint fight against terrorism. Finally, this senior officer will be operating in the region.'

They had taken a path into the park about ¾ of the way along Horseguards and were now walking along the south side of the lake.

David was silent for the moment as he digested what Tom had said.

'Tom, I don't know whether such a meeting is possible, and secondly whether such a joint operation would be considered. You know we like to keep our independence and operate alone.

I can see considerable benefits to you if it were to happen, but what Control's

reaction will be, I cannot guess. I can only make a request and get back to you.'

'I can understand your initial reaction David, it came as a bit of a surprise to me, but I can see some considerable joint benefits in the medium term.

If you could stress that this has been lifted at least two levels in priority, then perhaps your Control will realise that we are extremely serious as to our intentions.

Lastly, if such a meeting was agreed it could be held in one of our safe houses in North London. Of course, if that meets with your Control's approval, or somewhere else of his choice,' he added hastily.

They had turned right to cross the bridge situated in the middle of the lake which brought them to the north side and a short walk back to the Mall.

They discussed matters generally, and parted company at the bottom of Marlborough Road, David continuing north towards St James's Street, and Tom turning right along the Mall to make his way back to the office.

2010hrs Brinkley's Restaurant

Anna walked into the restaurant to find that the Minister had organised a table in a corner where they had reasonable privacy.

He ordered her a drink whilst she studied the menu and wondered how the evening would develop. A mix of grumpiness which would ease with wine or a list of complaints, as he vented his spleen about other government ministers, or the PM in particular.

Having just returned from the North East he was polite, friendly and in a semi-jocular mood, amusingly insulting about colleagues and self-deprecating on his own faults.

She realised where the evening was headed and for the first time found herself being critical of her own lifestyle and assignment, which rendered normality obsolete. Reflecting on her recent date with Harry, which had been very normal, she wondered what would be the reaction if she started to try and distance herself from the Minister; both from him and Control. There was no sentiment in the relationship, only duty to her country, but at what personal sacrifice?

Putting those thoughts to the back of her mind she smiled at the Minister and chose her meal.

2100hrs Clapham London

Harry sat in his local Chinese restaurant picking at his food. The owners had got to know him well over the years, and knew when to chat and when to leave him alone.

Tonight was one of those occasions as he doodled on a napkin.

The hieroglyphics he was sketching linked A to B to E to F by lines and question marks. His thoughts ranged around the Middle East and Gulf and who may be involved and what did they want to achieve?

His reflections were interrupted by the arrival of the next courses and he found himself thinking of Anna and wondering what she was doing and whether they would meet up again in a couple of weeks.

He stated to eat and told himself to put sentiment to one side. Any relationship that developed was to asssist the operation, nothing else. Remember that!

Tuesday 17th January 2006 1000hrs Mossad Control London

David Hadar had contacted Control as soon as he had arrived at the office and the meeting was scheduled for one hour later.

He sat down opposite Control and, after the usual exchanges, described the meeting with Tom Denman. After detailing what was being requested and why, he added some personal comments of his own.

'I actually think they are genuine and are not trying to drag us into something where we might have second thoughts. The point about our joint interests in combating terrorism is completely valid and they appear to be stuck at the present time, hence the request.

Even if you have the meeting with them, that in itself does not commit us, and further Intel may be offered at that time which we could find useful.'

'Alright David, I think I understand where they are coming from and thank you for your views and opinion. Let me think about it and I will get back to you, certainly within 24 hours. I need obviously to consider the bigger picture and also whether if this happens we meet in their safe house or somewhere of our choosing.'

He smiled, 'Perhaps our location and our bugs might be preferable to theirs.'

David smiled in response, and rose to leave.

'Thanks. I had said to Tom I would respond in 48 hours, yes or no.'

After David had left Control put through a call on a secure satellite link and spoke quickly in Hebrew. The call was finished within 4 minutes.

1000hrs Harry's office C10

Tom briefed Harry on his meeting with David Hadar.

'I felt David was supportive of what we are trying to do but, of course, it is not his decision to make. I stressed the elements of collaboration and sharing of Intel gathered during the proposed operation. He has promised to get back to us soonest, probably in about 24/48 hours.'

'Did you include the offer of our safe house for the meeting?'

'Yes, but there was no reaction, just a nod!'

'Fine. Let me know as soon as he gets back to you.'

1030hrs Minister's Office

Anna had not enjoyed dinner the previous evening, and had excused herself at about 10.00pm with an upset stomach and headache, which the Minister had accepted with bad grace.

She had started to question the value of her job as PA to the Minister, other than general political tittle-tattle and the odd covert monitoring of suspected home grown Muslim extremists. Most of these seemed to be in the public domain due to their very public Friday rantings against the country that housed, fed, and kept them, at taxpayers' expense.

She had decided she would ask for a meeting with Control to determine a short or medium term strategy, not only for her position, but also for her continuing career.

The atmosphere that day was abrupt and sullen as the Minister went about his duties, involving meetings both internal and external, which kept their face to face contact to a minimum.

For this Anna was grateful, and left at 5.00pm promptly to return to her flat, where, using her secure mobile, she phoned Control to request a meeting. This was agreed and scheduled for Tuesday, the 24th January, 1800hrs, at a travel agent, situated just north of the west end of Oxford Street.

1430hrs Mossad Control London

Control sat at his desk weighing up his options and what instructions he had received from Israel.

The request through David Hadar was not unusual in itself, but there were certain factors that had to be taken into account if he was to sanction such an operation.

Firstly, there would have to be a significant amount of trust, admittedly on both sides, if the operation were to succeed.

Mossad agents, in place, in sensitive positions, in the UK and Gulf, had to be carefully protected. Intel collected by both parties to be shared, plus additional material discovered by UK operative on the ground in the Middle East.

Attending the proposed meeting is not a commitment in itself, so Mossad could decline if not satisfied with structure, benefits and method of operation. Location of meeting would be a Mossad decision, plus their own bugs, he thought wryly.

He would sleep on the thoughts; if nothing negative arose he would advise David Hadar to make contact late tomorrow afternoon.

He wondered who would be at the meeting and whether their paths had crossed before. In the small, closed world of intelligence, that could happen from time to time. We will see, he thought.

1600hrs Nayband Marine Coastal National Park Iran

Approximately half way down the coastal area designated as a National Park the dhow anchored for the night.

Fayez was disappointed, in fact more than disappointed; he was angry.

The trials had gone badly. The divers clearly did not have the required skills for the operation. He would have to adjust his plans accordingly. If they did not reach the level demanded for a night operation, then that would place everybody in jeopardy. He started to think of ways he could get round their inadequacies and considered a number of alternatives in his mind. These ranged from minor operational considerations to significant irreversible change factors. He decided on one.

Under cover of the small cabin below decks he was able to prepare part of his revised plan, which he could implement at the appropriate time. Until then, training would continue on a daily basis until the dhow reached the lee of Lavan Island, on the North East side, facing Bandar-e-Mogham.

From here it would be about 70 miles to the Qatar North Dome Gas Field operations.

He joined the men for prayers, maintaining an air of brotherly friendship for the sake of the final target.

Tomorrow the dhow would continue its leisurely pace down the coast towards Lavan. As darkness fell Fayez insisted on a further training session before the evening meal, which was carried out with further grumbling and with limited success.

One of the divers, a Lebanese, argued that everybody was tired and that the night dive should be delayed to the next day, but Fayez insisted. Not a wise move, the Lebanese thought. There will be payback time for someone who knows nothing about diving.

Fayez had a discussion with the captain of the dhow about wind speeds, currents, the maximum speed that could be achieved by the dhow in an emergency, and for how long. With this information he thought through his options, based upon various conditions applying at the time of the operation.

With a group of people confined to a small boat for a fairly long time, tensions naturally arise and tempers fray. Fayez was aware that careful handling was required up to the operation, and contention must not be allowed to spill over and cause public dissent.

Wednesday 18th January 2006 1000hrs Mossad Control London

Mossad Control, Asher Roshal, picked up his internal telephone and called David Hadar to come to his office.
A knock on the door announced his arrival.

'Come in David. Sit down. I thought long and hard yesterday about the request for the meeting which I agree to. At this stage there is no commitment to co-operation, and we can always tactfully withdraw. Make contact this evening with them and suggest next Monday the 23rd. We will hold it at one of our safe houses in Hendon or Mill Hill and the meeting will be recorded. I want you to prepare a number of optional scenarios based upon existing Intel that we have from our various stations.'

David nodded. 'Can I ask a couple of questions?'

'Of course.'

'Will our people be working directly with the person concerned, or be in the background giving assistance when requested or required?'

'At this stage we don't know what their detailed request will be so work on both options. It had better be a well trained local operative who has first hand knowledge of the Intel, locations and people, otherwise we could be exposed. Get some basic criteria out to stations and draw up a list of possibles.

David nodded again.

'How soon do you think this will start?'

'Pretty soon I would imagine. They want to get moving as information is scarce at the moment. Top dog is probably breathing down their necks and demanding some results.'

'Right,' Control responded.

'I'll get onto it straight away and give you an update tomorrow morning.'

'Fine, here's hoping 'Good Luck' all round.'

David left Control's office and returned to his own to start preparing options, criteria for an operative, and arranging with Safe House crews for a building to be made available and prepared.

He would have plenty to do before he contacted Tom Denman late afternoon and agreed to meet at 1900hrs.

1100hrs Room C10 SIS(MI6) London

Harry was briefing Jane, within limits, as to what was being planned, assuming agreement with Mossad for a meeting was successful.

Whoever was involved would have to be wired, and, once location was known, listening teams would have to be briefed and deployed.

He asked Jane to draw up the usual checklist for such an operation and identify any gaps as the situation unfolded.

Tom entered the office as the briefing was taking place and waited until Harry had finished.

'Harry, we may have contact today, if we're lucky. I know it won't be difficult for us to arrange a safe house, but what if they insist of one of their own? That could provide some problems for our listening teams and they might want to check us out for wires?'

'Point taken and understood Tom. Dependent on their conditions I think they will want to meet on their territory. I know I would want that if a request came to us. We'll just have to modify our plans accordingly once we know and our teams will have to be responsive and flexible.'

'Let me know by safe line if you do hear tonight, and if so, meet here 0800hrs tomorrow morning. OK?'

Jane and Tom murmured assent and the meeting broke up, each working on potential options for the proposed meeting.

1500hrs Arabian Sea 35kms NW of the island of Lavan Iran

The dhow had continued its leisurely pace down the Gulf in a SE direction towards Lavan as friction between a number of the divers reached breaking point.

When a small group are confined for a long period contention develops, and destructive arguments can be generated over very small things.

This had happened between the argumentative Lebanese and another diver concerning the places used for sleeping at night. With hot weather it was often the case that places were moved so that a cooling breeze could be experienced by a different crewman every night. In winter the reverse was the case when the air was much colder.

After they had eaten at 1300hrs, Fayez had said that a dive practice would be held at 1700hrs. Following this the argument had developed and the two divers traded blows.

Fayez realised his authority was being directly challenged and he immediately intervened.

Insults and threats were exchanged and at one point the Lebanese turned on Fayez and delivered a stream of invective that no one in his position could accept.

At this point Fayez drew his silenced automatic and shot the Lebanese twice.

The remaining divers were immediately silent, and the crew members turned their backs and went about their duties.

Fayez spoke.

'My brothers, we are on a Jihad mission which must succeed. I am in charge and you will do what I say. Wrap him in some nets with heavy weights and tow him behind. When we make landfall tonight we will bury him. Allahu Akbar!'

The men responded quietly, now clearly afraid.

Fayez felt that his authority had now been restored and underlined, and that, Insha'Allah, he would have no more problems of this kind.

1715hrs Office C10 SIS(MI6) London

Tom had received a call on his mobile from David suggesting a meeting at 1900hrs in a small pub behind the Albert Hall.

He had agreed and advised Harry, so they confirmed he would call Harry later, and meet, as arranged, at 0800hrs the following morning.

The evening had a cold edge to it as Tom passed Exhibition Road on his way towards the Albert Hall. He pulled his scarf over his chin to provide some protection from the wind as he turned left into Kensington Gore, skirting around the back of the Albert Hall, and exiting onto Queen's Gate.

Entering the pub he saw David in a far corner, acknowledging him with a small hand gesture, before buying his drink and making his way over to the table.

'Evening David. I'm hoping we will be sharing some good news,' he commented with a wry grin.

'Could be. Let me explain as I don't have too much time.'

'OK.'

'The head man has agreed to the meeting you requested, but it will have to take place in one of our safe houses. The date will be Monday, the 23rd January at 12 noon. Only two people from each side. I'm assuming yourself and your key man. By the way what's his name?'

'Harry Spencer.'

'Right. The safe house address will be given to you on the morning of the 23rd, about two hours before the meeting. OK?'

'Fine, I'm assuming that will give us enough time to get there? Rough location? North, South, East or West?'

'Probably North, but subject to change.'

'Any other points at this stage?'

'No, we anticipate an open discussion at the time. Your objectives, location assistance, time expectations, contact networks, shared information, etc.'

'OK. I will take this back. Assume acceptance of date and time. Any variations as to attendees I will contact you, but I think it will be myself and the key man.'

'Fine. Is there anything specific we should be aware of before the meeting which requires some preparation or background research?'

'No. I think it will be open and frank, everything will be on the agenda, except those issues we both need to keep under wraps,' he joked.

David smiled.

'Point taken. Will contact on Monday re location. Good health.'

Shortly after some general conversation the meeting broke up and the two men went their separate ways, both thinking of the various permutations that would occur the following Monday.

2200hrs Arabian Sea Bandar-e-Bostaneh Iran

Under cover of darkness the dhow slid gently into a quiet bay east of Bandar-e-Bostaneh. The crew, without speaking, pulled the wrapped body in over the stern and placed it in the inflatable for its passage to the shore.

Fayez took three of the divers with him and the body, the others travelling in the other inflatable.

Arriving on a sandy beach the body was carried about 300 metres inland to a position behind a small grove of trees where a grave was swiftly dug.

There Fayez quickly gave an abbreviated burial oration which was sullenly echoed by the divers.

They then withdrew to the inflatables and returned to the dhow, casting off immediately and proceeding further down the coast under power and sail, finally dropping anchor at about midnight.

Everybody on the dhow was quiet; each shocked in their own way as to the chain of events that day, and nervous as to the future.

Fayez felt his control of the group was now confirmed and barring something unforeseen would now continue to the operation.

Thursday 19th January 2006 0930hrs Room C10 SIS(MI6) London

Tom joined Harry and briefed him on his meeting with David the previous evening.

'They are saying two from each side, and location is to be advised only at 1100hrs therefore giving us only an hour to get our teams in place. Perhaps we could be wired but I expect they will assume that. However if we are going to be working together, and you in particular, then perhaps we forget the listening teams and the wires and just go with it.

It could, in fact, demonstrate our trust in them and our confidence that we are all going to be absolutely straight on this op,' he commented wryly.

Harry thought for a moment.

'Time is not on our side given the one hour to make the meeting in their safe house. This is one occasion when we are going to have to start with our cards face up. At least that will be our stated position.

We can then assume they will do the same, otherwise we are going to be playing 'pass the parcel' with no bloody clue what's in it!

Additionally, I really want them to understand this is not some stupid attempt at infiltration into their network. We need their help, but hopefully we are both going to benefit from our joint op, both now and potentially for the future.'

Tom nodded and interjected,

'I was going to prepare some sort of timeline we can take to the meeting giving our Intel and thoughts to date, plus Whys? Where? What ifs? Connections? Etc. In that way it will indicate our seriousness, and trust in the potential partnership.'

'Fine. Run it past me 1400hrs.'

1030hrs Ministers Office Whitehall London

The minister was niggling away at Anna about some fairly trivial matter that had not been dealt with a few days before.

In reality an excuse to get back at her for her reluctance to see him on two recent occasions.

Anna was finding the situation increasingly uncomfortable and was hoping that the meeting with Control on the 24th would resolve a number of issues.

Meanwhile she would have to live with it, and when asked by the Minister agreed to dinner that evening, as he would be returning to his home and constituency on the Friday evening.

His manner improved during the day, but she did allow her mind to wander to the following week when she hoped or expected Harry to call.

1200hrs Room C10 SIS(MI6) London

Harry was trying to collect his thoughts in order to prepare a Sitrep for the Deputy's approval, and which would also serve as a clear starting point for the meeting with Mossad London Control on Monday.

The facts were scarce, the hypotheses numerous, all driven by no clear connection, either to a recognised or new terrorist organisation, or to anything other than a freak accident, which had little currency at the present time.

If, during the Monday meeting, it became evident that there may be a connection to terrorism, either home grown or Middle East based, then that at least would provide a basis for the joint co-operation.

It is common practice among a number of countries security services, considered to be on the 'same side', to share, when appropriate, Intel and resources for the common good.

This is such an instance and Harry felt that the scenario, background and benefits outlined would meet with the Deputy's approval.

Tom was building a timeline to present to the meeting, if required, albeit with significant gaps. If co-operation was forthcoming, then perhaps the gaps would start to be filled.

After lunch Tom joined Harry in building a file and operation timeline for Monday's meeting filling in gaps with possibilities or conjecture.

Although, at this stage, it looked fairly light on detail, the paucity of information gave additional reinforcement to the need for co-operation.

1530hrs Deputy's Office SIS(MI6) London

Harry knocked and entered, and after exchanging greetings led straight into the verbal presentation of his proposed tactics for the Monday meeting.

The Deputy listened intently, nodding occasionally in agreement, and on one occasion, towards the end, shaking his head.

'Harry, I'm in full and general agreement with one exception. Our own Intel is woefully light. Don't stress that. Say we are following a number of leads, which we will share with them, at the appropriate time. With their extensive Middle East and Gulf network, that is where we need their horsepower.

If there is a M.E. connection, they will either know already or have likely targets. That is where we want their assistance and co-operation. Understood?'

Harry nodded in agreement.

'OK, fully understood. I will brief Tom accordingly who will be my Number Two at the meeting.'

'Best of luck Harry, I look forward to the debrief afterwards!'

Harry returned to his office and brought Tom up to speed, particularly stressing the point the Deputy had made.

1645hrs Deputy's Office SIS(MI6) London

The Deputy was reflecting on his meeting with Harry when his telephone rang. Picking it up, his PA informed him it was the French Embassy on the line, a Monsieur Philippe Roberge. [It is common practice for relationships to be built over a number of years between allies as a result of various overseas postings.]

Accepting the call he greeted Philippe in French before reverting to English.

'To what do I owe this pleasure, Philippe?'

[The Deputy and his old friend, Philippe Roberge, went back over a number of years having first met when they were both stationed in Nigeria.

PR, as he is known to his friends, was now a senior officer in the DGSE, Direction Generale de la Securite Exterieure, the French equivalent of MI6.]

'Well, mon ami, you are aware of our continuing commercial relationship with

Big M, and I thought you should know that our source is indicating a developing relationship between them and your organisation.'

The Deputy answered in a similar jocular manner,

'Philippe, mon vieux copain, we have a particular project which is causing us a small problem and we think they can help. No more, no less. Our relationship with them and you remains a constant.'

'Do not forget that we have worked together before so if the need arises please call me. You know we French have more flexibility than you Anglo-Saxons!'

'I won't forget, Philippe', replied the Deputy laughing, 'I seem to remember your flexibility getting you into trouble on a couple of occasions in the past!'

'Trouble? Jamais! Merely a misunderstanding! Anyway, à bientôt, you have my number!'

The Deputy sat for a few minutes thinking about what had been said.

Clearly there was an on-board French asset in Mossad feeding back to the DGSE, but if the French had one in place could there be others? If the opposition also had an asset in place, that, by itself, could jeopardise any pending or future operation.

1715hrs Deputy's Office SIS(MI6) London

The Deputy called Harry back to his office and outlined the brief conversation he had had with the French

Embassy and possible implications. Such information to be kept between himself and Harry. This could make the relationship with Mossad more precarious, on the other hand it could, perhaps, be used as leverage in an appropriate situation.

2000hrs Harry's flat Clapham

Harry poured himself a beer, sank into his armchair, and dialled Anna's number. She answered almost immediately, and by the intonation in her voice sounded pleased to hear him.

'I said I'd call about now, so here I am. How are you keeping, busy? Is the Master working you hard? Mine is rushing me off my feet!'

'Do you mean Busy, productive? Or Busy, depleting an Amazonian rain forest with fairly useless Strategy papers that never get implemented?'

'Whoa, do I detect a note of cynicism in your voice? No, of course not. Why ever did I think of such a thing?!

They jokingly sparred in this way for a few minutes before Harry told her he was going to be very busy over the next ten days or so, which would push back their proposed date.

Anna sounded disappointed but readily understood that these things happen and said she was looking forward to seeing him again whenever that was.

Harry also stressed that he was very disappointed and would call her as soon as he could. After putting down their phones they both reflected on the problems of living the lives they did, and the near impossibility of normalcy.

VII

Monday 23rd January 2006

0900hrs Room C10 SIS(MI6) London

Harry was at his desk when Tom came through the door carrying three files.

'See you've got mine, yours and theirs. All identical?'

'Just checking. Jane finished them last night. How do you want to play this meeting?'

'I shall do all the talking. I realise that you have established a good relationship with David Hadar but what I want you to do Tom, is observe, listen and record. You know all the psychological tics and signs to look for. Watch their reactions to suggestions. Try and determine whether they are bluffing or saying what they think we want to hear. You know the drill. Afterwards I want to hear your appraisal before I make any comments. Understood?'

'OK. But what if I hear something I know to be incorrect?'

'Unless it has a real impact on what is being discussed, leave it. I need you to check every expression, including dead pan, in order for us to have picked up any nuance or slip they may make. Additionally we don't know the style and temperament of Mossad Control. He may be thinking he can call all the shots. In that case we diplomatically walk away.

Anyway we are going in cold, so we have to use our two man resource in the best possible way, plus don't forget I'm using an assumed name!'

'Understood' Tom replied before turning to check the files.

At about 1000hrs Tom's mobile rang, which he answered.

He copied down the instructions given and then turning to Harry said,

'A41, Hendon Way, turn off left at The Vale, park by Greenfield Gardens and await further instruction. Be there by 1145hrs.'

Harry rang the Deputy to advise him the meeting was on. The Deputy wished him good luck and asked to be updated soonest.

At 1050hrs they picked up the pool car with Tom driving, and drove across Vauxhall Bridge, passing Victoria

Station, up and round Hyde Park Corner into Park Lane. From there into Portman Square, then Gloucester Place, Park Road, and Wellington Road, the start of the A41.

They made good time as the traffic was reasonable in density, arriving close to Greenfield Gardens at about 1135hrs.

They parked and waited for Tom's mobile to ring, which it did at 1145hrs.

Tom answered, nodding as instructions were given.

'Yes, I see the maroon Ford about 75 yards ahead on the right. Follow? Right.'

After a number of left and right turns the maroon Ford turned into the drive of a large house, shielded from the road by a tightly packed row of trees.

Two men got out of the Ford and waved Tom and Harry to the front door where they were met by two further men who searched them quickly for wires, and whatever else they thought Tom and Harry might be carrying.

They then led them to a large room at the rear of the property where an oval table sat in the middle of the room with two chairs on either side.

Harry and Tom sat down, rising to their feet when David Hadar and Mossad Control entered.

Tom and David smiled and greeted each other, whilst Harry and Control shook hands and looked intently at each other.

Harry's mind was racing to see if he could recollect Control's face from previous years but could not immediately place him. His task was also hindered by the obvious remedial surgery that had taken place many years before, on Control's face. Could be burns, grenade fragments, he thought to himself, whilst maintaining a steady gaze.

Control waved to the chairs and the four sat down.

Harry passed a copy of the file to Control who slid it sideways to David.

'This is a very skinny Sitrep of where we are,' Harry commented, 'but at least it serves as some sort of basis for our discussions.'

Control and David nodded but made no move to open the file.

Harry continued,

'Let's get the introductions out of the way. Tom and David already know each other. I'm Harry Spencer. Been in the Service too long', he joked, 'and we need assistance on our current plot'.

Mossad Control smiled and said,

'Yes, David and Tom already know each other, but for you and me this is not our first meeting'.

Harry looked a little puzzled at this comment.

Control continued,

'You are Harry, but not Spencer. Your name is Baxter. You and I met and co-operated, to a reasonable extent, in Lebanon during a break in the civil war in 1982. We met in Beirut, at the airport, when you had arrived on an MEA flight from London on one of the first flights in, when the UN brokered a truce between the various groups including Hezbollah'.

Harry could not hide his surprise and remained silent as Control continued with a smile.

'My name is Asher Roshal, I've also been in my Service too long, and I will be listening to what you have to say to see if we can be of assistance to each other!'

Harry could not hide his surprise and recalled his short operation in Lebanon working with the Israelis in the South of Lebanon.

Following the UN brokered truce the Israelis had supported the Christian South Lebanese Army, which would act as a buffer in the South for Israel.

In The North a collection of militia including the PLO, Hezbollah, were supported and funded by Syria and Iran.

By June 1982 the Israeli forces were entrenched just south of Beirut with PLO and Syrian troops to the North.

'I remember you now, Asher. We spent about a ten days together gathering what intelligence we could north of Beirut in a very fluid and fast moving situation! I remember you covered my back very well on at least one occasion!'

'And you mine I also remember!' said Control. 'My subsequent tangle a year later with an AP mine changed my face a bit', he joked.

This comment let Harry off the hook as otherwise he was wondering how he could raise the matter of Asher's facial injuries.

'What can I say? My apologies for the alias, my boss wanted to keep our relationship neutral. We can forget that now. Incidentally, congratulations on your promotion!'

The atmosphere immediately thawed as old working arrangements kicked in, and the meeting progressed well from that point.

After about two hours of exchanging information and running through a significant number of alternative scenarios it was agreed that a number of assumptions and proposals would be put to their respective Services for approval and action.

It was very clear that there was a Middle East/Gulf connection arising from what little intelligence had been gathered in the UK, but which was now being reinforced by a significant number of unrelated observations, phone taps, and covert surveillance, pointing towards activity in the region, collected by Mossad teams on the ground.

Harry summed up from his side.

'Asher, your operatives have obviously picked up a number of unconnected events and Intel, that I think, and I believe you now also think, could have some connection to our current plot.

I think that we need to get on the ground with your people and work with them in order to add our bits to the puzzle, and confirm or otherwise, whether there are any future strikes planned, and if so where.

What I am proposing is that, if we submit, effectively a jointly agreed proposal, to our respective Services indicating common approach, interest, and mutual benefit, then it will probably be approved. Lastly, our joint operation must be kept at the highest level of confidentiality in both our Services; no one other than a

Needs Must, Level 1, can be party to these discussions, agreement and operations. Do you agree?'

Mossad Control agreed and said,

'Yes, lets work on the wording this afternoon, after we've had some coffee and sandwiches, so we can then submit at the same time and hopefully get fairly quick approval. The only shame is, Harry, that I won't be able to work with you on this one, as my face let's me down and is too recognisable! Except by you at 12 noon today!

Harry smiled and moved on quickly, 'What about those sandwiches and coffee then!'

Following a brief lunch, a detailed Sitrep was hammered out, reflecting the appropriate nuances that would push the right buttons in their respective Services.

Finishing at about 1630 hours, Harry and Tom left first, on this occasion Tom driving, against rush hour traffic which was already starting to build.

Tom drove, without starting a conversation, as he knew Harry was lost in thought, going over what had transpired and what were the likely outcomes once he presented his report to the Deputy.

As they proceeded down the A41 they were not aware of a motorcyclist maintaining station about 100 yards behind them. Reaching Vauxhall Cross the motorcyclist turned left into Albert Embankment in the direction of Lambeth Bridge.

1715hrs Room C10 SIS(MI6) London

As they sat down to summarise the meeting and agreed actions Harry turned to Tom, and commented ironically,

'One can never legislate for surprises, can one, bearing in mind I wanted you to observe, look out for the psychological tics, etc! Before I comment what was your reaction overall?

Tom thought for a few seconds and then said,

'Well, I thought it went well and they genuinely seem to want to co-operate fully. Let's face it; it's in their best interests. Plus with this sort of plot, they've got many more people on the ground than we have, so it makes real sense from our side.'

Harry interjected,

'With the coincidence of Control I think the landscape is much more defined than we imagined beforehand. Yes, they will want benefit out of the relationship, but my previous experience with him was good. He was dependable and he delivered. Personally, if he is recommending our proposal and it is approved, then with his backing we should get grade A assistance.'

Harry and Tom finalised the Sitrep document which would be discussed with the Deputy at a meeting Harry requested from his PA for tomorrow at 1000hrs.

1715hrs MI5 HQ Thames House Millbank

The motorcyclist, who had tailed Harry and Tom, parked his machine at the back of the building and quickly took the lift to the third floor.

Reporting to his controller he told him of the meeting held off Hendon Way, duration and time of return.

The controller was left wondering to himself why MI6 personnel were meeting with Mossad operatives in London when responsibility for home security rested with MI5.

Another occasion of the left hand not knowing what the right was doing, he mused. Perhaps, more importantly, why?

Both MI5 and MI6 guarded their respective turf with an obsession bordering on paranoia, and often took delight in political point scoring.

Low grade observation was in order, he thought, at this time. No point in frightening the animals at this stage.

Tuesday 24th January 2006 1000hrs Global Travel Agents, Eastcastle Street, behind Oxford Street

Anna had taken a days leave to attend this meeting which was being held in a rather run down travel agents behind Oxford Street. Certainly innocuous and did not attract a lot of passing interest.

She entered the shop to be met by the indifferent gaze of a woman behind the desk.

'Yes. Can I help you?'

'I've a meeting with the manager. Could you tell him Anna Harrison is here.'

The woman walked to the door at the back, entered and returned almost immediately.

'He'll see you now. Go through that door to his office.'

Anna knocked and entered.

Control was sitting at the desk and indicated to Anna to take the chair opposite him.

'Well, you asked for this meeting, so tell me what it's about.'

Anna marshalled her thoughts and started slowly to explain her thoughts and predicament.

'Perhaps not all of this will make sense immediately and perhaps it will not necessarily be in the right order, but I am not comfortable in what I am doing on my current assignment.

Firstly, you need have no concern as to my loyalty and love of country. My family has demonstrated that over many years.

I am not happy in the relationship that has been deliberately developed with my boss.

As you can see the amount of useful intelligence being gathered is low as he is being increasingly sidelined by his boss, and this is being reflected in his behaviour, heavier drinking and temper tantrums.

He is getting abusive at times in his attitude towards me, not physically yet, but I think it could happen, given time. That is not something I am prepared to accept.

I was wondering if I could therefore resign from my current position and be put in another region, different cover and assignment.'

Control did not reply immediately, and when he did the words were slow and deliberate.

'I fully understand the stress and strain that such covert operations put on people, but conditions and consequences were pointed out to you frequently during your training.

Let me make some observations, and ask you a few questions.

What you may consider to be low grade intelligence may just be the final link within the bigger picture that gives us a significant edge. I know you will have heard this many times but it bears repeating.

Additionally, one is never aware what tomorrow may bring. Events have a habit of happening, particularly when we least expect them. That is why we need to be ultra vigilant at all times.

With the constant pressure on our country from rogue states with increasing development within the nuclear field we must be on our guard constantly.

Do I make myself clear?'

Anna nodded.

'May I ask you a few questions?'

He continued without waiting for an answer.

'Are you involved in any relationship other than your boss at the present time?'

'No', she replied truthfully, 'But…'

'Yes.'

'I have a new friend who has asked me out again, but that's all it is at present. It's just been social, dinner, theatre, you know.'

'If that relationship were to develop them you would have increased pressure on the existing one which could put your present assignment in jeopardy. That would not be something I could accept.'

'I understand, but that is why I am asking to be reassigned. I am uncomfortable the way things are, and the way they are going. I have done this for a number of years. I need a rest and a change. Do you not see?'

'Whilst I hear the points you are making I cannot agree to do anything other than to consider what you have said, discuss the matter with Senior Control and come back to you.

Meanwhile continue as normal and we can discuss further within 7 to 10 days. Understood?'

Anna agreed and the meeting ended.

As she left, she glanced at the woman in the outer office, who was just closing a desk drawer. No doubt switching off the recording of the meeting, she thought cynically, but accurately, as the woman looked guiltily at her.

Control wondered what the background of the new friend was. When he spoke again to Anna he would ask further questions.

More importantly was the question of her continuing, or not, her current assignment as the Minister's PA.

Although she was right in the low strength of the Intel obtained, it did provide one or two pieces, from time to time, in the overall jigsaw. That, from Israel's' point of view, justified her continuing role.

Control would discuss the matter with his immediate superior, but could already guess the likely reaction.

1400hrs Deputy's Office SIS(MI6) London

Harry entered the Deputy's office to be greeted by his raised hand, indicating quiet whilst he was on the telephone.

'Yes Minister, I fully appreciate your concerns and the considerable public pressures you are working under.

Let me reassure you that that everything we are able to do with our current resources is focussed on a speedy resolution, albeit frustrated by a lack of forensic evidence.'

He stopped, holding the handset away from his ear, as the volume increased from the Minister, who was commenting on the collective incapacity and inability of the Department to come up with some quick and ready answers.

Speaking again, the Deputy said,

'I am as keen as you are Minister, in getting the right answers, and with our present activities and investigations believe that we are getting closer to understanding the possible connections, which are not confined to the UK.

No, I cannot expand on that comment, as to do so may be prejudicial to our operatives, and the scenario within which they are working.

Once I have solid information to share with you I will be contacting you immediately.

Thank you, Minister, for your support and understanding.'

The conversation was ended abruptly from the Minister's office and the Deputy replaced the handset with a wry smile.

'Hopefully he won't bother me for another week, but in the meantime Harry I hope you are making some progress, and will have something concrete pretty damn soon!'

Harry passed over the file and said,

'What's in the file is confirmation of what I am going to say plus recommendations as to action.'

'Fire away.'

'I'll keep it staccato as you have the file, but these are the essential points.

We held our meeting with Mossad yesterday which was held in North London.

Mossad Control turned out to be Asher Roshal who I worked with during the Lebanese Civil War in the 80s. He had been injured post our joint operation so I didn't recognise him, but he recognised me.

We got on well in the past and I trust him. We, and they put our cards on the table face up, and they are prepared to allow us to have direct contact with their people on the ground in the region.

Their Intel indicates some connected activity involving Qatar, Bahrain, Iran, and the UAE, and with what we have, plus their observations and reports, we think that two and two may make five.

To be honest our UK Intel is thin, so we don't have a lot to go on. This seems likely and is our best bet.

It is proposed that I go the Gulf, meet with their operatives, see the evidence, tapes, photographs, recordings, etcetera, and hopefully get a better picture of where this group is coming from, countries and nationalities involved, relationships, funding, et al.

I would start either in Bahrain or Qatar and probably be away about a week max. Bearing in mind the offer from London M, I think we take it, because even if we draw a blank, we will have established a firmer working relationship with them, which must be good for the future.'

The Deputy had listened intently whilst Harry had explained his reasoning and now spoke,

'Fine, in principle I agree. BUT, one important question.

How will you handle the question of the Minister's PA, now her boss knows your position in the Service?'

'Without divulging the connection between myself and Anna I asked Control for complete confidentiality of our joint op, and an information embargo in all their other sections.'

'Will it hold?'

I think it will, if not you'll have to replace me.'

'Hang on Harry; let me comment from a different viewpoint.

Even if the PA knew your real role, would that be problematical, bearing in mind you are both working on the same side, albeit with different agendas?

I think not. In fact it could well help this current scenario. Let it ride Harry. If it comes out, then you just acknowledge you've both been bluffing each other, but you're both on the same side!'

'I can see where you are coming from; I just like to keep certain things in tight compartments.'

'Fair enough, but I don't see high risk in this. By the way when are you seeing her again?'

'I spoke to her the other day, and said I was tied up and really busy for about seven to ten days, but would contact her after that. We were going to dinner or the theatre.'

'OK. Let me read the file and I'll give you my comments and decision by 1700hrs.'

The meeting over, Harry returned to his office thinking what the Deputy had said. He had a point. It could be of benefit. An interesting number of permutations came to mind, most dispensed with, but a few he felt, had mileage.

Initially, he wondered whether Mossad Control could keep the joint op confidential, and further, whether he would want to, if the connection was revealed.

That would be one of those bridges to be crossed in due course.

The Minister certainly had no knowledge that his private life was under scrutiny and on file by the Security Service, but would the disclosure make his PA's job that much more difficult? Only time would tell.

Harry hoped that the Deputy would approve proposal and implementation and glanced at the clock at 1645hrs.

1700hrs Room C10 SIS(MI6) London

Harry's phone rang. It was the Deputy.

'Harry, agreed and proceed. As quick as you like. Let's hope it bears results, we've got damn all on the radar here, and, you know who, will be spitting feathers unless we give him something fairly soon. Good luck, and keep me posted!

'Will do. Thanks for your support. Will coordinate with M and organise contacts and flights. Will not, repeat not, advise appropriate embassies on the ground of my actions. Keep it close at present. If I want help on the ground, I'll shout. But I don't think there would be any value including some defence attaché who has some time to spare, if you get my drift!'

'Agree completely.

I was going to say, this is really a one man op for the time you're there. Watch your back because you will be on your own, and dependent on M's cooperation.'

'I will try and fly down to the Gulf on Friday so I can get started on Saturday (their Monday) and not lose any time. I'm assuming M can get their people up and running for then.'

They finished their conversation and Harry started making some rough notes covering questions to M and briefing Tom the next day.

Wednesday 25th January 2006 1000hrs Room C10 SIS(MI6) London

Harry and Tom sat down, with Jane taking notes, to start to put in place some basic requests for Mossad London to assist SIS(MI6) in the proposed trip to the Gulf.

Harry opened by suggesting that a further meeting should be held between Tom and David to flesh out the indicators that had arisen in the meeting two days ago.

Tom went off to contact David Hadar, whilst Harry agreed some basic logistics with Jane, who then went to organise open airline tickets and various Gulf currencies plus US dollars.

Tom called Harry to advise a meeting had been set up for that afternoon at 1500hrs and he would meet Harry back at HQ at about 1730hrs.

Unexpectedly Harry received a mobile call at about 1045hrs from Asher Roshal, Mossad Control.

Harry, somewhat surprised, said,

'How did you get my number?'

'Harry, we have a number of ways, you know us! Anyway I didn't ring to chat about that. You and I need to meet again, and I was wondering where would be appropriate, and forget safe houses this time!'

Harry thought for a minute.

'If I book a hotel room, call you on your mobile, and you come straight to the room, ignoring reception, would that be OK? I know a little hotel in Bloomsbury that is usually discrete, but not for the sort of meeting you and I are planning!'

'I won't ask how you know that Harry, but sounds reasonable. We will probably need an hour. Check this number, it is a pay as you go mobile, so will not be operational after our meeting. Can this be arranged for tomorrow?'

'Yes, not a problem. What time would you like to meet? Noon?'

'Yes, OK, noon tomorrow. Give me a call about 11.15 with the address. See you then.'

The line went dead.

Harry called Jane to advise her of the two meeting taking place, Tom today, and himself tomorrow.

He placed a call to the Bloomsbury hotel reserving a room for 2-3 hours from 1100hrs tomorrow for the purpose of an interview. The resigned tone from the Reservations clerk indicated that this was not the first time such a reason had been given for such a short stay!

1715hrs Room C10 SIS(MI6) London

Tom arrived in the room looking a little nonplussed.

'Strange meeting. Their Intel is not much better than ours although there's more of it. Huge disconnects, and they are equally unsure as to what is going on. The one thing they are certain about is that something is being planned, but as to, where, time, date, group, not really any clue.

It was felt that when you have discussions on the ground, and the sharing of Intel, then this may trigger some possible connections. Following that, one may have some hypotheses that might bear some fruit.

The suggestion is you start in Bahrain, then to Abu Dhabi.'

Harry told Tom about his planned meeting with Mossad Control the next day and said they should meet back in Room C10 at about 1500hrs or when he got back.

Harry left that evening wondering what Control wished to discuss with him and what implications it would have on his Gulf trip.

Thursday 26th January 2006 1045hrs Hotel Coram St Bloomsbury

Harry approached Reception and advised them of his room reservation for an interview starting at approximately midday.

The young lady restrained the lifting of her eyebrow to a minimum, and enquired as the name of the person coming for interview.

When Harry advised her that the man would be coming directly to his room she had difficulty in hiding her smirk as she processed his credit card for the half day fee.

Harry took the lift to the second floor and entered Room 207.

At 11.15 he called Asher on his mobile leaving a message as to address and room number. He then called Reception to order some coffee and sandwiches to be brought up just before 12 noon.

He sat down at the desk and waited.

The coffee and sandwiches arrived just before noon, followed by a knock on the door at about 12.10.

Opening the door he saw Asher standing there with a quizzical smile.

They shook hands as Asher came in, removing his coat, and sitting in one of the armchairs.

'I think the young lady at Reception has a somewhat different idea as to why you and I are meeting,' he laughed.

'My apologies,' said Harry, 'She could hardly hide her smile when I was checking in.

However, first things first. Coffees, sandwiches, help yourself.'

Asher poured himself some coffee, took a sandwich and a bite.

'You and I will have to share something Harry. I don't think it will create any undue problems, but we should both be aware of it, so if does blow up in a small way, it will not come as a big surprise to anybody.'

Harry listened without comment.

'You may not be aware that Mossad has an asset working in one of your Ministries.'

Harry maintained a querying look on his face, giving no hint that he knew what Control was talking about.

'The asset has been in place for a number of years and holds a fairly senior position. Additionally, and coincidentally,' he smiled, 'You have been out to the theatre and dinner with this asset.'

Harry registered suitable astonishment at this point and exclaimed,

'Do you mean Anna?'

'Yes.'

Harry maintained his thunderstruck look for a sufficient length of time before asking,

'What can I say? I met her over Christmas down in Sussex, and, yes, we've been to the theatre and dinner on one occasion.'

Asher allowed the situation to sink in before he commented further.

'Anna does not know that I am telling you this today and I would ask you to keep it confidential until after your return. The position is that we have an internal situation to resolve, and I have told Anna that I will discuss it with her in about a week's time. I shall, at that time, advise her of our conversation today and our joint operation. Do we understand each other?'

Harry was trying to think quickly and responded,

'Fair enough. But is it absolutely necessary to tell her, at that time, bearing in mind the joint sensitivities of the overall situation?

I appreciate that there is no real disadvantage, but I am thinking that if we can keep the numbers tight on a 'need to know' basis, that is safer for all concerned.

I realise the decision is yours, and what you decide I will go along with, just keep me informed as to what your final decision will be!'

'Of course. I believe your Tom Denman met with David Hadar yesterday to discuss your starting point in the Gulf?'

'Yes. I can only describe the situation as fluid and very hard to pin down, but I think I will start in Bahrain and take it from there.'

'May I wish you well and assure you that our operatives will provide all the assistance you require. Please ensure that all Intel is shared, and that we are party to any proposals which may create activity outside of what we have agreed.'

Absolutely; I am sure your agents will provide a regular running report on my trip, and I will ensure that any Intel obtained, any peripheral relationships established, or any additional activity proposed or which we are forced to be party to, will be communicated through them to you.'

Good, we understand each other. Good luck for a safe trip.'

A number of additional logistical issues were discussed including country comms, fallback situations, crisis management and assistance, safe houses and country exits.

Asher left first, with Harry following about 15 minutes later.

The motorcyclist parked on the street about fifty yards from the hotel entrance noted the time, started his machine and left in an easterly direction.

His Controller would be interested in Harry's second meeting, so soon after the first.

1500hrs Room C10 SIS(MI6) London

When Harry met Tom he made no mention of the main item discussed and confined his briefing to the operational and logistical issues discussed at some length with Asher.

Tom was a little surprised, but thought it must have given both Harry and Asher a chance to catch up properly, after so many years.

The main part of their meeting was collating, in encrypted form, their Intel to date. Additionally, contact details in Bahrain, Embassy hotlines (in case of emergency), open tickets for Gulf travel, original and spare passports, driving licences (UK, International, Bahrain, UAE, and Qatar.)

Harry's BA flight was leaving the next day, Friday the 27th January, at 1030hrs, arriving in Bahrain at about 2000hrs local time.

Tom wished Harry the best of luck and said,

'Let me buy you a reasonably priced beer before you go home to pack, and if you want or need another pair of hands out there, give me a shout!'

Harry took him up on the beer, and at about 1900hrs headed home to pack.

Friday 27th January 2006 0900hrs Terminal 4 London Heathrow

Harry had checked in for his BA flight and was sitting in the lounge reading a paper and drinking coffee, when, to his surprise, he saw David Hadar walk through the door and cross over to his table.

'What are you doing here,' he said, very quietly.

'When my boss was talking over your trip last night he thought it would be a good idea for me to be involved, and to assist with liaison with our local people to ensure you get the very best service,' he said smiling.

'It would be a good idea if we could have discussed this,' said Harry testily, 'But what can I say at this stage? Not a lot!

Let's meet tomorrow morning, 0800hrs, with your local man, and see what we can determine from his observations.

We are not sitting together on the plane so my hotel is the Sheraton Bahrain Hotel. Ask at the desk for my room. I'll see you then.'

Harry was more than faintly irritated. This was the classic case of the tag along observer, not necessarily contributing much, but reporting back everything, good and bad. Plus, a lot depended on the individual's agenda.

The flight was uneventful and arrived on time, so Harry, with minimal delay through immigration and customs, found himself in the hotel in Manama by 2115hrs.

Saturday 28th January 2006 0800hrs Sheraton Hotel Manama Bahrain

He had slept fitfully, arising at 0600hrs, having showered, dressed, and had breakfast by 0715hrs. He spent the time before 0800hrs reading the local paper, Gulf Daily News, to get a feel for current sentiment on a variety of issues.

At 0810hrs David Hadar appeared and suggested they go to the Station Head's office for secure discussions. Harry agreed and they left in David's small hire car to an undistinguished looking commercial block not far away.

There Harry was introduced to the Station Head, a man who appeared to be somewhat reluctant to be talking to a member of SIS(MI6), until assured by David that the instruction he had received had come from the very top, and benefited both services.

From the transcripts of conversations overheard in Beirut it was evident that significant funding was being made available to a, as yet unidentified, group, who were planning an attack on the gas fields shared by Qatar and Iran.

Comments and observations by the Beirut station certainly helped, but the loose network of the targets involved, with no clear identification as to the grouping, was making analysis difficult.

The Bahrain Station Head, Amnon Shahar, was of the opinion that, although there was target identification; reason, method, timing, consequence, propaganda benefit, etc, were still clearly ill defined.

Analysis of Intel from a number of stations indicated various links with both Syrian and Palestinian individuals. However their movement around the Gulf had created more confusion, both in interpretation of likely actions, and reasons for the circuitous travel.

It was felt that the further meetings planned between Harry and the other Gulf stations involved would, perhaps, throw more light on a confusing mosaic of information.

Harry outlined the challenge facing SIS(MI6) in the UK following the Buncefield disaster, and the little Intel that had been collected by their regional office. Whilst the suspicion of terrorist activity was there, it had been almost impossible to determine the who's and why's. He spoke openly to reinforce the fact that two security services were working to a common purpose, and that both would benefit from such co-operation.

On what he and David had heard, discussed, and analysed, it was felt sensible to travel to Abu Dhabi that afternoon. They could then start discussions with that station chief the following morning, making best use of available time.

Harry and David caught a Gulf Air flight at about 1600hrs, landing in Abu Dhabi at 1815hrs. It was only a one hour flight, but Abu Dhabi is one hour ahead of Bahrain.

They travelled by cab to the Sheraton Hotel and booked in, agreeing to dine together at 2030hrs.

Whilst Harry was unpacking in his room he reflected on the meeting earlier in the day. Not much had been uncovered so far. Let's hope something more substantial emerges over the next few days, he thought.

When they met in the restaurant Harry decided to raise the issue of David's involvement, which without discussion or warning had irritated him.

'A point, David.'

'Yes.'

'I realise that your Control instructed you to accompany me on this trip, so my comments are not directed at you personally. It is just that I had no warning and frankly it's hacked me off. It gives the impression of 'tag along, report back.' Not something I'm too happy about, to put it mildly.'

'If I was in your shoes I'd probably feel the same, but let me add something which Control was very keen to stress.'

'OK.'

'Control spoke very highly of you. He likes and respects you. He also spoke of the times in Lebanon when you worked together, and when you really covered his back on more than one occasion, literally and physically.

He said he wanted your back covered, if needed, and that is why I was sent along.

Yes, I'm observing and listening, but there is no reporting back by me during this trip. Does that make the situation clearer?'

Harry was silent for a moment.

'Thanks David. Perfectly clear and understood. I appreciate your comments. What are you going to have to eat?'

They enjoyed their meal, and went to their own rooms reflecting on the fact that the trip would now be on a better footing, and, more importantly, understanding.

Sunday 29th January 2006 Abu Dhabi

Harry and David left the hotel by cab which had arrived to pick them up at 0830hrs.

David had told Harry it was 'one of theirs' and by a circuitous route finished up behind one of the old buildings in the commercial district.

The cab driver entered with his key and took them into a closed windowless room at the rear of the building. The A/c was gently whirring as they sat down and waited for the Station Head to join them.

After a few minutes a man entered, introducing himself as Dan Harpaz, Station Head. He had a pleasant manner, although his gimlet eyes indicated curiosity as to the present situation and cooperation.

After shaking hands, and acknowledging David quickly, he then turned his full attention onto Harry.

'I understand you have just come from Bahrain and discussed with our people some of the Intel that we have picked up over the last few weeks.

Let me be brief and to the point. What we have picked up here may be connected, it is very sketchy, we don't know what is actually being planned, but we have our suspicions. I have been instructed to share everything with you, and I understand you will share your findings with us. Let's hope we can make some sense out of this for our mutual benefit.'

Harry nodded in agreement.

'Absolutely.

I much appreciated the openness of our meeting in Bahrain and I am sure that we can work together on the same basis here. Bearing in mind your great coverage of the region, I would like, when we have shared and discussed the available Intel, to discuss what you think could be possibilities or probabilities arising from it.

As you are aware, our coverage and penetration on the ground is minor compared to your resource, and it was that that kicked off the discussions in London following Buncefield, which has led to these meetings.'

At this point another man joined the meeting carrying several files and a laptop, who was introduced to Harry and David.

What followed then was a detailed examination of intercepts, surveillance, most of which appeared to be from operatives based in Dubai.

It soon became clear that although the tracking of particular individuals had thrown up bizarre routings on airlines, there did appear to be some firmness in the Dubai observations, particularly the hiring of a particular dhow, which had not reappeared in Dubai Creek. Destination unknown.

Sifting through reports, explanation of Buncefield and political pressures, considering likely scenarios, listening to intercepts, took up most of the day without there being solid evidence as to what was really happening.

At about 1800hrs, Dan Harpaz, the Station Head, suggested they stop and convene again the next day at 0900hrs.

This met with consensus by all, and Harry and David were taken back to the Sheraton by the same cab driver who said he would pick them up at 0830hrs the next morning.

What they didn't see when being dropped off at the hotel was the parked car with one occupant taking a long range photo of them. As they entered the hotel the driver put down his camera, started the engine of his Ford and drove away down the Corniche. He stopped after about 300 metres, hitting an assigned number on his mobile, and started speaking very quickly, in French. After about three minutes the discussion was finished and he drove away.

Harry and David decided to have separate meals in their respective rooms as they had been together all day, and Harry felt like a run to clear his head, so afterwards he went for a jog down the Corniche.

As he passed the end of 'E' Rd he heard another runner coming up behind him, who slowed to match his pace as he drew up alongside.

'Great temperature for a run,' the stranger said with a slight French accent.

Harry nodded, not wishing to waste his breath.

The stranger then spoke causing Harry to a stop very quickly.

'Harry, you may need some extra assistance sometime, this is my number,' he said putting a piece of paper in Harry's hand.

'Don't look so surprised, you are not the only interested party with concerns in the region.'

With that the stranger jogged off in the direction of the Family Park.

As it was dark Harry could not fully make out what was written on the piece of paper so tucking it into his track suit he turned and jogged back to the Sheraton.

Once back in his room he opened the piece of paper.

A name and number. Alain Dubois. +33 432 22 33 44.

Probably DGSE, but why the offer of assistance? Sure they would have a presence in the region, but why the sudden contact?

He decided he would use his secure satellite telephone to call the Deputy for an update and a few questions.

After a few rings the Deputy answered, and once past the connection protocols they were able to speak freely. Harry however, was conscious of his position in a hotel room, and therefore referred to most matters in oblique terms.

'Not much to report, still early days, analysing market conditions and seeing if we have any real opportunities to hang our hat on. Hopefully much better idea in a few days, and will give you a full report when I'm back at base.

Main reason for call was I bumped across some French competition today who was, surprise, surprise, offering assistance if we found the going tough in the market place.

I was very surprised to hear from them and wondered whether you had any knowledge of this, or whether you had been discussing our activities at a trade show or somewhere?'

There was a slight pause before the Deputy answered.

'I had a contact from an old French friend of mine the other day suggesting they might assist, or joint venture in some way. I had not realised they were so enthusiastic to help, but bear in mind they have a significant presence in the market place, plus excellent relationships with our new current associates.

I suppose in some ways not surprising. However, they certainly don't need to know all our marketing plans, and I would suggest you keep them at arms length for the present. If competitive pressures become extremely severe then perhaps we should think again. Do you agree?'

'Absolutely. I was just surprised at their directness. Will act accordingly. Friendly but distant.'

They finished their conversation with the usual pleasantries and Harry sat down to think about this new dimension.

'Let's face it', he thought, 'If push comes to shove somewhere down the line then an additional reinforcement could be useful, in a non-attributable way!'

In London the Deputy was thinking about his conversation with Harry and the

position of the French now in the equation. Muddying the waters or could this be to the UK's advantage? He would call his friend Philippe, and suggest they meet for a chat.

It is a well known fact that so-called 'friendly' security services spend almost as much time watching their 'friends' as they do their 'enemies'.

Spheres of influence can produce some strange bedfellows and even stranger 'modus operandi' in times of need!

VIII

Monday 30th January 2006 0830hrs Sheraton Hotel Abu Dhabi UAE

Harry and David met after breakfast in the main lobby and quietly discussed the day ahead.

Harry had no intention of telling David anything about his contact whilst jogging the previous evening, and confined his responses to generalities.

They saw their cab pull in and climbed in for the short journey to their meeting.

Dan Harpaz opened the meeting with his colleague in attendance, carrying files and laptop.

'Harry, after we finished last night I was reviewing our discussions and some of our more recent Intel. In particular I was looking again at the reports from Dubai and the chartering of the dhow that has not been seen since.

We were trying to look for any sort of connection and we ran some dates and events through our system and came up with what, I think, you call a long shot.'

'What was it?' Harry enquired.

'On the 8th January there was a small explosion at the end of a jetty on Das Island. No significant damage done and a large tanker was moored on the other jetty, which would have made a better target. Remains of Iranian inflatables were found. However we couldn't really see the point, unless it was an indicator of something in the future.'

Harry nodded.

'We had the same piece of information back in London, but it seemed very insignificant, plus no claims of responsibility, unless, who ever they are, want Iran implicated.'

'However', Dan said, 'Let's assume that there is a positive connection between the chartered dhow and this event. Trying out their kit, explosives, team, etc? Plus, if there is going to be an attack in the North Dome/South Pars gas fields, then a dhow slipping in is going to be the best option. How many hundreds of dhows can we check in the Gulf?'

'True, but are they going to be able to get sufficiently close to plant their explosives without security picking them up?'

'You would be surprised how lax security is on the platforms. Certainly not too difficult, and with small inflatables on a dark night almost easy.'

'Forget the Iranian side, but aren't the Qataris concerned that something like this might happen?'

'Harry, you and I know that the Qataris have played a very clever game. They have acted as honest broker to the Saudis on a number of issues, been a conduit for continuing discussions and negotiations with the Iranians. Additionally kept right on side with the United States; remember US bases in Qatar during the Gulf War, and still there. Their positioning has been excellent and with huge revenues now starting to accrue from their gas field they are going to be major player, not only in the Gulf but in many parts of the investment world.

My own view is that you will probably have to raise the security issue with QGPC (Qatar General Petroleum Company) and/or Qatar Petroleum.

As you are going on to Qatar, can't your people organise a meeting with them on general security matters and you take it from there?'

'Dan, we have got very limited connections at present. Let's go with this. How can we try and narrow down our search for the dhow?'

Dan and his colleague looked at each other.

'One of operatives followed the Palestinian for a number of days through Iran, finishing up on the coast South East of Shiraz, when the Palestinian boarded the dhow. Our man couldn't follow so he returned to base in Bahrain.'

'Why didn't Bahrain mention this when I was there?' Harry exclaimed.

'Because the operative is back in Israel on compassionate leave', Dan explained.

'So if the plan is to bomb a platform, and make sure the blame is applied to Iran, then setting off from South East Iran is quite convincing and appropriate for any future story or publicity?'

'Yes. The accusation can be laid at Iran's door. Commentary from world opinion would seize on the connection and merely confirm most Western thinking of the instability of President Mahmoud Ahmadinejad.'

'Dan, many thanks for your help. As you said, Qatar next stop. We will have to run with what we've got. Flimsy but what else is there? I will contact our people and try and get a meeting with QGPC and see what security issues they think they have!

If you can trawl your Intel to see if there are any other small scraps that would be relevant I would be really grateful, no matter how small. Also, last observed position details of the dhow, numbers of personnel, size of dhow, anything that can help us in recognition. When we find it!'

Dan agreed, wishing Harry and David well. He promised them that he would ensure the trawl was completed, and suggested meeting at 1600hrs to review any items that had arisen.

1200hrs London SIS(MI6) Deputy's Office

The Deputy put through a call on a secure line to his old friend, Philippe Roberge, his DGSE contact at the French Embassy.

Philippe answered his phone with the usual pleasantries and said,

'To what do I owe this pleasure, mon ami?'

'You will recall our conversation the other day when you called me?'

'Indeed I do. How may I help you?'

'Have you briefed any of your staff in the region on what we were discussing, because contact was made with one of my staff in the UAE the other evening?'

Philippe did not immediately reply, but then said,

'I decided that as you and I have a significant interest with what is, or may develop, it seemed prudent to at least indicate to your man that he has some additional resource as backup if he needs it.

I can assure you that there will be no interference by us in your activities and I have given clear instructions to this effect.

I would not want any uncalled for actions by us to jeopardise your position and our own personal relationship.'

The Deputy had listened patiently and then said,

'Philippe, in some ways your command of English is better than mine, but let me spell out a few things.

One. Next time advise me of your actions before you implement them.

Two. Yes, we do have a joint interest in a challenge that we are currently facing.

Three. Interfere in our present activities and I will leak some of your less than successful ops to our newspapers, plus call off cooperation in all directions for a period of time, unspecified.

Four. I am sure you meant the best, but the status at present is critical, highly sensitive, and as clear as mud!

Do we understand each other?

A mildly crestfallen Philippe answered,

'Absolutely, my apologies. I did not intend to harm our excellent working relations and I will reinforce my instructions to my people on the ground. You have my assurance of that.

However, remember our offer still stands if it is required.'

Thank you Philippe, à bientôt.

The Deputy sat back in his chair and thought,

'I hope to God he keeps his word!'

1230hrs Abu Dhabi

Harry and David returned to the hotel with the same cab driver, who startled them, by saying he had seen somebody in a parked car, taking a photograph of them the previous evening.

'Why didn't you mention it this morning? demanded Harry.

'Because in our game here, everybody is photographing everybody,' he replied cynically.

'It could be the Iranians, Russians, the French, the Syrians, who knows, and who cares. We just get on with our job.'

Harry fell quiet, seeing no point in getting into an argument. He realised that that piece of information probably gave him the answer as to why he was approached during his jog the previous evening.

Harry and David ate lunch together mulling over what had been discussed that morning.

David commented on the upcoming trip to Qatar saying he would organise their meeting with the Station head before Harry followed up on the QGPC connection.

They organised their flights to Doha, Qatar for the following morning. David catching a flight at 0600hrs so he could brief the Station Head, and Harry getting in at about 1030hrs, going direct to the British Embassy to see if they could arrange a convenient meeting with QGPC.

Meeting Dan at 1600hrs they jointly read the fully detailed report produced by the operative when he had followed the Palestinian down the western coast of Iran until he had boarded the dhow.

They noted his estimates of crew and other personnel, plus numbers of large boxes and packages put on board.

Minor items had been thrown up by the Intel trawl, but did not add a great deal to the existing picture.

Harry and David returned to the hotel, packed and left each other to their thoughts for the following day's short journey to Qatar.

Tuesday 31st January 2006 Doha Qatar

Both flights were on time, David being picked up and taken to the meeting house on C Ring Road; Harry, arriving two hours later, going straight to the British Embassy in Rumeila.

David briefed the Station Head on the various meetings he had attended with Harry and indicated the line of thinking that was being pursued. Whilst recognising that Intel at present was not conclusive, the current path, at least, appeared worth following. Harry, having arrived at Embassy, met with the resident Intelligence officer and discussed with him where they found themselves currently, after deciding on this particular line of investigation.

He left out the French connection and went straight to the point of security on the gas platforms in the North Dome Field.

He asked for an appointment to be made with QGPC, at an appropriately high enough level, in order to discuss this question. He thought the tack of the UK North Sea platforms security review would provide a suitable reason for raising the issue.

Harry and David had agreed to meet at the Ramada Hotel at about midday where they had made reservations. It was also convenient for the meeting house on C Ring Road and not far from the Embassy.

David had set up a meeting for 1500hrs and they discussed his briefing of the Station head over lunch.

'Harry, the Station Head is Rami Peres, he has had a long career, pretty much all of it in the Gulf, one way or the other.

I have briefed him on your previous meetings in Bahrain and Abu Dhabi and at this stage he is not sure what additional Intel he may be able to provide.

I'm absolutely certain he's not playing his cards close to his chest in that respect, but he may have some useful background on the Qatari's position that may be able to assist you.'

'Right. My meeting at the embassy this morning was to get a time soonest for discussions with QGPC on platform security.

The Commercial Attaché is handling that and with luck I'll have that tomorrow.

If that is the case then I'll catch the British Airways flight back to London that leaves at 0200hrs Thursday morning.

As you're going back via Bahrain you can leave Wednesday evening.

David agreed and they planned to meet at 1445hrs as a car would pick them up to go to the meeting on C Ring Road.

At 1500hrs the Chevrolet swung off the Ring Road through some high automatic gates and stopped in front of the villa.

They were met and ushered into a rear room where the blinds were firmly in place, allowing no sunlight to penetrate. The A/C whirred in the background as the Station Head, Rami Peres entered, accompanied by a colleague.

He shook Harry's hand, looking at him with a slight quizzical smile.

'Well Harry, I understand from London that someone there thinks highly of you, and insists we give you maximum cooperation.

David has briefed me on your trip so far, the reasons behind it, the situation in the UK that kicked it off, and any links that might indicate group connections, reasons, future plans or exercises.

I'm happy with that, where do you want to start?'

Harry then gave an outline, in some detail, as to what happened at Buncefield and their suspicions.

With no group claiming responsibility it had become more difficult in trying to determine what was the purpose, future intent or otherwise.

This in turn had lead to the discussions in London and the meetings now held in the Gulf.

The hope was that perhaps in the myriad of detail contained in shared Intel there would arise one or two connectors that would help in the search.

Such cooperation would, it was hoped, would benefit both parties in the fight against any similar operations targeted against them.

The meeting continued for over two hours but analysis of available Intel provided no additional information.

In terms of Qatar's position in the Gulf, Rami then gave a short, but accurate, geopolitical summary of where he thought Qatar stood in the fluid mix of disparate countries and regimes in the Gulf.

In summary, a small country, punching well above its weight, supported by huge oil and predominantly gas revenues, acting as a link, buffer, sounding board and communication channel for many neighbouring countries and the West. Qatar was implementing gradual but progressive democratic moves, and establishing its presence as a significant international investment vehicle.

Harry thanked Rami for his time and assistance, but left feeling disappointed that further information had not been found or was available.

Returning to the hotel Harry and David agreed a Sitrep, so far, that each would present their superiors on return to London. This was interrupted by a telephone call to Harry advising that a meeting had been set up with QGPC for the following morning at 1100hrs.

1700hrs Lavan Island 7 miles off the SW coast of Iran

The dhow was sheltering in the NE side of the island having slowly made its way down the Iranian coast over the last few days.

The crew and divers were getting bored with the routine, pretending to fish and also carrying out practice dives to keep their training levels up.

Fayez called the divers together at the rear of the dhow after evening prayers and before they ate.

'My brothers, the time draws near to put all your practice into effect. I will tell you tomorrow when we strike against the Kuffar, but it is very soon.

Ask Allah for his help in this fight. Be strong, eat and sleep well. Allulah Akbar!'

The divers murmured their agreement and went about their evening meal, talking quietly but more excitedly amongst themselves.

Wednesday 1st February 2006 1100hrs QGPC Doha Qatar

Harry and David had agreed that Harry would attend the meeting at QGPC with the UK Commercial Attaché; David's presence would only add to confusion and create further problems as to identity and function.

After the opening pleasantries by them both, the Commercial Attaché then detailed the reason for the meeting, concentrating on overall security on the platforms, the gathering of intelligence by other resources, the sharing of that Intel, and the implementation of any security measures.

The man responsible for Security within QGPC listened to Harry as he explained, in general terms, some of the factors considered by UK security on North Sea platforms.

Dry run exercises, ranging from environmental activists to terrorist activity, were carried out on a regular basis, not only to test existing protocols, but also to determine response, in what might be considered a doomsday scenario. Ever since the Piper Alpha disaster, in July 1988, emergency and safety measures had been hugely strengthened, both in terms of rig safety, and also in response procedures.

Harry finished by asking a general question concerning North Dome security protocols and whether there were any systems or intelligence gathering in order to be one step ahead of any likely actions.

The response was guarded, political in tone, and indicated that the person was not particularly happy to be challenged in this area. He indicated that safety was of paramount concern, rules were rigidly enforced, and all security aspects were, and had been considered.

He thanked Harry for his comments and concerns but felt that overall risk was carefully monitored and controlled.

Harry then posed an awkward question.

'Do you think there is any risk by rogue Iranian elements against the North Dome Field?

The official replied in a testy fashion, indicating that he thought it totally unlikely, as this would also jeopardise the Iranian South Pars Field, thereby damaging their own interests.

Harry realised that there was little to gain by pursuing this line and merely nodded in agreement.

After a few more general comments and observations the meeting finished formally and Harry was dropped off at the hotel, the Commercial Attaché returning to the Embassy.

As Harry collected his room key, and made his way towards the lifts, a Qatari stopped him and introduced himself.

'We have not met before. My name is Ahmed Al-Marri, or that is how you will know me,' he smiled.

'Can we speak for a few minutes?'

Harry agreed and they went to a quiet corner in one of the lounges.

Ahmed started the conversation by saying,

'It doesn't really matter how I know, but I am fully aware of your discussions and their content today with Security at QGPC. This is something that is of great interest to me and my colleagues, and any way in which we can forestall any accidents, or other events on our platforms is of interest to us.'

Harry replied,

'Your English is excellent. How did you get to that level?'

Ahmed smiled,

'Two years in our London Embassy, possibly doing a similar job to yourself.'

Harry ignored the comment,

'In what way do you think we could co-operate together in this particular area?'

Ahmed replied,

'I shall be back in London within the next ten days. Could we meet then and discuss where we could be of assistance to each other? If you agree call me on my mobile, this is the number,' he said, handing over a piece of folded paper.

Harry took the piece of paper, and said,

'I'll call you in a week's time. I will have to clear this with my boss, but I think he will agree. We'll just have to see. I'll let you know, one way or the other.'

Ahmed rose, shook him by the hand, and said,

'I look forward to your call, have a good flight.'

He left Harry thinking about what was the real connection and reason for Ahmed's contact. He would have to do some digging.

He put a call through to the UK Embassy and spoke to the Commercial Attaché, asking him to run a check on Ahmed Al-Masri, whether or not that was his real name.

After agreeing to contact him at 1600hrs, Harry then met up with David for lunch to update him on the meeting at QGPC.

He did not, however, mention to David the approach from Ahmed.

He briefly outlined the scenario he had painted at QGPC and the less than enthusiastic response he had received from them. David said he was not surprised. He was of the view, that at this stage of their frenetic industrial development, Qatar was pushing such considerations to one side. Iran was benefitting substantially from the joint field. Why would they jeopardise such a position?

Harry agreed that that argument had some justification, but with the knowledge that they both shared such confidence was substantially misplaced.

After lunch Harry updated his reports that he would present to the Deputy on his return and checked in for his flight leaving Doha at about 0200hrs Thursday morning. David was taking an alternative route back to London via Bahrain on account of some unfinished business, and would be leaving at about 2000hrs that evening.

After writing up his reports Harry sat in his room feeling totally deflated and wondering how the investigation would move on from what appeared to be a stalemate.

There were no connecting lines to a number of disparate dots and the intervention of both French and Qatari contacts just further muddied the waters.

What did either of them think they would gain out of a very opaque scenario?

Harry was also tired of the various agencies apparently stonewalling in many areas.

He wondered what the Deputy's thoughts would be, particularly the French and Qatari contacts and whether he thought they should be followed up. From his point of view Harry thought that if they were approaching him, no doubt with their bosses' blessing, then there must be some mileage in following through, if only to see what could be revealed.

At about 1600hrs the phone rang and he held a brief conversation with the Commercial Attaché who confirmed that Ahmed Al-Marri was a middle ranking Qatar Government official ostensibly working in the Defence Ministry.

Harry thanked him for the information and his assistance during his visit.

He said farewell to David, thanking him for his co-operation, and said he would be in contact, either through Tom or directly himself, in the near future.

After eating a leisurely evening meal Harry left for the airport around 2130hrs, caught his flight to London, and slept fitfully until requested to fasten his seat belt due to the imminent landing at Heathrow at 0700hrs, Thursday 2nd February 2006.

2100hrs Lavan Island off the SW coast of Iran

The crew and divers had prayed and eaten and the divers were quietly talking amongst themselves.

Fayez could hear the odd comment and speculation as to when the operation would start and what it entailed. Some of the speculation was fairly accurate, a point he noted for consideration and action later.

He called them to him at the stern of the dhow and explained what was to happen, why, and when.

'My brothers, we can now strike a significant blow against the Western pigs that exploit our God given assets.

Our action will be broadcast around the world and the Kuffar will tremble at the strength that Allah has given us.

They will not know who has struck but they will know that, Insha'allah, we will not let our world and our culture, be poisoned by them. World Islam, God is great!

We will strike at one hour past midnight on Friday morning, our Holy Day.'

There was a general murmur of agreement from the divers and Fayez then continued to detail the operation, the teams and phasing.

Thursday 2nd February 2006 0830hrs London Heathrow Airport

Harry caught the Heathrow Express into London and went straight to his office where he showered and changed.

At about 1000hrs Tom Denman stuck his head round the door,

'Morning Harry, good trip?'

'Not really Tom. Am catching up on my report for the Deputy. Hope to see him later for an update and next steps. One or two odd things need to be examined and decisions taken on how we deal with them. Will give you a briefing after I've seen the Deputy.'

'OK. Do you want a strong coffee to help after the night flight?'

'Thanks. I think that might help, particularly when I'm explaining various things to the Deputy!'

Harry resumed his report writing, pausing only to confirm a meeting with the Deputy's PA for 1200hrs.

1100hrs 40miles WSW of Lavan Arabian Gulf

The dhow slipped gently through the water, creaking slightly as the wind tugged at the sail and rigging. A gentle, slightly frothy wake indicated that the engine was adding to its progress.

Fayez looked up at the cloudy sky, and thought that if this weather was maintained, then they would have ideal conditions just after midnight.

The crew and divers were going about their respective tasks, the divers checking their equipment, and the crew the position of the lanteen sail and rigging.

Fayez had calculated they needed to run for about 87 - 90 miles in order to bring them within three miles of the platforms, where they would then launch the inflatables. They had no more than 50 miles to go so would be in the area by 1800hrs at the latest, their average speed being about 7 knots. It would almost be dark by then, which coupled with the cloudy conditions and possible sea mist, would assist them in the operation.

Harry knocked and entered.

'Hullo Harry. Sit down. I hope you've got something for me because the station reports were very sketchy.'

Harry gathered himself.

'The sitrep is pretty disappointing with perhaps two exceptions. Let me start at the beginning.

We received good cooperation all the way through, but whatever Intel, we or they had, did not make any clear connections with our respective dots.

I didn't feel that they were holding anything back, and one positive target had been followed around the Gulf and had finished up in Iran. He was followed, but then boarded a dhow in Bandar-Kangan.

What was strange was the route this target took. He was all over the region. No real sense of purpose. I can only assume it was to try and throw off any surveillance and pursuit.

However we have certainly established some good working relationships and protocols for the future.

I have finished my interim report but would like to expand on that after you have heard about the two exceptions.'

'Fine, Harry. What are these exceptions?'

'One French and one Qatari. I was approached by the Frenchman in Abu Dhabi when taking an evening jog. It was completely out of the blue and frankly I wondered what the hell are they up to!

I know they have significant interests in the region but to make an approach like that just seemed so bloody infantile and for what purpose!'

The Deputy interjected at this point, and said,

'Harry, following that event I followed up with my opposite number at their embassy.

The response was that they were keeping an eye on your back and just wanted to let you know they were there if any back-up assistance was required.

I agree the approach could have been done differently, but you know how the French love a bit of drama!'

Harry didn't comment but then continued,

'The Qatari approach was a little strange, but he has proposed we meet in London in the next 10 days. He has had a couple of tours in their embassy in London, so we should have some background on him. Our Commercial Attaché did an initial check on him. He works in their Defence Department.

With respect to nailing something down in a positive way I'm frankly not too optimistic with the Intel we have, but something could come out of the Qatari connection.

Will you follow up on the French side to see if they've picked up something we've missed? It will benefit them if we can share Intel, particularly bearing in mind their relationship with Mossad, and our recent meetings both in the Gulf and London.'

The Deputy nodded, and said,

'Harry, do not forget I've got the Minister on my back, and we really need to come up with something positive that, frankly, I can shut him up with!'

He laughed, grimly,

'Maybe the background information on him will have to be brought forward, but I don't want to use that yet, if I can avoid it! What are your thoughts, plans, next steps?'

'Have a hard think, get a decent night's sleep, and come back to you sometime tomorrow or Monday. I need to do a complete review of what we've got, and where we are. Then I need to determine whether there are some other areas we should investigate.

Incidentally, has there been any contact from the Security Service (MI5)?'

'No. Why do you ask?'

'I was just thinking, that bearing in mind this situation is both on-shore and off-shore, whether we should see if they have any leads that could assist us, in any way.'

Harry immediately recognised the frosty look that crossed the Deputy's face.

'Harry, if I thought there could be some sensible co-operation then I would agree with you. With the lack of mature discussion in recent times then I don't see what can be gained. Most of that lot are playing politics, not defence of the realm! Defence of their backsides is their first priority. In addition, they are getting bogged down with all the PC edicts emanating from Whitehall. They've hardly got any room to manoeuvre at all!

No! Leave well alone for the time being. If something concrete appears and we have no choice, then that's a different matter. I don't want to be carrying the single can for a joint effort, which is what would happen!'

'Understood', Harry replied.

'I'll crack on if you don't mind and come back to you on Monday.'

'Fine, Harry, get some sleep in the meantime, review, and we will meet Monday, say 1000hrs, OK?

Harry agreed and returned to his office where he briefed Tom on his meeting and agreed they would meet Friday morning at 1000hrs to fully debrief and review.

Harry left early to return to his flat where he unpacked, slung his laundry into the washing machine, grabbed a light meal and was in bed by 2100hrs, where he slept fitfully, dreaming about a number of unresolved and confusing scenarios until 0700hrs on the Friday morning.

1730hrs Anna's Apartment Southwark

Her mobile telephone buzzed once, indicating a text. Reading it Anna immediately unlocked the cupboard, picked up the satellite handset, and answered the security question posed.

Mossad Control was brief and to the point.

'I said I would comment further on your new social acquaintance.'

Anna remained silent.

'He works for SIS(MI6) and is not a middle ranking MoD procurement manager. He could be a useful asset to us if turned, but that is not an order or priority. See how the relationship develops and report to me on a regular basis.'

Anna responded quietly, her mind racing.

'Thank you for that. I will keep you informed.'
The conversation finished she wondered if meeting Harry had been planned, or accidental. It had to be accidental looking at all the angles. However, she would have to be somewhat circumspect from now on. A pity, but necessary.

1830hrs 88miles WSW Lavan Arabian Gulf

The dhow had hove to, and was gently rocking as its sea anchor allowed a leisurely drift of about 1 knot per hour.
The prevailing wind in the Gulf is from the North West, and can be quite strong in February, however on this particular night it was just a gentle breeze.
Fayez gathered his divers together in the stern and held evening prayers before his briefing. His thought was bring them together through prayer, and extend that feeling into the Jihad they were about to undertake.
He spoke plainly and simply, focussing their minds on the task ahead, a mixture of sacrifice and reward as they struck a blow for Islam against the Western lackeys.
They ate lightly and talked quietly amongst themselves, aware now of the risks facing them, and the need for the rigorous training insisted on by Fayez.
The night was dark with little fluorescence on the water, and the gas platform lights and flared gases could be seen about two miles away.
At 2200hrs they started to prepare the inflatables with the electric outboards, making sure their oxygen cylinders were full and laying out their wet suits, masks and fins.
At about 2230hrs the various packages of explosives, fuses and timers, were brought up from below deck, Fayez assisting the divers, ensuring that the correct number were allocated to each inflatable.
At 2300hrs the divers suited up, checking each others equipment, then lowering the inflatables carefully over the leeside.

Fayez gave a short farewell address finishing with 'Allahu Akbar;' then kissing and shaking hands with each man in the Arabic fashion.

The divers climbed down into the inflatables, cast off and disappeared silently in the direction of the gas platforms in the South Pars Field.

Fayez had given the lead diver a short wave radio telephone to advise him, firstly, when they had arrived at the platforms, and secondly, when the charges had been placed.

At about 0020hrs, Friday, Fayez received the first message, Sahar (Dawn), that they had arrived by the platform and that each crew was close to the leg assigned to them.

He knew that the difficult task of placing the explosives would take some time so he sat at the stern of the dhow with his radio telephone and large holdall.

In the inflatables, the divers organised the various bomb packages, some for the main legs, and some for the linking web.

Silently they slipped over the sides of the inflatables, diving down to the agreed depths where water pressure would assist the focused explosions. Overall it was expected that the placement and setting up of the timers would take at least an hour.

When completed the lead diver would advise by radio and then return to the dhow. This would probably be between 0145hrs and 0215hrs with the timers set to 0415hrs. This would give the dhow enough time to be at least 15 to 20 miles away before detonation. That is what the divers had been told.

Fayez sat in the stern of the dhow thinking of his next presentation in Damascus.

This would be the big one.

This would establish him, once and for all, at the echelon of strikes against the putrid West.

He opened the large holdall and took out a 35 metre length of cable which he attached to the control box. At the other end of the cable was a small, black, egg-shaped antenna. Fayez gently let the cable down over the side of the dhow until the antenna was about 10 metres below the surface.

He sat, waiting patiently for the radio telephone to respond.

At about 0130hrs the radio telephone pinged, and Fayez picked up the handset. He heard the single word 'Qur'an' clearly repeated twice.

Turning to the control box sitting on the deck he turned up the controls to maximum and pushed the large red button.

The switch sent the sonar signal from the underwater antenna to the four timers on the explosives, strapped the legs and cross webs of the rig, about 2 miles away, taking about 3 seconds.

The explosion, which was seen before it was heard, lit up the dark night sky, followed by a thunderous roar as gas tanks and pipes exploded.

The divers, in their small inflatables, stood no chance.

The explosions created flaming whirlpools and vortexes which blew the craft and their occupants into the air, before they fell back into the maelstrom to be either drowned or suffocated due to lack of oxygen.

The gas platform was shrouded in flames and smoke.

Fayez stood in the stern watching the increasingly grim scene unfold in front of him.

During the long trip over to Iran he had installed override sonar switches inside the timers, so no matter what time was set his sonar switch would decide detonation.

He turned and shouted at the dhow skipper,

'There has been a huge accident. The explosives have gone off too soon. Pull up the anchor. We must be away.'

'What about the divers?'

'If not burnt to death, they will have drowned.'

'Should we not look for them?'

Fayez advanced down the boat, pulling out his 9mm automatic as he went.

He pointed it in the skipper's face, saying,

'If you do not want to be food for the fish, then pull up the anchor and let us away to Lavan.'

The skipper turned reluctantly and ordered the crew to make sail and engine immediately and steer a course ENE for Lavan.

Fayez sat in the stern, his automatic in view, providing sufficient intimidation for the skipper and near crew.

On the platform consternation and panic ensued, security and fire crews moving into action for the first time, attempting to initiate rescue procedures for the engineering staff to leave the rig.

A number of the rig staff were able to launch the rescue craft on the windward side as the prevailing wind drove the flames in a SE direction.

As two of the boats pulled away some of the engineers could see the tattered remains of an inflatable floating on the surface with clear markings of the Iranian Navy visible.

Some miles away the dhow moved at about 7 knots towards Lavan, the skipper and crew silent, wondering what their fate might be, following the probable deaths of the divers.

By noon the dhow was in the lee of Lavan Island, on its NE coast, a short distance to the mainland and the coast road.

When moored, Fayez spoke to the skipper and crew, explaining that with an operation like this, it is impossible to try and rescue people if it goes wrong. It had been tragic to lose the divers like this, but in a war, and this was a holy war, sacrifices inevitably had to be made.

He spoke with authority and menace, warning them all to forget what they had seen, to repeat none of this to their family or friends.

As the dhow approached the coast Fayez had telephoned his contact to arrange that he would be collected by car at the port of Bandar-e-Mogham that afternoon, and taken to the airport at Bandar Lengeh, from where, on the Saturday morning, he would take a flight via Shiraz to Tehran, and then to Damascus.

He paid off the skipper and crew and left the dhow at about 1500hrs, meeting his contact on the dock who would drive him the 90 odd miles to Bandar Lengeh.

Fayez was confident in his mind that with the publicity from this operation, then funding in Damascus would be readily agreed for his major Jihad against the West. He had already established some lines of communication which could be quickly activated if approval was given.

He smiled inwardly. This would enhance his position and perhaps a place on the Committee if he was successful.

Friday 3rd February 2006 0700hrs Doha Qatar

The news services had already picked up notification of the rig disaster and pieces was being quickly prepared for the local TV stations in Qatar, Bahrain, Abu Dhabi and Dubai.

It was the first disastrous 'accident' to have occurred in the gas drilling and collection North Dome project and speculation was running at 'red alert' as to cause.

The early broadcasts were specific in describing the 'accident', whilst at the same time allowing a very wide scope of analysis as to cause.

Commentary was, as usual, 'well balanced', as only the media can produce. Sonorous tones covered the tragedy, whilst unsubstantiated observations from industry 'experts' ranged from the probable/possible to the absurd.

Surprisingly, sabotage came someway down the list of causes, and was dealt with in a very cursory manner.

Because Qatar is three hours ahead of the UK, it was only picked up as a minor item by the overnight news teams in London, leaving more thorough coverage and analysis to the morning teams on BBC, ITV, and Sky.

QGPC had quickly responded to the incident by referring to a disastrous failure of specialist valves, thereby putting in train a sequence of events that had caused the explosion.

They had further added that they would be pursuing the manufacturer of the valves for complete compensation if it was shown to be a product rather than a process/operative malfunction.

UK Embassy staff in Qatar, and adjacent countries, had, as a matter of course, immediately notified the Foreign Office of the incident.

This resulted in Harry being called to see the Deputy as soon as he arrived in his office, C10.

0830hrs Deputy's office SIS London

As Harry entered the Deputy looked up from the report he was reading,

'You're no sooner back, than the balloon goes up!'

'Sorry, what do you mean?'

'Qatar, North Dome Gas Field. Big incident on a rig. Explosion, some dead, many injured. Rig shut down, probably a write off.'

'When did this happen?'

'This morning. About 0100hrs, local time. Information is very sketchy. Lots of conjecture. Accident, deliberate, equipment failure? The usual response by the media.'

'Our response at this time is what? Or what should it be?'

Harry, I think, dependent on some solid facts coming in the next 48hours that you need to be back on the ground in Qatar. This time you've got a damn good excuse for being there, bearing in mind the issues you raised with QGPC a few days ago.'

'Fine. But I need to discuss, in some detail with you, the question of the relationship and possible working with our French friends at DGSE, and how we are going to handle the new approach from the Qatari Defence contact.

I don't want to look like some third form amateur in terms of discretionary limits, levels of Intel sharing; all the usual operating parameters in fact.'

'Understood. Meet at 0900hrs Monday to cover all those points plus update on North Dome.

Incidentally, what plans do you have for seeing our Mossad friend?'

'I haven't contacted her since my return, but was going to telephone today to see if we might meet up tomorrow.'

'How are you explaining your recent absence?'

'Some boring M.o.D. contractual matters that had to be resolved on the ground. Nothing exciting.'

'Ok. But don't relax. She's smart. Remember she's been living a lie for a good number of years now.'

The meeting over Harry returned to his office, C10, to gather his thoughts and jot a few outline points on paper.

He was not worried, but certainly concerned, bearing in mind the increased complexity of the current scenario with the unknown inputs of additional players.

He rang Anna's mobile which after a short pause switched to her message service. He told her he was back and hoped they might be able to meet on the Saturday. He left his number and hung up.

He brought Tom and Jane up to date as far as he was able, and then held a separate discussion with Tom concerning the potential complication of DGSE and the Qatar operative, which would be discussed with the Deputy on Monday.

Some food for thought, but mostly speculative at this time. Events would drive knowledge at this stage, not the other way around.

Across London Anna had picked up Harry's message and was looking for an opportunity of returning his call.

The Minister was in and out of his office all morning at a series of short meetings, none of which appeared to improve his attitude, or temper. He was going up to his constituency this weekend which was also not contributing to his general mood.

Over the past few weeks there had been a general cooling between them, driven partly by his abrasive manner, and also a realisation by Anna that, although dedicated to her own particular operation, there were some sacrifices required that were above and beyond the call of duty. There had to be a balance and a life at the same time, which did not currently exist.

She called Harry at about 1pm, agreeing to meet at 7pm on the Saturday for dinner.

After completing the call Anna realised that she was genuinely looking forward to seeing Harry again, although now knowing what she did concerning his real activities, she would need to be careful.

1800hrs Bandar Lengeh. Iran

Fayez had been dropped at a small hotel in the town close to the airport, from where he would fly on the Saturday morning via Shiraz to Tehran, and then to Damascus.

After the call to evening prayers he sat in his room thinking of his presentation to the Committee and the way in which he would take credit for the recent operation and therefore the justification (and funding) for his proposed Jihad operation.

Fayez realised that he would have to take a very careful and methodical approach to his presentation so that the logic could be clearly seen by all. Emphasising the immense benefit of the world wide publicity to their cause would bring many new soldiers to join the Jihad.

One point that he must stress is that there had been no claims of responsibility for Buncefield, Das Island, or Qatar, and he wanted matters to remain so.

It made targeting of dissident or terrorist groups more difficult, and also added an element of mystery to the operations. 'Jihad' was enough.

Saturday 4th February 2006 0600hrs Bandar Lengeh. Iran

Fayez slept uneasily, thinking of the various scenarios available to him, which would require be consolidated and quantified before meeting the Committee on Sunday.

He rose early on the Saturday, arriving at the airport in good time for his flight.

Flights were uneventful, except for a two hour delay in Tehran, which meant his arrival in Damascus was pushed back to 2000hrs. However he used the time wisely, thinking through the various options available to him and laying out the broad outline of his proposal.

Arriving at his hotel at about 2200hrs, he telephoned his contact asking, that due to delays, if the meeting could be scheduled for 1800hrs the following day, Sunday. This was agreed, as certain members were also flying in from outside Damascus, and Syria.

1900hrs Anna's Apartment, Southwark

Harry was nothing if not punctual and rang the entry bell promptly at 7pm.

It was answered, after a slight pause, in a slightly mocking voice,

'My, you're punctual! I'm only just ready!'

'My apologies, old Army habits die hard!'

The door buzzed and he pushed it open, walking across the hall to take the lift to the first floor.

Exiting the lift, he saw her standing, smiling, by her apartment door.

'Come in. How are you and what would you like to drink?'

'I'm fine, and a glass of wine would be fine, as well.'

Anna poured two glasses of a dry white wine, and walked over to the sofa and chairs.

She waved him to a chair.

'Well, what have you been up to these last few weeks?'

'Oh, nothing exciting. Just fairly boring contractual stuff with some of our bases. Dotting Is and crossing Ts mostly! What have you been up to with the Minister?'

'Much the same, really. Fairly boring stuff, meetings, minutes, diary, you know the usual civil service justification for their self-important existence!'

'That sounds a bit cynical! On second thoughts you sound a bit like me on a good day!'

They both laughed softly, trying to get over a sense of nervousness that was holding them both.

Harry spoke first.

'I hope you don't mind but I've booked a table at La Barca again. We were a bit rushed last time after the theatre, so I thought a leisurely dinner might be a good idea. As you know their food is great so we can really pick and choose!'

'Great. What time have you booked for?'

'8 o'clock, but we can go earlier. I doubt it will be a problem.'

Anna glanced at her wrist watch.

'Why don't we have a second glass and I'll call a cab for 7.45 so you don't have to drive?

'Fine by me.'

They passed the time in general conversation gradually relaxing in each others company until Harry looked at his watch and suggested they had better get the cab to the restaurant, otherwise, as it was Saturday, they might lose the table!

As they sat in the cab Harry was conscious of Anna looking at him from time to time, and holding his hand quite firmly when alighting.

Their table was to the back and side of the restaurant, giving them a good view, but also providing a degree of privacy.

They ordered their meal and carried on their conversations, enjoying the moment aided by good food and wine.

Perhaps it was the occasion, being able to relax naturally, perhaps the wine, but at one point Anna suddenly shook her head, and as Harry looked at her he noticed her eyes were glistening.

'What's the matter?'

'Sorry Harry, just a number of things have built up over a period of time and I need to resolve them.'

'Is there anything I can do to help? If you want to tell me I'm happy to listen, and if I can be of any assistance, just shout.'

'No Harry, I don't think you can at this time, but thanks for the offer. I might take you up on it though, sometime.'

She smiled weakly at him and straightened up in her chair.

'How wimpish can I get? Sorry about that. Don't want to spoil the evening because I'm really enjoying it. A proper relaxing evening and I go all girlie!! Could I have some more of that delicious wine?'

She raised her glass as Harry poured some more wine and clinked glasses with him.

'Here's to us and thanks for a lovely evening.'

'It's not over yet', Harry jokingly protested.

The mood was quickly back on track, and time flew by as they ate, drank and enjoyed each other.

Just after 11pm Harry suggested getting a cab so they left La Barca, and went back to Anna's apartment.

In the cab Anna was quite quiet, but sat closer to Harry, her arm through his.

Back at her apartment Anna poured a couple of brandies and they sat talking quietly and listening to the background music.

Neither of them raised the issue referred to in the restaurant, Harry wondering how much of it was connected to the Minister or another scenario.

At half past midnight Harry reluctantly indicated that he ought to go home, advising he would take a cab, and collect his car, which was parked outside, sometime later on Sunday.

Anna walked with him to the door where Harry turned to kiss Anna on her cheek.

Whether it was lack of practice, poor footwork or what, Harry found his lips on hers in a delicate kiss which rapidly increased in intensity with Anna holding him in a tight embrace.

He pulled away and started to apologise, but Anna with her head on his chest still held him.

'I'm sorry'.

'Don't be Harry'.

She turned, still holding his hand and walked down the hall in the direction of her bedroom.

Later, outside in the road, about 50 yards away, the motorcyclist saw the lights going out in the apartment, noted the time in his log, started his machine, and rode quietly away.

Sunday 5th February 2006

0800hrs Dar Al-Yamin Hotel Damascus Syria

Fayez started work on the final version of his proposal that would be discussed at the meeting that evening at 1800hrs.

The meeting was to be held in a Committee member's house on the outskirts of Damascus in Jaramana, a suburb on the way to Damascus International Airport.

This would be convenient for Fayez who planned to catch a flight shortly after midnight to Bucharest in Romania if his proposal was accepted.

He ran through his proposal* many times, the success of recent operations, quantifying risk, cost, resources, challenges to the concept, benefits outweighing downside, publicity for the cause, a supreme Jihad. He felt confident the Committee would agree but realised there were always one or two who lacked boldness.

On a 'need to know' basis he omitted names and locations of resources in order to minimise risk of leakage, whilst recognising the severity of punishment if such a leak occurred.

*[Copy obtained of Proposal to Hezbollah Executive Committee; Translated from original Arabic. Some licence has been taken in the translation in order for the main points to be clearly understood.

'To my brothers, in our long and eternal Jihad against the Kuffar, I humbly submit my proposal for their kind consideration and agreement.

To date, Insh'Allah, we have been successful in all our operations.

Let me summarise.

Buncefield in Britain was a complete success, taking the Kuffar by surprise and leading to fear as to how this could have happened.

We did not take responsibility by publicly claiming the fact, which in turn created more panic and uncertainty with the authorities.

Because the authorities then increased their security actions it was wise to remove ourselves for a period of time, in order for them to relax when they were not able to find or prove anything.

We therefore decided to carry out two operations in the Gulf to prove that security can be broken by our soldiers anywhere in the world.

It was agreed that actions would be taken against two countries who are too close to the Kuffar. The Emirates, where the Emiratis are falling into the foul habits of the Westerners, and Qatar where their relationship with the Americans allows the infidels to have a large military base on their soil.

The first operation was carried out on an oil loading jetty on Das Island. Successful. With only one death.

The second, carried out against a gas rig in the North Dome Gas Field was a very big success, with loss of life and the rig. Unfortunately there was an accident with the fuses and our diver soldiers died at the scene. We prayed for them as heroes now in paradise.

I now will explain my proposal which I have planned and costed.

This action will take place in London and strike at the very heart of their government. It will create panic and fear in the leaders and the people, and serve as a call to the faithful to our Jihad.

We will use a similar system to Buncefield, only this time the bomb will be different and bigger.

We will hit the British Kuffar who have supported the Americans against our brothers in Iraq and Afghanistan, bringing death and misery to the true believers.

I will not explain all details, as some are too technical, but the way this will be done, Insha'Allah, is as follows.

Through our international network of brothers we can access sufficient Radio Active material which will serve as the basis for the bomb, used in conjunction with plastic explosive which will create what is called a 'dirty bomb'.

Besides causing a large explosion it will create radiation which makes people very sick and/or ultimately die, and contaminates an area for a long time, so it is unusable.

On this occasion after the event we will announce our responsibility. This will only be done once a high level of public panic has been reached.

I cannot give the exact timing when the bomb will be made and in place, but we are certain it is possible within two months.

Individual and overall costs are detailed on separate sheets.

Finally, the effect of this action will be registered and seen all over the world and the benefit to our World Jihad will be immeasurable.

I ask, humbly, that the Committee sanctions this action, and God willing, we achieve success.]

He lunched early, packed, and then rested prior to taking a taxi to the meeting house. Prior to his departure he prayed for success, and for retribution to fall savagely on the Kuffar.

0800hrs Anna's apartment Southwark

Harry woke first and glanced at the sleeping form next to him.

He lay motionless wondering why this had happened, and what was the likely outcome bearing in mind what he knew.

Anna stirred and rolled over, her arm catching Harry's shoulder.

She opened her eyes and looked at him. She moved closer into his shoulder and draped her arm over his chest.

Harry started to speak at which point a hand came up to cover his mouth.

'Don't say anything yet Harry.'

Harry nodded his head, her hand still on his mouth.

They lay like that for a little while until Anna suddenly sat up and spoke.

'Harry, I need to talk to someone and I'm going to put my trust in you.'

'OK. I'm listening.'

'Harry, I know you are not what you say you are in the MoD. I know that you work for SIS(MI6) and have been involved in various operations in the Gulf and Middle East. Don't ask me how I know, but it has an impact on what I do at the Ministry, and my total dissatisfaction with my professional and personal life over the last eighteen months.'

'And?'

'I have obviously become fond of you and what with everything else over the last few years and particularly recently I want to lead a semi-normal life, if I can.'

'So?'

'That is why I am trusting you and telling you my thoughts and concerns.'

Harry's mind was racing. He knew that she might have been told by Mossad Control or perhaps some connection through the Ministry. Then again perhaps she already knew that he had been briefed on her role and background.

If so, what was the purpose of it? Should he admit and also state his knowledge of her? Were SIS(MI6) and Mossad in cahoots wanting their teams to work closer together? If so a briefing might have bloody well helped!

Harry decided to play a limited response.

'You're right and you're wrong. Yes, I have had some security connections. Obviously due to my work that tends to happen, but not really to any great effect.

More to the point, what do you want to discuss or offload? I'm happy being a sounding board if you like, or giving, I hope, some sensible advice.

Why don't we get up, shower and discuss this over breakfast and coffee?

And before you say anything else, I'm very fond of you!'

Anna smiled at the last comment, and bent over and kissed him.

For a milli-second Harry thought about things other than breakfast, but then quickly moved out of bed in the direction of the bathroom.

They made breakfast and a large cafetiere of coffee, and after pouring the second cups, Harry said,

'The floor's yours. Do want to start? I'm going to listen and say nothing unless requested. The only thing I'm going to do is hold your hand. Is that OK?'

Anna smiled again, and sat quietly thinking as she marshalled her thoughts.

'I'm not going to go into a lot of detail, but try and explain why I find myself questioning what I have been doing these last few years.

Please don't be judgemental. I'm sure you won't be, but I've done a number of things I'm not proud of but were necessary at the time, out of a sense of duty.

As you know I am the Minister's PA.'

Harry nodded.

'I worked with him closely in opposition and have continued as his PA since his appointment.

Putting it bluntly, and like a lot of others in Westminster, we had an affair. This has cooled, by my making, and life is not very pleasant.

His temper is well known, and he is an emotional bully, taking no prisoners.

I've really reached the end and want to do something else, but I'm trapped in this job.

If I try to resign he will be vindictive and make my life a misery. I just don't know what to do.'

Harry had been listening closely and was wondering where this explanation was going, bearing in mind his knowledge of her origins, her placement by Mossad, and the clear responsibility she had to provide continuous Intel when it was available to her.

He was very aware of the limitation Anna had placed on her story and could understand why.

What he couldn't understand was whether her explanation had been triggered by stress or a possible nervous breakdown. Whatever the reason her impromptu, impulsive action was a clear sign of overload of one sort or another.

Harry chose his words carefully as a man who had just been given some fairly dramatic news, bearing in mind that it was likely he was now the third party in a ménage à trois.

'I don't know what to say immediately. I'll have to give it some thought. What I will say, however, is that I will help you any way I can. How I can I don't know right now, but you can rely on me.'

Anna looked up.

'Thanks Harry, I thought I could rely on you.'

'Anna, you've obviously been under a lot of stress which has been building up over a period of time. You've now allowed the release valve to blow. That is the first and best step.

Now you're recognising it and putting your trust in me, we can start looking at all the possible options.

No rush, take our time, plan carefully, think the options through, and all the time the benefit of sharing the problem/challenge will help your state of mind.'

Harry was playing for time. Keep Anna encouraged and onside. How he was going to handle this delicate situation would be tricky. He was seeing the Deputy on Monday who would want a sitrep of the situation. Whilst being obliged to give an overview he thought he could protect some of Anna's sensitivities. He also had to face up to the fact that he was becoming very fond of her, and the recent events had firmed up the relationship for both of them.

Harry had held Anna's hand through their discussion and now leant across and kissed her on her forehead. Her hand came up and rested gently on his cheek as they sat motionless for a short while.

Anna sighed and sat back, saying in a joking fashion,

'Well, now you've got part of my problem I feel better already!

I know, a problem shared is a problem halved. I'm grateful for your understanding and your offer of help, which I will take!'

She leant across the table and took his hand.

'Come on; let's go for a walk by the river. It's not a bad day and we need some fresh air.'

Harry agreed, picking up a coat from his car parked outside as they left.

A weak winter sun lightened the sky and the mood, and there was only a gentle breeze as they walked arm in arm along the Thames near Lambeth Palace.

Anna's mood appeared to have lightened considerably by the time they stopped for some lunch in a pub near the Imperial War Museum.

A gentle stroll brought them back to her apartment where Harry indicated that he should be making tracks, notwithstanding a great day and one he would be happy to continue.

'Look we've had almost 24hrs together and I love it, but I need to get myself organised before tomorrow.

You do understand, don't you?'

Anna nodded.

They were standing in her hall when Harry put his arms round her and gave her a strong hug followed by quite a long kiss.

'Remember, I'm here to help you, so give me call at any time. If I can't answer leave a message, and I'll get back to you as soon as I can.

Let's see if we can see each other mid week, OK? I'll call you.'

Anna squeezed his hand, thanked him and let him go.

She returned to the sofa, sat down, and let the tears run.

Anna knew she was in a cleft stick, and where the present situation would take her she had no real idea.

1800hrs Jaramana District, Damascus, Syria

The members of the Committee had arrived, mostly singly, in order not to attract local attention, and were now sitting in the Majlis room talking quietly amongst themselves.

The Chairman called for their attention and briefly explained that their brother Fayez would be presenting his report of recent operations and explaining his proposal for which he was seeking their support, agreement, and funding.

Fayez started his presentation using the trick of keeping his voice low so that a number of the committee were straining to hear what he had to say. This had the advantage of making sure they had listened when he would ask for questions at various points and at the end.

His description of the various operations, culminating in his final and very dramatic proposal, had their full interest and questions were raised at various stages and were particularly intensive concerning the London project.

After he had finished the committee asked him to leave so they could discuss elements of the proposal and funding.

There was a central core of about five people who would make the final decision, but the other members were always included in the wide ranging appraisal and Q & A sessions.

Fayez sat, drinking coffee, in another room, pleased with the way, he thought, the presentation had gone, and the general support and enthusiasm that the committee had seemed to express.

He was hoping that approval would be given that night, but any attempts to force the decision would be heavily resisted.

At about 2200hrs he was called back when he was told that the central core of the committee wanted to do some analysis of the funding and that therefore a decision would not be made until the afternoon of the following day.

Fayez was disappointed, but did not let the committee see that as he left and returned to his hotel, rearranging his flight for 24 hrs later.

He reflected on the delay and thought success was more likely with the funding queries, otherwise they would have probably rejected it out of hand, without further investigation.

The committee, meanwhile, was examining the funding and the sums involved, which were significant.

Questions were raised concerning individual amounts, Isotope material and shielding, logistics, frontier guard bribes, and what, within the total amount, was the sum attributable to Fayez.

The core group recognised the inherent dangers that Fayez would encounter, so having completed their investigation felt that what was apparently left was a reasonable amount to cover Fayez's operational management and high risk.

The chairman of the committee indicated that he would ask all of them to confirm or otherwise their agreement by midday the next day. Once that majority group decision had been agreed he would inform Fayez by 1600hrs.

Fayez had indicated, that if approval was given, he would fly to Bucharest in Romania at 0100hrs Tuesday the 7th February 2006, then to Kiev in the Ukraine, in order to finalise negotiations and start the difficult task of moving the Isotope across Europe.

***

IX

Monday 6th February 2006 0900hrs Harry's office C10
SIS London

Harry dialled on his mobile the number the Qatari had
given him in Doha. It was answered almost immediately
'Ahmed Al-Marri speaking.'
'Ahmed, good morning. Harry Baxter here. We met in
Doha when you said you were coming to London, and
gave me your mobile number. Hence my call.'
'Of course I remember you Harry. In fact I approached
you and suggested we might meet when I was next in
London. How are you?'
Fine, thank you. I was wondering when we might meet
and where?'
'What about tomorrow afternoon at about 4? I am staying
at the Hilton, Park Lane.'
Yes that's fine for me. Let's catch up then. See you at the
Hilton tomorrow at 4.'
Harry put down his phone and wondered where that
conversation would lead. Unknown territory at present,
but at least he could tell the Deputy that contact had been
made and a discussion would take place.
He was wondering what tack the meeting would take with
the Deputy when his internal phone rang, and the
Deputy's PA asked him if he could come earlier to the
meeting, say, in 10 minutes?
Harry agreed and collected his thoughts and files
together, before taking the lift to the Deputy's floor.
'Come in Harry.'
The door to the Deputy's office was open to his PA,
where Harry was standing, and the Deputy waved to him
to come through.
'Close the door and take a seat.'
Harry sat down and waited for the Deputy to continue.
The Deputy smiled sat back in his chair and said,

'The 'Boy Scouts' over the river have been on the phone suggesting that we should share some of our Intel due to a degree of overlap occurring.

You know my opinion of them at the best of times, but with their very obvious current political manoeuvring my last thought is to co-operate in any way whatsoever!'

Harry said nothing as he knew more was to follow.

'They have been angling behind the scenes for more direct funding, without any reference or communication with us, which indicates a total disregard for the big picture that includes both Services.

The self-centred charlatan currently occupying the top slot is clearly looking to his title in retirement, and has allowed too many of his decisions to be politicised, to keep his current, temporary, master Minister, happy!'

Harry was well aware of the persistent niggling operating problems between the Security Service (MI5) and the Secret Intelligence Service (MI6). Dependent on who were the Directors of the two Services at any one time rested the degree of cooperation that governed their actions, whether political, joint or single requests for resources and funding, and most importantly, operational issues.

Harry knew from past experience that the Deputy had little time for the current MI5 Director, believing he was self-serving, and that he was prepared to sacrifice anybody to his own self interest.

It was fair to say that over a number of years under the new Government that large swathes of the Civil Service had lost their independence, and had become highly politicised. This had been achieved with groups of non-elected Ministerial 'advisors' appointed within various levels of departments to ensure compliance with a Ministers wishes. The critical, independent stance of the Civil Service had therefore been severely undermined.

The Deputy stopped and changed direction.

'Harry, I've had quite a long conversation with my opposite number over there, and he's raised one or two interesting points, one of which includes you!

Dealing with them in no particular order.

1. They've observed some of the DGSE antics in London. I'll come back to that.

2. Although Buncefield occurred in the UK, our view is that it's an overseas Op, sourced and funded abroad. They think differently and want to be brought into the FULL loop. Not on my watch if I can help it! Clearly after some credit, if it ever occurs!

3. They have been monitoring all the usual suspects and nationalities in London and are offering that Intel to us, as they think there could be connections. I'm not so sure, but that's another matter.

4. In order to justify their existence they've been following our ops for a time. The excuse is there is clear overlap. Dereliction of duty if they didn't! Balls!

5. This is where you come in. They've been following you, and logged your overnight stay in Southwark on Saturday night.

He raised his hand as Harry tried to speak.

'Don't worry, I said I was fully aware of your movements having discussed and approved your operation before the event, and that he was not telling me anything that I didn't already know!'

Harry then spoke.

'I can assure you that it was part of my briefing this morning, plus that I have arranged a meeting with the Qatari for tomorrow afternoon, at his hotel.'

'Good. Now before your briefing let me cover DGSE.

I know they are more interested in what's happening in the Gulf and Middle East rather than here, which is why you got that nudge in Abu Dhabi. They mean well, but they do like to be dramatic!

The 'Boy Scouts' have been keeping an eye on them in the UK, but frankly a bit of a waste of time, and probably got up their Gallic noses!

However, if things develop further and you are back out in the Gulf again, then I'm suggesting you take their offer of help.

Don't forget they've got some long historical relationships in certain M.E. countries which could be useful to us, and, they are on our side, generally!

Harry agreed, and said,

'If I do go I'll want another meeting with you to clear Intel levels, etcetera.'

'Fine, now let's have your briefing and commentary. I am sure there are a number of things not included on file, or on our report database!'

Harry confined his comments to a number of verbal bullet points.

His meeting with the Qatari would just be a 'fishing trip'. Why the contact? What did they know? What did they want? What could they provide?

He dealt with Anna by limiting his observations to her stressed state and her admittal as to her affair with the Minister. He confirmed that she had said that she knew he was not just working for the MoD, but she had given no indication as to where this information had come from.

He had not indicated that he knew she was Mossad, and had kept his reactions to dealing with, and assisting with her mental upset.

Yes, he had stayed the night at her request and no, he had not detailed that in the file or report database.

One final point was that there did appear to be a genuine level of affection between them, and he was planning to see her on Wednesday evening the 8th February

The Deputy had listened without interruption.

'Well Harry, I don't need to tell you of the risks of mixing business with pleasure, but I am sure your experience will guide you.

Keep me in the loop on all things and if you want any input from or to DGSE, or telling the 'Boy Scouts' to back off, flag me. Understood?'

Harry nodded in agreement, then said,

'As I said, I have not indicated that I know she is Mossad, neither have I indicated my true position in SIS(MI6).

I don't intend to go down either of those paths currently. There can be no real benefit to full disclosure at present. Do you agree?

The Deputy agreed and the meeting finished.

1200hrs Hotel Damascus Syria

Fayez had not slept well going over the presentation in his mind and was waiting impatiently for the decision, Yes or No.

He had planned originally to take a flight shortly after midnight, but had taken an option on an earlier one, if the decision was forthcoming before 1530hrs.

Time dragged and he was exhausted from all his recent operations, travelling, and the presentation to the Committee.

Shortly after 1400hrs he received a call from the leader of the Committee.

The conversation was oblique, but he understood clearly what was intended.

Approval was to be given in two stages.

1. If the purchase and delivery of the 'package' was achieved then further approval would given. [If purchase was achieved but no delivery then the project would cease.]

2. Once the 'assembly' had been completed further approval would be granted for the 'assembly' to be located as proposed.

Fayez was asked twice if he fully understood what had been said and the limitations imposed.

He replied positively, then asking the caller to confirm the necessary first stage funding would be placed at his disposal within 48 hrs. As he explained purchase discussions would be starting very soon, and he would need sufficient funds at his disposal. This was confirmed and the call finished.

At this point Fayez was able to take his earlier flight option which would take him from Damascus to Bucharest, Romania, and then to Kiev in the Ukraine.

He left the hotel at about 1530hrs by taxi, passing the district of Jaramana, arriving at Damascus International Airport in plenty of time for his flight.

His flight schedule meant a two hour stop over in Bucharest, giving an arrival time in Kiev at about 0630hrs, on Tuesday the 7th February.

He resigned himself to less than enjoyable flights, but felt pleased that at least stage 1 was underway.

Tuesday 7th February 2006 0745hrs Kiev International Airport

Fortunately for Fayez the taxi ride to his hotel only took about half an hour.

He was staying at the Radisson Blu Hotel in Kiev and he was keen to get some proper sleep after a dismal couple of flights.

He needed to make contact with his suppliers to arrange an evening meeting, before sleep took over, so having checked in and arrived in his room he rang the first, Viktor Horoshko, followed by the second, Luka Koshara.

It was agreed they would meet at his hotel at 2000hrs and have dinner and discussions in his room.

Following the two telephone calls Fayez prayed, went to bed, and slept soundly for the first time in three days.

0900hrs Ministers Office Whitehall

Anna had arrived earlier in her office at about 0815hrs.

She was prepared for a busy day as the Minister had spent the Monday in his constituency holding 'surgery for local complaints and grievances, plus keeping his agent onside, and up to speed.

She had spent the balance of Sunday and all Monday reflecting on her new relationship with Harry.

Anna felt the time was right to start taking some personal decisions as to her present situation with the Minister, and the need to start, diplomatically, if she could, a cooling off period.

It would no doubt go through a messy phase; such scenarios always do, but needs must.

She thought that it was interesting that Harry had not denied his involvement with a Security Service, and equally interesting that he had not questioned her about the source of her information.

Perhaps he was holding back something, but her stressful situation had taken over in their thoughts and discussions.

The Minister came bustling at about 1000hrs, complaining loudly about constituents, trains, agents, fellow Ministers, MPs, the Opposition, et al, in no particular order.

This should be an interesting day, she thought. I wonder who he wants to deal with first?

He turned round quickly and in a much lower tone asked, 'Can we meet this evening?'

'No, it won't be possible, I've arranged to meet an old girl friend,' she lied.

'Can't you change the day or something,' he enquired testily.

'Perhaps. I'll let you know this afternoon.'

He turned and went into his office, shutting the door firmly behind him.

He reappeared a moment later, saying,

'I am at a Foreign Office dinner tomorrow night, so I am not available for anything after 5pm tomorrow.'

'Noted.'

She wondered how the discussion would go that evening if she agreed to his request.

She decided on a half-way house solution.

Keep the fictitious date, but meet for a drink and start the cooling off.

At noon Anna told the Minister they could meet for a drink at his apartment at, say 7pm, but that she would be going to meet her friend at 8pm.

He reluctantly agreed in a truculent manner and carried on reading his files which had accumulated over the last 24hrs.

One of the files concerned Buncefield, and the only update included was the fact that the trail appeared to have gone cold with no new information from either the Police or Security Services.

Muttering obscenities under his breath, he telephoned the Director of the SIS(MI6) and hectored him for about ten minutes, not giving the Director an opportunity to respond.

Putting down the telephone he felt better for his mouthing off, and left for lunch with a senior Ministry colleague.

1530hrs Room C10 SIS London

Harry glanced at the clock, rose from his desk, grabbed his coat and headed for the door.

At that moment Tom entered and raised his eyebrows as Harry made for the door.

'Just going to the meeting with our Qatari friend.'

'Do you want any backup?'

'Not for this one. Will fill you in later.'

'Good fishing then!'

Harry made his way towards Hyde Park Corner and walked the 150 yards up Park Lane to the Hilton Hotel, walking through the main entrance as Big Ben Struck 4pm.

He was walking towards Reception when he felt a tap on his shoulder, turning to see the smiling face of Ahmed Al-Marri.

'Mr Harry Baxter, Good Afternoon.'

'Harry is fine for me, if Ahmed is OK for you.'

'Absolutely fine, Harry. Why don't we go and have some tea in that lounge over there,' he said, pointing over Harry's shoulder.

Harry nodded and they took their places at a small table where an attentive waitress took their order for afternoon tea.

'One of things I like, when I'm in London, is to have the traditional British afternoon tea. It means I can eat less in the evening and convince myself I'm watching the calories!'

Harry smiled, curious to see where this meeting would lead.

They continued with general conversation until the waitress had served them and withdrawn, at which point Harry said,

Ahmed I'm very happy to have afternoon tea with you, but I would like to think, on behalf of our respective governments, that something a little more concrete might come out of this!

Where do you think we might help each other?'

'Harry, we keep a careful eye, as you do, on our near neighbours, as well as our enemies. I am not really concerned which Government department you work for, but there are areas of mutual interest in the Gulf where some co-operation could be useful.

Harry nodded.

'You came to Doha to talk to QGPC about rig safety and possible terrorist attacks. You met a professional brick wall, but within a week a rig is blown up.'

Harry interrupted him.

'What do you mean a rig is blown up?'

'Let me bring you up to date. In amongst the floating dead bodies was found a diver, only just alive, with bits of his aqualung attached to him. Also remnants of an Iranian Navy inflatable with electric motor were found

He was heard to say, before he died, words to the effect that the explosive charges had gone off before the fuses had been set.

Whether this is true we don't know. It may just have been the rambling of a dying man.

What we do know is that the rig has been lost; there were a good number of survivors but also an unacceptable level of fatalities.

From an industry standpoint we need to have answers, and a declaration that this was not an accident in order to calm Government nerves.

We are assuming this is a terrorist attack.

My initial approach to you was to try and gain some expert advice and collaboration. Events have now made this a necessity.'

'How do you think we can help? What sort of collaboration do you have in mind?'

'Perhaps you have advance intelligence that could help us forestall any similar events in the future. Perhaps you have advice that we could use to improve security on our rigs and the North Dome project in particular. Perhaps you have intelligence that could help us tackle rogue elements in the Gulf that are not happy with Qatar's progress.'

'That's quite a wish list, Ahmed. I don't know if the MoD can help in all those areas.

I would have to discuss what you have said with my immediate boss and see what is possible. These things can take time and can be rather bureaucratic, as you can imagine.'

'I understand, but can you raise the issues I have outlined to you, and see what sort of response you get?'

'I will, and when I have an answer I will call you on your mobile.'

They continued their discussion around the recent tragedy but Harry did not get any further detail as to the rig explosion. It was clear that a major investigation was underway by the Qataris, and yet again no group had claimed responsibility.

At about 1730 hrs Harry left and returned to his office to prepare a short report for the Deputy, and request a meeting in the next 48 hrs.

He saw Tom and briefed him on the meeting. Nothing could be done before an overall decision had been taken by the Deputy. Perhaps some sort of collaboration could be established, but if the gains were of no real consequence, then the proposal could be knocked on the head.

2000hrs Radisson Blu Hotel, Kiev Ukraine

Fayez had arranged for a light meal for three to be delivered to his room, one they could serve themselves without interruption.

Just after 8pm there was a knock on his door and he opened it to greet Viktor Horoshko and Luka Koshara.

Viktor he knew well, but Luka was an unknown quantity, however highly recommended by Viktor.

The conversation was general in nature whilst they ate and having poured three coffees Fayez then focussed on specifics.

Viktor, do you have proper access to the product I require, and have you the necessary packaging to ensure that it can be transported safely?

Viktor said it would take him about two weeks to put all the necessary items in place and to have a product that could be safely transported across Europe.

In terms of funding it would be 50% up front, and the balance on delivery to the logistics organisation organised by Luka.

Fayez then questioned Luka as to the transportation of the two packages, its packaging (shielding), and deception of what was being carried.

The initial thinking was for a two tonne truck with the containers hidden in large packing cases at the front behind the cab, identical to the remaining cases being carried in the truck.

The cases at the rear of the truck would contain new tools and farm implements suitable for the cursory inspection that would take place with 'friendly' border posts.

Timing would be critical for crossing the border from the Ukraine into Lithuania and also from Lithuania into Latvia. Luka would be ensuring that 'informed' border guards would be on duty at specific times to assist the border crossings.

Luka insisted on a similar payment schedule, as a number of payments needed to made in advance, to ease the passage of the packages across three countries.

Viktor was questioned as to the source of the product and he advised that in a number of the old Soviet bloc countries various thefts had occurred in hospitals, resulting in the loss of X-Ray machines, or parts thereof, containing Caesium-137.

Such thefts had been placed in shielded storage, awaiting a purchaser, in this case Fayez.

The utilisation of such material encased with plastic explosive does not create a conventional atomic bomb. It falls under the description of an 'Improvised Nuclear Device' (IND), designed to contaminate an area and create fear and panic in the local population. Because of the contamination the area cannot be safely used for a number of years, this information in itself creating further fear and distrust.

The three men discussed in great detail all the elements of collection, shielding, transportation, bribes and commissions, until Fayez was satisfied that the plan was feasible and sufficiently flexible to accommodate changes in dates, routes, and therefore border crossings.

Payment terms were agreed with the promise that the initial payments would be made within seven days to their nominated bank accounts in Macau.

1910hrs Ministers apartment Onslow Gardens South Kensington

The doorbell rang and the Minister answered it, admitting Anna and giving her a perfunctory kiss on the cheek.

He was clearly in an abrasive mood, judging by his opening remarks.

'Well we'd better have a quick drink so you won't be late meeting your friend.'

'As long as I leave by ten to eight it will be fine.'

He poured her a glass of wine, himself a Scotch, which he drank immediately before pouring a second.

He said nothing, so Anna decided to break the silence.

'I've been thinking about us for a little time, and think we ought to give each other a break.'

'What the hell for?' he responded angrily.

'Because, frankly, we live in two totally different worlds. You're a Minister and I'm your PA. I think we should get on with our own lives. It's highly unlikely our relationship will change from what it is now, and I think I want something different.'

'Is there somebody else?' he asked quietly, but menacingly. 'If there is, you know I will find out.'

'No' she lied. 'I'm not interested in playing games with you, and if you want me to resign, I will.'

'Of course I don't. How would I bring anybody up to your knowledge level and how the 'circus' is run and organised?

He was backing off a little, watching her intently to see if she was lying or not.

Anna was grateful for her training and experience in handling such scenarios, and allowed him to see a little femininity as she brushed some imaginary moisture away from her eye.

Anna responded quietly.

'You would, nobody is indispensible. I am prepared to continue working as your PA if you want me to, but I think our relationship has to be a professional one.'

The Minister was thinking that if Anna continued as his PA there would still be a chance to renew their old relationship, so he agreed diplomatically, thanking her for her honesty, and hoping she would have a pleasant evening with her friend.

Anna smiled politely and left at about 1945hrs, thinking, that although he was a manipulative, scheming bastard, whose words she would never trust, that paradoxically, she was probably out of a similar mould.

As soon as she left she called a girl friend that lived in Fulham, and asked if she could call by.

Her friend was delighted to hear from her so they met up and went out for a Chinese meal locally, catching up on events and friends, nothing being discussed on the subject of Ministers or Government departments.

The Minister sat nursing the latest in a series of strong Scotches, becoming more bellicose and self centred as the alcohol took effect.

His thoughts ran around their recent relationship and the gradual cooling that had occurred. Was she involved with somebody new? He'd talk to Internal Security and Vetting tomorrow to run some spot checks and random samples to include her. Must be fair. Not to include the Minister's PA would be grossly unfair!

Maybe she was right. Maybe he was getting too old for sort of thing. Bearing in mind his position in the Cabinet perhaps he should concentrate on getting a promotion at the next reshuffle. The PM owed him several favours, and the black mark against him for Buncefield was starting to fade, in the absence of any group claiming responsibility.

He warmed to these ideas, whilst finishing his Scotch.

He poured another, sipping and thinking along these hazy lines, until sleep overtook him. He woke at 0200hrs shivering, and went to bed with a thumping head, that two Ibuprofen did little to ease.

2300hrs Anna's apartment Southwark

Anna let herself in and went to her secure telephone.

Dialling a number, she then punched in a security code before leaving a brief report and update on her continuing professional relationship with the Minister.

'Tomorrow is another day' she thought. 'What the hell's next?'

Wednesday 8th February 2006 1000hrs Minister's apartment Onslow Gardens South Kensington

Archie Preston was a well known exponent of climbing the greasy pole. He had started his professional career as a cub reporter on one of the broadsheets, and had quickly acquired the gutter skills of sniffing out scandals.

Physically he was unprepossessing, being a thin shadow when compared to the Minister.

Their paths had crossed at a Party Conference in Blackpool where he had passed to the Minister an interesting titbit concerning a fellow member of the Shadow Cabinet, just in time for him to threaten publication unless the unfortunate MP withdrew his challenge to a party position.

Archie had kept close to the Minister over the years and was rewarded with an unelected 'Political Advisor' role when the Minister made Government.

He had kept his hands dirty over the recent past, carrying out tasks for the Minister that required discretion, and an ability to sail close to the wind in order to achieve the required results.

The Minister was outlining what he wanted him to do.

'As you know, security is very much a number 1 priority at present, and I am asking you to carry out an internal review of senior staff, both elected and non-elected, to ensure that there no existing or potential threats that we could come to regret if they lay undiscovered.'

'Certainly Minister. But I would welcome a note from you outlining the brief and the content of Terms of Reference/Rules of Engagement,' he said, smiling wolfishly.

The Minister glanced sharply at him.

'There are times Archie, when I think you ought to be more flexible in your approach. I'm sure there are some episodes in your career that would not benefit from exposure to the light of day.'

Archie sat and stared back at the Minister, with a smile playing on his mouth.

'With respect Minister, I am sure that a number of your Cabinet colleagues would be fellow passengers in the same boat.'

He knew he was on solid ground. He had put away, in safe keeping, a few details that could always be leaked, and which would make the Minister's life a little less pleasant.

And they both knew that.

'Can you indicate who I should start with?' he asked.

'Permanent Civil Servant, elected Number Two and Three, PA, your opposite in Strategy.'

'But....'

'Yes?'

'Your PA?'

'Yes. Absolutely. I must be fair; otherwise accusations of favouritism will be levelled at me.'

'But.....'

'Yes?'

'Doesn't matter. Do I need to make contact with SIS(MI6), MI5, etc?'

'Not at all. This is an 'internal only review' with a limited scope of reference. Do you understand?'

'I think so but can I have some clarification as to what I am looking for.'

The Minister sat back and looked at the ceiling in exasperation before replying.

'You're the last person I thought I would have to instruct as to what we should be looking at.

Elementary things, drinking, drugs, socialising with whom, peccadilloes, boyfriends, girlfriends, all the usual suspects.

Is there any chance of any of them being compromised by unfriendly states?

All the things you used to scoop up in handfuls when you were a reporter.'

Archie nodded his head in agreement thinking it a little odd the Minister wanted him to check up on his PA. However....

The Minister dismissed him, and he went back to his office to draw up a mini

hit and check list to put some shape to the task.

1000hrs South Kiev Ukraine

Viktor met Luka at a warehouse in a rundown area in the south of Kiev.

At the back of the warehouse covered in tarpaulin were two packing cases, each just under 1 metre long by 750mm by 750 mm.

Each contained approximately 25 kg of Caesium-137 in a heavily shielded Lead Pig, its walls over 2cms thick.

Viktor had organised delivery of the product from Sevastopol where 'fraternal' connections had obtained it as a consequence of the closing down of Soviet military facilities on the Black Sea.

Luka now explained in detail the route and timing of the shipment from Kiev in the Ukraine to Riga in Latvia, crossing Belarus en route.

It is just over 1100kms from Kiev to Riga, and the trip was planned to take three days.

Flexibility was essential, as 'friendly' contacts at the two borders would have to be notified as to approximate crossing times.

In the first stage the truck would leave Kiev, taking the E101 in a NNW direction, then linking up with the M01, bypassing Chernihiv, on the way to the border with Belarus. Skytok would be the last town before the border, 220kms from Kiev. This distance would be covered in a morning, ensuring that the consignment would arrive at the border at a busy time when border staff were more inclined to wave shipments through. Contacts would have been advised and would ensure rapid processing.

Once in Belarus they would proceed to Gomel, 50kms from the border, and stay the night just north of the town with pre-arranged contacts. The consignment would then be transferred to a Belarus registered vehicle and the original truck garaged to await the return to the Ukraine.

Day 2 would be 300kms on the E271 from Gomel to Minsk, and then on the P3 250kms to Braslau, 20kms short of the border with Latvia. Once again, the two drivers would spend the night with friendly contacts.

Day 3 would be the crossing into Latvia on the P68, border contacts again being advised to ensure smooth transit.

Once in Latvia they would drive the 40kms to Daugavpils where the shipment would be transferred to a Latvian registered vehicle, the second vehicle being garaged to await a return to Belarus.

The Latvian vehicle would then drive the 235kms on the A6 to Riga, arriving mid afternoon, just south of the city. They would stay overnight.

At this point, Luka explained, the operation reaches a critical stage.

The two packages are to be transferred to a vessel in Riga Port and this is where the operation must run as smoothly as possible.

Port contacts will have been paid, and it is to be hoped that a cursory inspection would have taken place of the three packages at the rear of the vehicle.

The ship's cranes would lift the packages into the hold, and at that point their involvement would cease.

The ship would later transfer the packages to a fishing boat, planned to be met off the coast of Holland.

The drivers would then return to Kiev, changing empty vehicles as previously scheduled.

Viktor had listened closely to Luka's schedule and confirmed that Luka's younger brother would be one of the drivers on the delivery assignment.

Luka would maintain contact throughout, with regular reporting points, confirmations and advice of completion to Viktor. Balance of payments would be secured on completion.

Assuming all border contacts had been briefed then the delivery schedule would commence at 0800hrs, the morning of Monday 13th February 2006.

Viktor and Luka shook hands wishing each other good luck for the operation.

1945hrs Beachamp Place London SW3

Harry walked into the Lebanese restaurant, Maroush, situated in Beauchamp Place, SW3.

He and Anna had agreed to meet there. He'd been recommended it by a colleague, so as it was unknown to both of them they'd decided to try it.

It being comparatively early there were few diners, so they were able to choose a quiet corner where they could talk, without being overheard.

They kissed each other affectionately on the cheek as they met, and held hands as they walked to their table.

Smiling at each other as they sat down, Harry said jokingly,

'We really must stop meeting like this, people are beginning to talk!'

Anna smiled a trifle weakly.

''Almost a joke Harry, but a bit too close for comfort bearing in mind recent conversations with my boss.'

'Sorry. Didn't mean to be insensitive. Just very happy to see you again.'

'Me too. Situation is a trifle delicate and may be for a few weeks or months yet.'

'How about some dry white wine then, and a change of subject?'

'Fine. You choose.'

Harry ordered the wine and they drank whilst studying the menu.

Having ordered their meal Anna looked directly at Harry and said,

'Do you mind if I ask you a few questions, as I really would like us to be honest with each other.'

'Fire away.'

'When we were talking the other day I said I knew that you were connected to a particular government department.'

'Yes, and I replied that in my line of work I will obviously have certain connections and contacts with that department.'

But Harry, why no question to me as to how I know you have those connections?'

There was a short period of silence before Harry replied in careful, measured tones.

'Anna, the sort of business and world that you and I work and live in has a population that spends a lot of its waking hours listening, and watching everybody else.

Obviously, you know a number of things about me, which I could probably match in a number of things I know about you.

There is, however, one essential thing that I am aware of.'

'What's that?' Anna interrupted.

We're both on the same side, and bearing in mind I'm very fond of you, I'd like to leave it like that, if that's OK with you?' he said, smiling.

Anna dropped her head, looking at the table seriously.

Then she looked up, a smile playing on her lips.

'Alright Harry Baxter, I'll go along with that. For now. But a woman's prerogative, I may change my mind!'

Harry smiled back, happy he had been able to defuse the situation for the time being.

They dined, drank, enjoyed each other's company and following a cab ride back to her apartment, without a word being said, went arm in arm to her bedroom.

Later Harry leant over, kissed her on the cheek and left quietly to return to his apartment.

Anna lay there, pretending to be almost asleep, wondering where this relationship would go.

Harry made a mental note to update the Deputy, both on the Qatari proposal, and the developing situation with Anna.

Thursday 9th February 2006 0900hrs Deputy's Office SIS London

Harry had brought the Deputy up to date on his discussion with Ahmed, the Qatari Defence contact, and what had been requested by way of cooperation.

The Deputy responded by saying he saw no reason why simple cooperation should not be extended, certainly within the area of rig security, but in terms of those areas including security, then public domain information, at the present time, would be the extent of the working relationship.

On no account could the Department's security be put at risk or jeopardised by sharing sensitive information, particularly at this level.

Harry had already guessed what the Deputy's response might be in this area but then explained the questions that had been put to him by Anna and his response.

The Deputy listened and then commented,

'Harry, you are, as I'm sure you're aware, skating on very thin ice, almost to the point where I should assign you elsewhere.'

He put up his hand as Harry opened his mouth to speak, 'Let me finish.

I have to balance a number of factors at this stage.

If I re-assign you, how long is it going to take to bring the new man up to speed?

You have other important and ongoing connections that, I think, counterbalance the downside of your developing relationship, which perversely, has a strategic advantage within our current investigation and accompanying threats.

Continue, but I want a clear acknowledgement by you, that if the situation becomes, either untenable, because of your relationship, and/or, it is risking the other contacts and the investigation, I will have no alternative but to reassign you.

Is that clear and do you fully understand our relative positions?'

Harry agreed. He had to. The argument was logical. If the positions had been reversed he would have said the same thing.

'Agreed. No argument. I will call Ahmed and try and see him today sometime.'

The meeting over Harry went back to his office C10, and brought Tom and Jane up to date with the exception of Anna.

He and Tom then shared some thoughts around the information Ahmed had given him concerning the Qatar North Dome rig disaster, and why no group was claiming responsibility.

The normal pattern for terrorist groups has been to garner maximum publicity for their cause, and for texts and videos to be released to the TV news channels so that there is a world wide awareness of the atrocity committed. By the publicity generated the terrorist organisation hoped to benefit by future recruitment to their group.

The evidence of remains of an Iranian Navy rigid inflatable was not really explainable. The North Dome/South Pars field was a joint operation between Qatar and Iran. Was there a dissident group in Iran determined to spoil the existing partnership? And to what end? Internal regime change in Iran?

At about midday Harry called Ahmed on his mobile and they arranged to meet at Ahmed's hotel at about 1730hrs.

Ahmed smiled as he finished his telephone call with Harry, and turned to the other two men who were seated opposite him in a house in Ealing.

'Well my brothers, we take another step along the road. That was my contact I had told you about in the ministry, agreeing to a meeting with me in London later today.'

The two Pakistanis, Tariq Hashmi and Atif Masood, looked at each other and smiled.

'He believes that you are working with him on rig security and prevention of possible terrorist attacks.'

'Yes, my position in the Qatar Defence Ministry is proof, and our meeting in Qatar and recently in London, via the Embassy also confirms that.'

They both nodded, satisfied with the explanation and how events were moving.

'The packages will be here in less than three weeks. Do you have the reception facilities organised, with all the necessary equipment for fabrication?'

'Yes, it is proceeding well and will be completed within seven days.'

'When do we expect Fayez?'

'Sometime in the next ten days. He will be staying at a hotel not far from the factory.'

'Have you been told how our package is to be used?'

'No. Fayez said he will explain everything when he arrives. Although he has asked us to obtain maps and drawings of certain areas of London.'

Ahmed rose from his chair.

'I will return to my hotel to prepare for my meeting. I must put together some facts and figures that will interest our Ministry man. I want him to remain very interested!'

They shook hands and embraced before Ahmed left.

Ahmed hailed a black cab that was passing at the end of the road and journeyed into his hotel, all the while thinking of ways to maintain Harry's interest without revealing his own hand.

[Ahmed had been recruited about 8/9 years ago, when studying at a European university that had a very active Islamic Society. Visiting mullahs delivered strong virulent messages against Western society, its perceived attacks against Islam under the pretext of regime change and democracy, a lax, immoral society, against which followers of true Islam should protect themselves.

To a young, impressionable mind the message was clear and unequivocal. As a Muslim he should follow. He did.

After he graduated in Middle Eastern politics he was encouraged to join the increasing Qatar Government payroll as a potential permanent civil servant in the Defence Department, with all the free benefits of housing, healthcare, education and travel that such a position can bring.

As he slowly climbed the promotional ladder his previous contacts from university ensured he stayed committed to the cause; actions by the US and UK governments in Eastern Europe, Gulf and Middle East, further confirming his convictions and making him, privately, extremely radical. He became what is euphemistically called 'a sleeper'.

When he was approached to commit to assisting a group in their attack against Western interests he needed little persuasion, and was a willing recruit to the potential action in a Jihad.]

Ahmed paid off his cab and entered the hotel, hurrying across the lobby to collect his key from reception.

What he hadn't noticed was the motorcyclist who had tailed his cab from Hounslow, and who had pulled up about 50 yards from the Hilton Hotel, Park Lane.

1730hrs Hilton Hotel Park Lane London

Ahmed and Harry greeted each other in the main lobby where Ahmed had been waiting.

They took themselves to a quiet corner of the lounge where Ahmed ordered coffee and passed a few minutes commenting on the difference between London and Doha weather at this time of year.

After Ahmed had poured their coffees, Harry opened the conversation,

'I'll get straight to the point Ahmed.

I took what we had discussed straight back to my boss and he's quite happy with a conversation about rig risk, improving safety procedures (we have some real experts for that), anti-terrorist systems, defence and evacuation. In fact anything in that area where we could sensibly work together, to achieve a greater level of security that currently exists, and which would be transferable between the Gulf and our North Sea operations.

If, however, we are talking about possible sharing of security information that could be fed to my department from the security services for the prevention of terrorist attacks, then that cannot be made available under any circumstances.

The exception to that is if the information is already in the public domain.'

Ahmed had looked pleased at Harry's initial comments, but had changed to disappointment by the time he finished.

Ahmed thought quickly.

'I appreciate what you have said Harry, so we will have to work on the basis of your boss's ruling, which I can understand, bearing in mind Government department security issues,'

Adding hastily, but smiling,

'Our own departments get completely paranoid from time to time!'

Harry responded in a similar vein, and said,

'Perhaps we should try and schedule a meeting with some of our experts at the Department of Industry so we could draw up a list of those areas, we, and you, want to cover so we can bring some focus to our joint interests.'

Ahmed responded quickly,

'Now it's my turn to have to go back to my boss and get his approval for what is suggested. Once I have that I'll contact you. Which telephone number should I call you on?'

Harry gave him the number that filters all Whitehall calls, without giving direct access to any Ministry.

Harry said he would look forward to his contact and left the hotel at about 1830hrs. His departure was noted by a young man sitting reading a paper in the lobby who left shortly afterwards, mounting a motorbike parked just round the corner in Hertford Street.

The rider moved off quickly, around Hyde Park Corner and down Constitution Hill, past the Palace, along Buckingham Gate, and finally down Horseferry Road to Millbank, home to the Security Service (MI5).

He entered the building and made his way to his line Officer to report on observations in Ealing and the London Hilton.

What the Qatari was up to with the two Pakistanis would need further observation, perhaps phone line tapping, or some listening devices planted on their property.

Additionally what was the relationship between the Qatari and an officer of SIS(MI6)?

Perhaps it was time there was some inter-departmental liaison and discussion.

The Line Officer took his verbal brief, produced a bullet point report, and took it into his Sector Director, who having read the main points, said,

'Should be an interesting conversation tomorrow morning with 'Supermen'. This might be a good opportunity for them to recognise they don't know everything. Secondly, with this information they've got a real problem on their hands if they've started dealing with the Qatari on a professional level.'

The Sector Director sat back in his chair, put his hands behind his head, smiled at the Line Officer, and said,

'With the Intel we've been collecting over the last few weeks and months we're starting to see some action. Curious though it may be, it's difficult to see exactly where it's going. But it's going somewhere, and that's what we've got to find out. Whether the 'Supermen' want to willingly work with us 'Boy Scouts' is another matter!'

(With the clear cut division of responsibility between the Secret Intelligence Service (MI6) and the Security Service (MI5), namely Worldwide for MI6 and the UK for MI5, it is paramount that they work together on operations that include both overseas and UK elements).

Friday 10th February 2006 0930hrs Deputy's Office SIS London

His telephone rang.

His PA advised it was the Assistant Director MI5, who wanted to speak to him.

The Deputy responded in a courteous manner, his beef was with the Director at the very top, not the man he was talking to.

The gist of the conversation between them was a request from the Assistant Director for an early meeting, to discuss a number of elements that clearly involved both Services.

Queries from the Deputy produced some specific points and overlap from the Asst Director, and although he was somewhat reluctant, the Deputy recognised that a meeting would be necessary, in order to clarify current positions, priorities, and precedent in future actions.

The meeting, given its priority, was arranged for 1500hrs that afternoon at Thames House.

Following the phone call the Deputy contacted Harry and told him to be available for the scheduled meeting, but also to see him for an update/Sitrep at 1200hrs.

Harry wondered what had developed, but was not surprised if overlap between the two Services had occurred. It wouldn't be the first or the last.

He reviewed his own notes, reports, meetings, and recent discussions with a number of people of interest.

He called in Tom for any additional information from his side, or any Intel that may have come in from overseas, or from one or more of their regional 'moles' in the UK.

He noted the essentials for his meeting with the Deputy and reviewed the day's Intel from those overseas stations which have, or may have, some connection with their operation.

Harry wondered what the Security Service had turned up, and where it fitted in their complex matrix.

1500hrs Security Service (MI5) Thames House Millbank, London

The Asst Director shook the Deputy's and Harry's hands, and led the way to Meeting Room D5.

Once they were seated, coffees and teas poured, he opened the discussion.

'There have been a number of overlaps recently, involving persons and targets of joint interest, so I felt it would be sensible for both departments to sit down, share Intel, objectives, etc, in order that we don't fall over each other, and jointly have a clear idea of what we want to achieve.'

The opener had been delivered in a slightly sarcastic but humorous tone, and Harry hoped that the Deputy would not rise and take the bait.

On the contrary. The Deputy adopted a very friendly and accommodating tone, hoping that they would be able to maximise their efforts by sharing what Intel was available to them both, and to build up a clearer picture as a direct result.

He said he thought that the waters were muddy enough with the variety of current threats to warrant a full and frank exchange, in order to build a clear picture of what they were jointly up against, both within the UK and overseas.

Harry smiled inwardly to himself. He had heard the same approach adopted by the Deputy to the previous Asst Director. Get as much information as he could without releasing as much from SIS(MI6). Oh, how the politics play out!

The Asst Director was accompanied by a line Officer who then started to read from some recent reports concerning both the Qatari, Ahmed, and Harry.

Harry mentally sat up this point, and listened closely.

The nub of the report covered Ahmed's meeting with the two Pakistanis, his return to London and subsequent meeting with Harry.

Obviously, Harry thought, a double game, whatever the reason.

He interrupted at this stage.

'What do we know about the Pakistanis?'

'Not much at present. They do not appear on our watch list, but have the house and a couple of warehouse businesses, storage, cars, machinery, jobbing engineers, repairs, etc.

With these developments however, we have now included them on our watch list, plus phone tap and future bugs.'

'Do you have any idea what the Qatari is up to with them?'

'Nothing at present. We are only talking of this development in the last week. Incidentally what discussions are you having with him, and what do they cover?'

The question was direct.

Harry looked at the Deputy who nodded his agreement.

'There have been a couple of incidents in the Gulf that, we think, could be terrorist linked.

The most recent, a big one was in the offshore gas field off Qatar. I visited QGPC on the pretext of rig safety and security, and was approached by the Qatari, who is an official in Qatar's Defence Ministry.

We agreed to meet in London on his next visit which is now.

He wants us to provide assistance in safety, counter terrorist systems, etc.

The final point he raised was whether we could share information as to possible terrorist threats and connected

Intel. He was told the first area was possible. The last never.'

'How are we going to jointly handle this, then?' the Asst Director asked.

The meeting then examined the two separate lines of Intel from the respective agencies over a period of time; the Security Service commenting on monitoring of the Minister, his PA, Harry's meetings with Mossad and other agencies, the accidental discovery of Harry's relationship with Anna, the coincidence of the Pakistani meeting with the Qatari, and his meeting with Harry.

SIS(MI6), in turn, updated as far as they wanted to, on the various overseas meetings and shared Intel, commenting briefly on the Das Island and Qatar 'accidents'. Harry also added that if any of the disasters had been terrorist led, nobody, to date, had claimed responsibility.

In terms of future actions it was agreed to have a twice weekly update of shared Intel, unless code Red demanded an earlier response, and coordination.

It was also agreed that Harry would maintain the existing contact and try to develop a closer relationship with the Qatari, Ahmed, and see if he could be drawn as to his other connections, activities, or operations.

Hints, as to Intel of possible low level terrorist threats should be given, to see if this drew out any more information from the Qatari.

It was forcefully delivered by the Asst Director that he hoped this would be the start of some meaningful cooperation between the Agencies, putting to one side their political competitiveness of the past.

The Deputy murmured his agreement, and looked forward to sharing solid Intel and action with the Security Service.

No comments were made as to Harry's involvement with Anna, and her own intelligence allegiance was not raised by SIS(MI6).

The meeting ended on an apparently positive note, and the Deputy and Harry left to return to SIS(MI6) HQ, at Vauxhall Cross.

The Deputy was quiet until they were halfway across Lambeth Bridge.

'Harry, you heard what I heard, and they've obviously got the men on the ground to pull in faster Intel than we can. Fine, we'll work with them. But let's just watch our backs. The men doing the work I can trust, I think. The men at the top pulling the strings, I'm not so sure.

Old habits die hard, and in the past they've never missed a political trick, if it was there.'

'OK, but from my side it's just another op. I'll go along with it unless something starts to stink. Then you'll know about it, and you can take it up to the top.

What interests me now is what Ahmed is up to. I think we'll have to do some digging into his past, and present.'

Right Harry. I'm catching a cab from here to go to London Bridge. Keep me updated at least every other day. 'Bye.'

The Deputy hailed the cab on Albert Embankment as Harry walked on down towards Vauxhall Cross.

Sunday 12th February 2006   1230hrs Battersea Park London

It was a cold, crisp, sunny winter's afternoon and Anna and Harry went for a long walk through the park finishing up at a local pub that served great Sunday lunches.

After a traditional roast beef lunch they walked back through the park as the sun slipped towards the horizon and the air grew noticeably colder.

The increasing chill was also noted by the observer standing about 75 yards away from Anna's apartment, who noted with relief that Harry left at about 1815hrs to make his back to Clapham.

Times were noted in his log which would be on Archie Powell's desk by 0900hrs Monday morning.

***

X

Monday 13th February 2006 0930hrs Minister's Office Whitehall

The Minister's direct line telephone rang.

Answering it he heard Archie Powell asking what time it would be convenient for him to come to his office.

Glancing at his diary he said,

'1.30pm this afternoon', then immediately replaced the receiver.

He glanced towards his outer office where Anna was working, and told her to take a late lunch as his 'Political Adviser', Archie Powell, was coming at 1.30pm to discuss constituency matters.

Anna readily agreed. She couldn't stand Archie Powell, who she thought was a slimy, devious untrustworthy specimen, but unfortunately, within the political jungle, natural selection had not reduced their numbers.

1100hrs Room C10 SIS(MI6) London

Tom sat down facing Harry.

'What's the Sitrep?' he asked

'Several interesting threads, some of which need some fairly fast follow up. Let me bring you up to speed.'

Harry updated Tom on the recent meeting with the Security Service (MI5), the proposal for cooperative action, and finally, the situation with Ahmed and the Pakistanis.

'We will have to use the 'Boy Scouts' for any surveillance on the Pakistanis, but that doesn't stop our own on Ahmed.

We need to get some further background on him and them, and what/who was the link and for what reason.'

'Tom, can you start digging into Ahmed's background, contacts, family, etc? Use our man on the ground in Qatar. Tell him its priority 1. Do not indicate Pakistani contact in UK. I will ask our boys to dig in that area. Alright?

Ahmed is supposed to contact me soon for a meeting, so would like to have more of a profile when he does.'

Tom left to start his investigations, while Harry sat and thought through a number of possible scenarios in his mind. None had the solidity he wanted so he summarised what he had suggested to Ahmed, and considered options if he agreed to such cooperation.

1330hrs Minister's Office Whitehall

Archie Powell sat down in the chair across from the Minister and smiled unctuously.

The Minister sat stony faced, looking at him, having closed his office door to indicate no entry.

'Well?'

'Some basic information I thought you should have.'

The Minister said nothing so Archie continued.

'In your Department there are several interesting situations, developing and ongoing.

Some of these facts I have gathered over a period of time, not just recently, in case you should require such information for some reason,' he said, smiling wolfishly.

Still the Minister said nothing.

'Two senior permanent Secretaries are involved in affairs, one heterosexual, one gay. A minor minister is taking 'commissions' from two private organisations to provide details of pending legislation that could affect their markets. Another has cultivated an expensive drug habit, and lastly your PA is seeing somebody.'

The Minister was quiet for a moment digesting what had been said.

Then he spoke, quietly at first but with his voice gaining in volume as he responded.

'Archie, I thought you were a professional, but these amateurish comments disappoint me. Frankly you are bloody useless.

Nine tenths of the information you have given me I've known for the last two to three years. In addition there are at least three or four other situations you have not discovered.

Now who is my PA seeing?'

'I'm not sure at present. I'm working on it.'

'So what do you know so far?'

This man went to her apartment, they went for a long walk across Battersea Park, had lunch in a pub, went back to her apartment and he left at about 6.15pm.'

'Fanbloodytasic, Sherlock. Hardly a raving bloody affair is it?

For Christ's sake go and do a proper review, otherwise your name will be mud for trying to take fees under false pretences.

Now bugger off, and let me get on with some work.'

Archie left, suitably chastened, vowing that any further information he discovered would have the Minister eating his words.

The Minister wondered who the lunch date had been, but thought that Archie would bring him the answer before long, particularly after his outburst.

1530hrs, Room C10 SIS(MI6) London.

Harry's phone rang.

It was Ahmed coming through the general filter switchboard.

'Afternoon Ahmed.'

'Harry, good afternoon.

I am ringing to see if we can meet soon.'

When were you thinking of?

'Tomorrow or Wednesday.'

'Wednesday would be best for me.'

Good. What time?'

Can we say 1130hrs at the Victoria & Albert Museum, Cromwell Road? We can always get a bite of lunch if our discussions go on.'

Fine. See you at the main entrance?'

'No. Go to the galleries. Constable collection.'

'See you there.'

The conversation over, Harry contacted Tom to put more pressure on their man in Doha, so that if further intelligence was available he would have access to it, before the meeting on Wednesday.

Tuesday 14th February 2006 1000hrs President Hotel Athens Greece

Fayez had been staying at the President Hotel since the 8th February, when he had flown in from Kiev on Aerosvit Ukrainian Airlines.

He had used a Greek bank in order to receive and transfer certain funds for the operation.

Few questions were asked as to source and reason for transfers, Greek authorities apparently being comparatively relaxed in this area.

After completion of the various financial matters that took a few days, Fayez was able to relax and enjoy, with discretion, some of the distractions of Greece's capital city.

He had planned to break his journey in this way, subsequently flying from Athens to Amsterdam, where he would stay for a few days, before his final leg from Amsterdam to London Heathrow, arriving on Sunday 19th February.

He had arranged to track the 'package' with regular reports from the 'delivery company', and would receive updates following the border crossings.

His KLM flight to Amsterdam was departing at 1700hrs, arriving on schedule at 1930hrs, which meant he was in his room at the Hotel Hegra by 2115hrs.

He hoped the delivery was maintaining progress, if so, it would arrive in Riga tomorrow, the 15th.

1420hrs Room C10 SIS(MI6) London

Tom entered carrying a file and a memory stick.

'Harry I've got some Intel from Doha, and further background on you friend, Ahmed.

'Good. Give me the basics.'

'It appears that his family is a Qatari father and Palestinian mother. His father died when he was about ten, but Qatar looked after him well as he was apparently very bright at school, and eventually went to university both in Doha and London.

Having got the universities, started to trawl our database here, and threw up some interesting facts.

Special Branch had a minor interest in him due to some Islamic society demos and a bit of agitprop.

After that he seemed to drop off the radar for a year, but then reappeared in support of Palestine and anti-west marches.

Completed his degrees, returned to Qatar, started in the Government and moved into the Defence Department. No further reports on any political activity.

Story is, due to his mother's influence, he's a very keen supporter of Intifada, but seems to keep it under wraps in his present Defence job in Qatar.'

'Any indications as to why he's in contact with the Pakistanis?'

'Not at the moment. I'm chasing up our contacts in the 'Boy Scouts' to see if they have found out anything more and, if they've got the line tap or listening post scheduled.'

'OK. Chase them. Say it's definitely Priority 1. Any way they could speed things up would be much appreciated, etc. You know the flannel!'

Tom smiled, and said,

You, smoozing the Boy Scouts! That's a first!'

Harry smiled back,

'Never forget Tom, the shovel is mightier than the sword!'

Tom left to continue his investigation.

Harry wondered whether they could get their own listening team on the ground quicker, but realised that would start a pissing contest almost immediately.

Tom returned unexpectedly in about 15 minutes.

'Update on the Pakistanis.'

'Good.'

'Their boys had already started to run a check on them.
Their names are Tariq Hashmi and Atif Masood.
Basically small engineering business, factory, storage, no
convictions or black marks against them as yet.
Tariq, 45, born in this country. Atif, 40, immigrant,
related through marriage to
Tariq, came to the UK three years ago.'

'The first question is why would Ahmed have a
connection to them?
That's the odd one.
Start running background checks on their engineering
business. Find out who they do business with. Then get
checks started on them. Start expanding the net into their
community. Find out who they mix with. Do they have
any radical political or religious connections or
affiliations? Let's spread the net into their wider family.
Get your oppo to crank up the whole thing, big and fast!'

Tom nodded and left.

Harry hoped the phone tap or listening post would be
activated soonest. That can always contribute to the mix,
no matter how guarded the overheard conversations.

He started to think about his meeting on Wednesday with
Ahmed, and how that might go.

A little bit like fishing; fly on the water, lure if you can, if
hooked play carefully, gently, patience is essential, wear
the fish out, remember the limitations of the line, and
finally, perhaps success, unless a wily fish who suddenly
dives, breaks the line and escapes.

Keep that in mind, Harry thought, tomorrow.

1900hrs Anna's apartment Southwark

Anna was sitting quietly, drinking a glass of Sancerre,
thinking about her life, Harry, her loyalty to her country,
and her current assignment.

She recognised that her affection for Harry was growing,
but in the current set of circumstances it was an added

complication that she was starting to think only created more confusion.

Bearing in mind what she was supposed to be doing in terms of intelligence gathering, commercial, governmental, strategic, tactical, she saw no problem, assuming she stayed where she was.

The added pressure of withdrawing from the relationship with the Minister would probably resolve itself by him replacing her.

In that eventuality she would then be able to turn round to Control and insist on a new assignment and posting.

Therefore, continue with the new status quo, one, with Harry, and two, a purely professional relationship with the Minister.

One would continue to be pleasant, the second a professional accommodation until resolution. She hoped.

Harry and she were meeting on Wednesday evening and she realised how much she was looking forward to it.

Wednesday 15th February 2006 1000hrs Room C10 SIS(MI6) London

Harry had verbally updated the Deputy on recent Intel and activity, and what was happening in terms of widening the intelligence gathering net.

The Deputy had responded by telling Harry to keep up the pressure in all directions, both internally and externally. Remember, he warned, I have pressure from the top down as well.

Harry appreciated the difficult political game the Deputy had to play, and the fact that he shielded and ran interference for Harry and others, so they could get on with the job, with minimum intervention by Government jobsworths.

At 1100hrs Harry left to go to the V & A, on Cromwell Road.

He was a few minutes late, but soon found Ahmed in the Constable Gallery sitting on a padded bench looking at the pictures.

Greeting him, he sat alongside looking at the paintings, and engaged in quiet conversation, in the manner of two art aficionados.

'Well Ahmed, what is the response from your organisation?'

'Some progress I feel, but we need to establish some overall parameters.'

'You have just taken the words out of my boss' mouth!

The invitation still stands as to discussions with our Department of Industry to draw up areas of cooperation, and then to detail some of those areas so that experts from both sides can be included.

In that way I think that some real progress can be made.'

Harry was hoping that Ahmed would accept his proposal. This would get him on side, superficially at least, and provide a greater opportunity for surveillance and in-depth appraisal.

Contacts both in Qatar and the UK would then start to become available, and this in turn would help the investigation into the Pakistani contacts.

Ahmed looked at one of Constable's paintings as he replied,

'Harry, let's take your suggestion as a starting point. We have to start somewhere!

If you can send an official invitation to the embassy on the basis you have just outlined, I think we should get the discussions started as soon as possible.'

'Excellent, I'll get the bureaucratic wheels in motion as soon as I get back to my office.

Now that's agreed, how about a quick lunch?'

Ahmed declined, excusing himself on the need to catch up on some reports and admin.

Harry was quite happy to get back and put the wheels in motion through the Department of Industry so that time would not be lost, and pressure and contact would be maintained.

He wondered what would eventuate with further discussions, and whether there would be any explanation as to Ahmed's connection with the Pakistanis.

Ahmed left, wondering where the proposed meeting would be useful to him and his 'brothers', but thought that any inside contact could be beneficial in the long term.

1830hrs Harry's apartment Clapham

On a previous occasion Harry had said it was about time Anna came to his flat, and sampled his cooking.

That had made Anna laugh, as Harry had certainly never given the impression that he was a cook. More likely eating out, or a Take Away!

However he had persuaded her to risk it, and he was immersed in following the recipe in his only cook book as his doorbell rang.

Thinking it was Anna he answered it, to be confronted by a door to door salesman, or so he was told, of home security systems.

In measured but forceful tones he declared no interest and closed the door firmly, returning to his cooking preparation.

The salesman took note of the number of the apartment on his pad and walked up the road to his parked car.

Opening the door he sat in the passenger seat, facing the apartment, and settled down to wait.

Shortly after 7.15pm he saw Anna alight from a cab, and make her way to the apartment which she entered after a short pause.

Harry gave her a swift hug and a kiss on both cheeks as he let her into his apartment.

'Hullo, and it's very nice to meet you again', he joked as he took her coat.

She smiled affectionately at him as she took his arm and looked round his very masculine apartment.

She noticed how neat and tidy it looked, almost unlived in, a typical layout you might see in a furniture store.

But, she mused, not unsurprising, bearing in mind the life he lead. Not a great deal of time to move up from basic functionality!

'Let me see how the great chef is getting on', she said, walking towards the kitchen.

Harry blocked her path and said in a mock French accent,

'Zee creation murst not be seen before the Maestro has completed it.

As your Maitre D' however I can offer you an aperitif meanwhile.'

She laughed.

'Alright, a dry white wine would be nice.'

'Immediatement, Madame.'

He turned and disappeared into the kitchen, closing the door behind him.

Harry reappeared in a couple of minutes carrying two glasses of white wine, passing one to her and then suggesting a toast to the cook!

Anna smiled; she was happy and relaxed in his company, and there was a high degree of normalcy in the situation that she hadn't experienced for a long time.

The dining table was laid with mats and napkins with a single candle between the two settings, positioned opposite each other. He lit the candle and turned off the room centre light which produced a warmer atmosphere.

Harry then produced the starter, it being simple halves of Ogen melon, with a little Port sitting in the middle.

He ate his melon a little anxiously, frequently looking at his watch, before clearing the plates and disappearing into the kitchen.

When Harry reappeared, he was carrying two plates on which sat poached trout, which was then accompanied by two dishes containing new potatoes and peas.

He was now more relaxed, and poured further glasses of the white wine to accompany the main course whilst engaging Anna in amusing and lively conversation.

They finished the meal with cheese and biscuits and a little Port left over from the first course.

The time passed all too quickly and at about 10.30pm Anna looked at her watch and said,

'I think I'd better make a move now and call a cab. I have an early start tomorrow.

Harry I have appreciated this evening. It's been a lot of fun, and do thank the chef. Mouth-watering!'

Harry was disappointed, but accepted that mid week had its own restrictions of which he was only too aware.

For him the cab came, it seemed, with indecent haste, as he led Anna to the door.

Before she left he kissed her, and held her in a long embrace. No words were exchanged, but he thought he saw a little moistness in her eyes.

He waved goodbye as the cab went up the road towards Clapham High St.

The 'salesman' sitting in his car noted the time on his pad, waited until Harry had disappeared inside, started his car, and drove gently away towards the main road.

'Boring', he thought to himself. 'Never mind, the evening rate payment will come in handy. If they want to waste money on things like this, that's their lookout!'

Thursday 16th February 2006 0600hrs Factory Hounslow West London

The truck drew up at the entrance to the factory as the doors were opened.

It reversed carefully into the factory, and edged slowly towards the wall at the back.

As it neared the wall one of the men standing there pressed a switch and a section slid back to reveal a space approximately 20ft deep by 50ft wide.

The large cylindrical object in the back of the truck was lifted and removed by a mobile crane and placed in the far corner of the space revealed.

Other smaller components were stacked adjacent to the large cylinder, the crane withdrew, the switch was thrown and the section rolled back to its original position.

The two Pakistanis withdrew to their small office and sent a text to Ahmed advising 'last but one delivery received'.

All elements were now in place, awaiting delivery of the vital package sometime around Monday 27th February.

Atif Masood had studied Engineering at the National University of Sciences and Technology in Islamabad, Pakistan, and had maintained contact with many of his classmates; some of them highly qualified in various science and technology disciplines.

A few had become highly radicalised Muslims over the years, and Atif had identified two, now resident in the UK, who would be able to carry out the element of engineering required with diligence, and a passion for achieving some sort of retribution against the West.

Tariq was different; still a Muslim but without the radicalisation of Atif.

His interest was money. What they were doing would bring him, tax free, the sort of sum that would take him probably three or four years to earn through his business.

At 0730hrs the other workers started to arrive, carrying on with their minor fabrication assemblies, only aware of the separate engineering unit behind the rear wall as a place where 'no questions asked' jobs were carried out on a cash only basis.

1000hrs Hounslow West London

At a junction box, about 50 yards from the factory entrance, a BT van was parked and an engineer was working on one of the circuits.

Working quickly he finished in about 10 minutes before loading his van, and driving up to the factory gate.

There he approached the office and requested access to the main BT connection box situated near the window. The reason given was that a local company had complained of crossed lines, not apparent to the Pakistanis, but clearly evident to the other company. He had rectified the fault in the street junction box, but needed to check their internal connections as well.

The Pakistanis reluctantly agreed, and moved out so he could complete his testing.

Working rapidly again, he apparently checked the lines, and installed a small device in the junction box which was then concealed by its cover.

He advised the owners that everything was now working normally, with no risk of crossed wires and poor connections.

Placing his tool kit in the van, the BT engineer called base, advising that both the 'tap' was operational, and that the omni-directional mike (ODM) was located in the office.

This information was relayed to Harry's office, where Tom and Jane were then able to set up recording equipment which would receive both sources, carried by BT, but diverted from the exchange along secure lines to SIS(MI6).

1500hrs Room C10 SIS(MI6) London

Harry made it clear to both Tom and Jane that transcripts of 'taps' and 'hifone' were to made available every two hours with any particular observations or 'spikes' highlighted.

It would not be possible to maintain a 24/7 listening mode, so he hoped that the Security Service across the river would be able to monitor the situation more closely, particularly with their sophisticated kit at GCHQ, Cheltenham.

Tom had already discussed cooperation with his opposite number following the recent meeting and was assured that analysis and observation reports would be made sent as soon as they were available.

Harry went to see the Deputy to give him a quick 'Heads up' on current status with the Pakistanis, and the cooperation in place with the Security Service.

'Fine Harry, but watch them all. You know my reservations. If something comes out of left field and takes everybody by surprise, then we'll suddenly be on our own!

Nothing to do with us, they'll cry. At that point watch your back, and be prepared!'

Harry nodded.

He wasn't going to argue with the Deputy at this stage.

'Let's see what develops first' he thought.

'I've made approaches to the Department of Industry to extend an invitation to the Qatar Embassy, addressed to Ahmed Al-Marri, for discussions on areas of rig security and safety, both onshore and offshore. They will pull something together with areas of specialisation that could form a basis for a discussion seminar within the next two to three weeks.

With that proposed I can maintain regular contact with Ahmed, and see if I can spot any connections to the Pakistanis, above and beyond what our taps may throw up.'

The Deputy nodded,

'Keep me up to speed Harry, day or night, if need be.'

Sunday 19th February 2006 1745hrs London Heathrow Airport

The BA flight was only a few minutes late touching down and Fayez was quickly through Immigration on his Dutch passport, although his suitcase took considerably longer to make its way to the Arrival Hall.

He was staying at the Holiday Inn, Brentford Lock, 600yds from the Great West Road, giving easy access to the airport, and also convenient for his meetings and contacts who lived and worked in Hounslow, West London.

He texted the Pakistanis that he had arrived, and also sent a separate one to Ahmed. He suggested that they all should meet at about 1030hrs the next day, Monday. Location was understood and not mentioned in the text.

***

XI

Monday 20th February 2006

1030hrs Factory Hounslow West London

Tariq and Atif sat in their small office waiting for Ahmed and Fayez.

They were both quite nervous. They had known Ahmed for some time but Fayez was an unknown quantity. They had no real background information of him*, other than the scarce details that Ahmed had provided.

Ahmed arrived within five minutes, but Fayez was late by a good fifteen minutes. Quite deliberately so; he wished to make an entrance and establish his seniority and authority from the outset.

Fayez entered the factory at 1050hrs with greetings and introductions being quickly dealt with.

He took charge of the meeting, telling Ahmed that now introductions had been effected he could go.

Ahmed was not particularly happy in being dealt with in this way, but understood the protocol and the need for limited information.

Ahmed left, returning to Central London.

Fayez turned to Tariq and Atif,

'My brothers, we are going to strike at the very heart of the Kuffar.

I cannot give you all details today, but we will discuss what I require and what will be happening over the next four weeks.

You heard from Ahmed what I wanted, yes? I want maps of Central London showing the water mains drainage and sewers. You have them, or can get them quickly?'

They both nodded in agreement.

'Then I want contact with one of our brothers in the Water Company. Do you have one?'

Atif and Tariq looked at each other,

'Yes', Atif replied. 'He is one of us. A true believer who wants revenge for what the Kuffar are doing against

Islam around the world. I also have the physics engineer you want for the delivery. He is a true Jihadist.'

'Good. The delivery will take place next Monday or Tuesday. Is everything ready for its arrival?'

'Yes', they replied.

*[It should be understood that with networks like these populated by people such as Fayez, then the basic rule is to keep confidentiality by 'the need to know' premise. By keeping such information tightly compartmentalised if one link of the chain is broken it does not affect every other one. The big picture is broken down into small individual bites, deliberately limiting and preventing connectivity.]

At this point Tariq said the delivery must be made before or after working hours, in order that their small number of staff were not aware of what was being done.

Fayez agreed to organise the delivery in this way or perhaps to arrange delivery for Sunday, the 26th February.

He then said that In future any reference to the project would be by its name, 'Sabah', meaning 'Morning'.

Tariq then told him he had the maps, so they were rolled out on the desk for Fayez to study.

Knowing his target Fayez quickly identified the options available to him.

There were two.

One option was too close to the target, the other appeared more suitable although it was the oldest, and therefore, perhaps, more prone to damage.

However, with what was planned, it was the most appropriate option and would serve the cause.

He asked Atif to arrange a meeting for Tuesday, after 5pm, with the water engineer, not at the factory, but in a convenient store car park locally.

A separate meeting was to be organised with the physics engineer for Wednesday at the same time, 5pm, but at a different location.

Fayez then lectured them to keep completely confidential anything he said, or what they saw.

He described what they were planning as a huge blow against the decadent and venal West who were attacking and killing Muslims indiscriminately in their so called fight against terrorists. In fact it was a war of the West against all Muslims. They had to fight back to defend themselves.

Atif was impressed with the passion and words used by Fayez, but Tariq was a little more sceptical.

He knew money, big money, was involved in these sorts of operations. Fayez was not doing it just for his faith. A handsome return would be the result if the operation was successful.

Fayez did make one comment that focussed their attention and mind.

He said that because it was a Holy War, extreme measures need to be taken from time to time.

He said that because of an irresponsible challenge to him on a previous operation he had had to shoot the challenger. If a similar situation arose he would do the same again. Had he made himself quite clear?

Tariq looked at Atif before replying.

'I would hope it would never come to that, my brother. We are with you in this fight. You may count on us for total support on this mission.'

Fayez thanked them for their apparent loyalty and said he would now return to his hotel until the meeting scheduled for the Tuesday. He would return to the factory after 5.30 pm to avoid contact with their employees.

After he had left Tariq questioned Atif as to his views on Fayez.

Atif was younger than Tariq and was generally more committed.

Atif spoke passionately about his faith and what he wanted to achieve in his own small way in the global Jihad.

Tariq nodded and apparently agreed. This was not the time for argument or dissension.

He felt that if they were successful and received the money promised, then that plus his small house and savings would be enough for him and his family to retire to Pakistan, sooner rather than later.

They carried on a general conversation discussing arrangements to be made, locations to be decided for meetings, the delivery the following week; and all the time the highly sensitive ODM was passing their commentary down the line to the Security Service and the SIS(MI6).

1400hrs SIS(MI6) Vauxhall Cross London

In a room close to C10, Jane had been logging the recordings coming down the line from the Security Service.

Because of the technical link up between BT, the Security Service and SIS(MI6), there was a time lag in reception, so conversation recording was not in real time. It was normally about 10-15 minutes after the event.

In addition to the delay, it was also necessary to get translation of Urdu and lingua franca.

Harry had been chasing Jane for some up to date reports of the discussions taking place at the factory. Working quickly with the translator she had been able to prepare some abridged versions for Harry's meeting with Tom, scheduled for 1515hrs.

Translation is difficult when 'slang' or 'patois' is used and quite different interpretations can be applied to the same words. Confusion can therefore arise, and specialist regional interpreters are vital in providing clarification in such situations.

1515hrs Room C10 SIS(MI6) London

Harry ran his eye down the abridged report. Some editing had been done but the main points were there for all to see and query.

What had been said in the factory raised more questions than answers.

Harry asked Tom,

'Do we have anybody on the ground to see who's coming and going?'

'Not at present. After we had tailed Ahmed back to his hotel, we thought it best to keep a low profile until things firmed up a bit. I think we're there now. Don't you?'

'Yes. Agreed. Get two on the ground tomorrow. We need to start following, besides listening.

Now can we make sense from what we've heard so far as to what they're up to?

Let me summarise.

Ahmed came and went. Brief visit. Possibly only for intro.

The new boy Fayez. What do we know about him? Damn all. Let's start some digging now, background, history etc. I'm interested in his veiled threat connected to his previous shooting.

Why his interest in water mains and sewers?

Why do they need a water engineer?

What are they expecting next week? What are they going to make?

Why do they need a Physics Engineer?

We've all heard the Jihad propaganda before. They clearly want to make a big splash (excuse the pun!) with what they're planning.

AND finally, I have no doubt they're serious.'

'I'd better start digging straight away', Tom replied. 'Plus, I'll organise the two man team for surveillance tomorrow.'

'OK Tom, I'll start making a list of possible targets in the water main system. Probably need to call in an expert. Then I'll keep the boss in the loop.'

The two men got on with their immediate tasks, Harry hating this stage in any operation when one was fumbling in the dark, desperate for hard facts. The hard facts always did arrive, but not always at a time of your choosing. That's when things can go horribly wrong.

If one had to fight, even with odds stacked against you, it was always preferable for it to be on a field, and at a time, of your choosing.

1630hrs Hilton Hotel Hyde Park Corner London

Ahmed was seated near the window looking across the expanse of Hyde Park.

He had completed the introduction that morning between Fayez and the Pakistanis, but was a little disappointed that he had not been included in the discussions.

He was well aware of security protocols within their international group, but felt he could have provided additional assistance and intelligence, bearing in mind his on going connection with Harry Baxter.

Another point played on his mind. Fayez himself.

He was aware of some of Fayez's background and activity, but he was not an admirer of his style which was highly autocratic. This, in itself could create problems and areas of weakness, due to his usual inflexible, one solution, response to most things.

Additionally, he had a natural suspicion of his real reasons for his position in the Jihad. Significant funding was extended from the Committee to fund such activities, and it was understood that the senior organisers would be paid well for their planning, implementation, and risks involved.

However, Ahmed was concerned that Fayez was perhaps more interested in the monetary return than the war against the West.

He would do nothing at present but would certainly keep Fayez and the operation under close review.

His mobile rang.

It was Harry advising that the Embassy should receive an invitation from the Department of Trade and Industry within the next few days concerning the proposed meeting on rig safety and security.

Ahmed thanked him for his message and promised to respond quickly once the invitation had been received.

Tuesday 21st February 2006 0630hrs Harry's apartment
Clapham

Harry woke with a start from a confused dream, thinking
to himself that reality wasn't that very different, bearing
in mind the current situation.

He needed to up the game from their side and would
require further resource and assistance from the Security
Service (MI5) in order to cover different locations and
individuals currently outside their remit.

He entered his office, C10, at about 0800hrs and drew up
a Sitrep for the Deputy including the additional resource
required. It would require the Deputy's sign off before
approaching his counterpart in the Security Service
(MI5).

Tom arrived at about 0845hrs and Harry suggested they
formulate an action plan on the assumption of the
Deputy's agreement.

Meanwhile Tom agreed to brief two surveillance teams in
order that they were ready to move, once clearance had
been given.

The Deputy called Harry and said,

'You have clearance, go! Keep me posted. Watch you
back, in both directions!'

Harry rang his oppo in the Security Service (MI5) to
crank up the joint operation, and to provide two more
surveillance teams in addition to his own.

His opposite number already had one team on the op, so
briefing and getting up to speed would be comparatively
easy. He agreed to coordinate the surveillance under
Harry's control, unusual, because that would normally be
his responsibility on UK soil, but deferred to Harry due to
the foreign overseas elements involved.

Harry decided that Tom should accompany one of the
surveillance teams and report directly to him as events
occurred. He imagined that at some point in the near
future the pace could quicken quite dramatically, and he
would need to have current status as it happened.

1100hrs Factory Hounslow West London

Tariq and Atif sat in their office talking about organising the meeting at 5pm for Fayez with the water engineer.

They had decided they would meet in the Ivybridge Retail Park on Twickenham Rd, Isleworth about 2 miles from their factory. It was a large retail park with all the usual outlets, parking being no problem, and an ideal place for such a meeting.

Tariq called the water engineer, Tahir Hosni, on his mobile number giving him the location and time. All this information was picked up by both the tap and hifone.

Atif used his mobile to call the physicist, Saif Jarwar, and suggested the meeting for Wednesday should be held in the Staples Corner Retail Park, on the North Circular Road, which he knew would be convenient for the engineer.

This time only the ODM picked up the message.

1200hrs Room C10 SIS(MI6) London

Harry and Tom were reading the latest transcripts from the tap and ODM, and planning how the surveillance would be carried out that afternoon.

They knew Fayez was initially going to the factory, and would then go with Atif and Tariq to the meeting in the retail park.

There would be no chance to overhear what was discussed, but infrared photos would be possible, which after finessing, would enable identification of the water engineer, Tahir, and Fayez.

The same plan would be adopted for the following day with teams following both Tahir and Saif to determine where they lived. This in turn could provide more background intelligence.

The two surveillance teams would be deployed on motorcycles, these being much more flexible in following cars, particularly in London traffic.

Harry briefed Tom thoroughly on what results he wanted from the operation that afternoon and asked for an update as soon as it was finished. If it included further tailing of targets, then so be it. Just ensure maximum Intel was obtained on all participants, location, actions, photographs, contacts, etc.

1715hrs Factory Hounslow West London

Fayez entered the factory just after the last employee had left, and joined Tariq and Atif in their office.
'Everything is arranged?'
'Yes, we can leave in about 10 minutes; the meeting place is only a short distance away.'
After short conversation concerning the water engineer, Tahir, they left in Tariq's plain white Ford Transit van to go to the retail park on Twickenham Road.
Fayez had the maps and drawings with him of London water mains and sewers which he wanted to discuss with the engineer, and also determine points of access into the system.
The Ford Transit swung into the retail park and drove slowly round the perimeter. As they approached a solitary parked car its lights flashed and they drew up alongside.
The driver of the car, Tahir, left his vehicle, and entered the side door of the van, joining the three now sitting in the back.
Greetings were exchanged and introductions made.
Fayez spoke first.
'Do you realise, my brother, the fight we are taking to the Kuffar, the unbelievers? This action is a Jihad to which we are committed. Are you?'
'Yes, my brother, Allahu Akbar.'
'Allahu Akbar,' they all replied.
Then Fayez unrolled his maps and drawings and started to question Tahir on his knowledge of the networks.
He wanted to know which were the easiest to gain entry, to and how that could be done.

Did Tahir have access to company trucks and equipment and would they be able to use them on this mission?

Did he have access to and could he operate a self propelled pipeline crawler pig?

Bearing in mind the size of the overall 'package' could they gain entry of a size to accommodate it?

The discussions were long and detailed with Fayez and Atif taking notes, until Tariq noticed they were one of the last vehicles in the retail park.

Tahir got down from the van to go to his car, as did Fayez in order to take his seat in the front of the Ford.

What they did not notice was a dark clad figure on the far side of the car park holding a telescopic lens infrared camera taking shots of them during this time.

The van and the car went their separate ways as two motorcycles, one with a pillion passenger, quietly started and maintained station about 100yards behind each vehicle.

Tariq drove to a nearby station where Fayez picked up a cab to take him in to London, and where Atif left to take the Underground home. Tariq drove home, tailed at a respectful distance by the motorcycle, which left after seeing him enter his house.

Tahir was followed to his home, just off the Chertsey Road, where the address was noted, and the surveillance team returned to base.

Both teams quickly engaged the technical staff in blowing up and increasing definition of the infra red shots which would accompany the report to Harry.

Tom spoke briefly to Harry advising what had happened, and that there would be a detailed report plus infrared shots.

In the meantime they were starting to run more detailed background checks on Tariq, Atif, Tahir and Saif, and now Fayez.

Harry agreed with Tom as to further checks, and thought to himself that he would follow through with Mossad tomorrow to see if their database could throw up any background, connections, previous activity etc, with the five targets. They agreed an early meeting for the next day at 0800hrs.

Wednesday 22nd February 2006 0745hrs Room C10 SIS(MI6) London

The infrared shots had been put on Harry's desk overnight and he was studying them as Tom came into the room.

'Not bad at all, the 'touch up' boys have done a good job considering the distance, time etc.

Quite a few from different angles, as they moved from one vehicle to the other.

At least we know now what some of them look like!

Can you see how the various checks are going? I want anything and everything, houses, business, UK born or not, Immigration status, company activities, accounts, political party membership, any known radical group connections. Everything over the last 3-5 years. You know the drill; everything from collar size to inside leg measurement!'

Tom left to pull in Jane on the exercise, and to get the IT boys cracking on sifting through their billions of terabytes of data, working in partnership with GCHQ.

Harry read the report. Not much detail at this stage, but at last they had some hard targets to work on.

1100hrs Factory Hounslow West London

Atif and Tariq were discussing quietly the contents of the meeting the previous night with Tahir.

'Do you think that Tahir can provide all that Fayez requires?' asked Atif.

'I think so. But, providing what Fayez wants, and gaining entry to where he wants to go, are two totally different things.

Do you think your physicist can do what Fayez wants?'

'He has indicated his type and level of work in this area. He was educated at one of the top universities in Pakistan and is supposed to one of the best men in this field. Fayez can question him this evening.'

They speculated further on what Fayez would require, and also that the 'package' delivery could be organised after factory hours so as to avoid any suspicion from their work force.

All this information was being transmitted down the tapped BT lines to London SIS(MI6) and MI5 bases, where translators worked as quickly as possible to prepare transcripts of the conversations. Voice recognition software was helping, but this could not provide the nuance of actual conversation.

1500hrs Room C10 SIS(MI6) London

Harry called Anna on her mobile and excused himself for next few days, saying this was due to an exceptionally heavy workload and some travel. He said he would call before the end of the week and hoped they could meet up on the Saturday.

He called in Tom to confirm the same M.O. for that night and that a bug had been fixed to the Ford Transit. [This had been done by 'Traffic Police' supposedly checking car tax discs in the industrial estate; one inspecting the vehicle (and placing the bug), the other confirming registration details with the company.]

He observed to Tom that Ahmed did not appear to have any involvement with the Pakistanis and Fayez since the first meeting. Events apparently being controlled by Fayez alone.

Tom left to join the surveillance team and Harry asked for an update as soon as the op was finished, whenever that would be.

1720hrs Factory Hounslow West London

Fayez arrived and the three of them left almost immediately in the Ford Transit to go to Staples Corner Retail Park to meet the physicist, Saif.

The surveillance teams kept station at a discrete distance behind the van assisted by the bug, which gave a GPS position, in addition to its listening capability.

Just after 1810hrs the Transit turned into the retail park and travelled slowly around the perimeter looking for a place to park. Having picked a slot in the NW corner they waited for Saif who had been give the van registration number by Atif.

A gentle tap on the door window indicated his arrival and the four of them sat in the rear of the van for their discussions. Tariq was deputed to keep an eye on the car park, and advise if any vehicles came and parked too close for their comfort.

Atif introduced Saif to Fayez who looked sternly at a slim, sallow, unprepossessing individual, who sat, looking somewhat shifty, between Atif and Fayez.

Fayez spoke in a similar vein to the previous night, but this time adopted a more aggressive tone.

Saif sat listening, his eyes flickering around the group, his nervous disposition plainly evident to all.

Suddenly Fayez changed tack,

'Do you have experience in handling Caesium-137?'

'Yes, but limited. And only under proper shielded conditions.'

'In our Jihad against the infidels we are having to adopt drastic measures.

In this particular situation we need to construct, as the Kuffar call it, an Improvised Nuclear Device (IND).'

He paused.

'Can you design it and construct it, so it can be detonated by a delayed timer?

Only say yes if you can, not if you think you can. Do you understand me?'

 Saif thought briefly before responding.

'Yes I can, but only if the things I say are necessary to build it are provided for me. There is no cheap route to prepare such a package, and proper radiation protection is vital in the construction. I have no wish to die from radiation poisoning.'

Atif and Tariq looked at each other, suddenly conscious of their own involvement in something that was clearly dangerous for them, as well as the designated targets.

Fayez looking steadily at Saif,

'No Jihad, my brother, is without danger. Think of the blow you will be striking in the name of Allah. Whether now or at some other time, we, as his soldiers, will be in paradise.'

Saif raised his hands, almost as in prayer, and nodded in agreement.

'May I speak to you alone concerning my fee? That is equally important to me,' he said smiling bitterly, 'and my family.'

He exited the van followed by Fayez and stood near the rear door.

Whilst they held their brief discussion infrared photos were being taken from across the car park by one of the surveillance teams, the other preparing to monitor Saif's car when he left.

Fayez and Saif shook hands to agree the payment terms before entering the Transit again.

Atif and Tariq explained that any work to be carried out in the factory would have to be at night, starting after 1800hrs and finishing by 0600hrs, to avoid any problems with their work force.

It was agreed that Saif would come to the factory the following week, probably Tuesday, this to be confirmed by Atif.

Saif left to return to his car and drive home, the second surveillance team noting his car registration number and home address, his house being located less than a mile from Staples Corner.

Atif and Tariq dropped Fayez at a cab rank near Staples Corner at about 200hrs and drove back to the factory, both quiet, but deep in thought.

A number of thoughts were whirling around Tariq's head; one in particular concerning personal safety kept cropping up, linked to his pathological abhorrence and inability to suffer any sort of pain.

He was becoming increasingly unhappy with what he and Atif were involved in. He knew Atif was an idealist, swept up in the Jihadist cause. He was only interested in what this venture could bring. Retirement back in Pakistan.

The situation, and what was likely to happen over the next few weeks, would require some very careful managing. No slip ups.

Tariq hoped that Atif would be equally concerned about the managing and supervision of what could be very dangerous. He had no wish to enter Paradise at an early date!

Once at the factory they went their separate ways, the surveillance team returning to base.

2030hrs Room C10 SIS(MI6) London

Harry was updating himself on the previous day's reports when he received a mobile call from Tom.

'Some great shots tonight of both of them. Thought I would let you know. Something to look forward to in the morning once the enhancement has been completed,'

'Well done. Have we started an Intel trace on Fayez back through his hotel details and then Immigration at London Heathrow?'

'Yes, Jane has got most of that. Should be available tomorrow. From what I hear, not a lot of hard facts. We may have to ask some of our friends if they have anything more solid.'

'Fine, Tom, see you tomorrow.'

Thursday 23rd February 2006 0945hrs Hilton Hotel Hyde Park London

Ahmed telephoned Atif.

'Is everything going well?' he asked cautiously.

'We think so, but there are some technical problems that will need to be sorted out. We will know more next week after the delivery has been made.'

'Is Tariq happy with the way things are going?'

'Yes, but he is concerned about the problems I have mentioned.'

Well my brother, in such a fight there will always be some danger. God is great. He will protect you.'

Finishing the conversation Ahmed wondered how Fayez was handling their concerns, and what would eventuate after the delivery the following week.

He then telephoned the embassy and was advised that the invitation had arrived from the Department of Trade and Industry, suggesting two alternative dates in the week commencing Monday, the 6th March 2006; the first, Tuesday the 7th, and the second, Thursday the 9th.

1015hrs Room C10 SIS(MI6) London

Tom was explaining to Harry who the two people were in the enhanced infrared photos when the telephone rang.

It was Ahmed coming through the general switchboard number Harry had given him.

Harry lifted his hand to indicate silence.

'Morning Ahmed.'

'Good morning Harry. I have received the invitation for the suggested meeting. I see two dates are offered. Thursday the 9th would be best for me. Is that convenient for you?'

'Absolutely fine for me, Ahmed. Shall we say 1000hrs at the Ministry?'

'That would be good for me. Thank you Harry. If not before, see you then.'

Harry filled in Tom on the conversation and said they would have to work with a couple of Department of Trade officials to put together some sort of agenda.

Harry was delighted that they now had some good photo ID of most of the players, and looked forward to further background on all of them, once the trawl had been completed through their own and GCHQ databases.

Dependent on their own results they may then spread the net with some of their close intelligence community friends to see what additional Intel could be contributed.

Harry then telephoned the Deputy to keep him up to date, whilst Tom left to put some time pressures on the Intel gathering, if at all possible.

Harry decided he would get Tom to have an 'off the record' discussion with David Hadar at the Israeli Embassy to see if they could shed any light on Fayez Al-Hourani. Background, activities, anything.

He contacted Tom, told him what he wanted, and asked him to action soonest.

Tom immediately telephoned David on his mobile number, stressing that it was important they had an early meeting. It was agreed they would meet in Kensington, that afternoon, at about 1730hrs.

1200hrs Holiday Inn Great West Road London

Fayez had just received an update on the package delivery which told him everything was on track, and the scheduled arrival in Hounslow would be Monday, the 27th February.

He gave instructions for the delivery to be scheduled for 1830hrs Monday. Not earlier.

He had deliberated on the two recent meetings and felt satisfied that they could both carry out their required functions; the main concerns would be one of credibility gaining access to the water main/sewer, and the technical competence in manufacture and delivery of the IND to its destination.

Fayez was satisfied with his commercial negotiations with all parties; he had driven down the price requested without exception, the additional margin being deposited in his overseas account.

After this operation and with his enhanced reputation he would consider living in Lebanon, just outside Beirut, close enough to civilisation, but also with easy contact to Hezbollah.

1730hrs Kensington London

Tom and David met in the arcade that runs down to the Underground in High Street Kensington, and moved into a coffee shop for their discussion.

Sitting over a cup of coffee Tom outlined to David what they wanted in terms of some solid Intel on Fayez Al-Hourani.

Were any of the Mossad stations able to give any background or detail on him that would assist in building up some sort of a profile that was non-existent at present?

David countered this request with his own, one in terms of an update, and also what was happening currently.

Tom had to remain fairly guarded, but was able to indicate that the situation had moved up a couple of notches, and was certainly at Amber.

David said that he would report to his Control and see what could be found and released under their agreed understanding. What he didn't say was that he was sure Control would escalate their own Sitrep, and react accordingly.

Tom thanked him and asked that he revert soonest, which he promised to do.

1930hrs Near Harry's Flat Clapham London

Harry had received a call at about 1830hrs on his mobile from the Deputy advising that contact may be made by the French. He had given Harry no further information, just to expect contact.

As he was walking alongside Clapham Common, immersed in his own thoughts, on the way to his flat, he was gently tapped on the shoulder.

He turned, to be greeted by a man who smiled and said,
Bonjour Monsieur, Alain Dubois. You remember? We met in Abu Dhabi! Only on that occasion we were both jogging!'

Harry did recognise him, and replied,

'Yes I do. But what the hell are you doing here? I thought my boss had spoken to your boss?'

'Indeed he has, and quite recently I believe. I think I can help you with your particular current problem.

I know quite a lot about one of the players which could be of assistance to you. Why don't we have a short conversation over a drink? Neither of us can cause a problem doing that, I think?

Harry agreed to that, albeit reluctantly, a little miffed that the French were still sticking their oar in. However their fields of operation and spheres of interest often overlapped, so hardly surprising. Anyway it might prove useful.

They entered a pub on the East side of the Common, the Frenchman buying the drinks, and made their way to a quiet corner at the back of the Lounge Bar.

The Frenchman opened the discussion,

'We have often come across Fayez Al-Hourani who has been involved in a number of operations that took our interest.

Although he puts himself forward as a Jihadist his sole interest is money.

You will not find him risking his own life! Paradise can wait!

We know he is in London on an operation, which is obviously your interest. We also know that it is being funded from Hezbollah. Details to us are not clear, but perhaps you have more information?

It was felt that our information may help you. As you say, $2 + 2$ might make 5!'

Harry was curious as to why the French were involved at all, but took a pragmatic view that the Deputy thought the cooperation was worth it.

'Alain, you're right. We do have a keen interest in Fayez. We have partial Intel on a planned attack, exact location and timing, as yet, not known.

I'm happy to share some Intel with you but I don't want you under our feet when the action starts. Is that clear?

'Absolument, my friend.'

'Fine, let's trade. You first,' Harry said, smiling.

The information provided by Alain, added to what Harry knew, started to build into a reasonable profile of Fayez, his previous operational style, motivation and obvious pathological traits.

Harry, in turn, then gave a guarded and précis version of where they were at present, but without location, timings, etc.

He wanted to discuss this new intervention with the Deputy before taking it any further.

They parted around 2100hrs, Alain having given Harry his mobile number, if he wished to make contact.

Harry indicated he would, subject to sign off from his boss.

He made his way home thinking of the plusses and minuses of having the French in the mix!

Friday 24th February 2006 0900hrs Room C10 SIS(MI6) London

Harry gave Tom an abbreviated update on the meeting with Alain Dubois the previous evening, and told him he was seeing the Deputy at 1000hrs to get clarification and sign off before proceeding any further down that particular road.

He did, however, give Alain credit for filling in a lot of the background on Fayez, so a clearer picture was emerging of his motivation, method of operation, and organisation funding.

Tom would then be able to add to their database all the additional factors concerning Fayez once Harry completed his report.

He also updated Harry on the most recent taps and expectation of the delivery to the factory on Monday at 1830hrs.

1000hrs Deputy's Office SIS(MI6) London

Harry looked quizzically at his chief as he entered the office.

The Deputy smiled,
'Sit down Harry. I will explain.
I met my old contact at DGSE yesterday and had quite an interesting conversation; hence my very brief call to you late yesterday.
I believe your old jogging 'friend' from Abu Dhabi was going to contact you. Did he?'
'Yes he did. On Clapham Common, as I was walking home.'
'Good. Did he provide some useful Intel?'
'Yes, which I have passed on verbally to Tom this morning, prior to seeing you.
Could you explain where we are going with this and where our French friends fit in?'
'My thinking, Harry, is this.
We could well have a Category 1 incident very soon, with potential loss of life, and we have not yet been able to get a real grip on the status until very recently.
Our French friends appear to have more detail than us concerning two of the major players.
Let's use them in any way we can that will enable us to respond more quickly, and deal with any potential incident before it happens.
Additionally, and I am sure you are aware of this; their modus operandi may be slightly more flexible, and less conventional than our own. They do not appear to have the same public strictures that contain us within our relationship with our political masters.'
Harry nodded. He could see which way this was going.

If the French were involved due to the shared overseas connection and something went wrong, then blame could be shifted from the department to DGSE.

Political 'Damage Limitation' was the name of the game.

If, however, everything was successful then shared credit would be the order of the day.

The Deputy and Harry discussed a number of scenarios, mostly hypothetical, drawing on the Intel to date, and possible outcomes.

Harry returned to his office to finish his report covering the previous evening and to telephone Alain Dubois to arrange a meeting for Monday, the 27th February at 1400hrs in Chiswick.

1430hrs Ministers Office Whitehall

The Minister was not in a good mood.

He had spent an unfortunate morning at Cabinet where colleagues had been less than supportive to his proposals; in fact some adopting the pained look of tolerance normally only extended to less than average intelligent teenagers.

'Condescending bastards,' he muttered to himself as he entered his office.

He called in Anna to organise the few papers that were left over from his red box and to arrange his diary for the following week.

He had received no further reports concerning her from his tame ferret, Archie Powell, other Department personnel information not being of real interest.

The atmosphere between them was somewhat strained, but kept just on the side of civil, from his side. He was clearly not wishing to jeopardise the day to day operations of his office, and perhaps drive her into an early resignation, which could be severely damaging in the short term.

He was travelling to his North East constituency this weekend for his local 'surgery', and would be on parade with his wife at a local Party dinner at which he would be speaking. Neither event was guaranteed to improve his demeanour.

The Minister left at 1515 hours in his official car to go to Kings Cross station, his train for Newcastle leaving at 1600hrs.

Anna finished her paperwork by 1700hrs and joined the group of early leavers from the Department.

As she walked down Whitehall towards Westminster Underground station her mobile rang with a text from Harry, asking if it was possible to meet up on Saturday, that he would telephone her later, and that he hoped the answer would be Yes!

She smiled whilst reading the text, and then replied by saying she was looking forward to his call later, but was not sure what her response would be!

1930hrs Room C10 SIS(MI6) London

Harry had been discussing with Tom the planned surveillance for next Monday at Hounslow and the need for some close quarter observation.

They looked at the factory location, the proximity of unoccupied adjacent buildings, and any cover or observation points they might provide.

Would it be possible to rig up very small high definition CCTV over the weekend which could cover the factory approaches?

Could they access the factory from the rear to achieve similar observation internally?

They had micro cameras, similar to medical versions that are put down patients throats, which can be positioned high up in a factory giving a wide angle view of activity.

A team had been briefed to carry out such an installation, if physically possible, over the weekend so Harry and Tom would be able to see the results first thing Monday morning.

Tom left for the weekend and Harry left his office at 1945hrs, calling Anna as he made his way home.

Their conversation was brief but a happy one, as Anna, with mock reluctance, agreed to meet Harry at 1930hrs on the Saturday.

Harry would pick her up at her apartment; they would go to one of the major cinemas in Leicester Square, followed by a Chinese meal in Gerrard Street.

Saturday & Sunday 25th & 26th February 2006

The installation team had been completely successful over Friday, Saturday and Sunday nights in penetrating the factory and installing the micro CCTV.

In addition the factory approach was also covered with a direct and a side-on camera located on an adjacent building.

Controls, including zoom facility, would be available adjacent to Room C10.

****

XII

Monday 27th February 2006

0900hrs Room C10 SIS(MI6) London

Details were being hammered out concerning the two surveillance teams for Monday evening.

It would be vital for all personnel to be in position no later than 1600hrs in case any variations were suddenly called on the delivery schedule.

Intercepts on the taps and ODM were continuing, providing a steady stream of commentary for analysis.

GCHQ had been able to contribute in terms of intercepts. It had collected a number of text communications from inbound UK traffic, and assembled a summary* that gave clear evidence of the passage of Caesium-137 from Kiev to London. All the texts had been received by an unidentified foreign mobile phone that they were attempting to track, and locate, by intersections of signals from mobile phone base stations. The obvious assumption was that it was Fayez Al-Hourani. They were confident this would be confirmed in the next 12 hours.

- -
- - - - - - - - - - - - - - - -

 Elements of information and data have been heavily redacted and a summary report of events inserted.

Monday 13th February 2006 – Monday 27th February 2006

Movement of Caesium-137.

13.02.06. Transportation of product from Kiev to Belarus proceeded   satisfactorily   and   to schedule.xxxxxxxxxxxxxxxxxx No holdups at border post.xxxxxxxxxxxxxxxxx

14/15.02.06. Uneventful passage through Belarus. Problem at border with Latvia. Border Guard indicating incorrect manifest. xxxxxxxxxxxxxxxx Manifest correct.xxxxxxxxxxxxxxxx Matter resolved by payment of 'border' commission/fee.xxxxxxxxxxxxxxxxxxxxxxxxxxxxxxxxxx

Riga required 'Entry' fee and further fees to obtain loading asSIS(MI6)tance.xxxxxxxxxxxxxxxxxxxxx

16.02.06. Loading onto cargo ship completed. Drivers and vehicle commenced return journey.

Friday 17th February 2006 – Sunday 19th February 2006

Cargo Ship left Riga and proceeded westwards, passing Denmark and Sweden until laying up off shore Holland, distance 6 miles, whilst transferring packages to Irish registered fishing boat on the 19th.xxxxxxxxxxxxxxxx. Transfer completed.

Sunday 19th February 2006 – Thursday 23rd February 2006

Irish registered fishing boat sails from offshore Holland, down the Channel, around Lands End, and up the west coast of England and Wales to the west coast of Scotland, namely Stranraer.xxxxxxxxxxxxxxxxxxxxxxxxxxxxxxxxxx. There is a regular Belfast/Stranraer ferry service and a number of fishing boats based there, so no problems for unloading onto transport destined for London.

Thursday 23rd February and Friday 24th February 2006

Transportation to London and delivery to warehouse in Kilburn.xxxxxxxxxxx. Delivery from Kilburn to Hounslow warehouse on Monday 27th February 2006.

END

Tom would be responsible for infrared photos, riding as passenger on one motorbike, the other a roving brief, dependent on what happened at delivery.

Harry had checked the installed CCTV and was surprised to discover the separate assembly room at the back of the factory cut off from the main area.

The installation team had located one wide angle micro camera high up on the rear wall of the factory, this now showing clearly the separate enclosed area.

1100hrs Factory Hounslow West London

Atif and Tariq were careful to ensure that there would be no overtime working on the Monday and made sure that any fabrications were placed to the side of the factory to ensure easy access to the rear that evening.

They gave as an excuse a planned visit by the Health & Safety Executive which could take place at any time, and that they wanted to give the best possible impression to the inspector.

They were both suffering from nerves, not being helped by Fayez arriving early at about 1500hrs, when he had previously advised he would be there post 1700hrs.

1400hrs Chiswick London

As the train made its way towards Chiswick, Harry had been thinking about the previous weekend.

He and Anna had enjoyed the film and dinner, and on this occasion gone back to his flat in Clapham.

They woke on the Sunday morning, quietly resting in each other's arms, relaxed, as only a contented and sated couple can be.

They breakfasted leisurely, which was followed by a walk on the Common, a late pub lunch, and then a reluctant parting.

A normal life could be catching, Harry thought, whilst wrapped in her own thoughts, Anna was thinking much the same.

The train ground to a halt, shaking Harry out of his reverie.

He exited Chiswick Park Underground Station and crossed the road heading towards the Sainsbury's Car Park.

He saw Alain Dubois standing next to a French registered Renault and walked over to him, shook his hand, and then joined him in the car.

'Alain, first things first.

We need to have some Intel pretty damn quick on one of the players. If you have it, have you clearance to pass it to me? If not can you get it?'

'Harry, tell me who the player is, and I will tell you if we have the Intel or not. If we have, then I am sure I can pass it to you.'

Ahmed Al-Marri, Qatari.'

Alain thought for a moment.

'I'm sure we have something on him, but Harry, we need to trade a little,' he said smiling.

'What do you mean?'

'We cannot give something for nothing!

Let's assume we have some Intel on the Qatari. I'm happy to share that with you, but he is probably just as interesting to us, as he is to you.

You and I have some mutual 'friends' in the same line of business as us, and who have helped both of us in a number of ways. They are interested in him too.

What would be sensible, and what my boss has suggested to your boss is that I should 'assist' you as a kind of backup.

Don't forget, we have a reputation for being very flexible when required!'

Harry thought for a brief moment.

'My boss mentioned something similar to me, and suggested some cooperation if you mentioned it.

Looks like it has received the Papal blessing from both sides of the Channel!

But I do want that Intel soonest. Agreed?'

'Agreed' Alain said, as he extended his hand which Harry shook.

'Final point.

What I would suggest is that you ignore me. Assume I'm your shadow following you around. Don't concern yourself in any way. Just remember I'll be close!'

Harry adopted mock surprise as he said,

'Well, it's amazing what comes out of a conversation I've never had!

I'll say goodbye then!'

With that he got out of the car and retraced his steps to the Underground station.

Harry liked Alain's style, and felt quite comfortable that he would have some ready backup if needed, albeit of the unconventional variety.

He returned to Vauxhall Cross to continue CCTV observation over the next few hours.

1815hrs Factory Hounslow West London

Fayez kept looking at his watch as the minutes ticked away.

At about 1830hrs his mobile buzzed, indicating a text, which advised arrival in about 20 minutes.

In Vauxhall Cross observers of the CCTV were wondering if the shipment had been delayed.

Surveillance teams were standing by in suitable vantage points close to the factory.

A nondescript ten ton truck made its way slowly down the road towards the factory before turning across the road and reversing up the slight incline towards the factory doors.

Tariq had observed the arrival from the small office window and went out to help the driver of the truck reversing into the factory.

Atif had been opening the sliding wall at the back of the factory, and positioning the mobile crane to lift and place the two packages.

Very carefully each box was lifted, and then placed on the left hand side of the available space.

As soon as this was completed, lights were extinguished, and the sliding wall closed.

The driver entered his cab and disappeared into the night, not aware of a tail following at a discrete distance. The vehicle returned to a street in Kilburn where the driver parked, and entered a small block of flats, the tail noting the address and vehicle registration which would provide some ownership details.

There was a feeling of disappointment at Vauxhall Cross as CCTV had not shown more, but at least they now knew delivery had been completed, and an opportunity now existed for further covert investigation.

Harry called up Tom to organise, if possible, a small two man crew to gain entry that night to determine, if possible, contents of both packages, and most importantly, leave no trace of entry and investigation.

Tuesday 28th February 2006 0900hrs Room C10 SIS(MI6) London

Tom was briefing Harry that it had not been possible for a crew to gain entry during the night and examine the packages.

Harry reluctantly accepted that the entry crews required more notice, plus preferably a reconnaissance and/or drawings of where they were going.

He turned their discussions in another direction.

'Tom, I've been thinking about two of the major players, namely Ahmed and Fayez.

I've been having discussions and meetings with Ahmed, so he thinks things are progressing satisfactorily between us.

Conversely, he has never met you.

What I intend is that I will maintain a continuing contact with him, i.e. this pending meeting with the department of Trade, and other areas of supposed cooperation, but that you will start a covert surveillance of him, covering all other times.

In the case of Fayez he has no knowledge of me, so I will start a similar cover of him.

In this way I hope that we can secure additional Intel which will help us overall.'

Do you agree?'

Tom could see the logic behind the suggestion so agreed that starting Wednesday the 1st March he would cover Ahmed during the 'after hours' period, as best he could.

Harry left his office to quickly brief the Deputy, whilst in Knightsbridge a meeting was shortly about to start in the French Embassy.

1045hrs French Embassy, Knightsbridge London

Philippe Roberge, Head of DGSE, London, called Alain Dubois into his office.

After exchanging the usual greetings and pouring coffee, Philippe was brought up to date by Alain following his recent meeting with Harry.

Alain explained that they had reached an accommodation of understanding and that he, Alain, would be acting as a sort of 'shadow' to Harry.

He outlined his reasoning that also contained a small political element that he knew would appeal to Philippe.

By adopting this somewhat unconventional approach, which effectively had the approval of both Philippe and the UK Deputy, then, if successful, the French would gain some kudos. If it was not successful, then it would stay under wraps. No loss to either party.

Philippe was happy to go along on that basis, but warned Alain not to be too enthusiastic or too unconventional, as there was still a high degree of risk in what and who was being tracked.

1400hrs Room C10 SIS(MI6) London

GCHQ had reported successful identification of the mobile telephone.

Yes, it was definitely Fayez, and triangulation had pinpointed its position to his hotel.

GPS surveillance, through his mobile, would now be applied to monitor his movements, this being of considerable assistance to Harry from now on, which would speed up tracking.

Recent reports indicated small amounts of information being picked up from the listening devices at the factory, the most relevant concerned the planned visit that evening by Saif, the physicist, at 1830hrs.

Tom planned to cover Ahmed that evening, and see if he was also going to the factory, so left to take up station at the Hilton.

Harry decided he would cover Fayez, to see if he was involved in the factory meeting, but decided to initially check on the CCTV to see what activity there was before going to Hounslow.

At about 1630hrs he changed his mind and left by car, carrying with him a laptop connected to the surveillance CCTV through SIS(MI6) Comms department.

He would therefore be able to park a little distance away from the factory, and observe, but near enough to get there in less than 5 minutes if so required.

1830hrs Factory Hounslow West London

A small van approached the factory driven by Saif. He flashed his lights and the main doors were opened to allow his entry.

The van proceeded slowly to the rear of the factory where the rear wall had been slid back revealing the separate fabrication area.

Saif got out, greeting Tariq and Atif, and requesting their help in unloading the van.

Opening the rear doors they saw the boxes of plastic explosive piled on top of each other.

Working together they moved the boxes to a convenient position adjacent to the two large packing cases, before retiring to the office, after closing the sliding partition.

A brief discussion followed, with Saif confirming he would be back at the weekend to start 'fabrication'.

A short distance away Harry had seen, through his laptop, linked to the CCTV, the arrival and departure of Saif, but no obvious sign of Fayez.

He was still around; they knew that, staying at the Holiday Inn. Obviously the paymaster, wanting to see everything in place before part, or full payment.

He would meet up with Tom the following morning and plan for continuous surveillance of Ahmed and Fayez.

Everybody needed to be up to speed as far as possible, and there were still some fairly large missing links in the chain.

Wednesday 1st March 2006

0900hrs Room C10 SIS(MI6) London

'Tom, can you get Jane and meet in my office, say, in 10 minutes?'

Harry had caught up with Tom as he exited the lift and made his way towards Room C10.

Tom nodded, and turned left down a corridor leading to Jane's office.

Harry spent the next few minutes marshalling his thoughts as to how he would present the current situation to both Tom and Jane, and whether he would give full disclosure concerning Alain Dubois.

Tom and Jane entered and sat down waiting for Harry to start.

'Right,' he said,

'Two things we do know. One, Fayez, Palestinian, is here in London at the Holiday Inn, near the Great West Rd, paymaster and organiser. Two, Ahmed, the Qatari, is clearly involved and is certainly not on our side, as he is working with Fayez and the Pakistanis.

We cannot move yet, we are not sure what is planned and with their usual, irrational thinking we don't want them turning anything into a suicide mission.

Ahmed knows me, that's why I want you to handle him Tom.

Fayez does not know me, that's why I'll handle him.

Tom, I want you to tail Ahmed, and keep him under surveillance as much as possible. You'll need a small team, ring the changes frequently. He's staying at the Hilton, Hyde Park Corner. Make sure he's tailed by motorcycle if he goes to the factory in Hounslow. Have a car observation point at the factory. We need to build the case.'

Tom agreed and said,

'If I focus on the factory, and the bike team on tailing, then effectively they would hand over to me once Ahmed arrives at the factory.'

'OK.'

Harry then went on,

'I'm personally going to put Fayez under immediate surveillance at his hotel and also when he goes to the factory, with assistance from a small team, similar to yours Tom.

If he's the paymaster, then when does he pay, and does this give us an indication of the timing of their operation?

Jane, notes of meeting for file, cc the Deputy, plus immediate request for two small surveillance teams as discussed. Understood?'

Jane nodded and rose to leave the room.

'One more thing, Jane. Get me details of Fayez's room at the hotel. Number and floor.'

She nodded again and left.

Harry turned to Tom.

'We need to get a firm angle on these two. Ahmed is very canny, and I would think the idealist, if he's prepared to play the sort of game he's been playing with me.

Fayez being the money man might be less of an idealist. If previous form is anything to go on, then the money men have always been skimming a fair amount off the top and bottom for their own personal pension fund!'

'Could be,' Tom responded, 'Right, I'll be away to organise my surveillance detail and report to you either daily or a 'priority' basis.'

'Good luck to us both then. Talk soon.'

Tom and Harry were then involved for much of the day in organising their respective teams, comms, shifts, which included elements from the Security Service (MI5).

It was planned that surveillance teams would start on Thursday, the 2nd of March, and Jane confirmed that a room could be booked for Harry, at the Holiday Inn, commencing Monday, the 6th March.

Thursday 2nd March 2006 1030hrs Holiday Inn Brentford Lock West London

Fayez telephoned Tariq from his hotel to arrange a meeting for later that day at the factory. 1830hrs was agreed.

At the same time he asked Tariq to telephone Ahmed and ask him to come to the factory the following day, Friday, at the same time, namely 1830hrs. If there was a problem Tariq should inform him.

Putting down the telephone Fayez was thinking of ways and means to reduce, if he could, the payment to Tariq and Atif.

His excuse would be that restrictions were being placed on him by the Committee, as overall levels of funding were down. He would have to be careful in this area as he did not know what Ahmed knew of the funding trail and levels of expenditure agreed.

He had already placed significant sums in overseas accounts, and he was looking to this operation to bolster those amounts.

With his reputation enhanced by a successful operation, and sufficient funds with which to buy some influence, he hoped that it would not be long before his position on the Committee was assured.

With that position achieved, and his experience in planning and funding operations, then it would be likely that he would have access to further funding, and therefore the opportunity of increasing his personal wealth.

1745hrs Holiday Inn Brentford Lock West London

Fayez took a taxi to the factory. One of the surveillance teams followed on motorbikes, and logged times of departure and arrival.

The other surveillance team was detailed to cover Ahmed who did not leave his hotel, the Hilton, Park Lane, all day.

One of the team, who knew which floor and room Ahmed occupied, realised in a brief recce, that Ahmed was 'entertaining' and would no doubt be indisposed for at least 18hours.

1830hrs Factory Hounslow West London

Tariq and Atif were waiting for Fayez when he arrived just after 1830hrs.

Atif took him to see what Saif would be doing with the various modules and components in the isolated fabrication area. He was told Saif would be working on both the next Saturday and Sunday nights.

It did not mean much to Fayez looking at a collection of metal objects, but the passion with which Atif spoke, and his simmering hatred of Western culture pleased him.

'A true Jihadist', he thought, 'who would probably give his life for the cause.'

Then, in a roundabout way, he raised the question of payment and the amount.

He fabricated the story of reduced funding, and was interested to see that a possible reduction did not affect Atif as much as is did Tariq, who became quite angry.

Fayez lied to him, hinting he might be able to persuade those that controlled the funds to honour the original commitment. He hoped so, but could not guarantee.

He thought he would let the idea sink in over 24hours before they all met the following day, Friday, on that occasion with Ahmed.

Friday 3rd March 2006 1000hrs Hilton Hotel Park Lane London

Ahmed woke up with a throbbing head as his telephone rang.

As he regained consciousness he started to regret his actions of the day and night before.

He had previously succumbed to temptation a few times, and as a devout Muslim, hated the way he had reacted to the two women, but consigned them to being 'sharmuta', which partially salved his conscience.

It was Tariq, calling to see if he could come to a meeting at the factory that evening, after 1830hrs, to meet with Fayez, himself and Atif.

Ahmed agreed truculently, then went to the bathroom to relieve himself, take a couple of Panadol, and returned to his bed, asking Reception to wake him at 1600hrs.

1200hrs SIS(MI6) London

Surveillance teams were already in position, with relief crews standing by, dependent on duration of operations.

Because of little activity at the factory, and hardly any movement by Ahmed or Fayez, Harry advised the Deputy that he would be away for the weekend in Sussex. He would be contactable at all times over the 48 hrs, therefore no more than 1½hrs from Vauxhall Cross, if required to return.

The Deputy did not question him at all, merely agreeing to his request.

1600hrs Hilton Hotel Park Lane London

Ahmed woke up when called by Reception, without his headache, but his senses numb, his stomach empty, and feeling morose.

He called Room Service to bring him some food and coffee while he showered and dressed, and left the hotel, feeling a little better, at about 1730hrs by cab.

1830hrs Factory Hounslow West London

Fayez was already there with Tariq and Atif when Ahmed arrived.

He acknowledged their greetings in an unfriendly way, doing little to hide his poor disposition.

Tariq took him to see what Saif would be working on over the weekend. Fayez neither knew nor cared. His only interest was hitting Western interests where it hurt, and drawing attention to the decadence of the West and the Holy War true Muslims and Jihadists were involved in.

They sat down with some coffee to discuss certain matters raised by Fayez and challenged by Tariq.

As far as Ahmed could determine, Fayez was trying to pay less to Tariq and Atif with what had previously been agreed. Naturally Tariq was challenging this.

Fayez went into a lengthy explanation of the reasons for the reduction, limited funds, need to reduce costs, cash payments made in transit of packages considerably higher than envisaged, a litany of excuses.

Ahmed listened, his temper aggravated by his poor stomach, just kept in control, as he realised that some of his previous suspicions concerning Fayez were well founded.

Tariq moaned again about the injustice of it while Ahmed sat silently for a few minutes before he spoke.

When he did his voice was low, but menacing.

'I've heard what you have said Fayez, and I will say one thing.

You are a liar.

I know what the details are for any operation, such as we are involved in now. Having agreed an original funding there is always a significant extra amount added to take care of the things you have referred to.

Fixed sums, such a Tariq and Atif here, should be no problem.

I suggest you go away and do your sums again, before we meet next week.

I do not intend to discuss this with you any further at this time.

Do you understand?'

At the end of his comments he stared glacially across at Fayez, before turning to Tariq, saying,

'Get me a taxi Tariq. We will discuss this matter again early next week.'

Tariq hastened away followed by Ahmed, as Fayez inwardly fumed and stared aggressively at Ahmed's departing back.

When Tariq returned Fayez was diplomacy itself, saying he could not accept what Ahmed had said, and would see what could be done to ensure they received full payment.

Tariq and Atif must leave it with him, and he would report back the following week.

Fayez also left by taxi, fuming inwardly at what Ahmed had said; but there was little he could do.

He would have to think carefully of his words and actions over the next few days.

Saturday 4th March 2006 1100hrs Southwark London

Harry picked up Anna from her apartment in his car and drove leisurely out of London on the A3, passing through Clapham, Balham, and eventually onto the Kingston Bypass, before turning off onto the A24, via the A243; ultimate destination Storrington.

They wanted a weekend away from London, no hassle, just some country air, walks, food and wine.

Harry knew of this small country hotel, sitting in its own grounds, recommended by his Sussex friends, who had entertained him at Christmas, and who had been the reason he had met Anna.

They were both tired and needed a break, away from their respective stressful situations.

Harry had been looking forward to this time away, he hoped Anna felt the same; she seemed to be relaxing by the hour as they drove through Surrey and Sussex.

They arrived just after 1pm and had a sandwich lunch in the bar; Harry's accompanied by a glass of the local beer, Anna's a glass of dry white wine, looking out over the hotel's manicured lawns and low hills in the distance.

They took a short walk in the grounds after lunch; it was chilly, but a weak winter sun took the edge off the temperature, making it very bearable.

When they came down to the dining room they found an apple log fire burning in the walk-in fireplace, the aroma adding the ambience of the oak beamed room.

They ate quietly and leisurely, enjoying each others company, with the local produce enhanced by some very pleasant wines.

They spoke about anything and everything, avoiding any reference to their work. For this short period they could ignore the usual external pressures.

1830hrs Factory Hounslow West London

Saif had arrived at the factory, being let in by Atif.

He went immediately to the fabrication area at the rear behind the sliding section and started work on the various components required for their operation.

It was fairly boring work so Atif soon lost interest and went back to the office to watch the small television he had brought in.

It would be a long night, Saif probably leaving at about 0400hrs.

A short distance up the road a man in a car had noted Saif's arrival.

2200hrs Country Hotel Sussex

After dinner Harry and Anna had moved through to the lounge where they had coffee and liqueurs, and held a short conversation with another couple who were also staying overnight.

At about 2230 hrs Harry looked enquiringly at Anna, who rose from her chair and they walked hand in hand up their bedroom on the first floor.

They entered their bedroom to find the bed covers turned back, subdued lighting from bedside lamps, a form with which to order room service breakfast for the Sunday morning, and finally, a rose and chocolates lay on the covers.

Harry laughed quietly.

'No, I didn't ask for all this. But it is quite nice, in an over-the-top type of way!'

Anna smiled back at him.

'Oh come on Harry, you know you're an old romantic at heart. Admit it! You requested this, but I will admit it's quite nice!'

Harry turned towards her, with mock seriousness,

'Damn! My cover is blown. I admit it, but do I, at least, get a hug?'

Anna moved towards him, smiling,

'Come here.'

They embraced, her arms around his neck, his arms around her waist.

Anna kissed him, gently at first, but then in a more intense way as Harry reacted to her.

They broke away from each other, Anna looking at Harry as she switched off one of the bedside lights, then gently guiding his hand to the zip at the back of her dress which he gently pulled down.

Sunday 5th March 2006 0400hrs Factory Hounslow West London

Saif left the factory and drove home reminding Atif he would return at 1830hrs that evening.

His departure was logged by the man in the car, about 200 yards from the factory.

0915hrs Country Hotel Nr Storrington Sussex

Harry was the first to stir, so he lay there, quietly watching Anna.

A short time later Anna opened one eye to see Harry watching her.

'How long have you been awake?' she asked.

'Not long. Just taking in the view!' he said, smiling.

She raised a hand to smack him which he caught, and then he held her in a bear hug while he kissed her.

When he let her go she laughed and moved closer, so she lay against his shoulder.

'I didn't order breakfast last night. Shall I do it now?' Harry asked.

'No', she said in a small voice. 'Hold me tight.'

It was a late breakfast when it came at 10.30, but after a shower and getting dressing, the crisp, sunny weather begged for a walk, which they did for an hour and a half, bringing some colour to their cheeks.

A late lunch at 3 o'clock reminded them both that the weekend was running out of time, so reluctantly they packed, and left their little oasis at about 5pm.

1830hrs Factory Hounslow West London

Saif was logged in again by the man in the car; this time situated 150 yards past the factory, observation being maintained by the rear view and wing mirrors.
This time the 'caretaker' was Tariq, who was even less interested in what Saif
was doing than Atif.
Tariq watched TV, ate, slept, and let Saif out of the factory at about 0430hrs, this being noted again by the man in the car.

1900hrs Anna's apartment Southwark London

When Harry dropped Anna off at her apartment he noticed she was quite quiet, almost withdrawn, but she held him, it seemed, in an overlong tight embrace before she kissed him several times.
She then bade him goodnight in a slightly broken voice, leaving her hand on his arm until he turned away to go to his car.
Harry drove home, happy and content from the weekend, feeling that their relationship was proceeding well, despite its obvious complexity.
A man sitting in a car about 75 yards from Anna's flat logged the time of arrival , as he had logged the time of departure on Saturday.

XIII

Monday 6th March 2006

0800hrs Room C10 SIS(MI6) London

Harry called the Deputy's office, leaving a message asking for an early meeting, say 0915hrs, if convenient.

He had decided there was a part solution, and perhaps one that might draw action from the 'players' on the other team.

There was always a risk that things could go belly up, but that was probably a risk worth taking bearing in mind the current circumstances.

0915hrs Deputy's office SIS(MI6) London

'Good morning Harry, what do you want?'

'Your agreement that I can bring in Fayez Al-Hourani to one of our safe houses for questioning.

We need to draw them out, and if they think we have one of their key players they may make a mistake.'

The Deputy thought for a bit before replying.

'Yes Harry, I agree. BUT, he emphasised, 'Remember, this sort of thing sometimes turns round and bites you, so have a contingency plan in place, in case.'

'Well, as you know, I have my unconventional back up, so the actual pull op should be pretty fail safe. It's what happens afterwards is the unknown.'

'Keep me posted Harry, particularly if you get anything substantial from the questioning.'

'With assistance from the Met, I plan to bring him in tonight. I'll let him stew overnight in the safe house and question him tomorrow.

If there's anything interesting I'll get straight back to you.'

Agreement obtained, Harry went back to Room C10 to plan the evening 'arrest', and how best to handle it, with the least amount of fuss and disturbance at the hotel.

He called in Tom for an update on the Hounslow factory and heard about the two overnight visits by Saif over the weekend, and one very brief visit by Ahmed on the Friday evening, when Fayez was also there.

Conversation and argument picked up by ODM had been brief, part Arabic, part Urdu, and part English. Payment, amount, reduction, argument!

Harry explained to Tom that the cover used to pick up Fayez would be the UK Immigration Service.

Accompanied by a Met Police Officer he would take Fayez for questioning about some irregularity in his passport picked up at Heathrow.

Having provided the hotel address as his contact point whilst in the UK on the immigration form, it had been easy to trace him, hence the visit and request to return to Heathrow for questioning.

From the hotel it would be about half an hour to the safe house.

Tom then left to organise the details for the surveillance teams, involving both MI6 and MI5, and to brief those covering the Holiday Inn at Brentford Lock to be aware of the evening operation involving Fayez.

Harry called Alain and advised him what was happening. Additionally, he asked him to keep a very low profile, if he was shadowing!

1630hrs Holiday Inn Brentford Lock West London

With a Met Police Officer in tow, Harry walked into the hotel and went straight to Reception.

'I believe you have a Mr Fayez Al-Hourani staying in the hotel? Is he in his room?'

The receptionist referred to the guest register, confirming the name, room number and current occupation, looking slightly alarmed at him and the policeman.

Harry leant forward and said quietly, with a small smile on his face,

'A simple matter of an immigration irregularity, which will have to be cleared up at Heathrow. Should be no fuss and bother for the Hotel. It's our problem to sort out.'

He and the police officer went over to the lift and took it to the third floor.

They walked down the corridor to room 314 and tapped on the door.

Fayez opened the door, and appeared startled to see Harry and a policeman.

'Yes?' he enquired.

'Mr Fayez al-Hourani?'

'Yes, what is it?'

'UK Immigration Service. London Heathrow. There appears to be a problem with your passport, and therefore your Visit Visa. You provided this address so that is how we were able to trace you.

You will have to come with us to Heathrow to resolve this, as that was you point of entry. Hopefully it should not take long. We have a car waiting downstairs.'

'Can't this be done tomorrow morning, or some other time?'

'I'm afraid not Sir. These matters have to be dealt with as soon as they are notified, otherwise an Offenders Notice is issued, and you could, at that point, be liable to arrest, and any subsequent punishment that a sitting Justice of the Peace may decide.'

Fayez was not prepared to resist on the basis of what he had just heard, so collected his coat and went with Harry and the police officer downstairs to the waiting car.

As Harry passed Reception he waved to the receptionist and smiled, which she returned, pleased to see him and the police officer leaving the hotel premises.

He smiled to himself when he spotted Alain sitting reading a paper on the far side of the Reception area.

The car, a black BMW, with a uniformed police driver was sitting just outside the entrance, its engine running.

Fayez was shown into a rear seat, along with the police officer, while Harry sat next to the driver.

The car moved off and joined the rush hour traffic, its blue light flashing, but no siren. It turned onto the A4, the Great West Road, but turned East, away from the direction to Heathrow.

As Fayez was about to ask why, the police officer grasped his wrist, and he felt the short sharp pain of a needle entering his arm.

He started to remonstrate, but blacked out within seconds.

'He'll be out for about two hours' said the officer, as Fayez slumped back against the seat.

Now the car picked its way quickly through the traffic as it headed eastwards, before turning right down Redcliffe Gardens, then along the Embankment to cross Lambeth Bridge, down Lambeth Rd and Brook Drive, finally turning into West Square, and pulling up outside a house on its NW side.

West Square was dark so they had no problem in quickly bundling Fayez inside, taking him to a basement room that contained a table with a bottle of water sitting on it , a chair, a single bed with one blanket, a bucket, and no windows.

It was cool, not cold in the room, and he was laid on the bed and the blanket thrown over him.

They left him, but the light remained on, controlled by a switch outside the room.

About an hour later Fayez woke up with an aching head and in his half drugged state tried to open the door, which was locked.

He banged on the door and shouted, quickly realising that it was pointless as the room was obviously sound proofed.

He looked at his watch to see what time it was, only to realise it had been taken off him, so he had no idea how long he had been there.

He found the bright single bulb irritating but could do nothing about it. He was hungry, his stomach was looking for food; he was thirsty, aggravated by the drug injected into him. The water on the table went some way in alleviating that.

Fayez resigned himself to try and get some sleep. He had no idea of what to expect.

After about a quarter of an hour as he started to drop off to sleep, an ear splitting sound erupted, which woke him with a start.

He stood up and the sound ceased.

He tried to sleep again.

As he started to drop off, the sound erupted again.

He realised that sleep was impossible, so sat at the table with his head in his hands, until it slipped through them with fatigue, and the sound erupted again.

[Sleep deprivation is a well known tool prior to interrogation]

After how many hours he did not know, he snatched a short sleep before being woken by the light going off as the door banged open, then to be closed almost immediately, and the light coming on again.

He blinked under the glare and saw that a plate of meat and potatoes had been placed on the floor.

His hunger was gnawing at his stomach so he quickly bolted down the food and drank some water.

He felt desperately tired, and was fearful of what would happen next.

Fayez was not one of Nature's warriors; good at telling acolytes about their place in Paradise, and the strength that comes from being a Fighter for the Jihad.

For him, home comforts and money were the drivers, with a passionate defence of his own skin and little exposure to real danger.

He prayed, for his own safety, and getting out alive. Nothing else.

Suddenly the light went out. He could see and hear nothing. His heart was pounding. He could feel the sweat breaking out on his top lip and under his arms. He started to shiver with fright. He could not see the bucket in the pitch black. He wet himself.

Tuesday 7th March 2006

0830hrs SIS(MI6) Safe House West Square London SE

Suddenly the door crashed open and two highly concentrated beams of light blinded him.

He felt himself being picked up and put in the chair. He felt his damp trousers clinging to him as they taped his legs to the chair and his hands behind the back of the chair. His shoulder joints ached in this uncomfortable position. If he tried to ease the stress it created more pain. Up to now there had been silence.

One of the interrogators suddenly slapped his face. He recoiled and tried to lower his head. As he did so pain creased through his shoulders.

He was slapped again and he tried not to recoil which was difficult, but the pain in his shoulders was less.

A question came out of the dark.

'Name?'

'Fayez Al-Hourani.'

'Nationality?'

'Palestinian.'

'Reason for entry into the UK?'

His mind was racing.

UK Immigration Service? This was not what, he understood, was the usual benign, considerate, inclusive, non-intrusive style, he had been told about.

'Visiting commercial contacts.'

'A further hard slap was followed with the comment,

'Don't lie. We have had you under surveillance since you arrived in the UK.

What is happening in the factory in Hounslow, and what is you relationship with the two Pakistani owners?'

Fayez, the born survivor, had quickly realised he was being interrogated by people in a Security capacity with clearance to carry out specific levels of interrogation.

His animal cunning kicked in.

'If I am able to help you, can we trade information for my freedom? If not then I shall remain silent, no matter what you do to me.'

The last statement was a hollow boast. The last thing he could stand is personal pain. Under severe duress of that kind he would crack, and he knew it.

Another slap came out of the dark.

The two strong lights were making his eyes hurt when suddenly they went out and silence followed.

His nerves were on edge, wondering what was going to happen next.

Suddenly he felt his throat gripped strongly from behind, making him choke and gasp for air.

'You realise I could break your neck', a voice said quietly behind him.

Fayez tried to move his head, but all that happened was that the grip tightened, making it almost impossible to breathe.

His neck was suddenly released, allowing him to gasp and draw in air to his depleted lungs.

Water splashed across his face, the door opened and closed, and he was left in blackness.

About ten minutes later the light went on and the door opened.

Harry entered quickly looking grave, followed by one of the policemen, now in civilian clothes.

'Release this man immediately. Take him next door for a shower and change of clothes. If I find that unnecessary force has been used on him I shall submit a full report to your superiors for disciplinary action.'

The officer, apparently unhappy with what had just been said, untied Fayez and led him quickly next door to a shower room which also had a selection of clothes hanging on hooks.

The officer stood looking at Fayez aggressively, as he showered and dressed
himself.

Fayez was led back to the interrogation room where Harry was sitting at the table and indicated he should sit down on the chair facing him.

Harry dismissed the officer with a wave and an instruction to wait outside the closed door.

Turning to Fayez, he said,

'My apologies, some of these officers watch too much television and allow their enthusiasm to take over.'

Fayez said nothing. Relieved that, apparently, a civilised approach was replacing physical punishment.

'However, what is clear from our intelligence and surveillance teams is that you and the Pakistanis are actively involved in what could be described as a terrorist attack on this country.

Now, as a result of my intervention, you have been saved from some fairly strong treatment being handed out by some of our Security people.

What I want you to understand is that I detest you myopic, cowardly, supposedly truly devout Islamists, involved in a world Jihad, with a passion equal to yours, and if I do not get the answers I want to my questions, then I will be quite happy to hand you back to my enthusiastic colleagues.

Do I make myself clear, and do you understand what I have just said?'

Fayez nodded, his mind racing as to how he was going to respond.

'Frankly you bastards make me sick. If you got your pathetic little 13th Century minds in gear you'd understand what stupid blind adherence without question can do, in causing indiscriminate suffering to so many people.

Now, I'm going to start asking you questions and I want some true answers. Don't lie to me. I can smell a liar at 20 paces, so don't go there. Plus, I cannot be bought and neither can my colleagues. So don't even think about that as a way out.'

Harry started his questioning by hinting that he was aware of some of Fayez's activities in the Gulf and queried what had been the thinking behind those operations. Then what was the connection that had brought Fayez to the UK?

What Harry was not aware of was Fayez's connection from the very outset with Buncefield.

Fayez thought his only hope was to drag out the questioning for as long as possible, so he answered by giving only very small pieces of information, and trying to indicate that he was a comparatively small cog in the machine.

Initially Harry accepted the stalling tactics, as he knew this was quite normal, before either fear, or cooperation kicked in.

Suddenly he threw in a direct question.

'Do you report to Ahmed Al Marri? Is he the top man?'

Fayez, tired, and now with slow physical and mental reflexes, reacted,

'No, he reports to me, although he is a leader in our operation.'

'So you are the money man?'

No reply.

'I can assume by no reply that you are.'

'Is he a true Jihadist?'

This time there was a reply.

'Yes.'

Harry abruptly got up from the table.

'I need better answers than what I have been given.

Think on; if not, your life will be very uncomfortable again.'

He left and the door clanged shut and almost immediately the light went out.

Fayez had no idea what time it was, Harry had not been wearing a watch, so feeling his way across the room he climbed onto the bed and pulled the blanket over him.

About two minutes later the light came on as the door slammed open and a plate was pushed in on the floor. The door closed and the light went out.

Fayez got down on his knees, and crawled across the floor in the direction of the door, feeling for the plate of food.

He was almost there when the light came on, the door opened, the plate was snatched away and the door slammed shut as the light went out again.

The interrogation team were able to monitor what Fayez was doing by their infrared pinhole cameras installed at the junction of ceiling and wall of the holding room.

[Such techniques were used by North Korean and North Vietnamese forces on POWs, and have been used in UK Special Forces training in the past.]

1200hrs

Harry returned to Vauxhall Cross and caught up with the latest reports on the factory surveillance which was not revealing anything new.

1600hrs

Harry returned to West Square and started the process
with Fayez again.

In Harry's absence sleep deprivation had been maintained
with noise, lights on/off, and intimation of harsh
treatment if he did not cooperate fully in the near future.

Fayez had tried to think during this time, and he had
decided that if he was to have any chance of freedom he
would have to provide information that would preferably
incriminate others, and show him to be of no real worth
in the organisation.

Regrettable though it was, Ahmed Al-Marri would be that
person, and the Pakistanis as secondary bait.

Slowly, under further questioning by Harry, Fayez started
to draw a picture that clearly implicated Ahmed Al-Marri
as the centre of the wheel, guiding and instructing his
followers and 'soldiers' in their Jihad.

Fayez focussed on the activities in the Gulf, slowly drip
feeding information that built a solid framework around
the two incidents, Das Island, and the North Dome Gas
Field.

In his description, Ahmed was the link between fund
providers for the operations and 'soldiers', the decision
maker as to targets, the leader who would manage the
operations and who sat on the Committee on an ad hoc
basis.

His story telling was credible, but Harry knew from
previous Gulf and Mossad Intel that it was not
completely true, profiles fitted, but were not necessarily
assigned to the right players.

However, further information was being made available,
so useful analysis would arise from that.

1800hrs Factory Hounslow West London

Tariq had called Fayez on his mobile to arrange a
meeting as soon as possible in order to resolve their

outstanding issues, but had not made a connection as the phone switched to answer mode.

He tried again at half hourly intervals until 2200hrs, without success, and then decided to leave it until the following day, Wednesday.

He found the lack of response irritating, and wondered if any problem had arisen.

Wednesday 8th March 2006 1030hrs Factory Hounslow West London

Tariq had telephoned Fayez several times on his mobile without success so telephoned the Holiday Inn and asked to be put through to his room.

He had been told to use the mobile at all times, only ringing the hotel direct in an emergency. Tariq considered this an emergency.

Reception advised him that Fayez had left with the UK Immigration Service on Monday afternoon and had not returned. They understood that there was a query with Fayez's Visit Visa.

Meanwhile they had put his clothes and belongings in safe storage.

Tariq immediately phoned Ahmed and told him what had happened. Ahmed said he would be at the factory by midday.

Ahmed put down his mobile and thought about what he had just been told.

He telephoned Fayez's mobile to hear what Tariq had experienced about a dozen times.

He then rang the Holiday Inn and was given identical information to that which Tariq had given him.

He took a taxi to the factory and joined Atif and Tariq in their office.

1215hrs Factory Hounslow West London

Tariq was concerned, bordering on suspicious, as to Fayez's whereabouts.

He was thinking that perhaps Fayez had done a runner, and that they would be unlikely to receive any, or all of their costs and amounts due to date.

Ahmed was thinking a little differently.

What if the Immigration Service had been a front in order to pull in Fayez?

What if the UK Security Services had picked up enough information for them to pull in one of the major organisers?

How this had come about he did not know, but if they had pulled in Fayez then it was fairly certain they would have the factory under surveillance as well.

Ahmed spoke,

'I am assuming that the Immigration Service detainment is false, and is a cover.

I can only assume that Fayez is now being interrogated and we have no idea to what level. We do not know what information he has already given; therefore we must make certain decisions.

Tariq, contact Tahir and Saif.

Get the package away from here this evening. Take it somewhere where it can be stored and well hidden.

Saif, go outside and see if you can see anything or anybody that might indicate we are being watched. Parked car or van with driver. That sort of thing.

If you see something, do nothing, but come back and tell me.'

Saif left the office.

Tariq rang from his mobile and arranged for both Saif and Tahir to be at the factory no later than 1900hrs and for Tahir to have organised an appropriate vehicle.

The more Ahmed thought about the situation the more he became convinced that Fayez had been pulled in for interrogation. Fayez had made no contact with the Holiday Inn following his arrest. His clothes remained there and there had been a complete lack of any communication.

In that case, Ahmed thought, perhaps we need to act in a similar way.

That would depend if the factory was under surveillance; perversely he hoped it was.

At about 1730hrs Atif returned.

Ahmed told Tariq and Atif that they would stay the night at the factory to ensure the package got away safely and also to check on any possible surveillance operations directed at the factory. He hoped that by staying the night it may draw more attention from any surveillance team

Atif explained to Ahmed that he had walked around the local streets in a random manner looking for possible observers adjacent to, or not far from the factory.

He had spotted what he thought was a possible target and when approaching from a different direction noticed what could have been a handover between details.

A different car and driver had replaced the former, who had then left.

The new driver moved his position to one about 200yds the other side of the factory, which still provided a clear field of observation.

Ahmed asked Atif to run a further check at about 2200hrs to see if the same car was there or if it had been replaced.

At 1830hrs Saif, the physicist arrived, closely followed by Tahir driving a truck with covered sides.

With supervision, by both of them, the package was loaded successfully onto the truck and departed at about 1945hrs.

The departure of the truck was logged by the current observer located about 200yards away.

As they were all staying the night at the factory Tariq went out later to get some food.

At 2145hrs the observer in the car reported in that it appeared that several persons were staying at the factory and that subsequent details should be aware of this.

At 2215hrs Atif went for a discrete walk in the industrial estate, noticing the same parked car.

When he repeated the exercise at just gone midnight he saw that the detail and position had been changed.

He advised Ahmed of what he had seen on both occasions. Ahmed thought to himself that this might provide them with a suitable opportunity.

**

Thursday 9th March 2006

0615hrs Factory Hounslow West London

Tom was sitting in his car about 200 yards from the factory, pretending to read a newspaper.

He was tired and looking forward to handing over to his replacement at about 0800hrs, when there was tap on his passenger door window.

He turned and his stomach sank, although his face merely registered enquiry.

Tom wound down his window to be confronted by Ahmed's face, a few inches from his own.

Ahmed spoke quietly,

'Get out of the car, slowly, and walk with me back to the Ford car 50 yards behind you.

Do not make any sudden move otherwise you will be shot. My silenced automatic is pointing at you right now the other side of your door. Do you understand?'

Tom tried to bluff,

'But, I am just sitting here........................!

'For the last time do you understand?'

The look on Ahmed's face convinced Tom to nod his head in agreement.

He exited his car and walked slowly back to the Ford with Ahmed a half step behind him.

Ahmed nodded for him to get in the back where one of the seats was already occupied.

Tom got in, where his mouth and arms were immediately taped, and he was pushed down towards the floor where he could not be seen from outside.

The Ford drove off normally, and exited the industrial estate towards London.

Ahmed, sitting in the front, leant over and said quietly,

'You and others have been watching the factory recently, probably over the last two weeks. You are obviously working for a Government Department, but that is not my main interest. I will tell you when we reach our destination.'

With that he turned to the front and said nothing for the remainder of the journey.

Eventually the car pulled up in a quiet, poor street, just off the Pentonville Road, near Kings Cross Station.

Tom was bundled inside and taken into a darkened room at the back.

There he was tied to a wooden chair, the tape still covering his mouth.

He winced in pain, as Ahmed slapped him, hard, across his face.

Ahmed spoke quietly, but with menace,

Let's be quite clear. I know you are a member of one of the UK's security services. Which one doesn't interest me.

I could kill you now, and it would not bother me. Your body would be dumped in one of the canals near here, and nobody would find you.

However, I am going to use you as a trade.

A man called Fayez AL-Hourani has been detained and arrested, and I want him released to me.

You will be that exchange.

My contact on your side is a man who pretends to be part of the Ministry of Defence, but he is also in a Security Service.

That man is Harry Baxter, who I shall call, when I am ready to negotiate an exchange.

Meanwhile, do not try to escape; you will be fed and given water, and if I do not achieve a satisfactory arrangement with Mr Baxter, you will be killed. Do you understand?'

Tom nodded, his mind racing, wondering what, if anything, he could do.

The two men assisting Ahmed had watched sullenly whilst he was speaking.

One now walked over and spat mucus straight into Tom's face, sneering at him as it dribbled slowly down his chin onto his jacket.

The other kicked both of Tom's shins, very hard, bringing tears to his eyes, as he fought to stifle a cry.

Ahmed turned, and left the room with one of the men, the other remaining and taking a chair and newspaper to the far side where he could observe Tom from about 12 feet.

0930hrs Room C10 SIS(MI6) London

Harry ran into his office to be confronted by a very worried Jane. She had called Harry on his mobile advising potential Priority 1 alert.

'What's up Jane?'

'Tom. He was on surveillance duty in Hounslow, and was supposed to hand over to his replacement at 0800hrs.

When the replacement arrived, no Tom, but car still there. No contact by mobile.

Trying to get a fix through GCHQ, but nothing yet. If he's been taken then mobile may have been thrown away.'

Harry sat down, his mind racing.

'What happened at the factory last night?' he asked.

'Status reports say truck came and went about 1830/1930hrs, and people stayed at the factory overnight as far as we can tell.'

'Get somebody to Hounslow to find out if the owners are there. Perhaps we should pull them in for questioning. Chase up GCHQ on that fix. Stress its Priority 1.

I'm going up to brief the Deputy.'

Jane turned away to chase GCHQ and Harry went upstairs to the Deputy.

Harry walked into the Deputy's office unannounced, apologising as he did so,

'Sorry to barge in, but your PA said nobody was with you.'

'What is it Harry?'

'I was going to ask you for a meeting later today to discuss the interrogation of Fayez Al-Hourani, but an event has overtaken us. Tom Denman has disappeared, and we think he has been taken by the other side. We've given it a Priority 1 status.'

'What happened?'

Harry gave a brief explanation as to what he thought had happened, but had no hard evidence to back it up.

He speculated that the surveillance had been blown, Tom taken, and what might be the consequences.

If the other side quickly realised that Fayez had been detained, or knew that already, then they might well be in a tit-for-tat situation where a trade might be the only sensible resolution.

The Deputy replied that all efforts were to be made to get Tom back, safely.

'Negotiate for ever if you have to, but make sure he's brought back alive.

Some of these committed head cases have no compunction in slitting throats.'

Harry assured the Deputy that he and the various teams would do all they could to get Tom back safely.

He then hurried back to his office.

'Jane', he called, 'Any info back from GCHQ yet?'

Jane came into his office,

'Not as yet. They cannot even get a signal, let alone a possibility of co-ordinates. Our view is it's been thrown away.'

'Have we got someone going to the factory?'

'Yes, they're on their way. Any specific instructions?'

Yes. Tell them it's a Local Authority inspection to confirm owners and lessee details. If they are not there, check with somebody when they were last seen.

Plus any other information that might be considered relevant.'

Jane left to telephone guidance to the team on the ground, as Harry sat in his office, not wanting to contemplate the real downside of such situations.

He decided to go to the safe house and see if Fayez, perhaps under a little pressure, may have any knowledge of likely places where Tom could be taken.

1130hrs SIS(MI6) Safe House West Sq London SE.

Harry entered the safe house and queried the current status of Fayez, who was being continuously monitored with infra-red cameras.

He was told that Fayez was not in good shape, obviously having had no previous experience of this type of interrogation, nor, it would appear, any training in order to cope and withstand it.

The light was currently on in the 'interview' room and Fayez was lying exhausted on the bed as the door clanged open and Harry walked in.

'Get up. Sit at the table' he instructed.

Fayez half stumbled from the bed to the chair.

'You've given me some information, but most is worthless; however when I speak eventually to your people I will tell them you have been extremely helpful, and you and I know what that will mean, if you ever see them again.'

Fayez looked at Harry, his eyes red rimmed, the lines of fatigue etched in his face.

Although Harry had good reason to hate him, instead he found him pitiable, a worthless individual driven by money, trying to ride on the back of a so-called religious, fanaticism driven, international terrorist group.

'Where are your brothers at the factory living?'

'I don't know'.

'You're lying. Because we know.'

'I'm not', he replied wearily.

'Where is your other colleague staying?'

'Which one?'

'The one, I think, is called Ahmed.'

Fayez reacted, but slowly.

'He came to the UK like me, and is staying in a hotel in London.'

'Why didn't he stay in your hotel?'

'I don't know.'

'Where else would he stay in London, if not in a hotel?'

'I don't know.'

'Fayez, unless I start getting some answers I will allow my colleagues to start the treatment again. And you won't like that.'

Fayez looked at him fearfully and replied dully

'I do not know the answers to your questions, and the treatment won't change that.'

Harry looked at him, suddenly banging his fist on the table that startled Fayez, rising and leaving the room. The door then clanged shut and the light went out.

Harry returned to Vauxhall Cross to find that Jane had distributed details of Tom to MI5 and the Metropolitan Police as someone who had been abducted.

The instructions accompanying the details said that contact should be made to (Telephone number) in the event of a sighting.

With such a standoff and impasse it is usually the case that progress can only be made if contact is made from one side or the other.

In such operations publicity is a nightmare, as speculation and conjecture can often take over, being driven by the insatiable, rolling, 24hour news bulletins.

Events can then take on a murky, ill defined hue, with commentary often falling into the 'why ruin a good story with the facts' category, by enthusiastic, but often ill informed commentators.

Harry, aware that events were in the initial phase, thought that something must break from somewhere within 24-36 hrs and discussed what he had done to date with the Deputy late that afternoon.

There was natural heartfelt concern for Tom, but he was a well trained officer, and would be able to withstand considerable punishment, both mental and physical over a sustained period of time.

Friday 10th March 2006

0915hrs House Nr Pentonville Rd London N1

Ahmed punched Tom again. Hard.

Tom coughed, his head dropping towards his chest.

Ahmed was trying to find out which Service Tom was a member of, and whether this had any connection with a Mr Baxter.

He was being careful in the punishment he was handing out to Tom, confining it to the body and feet, so if Tom was eventually released, there would be no signs of facial beating.

Tom was pleading ignorance of any knowledge of any Security Service, and was sticking to the line that he was a member of the Immigration Service involved in their ongoing operation against the employment and trade of illegal immigrants.

Because of the high concentration of ethnic minorities in this part of London, it tended to act as a magnet, or clearing centre for such illegals.

He could not understand why he had been detained in this way and was switching between indignation and partial crying to indicate his anger and confused fear.

Ahmed half believed his story, until in an exchange immediately following some sole beating, Tom let slip that he didn't know 'Harry'.

Ahmed hit him again across the soles of his feet as he said,

'How do you know his name is Harry? I've only referred to him as Mr Baxter, you lying pig!'

With the connection established, Ahmed left Tom to further treatment from the two other thugs, who quickly tired as Tom slid into semi-unconsciousness.

They revived him with throwing filthy water into his face from a bucket.

He came to, but pretended to be punch drunk and only semi-coherent in his speech.

He did not know what to do other than try and survive.

1500hrs Room C10 SIS(MI6) London

Harry was stumped. No reports from the Met as to any sightings.

The team investigating the factory had drawn a blank.

The two owners were not there, and the engineering staff had heard nothing.

The team then followed up at the known addresses of Tariq and Atif. Again nobody there. A bulletin was issued with photos and description to the police.

Harry saw the Deputy at about 1700hrs and said,

'I just hope the other side contacts us, because we're in a waiting game now.

Until we get some sort of a lead we have nothing to go on at all.

All I have is Ahmed's mobile phone, and that is switched off, therefore no identification and no coordinates.

Tomorrow being Saturday I shall put myself on duty in case there is any contact whatsoever. We need something, quickly.'

The Deputy asked to be kept in the loop on a regular basis, and commiserated with Harry, endorsing his concern for Tom.

2000hrs Harry's apartment Clapham London SW

Harry had bought a takeaway at the Chinese and sat eating it mechanically with no appreciation of taste, his mind flitting back and forth over recent events, and Tom's current predicament.

He watched the news on television and went to bed at about 2300hrs, sleeping fitfully, until about 0630hrs the following morning.

Saturday 11th March 2006 0800hrs Harry's apartment Clapham

His mobile rang on the table next to the sofa, and Harry reached across to answer it.

It was Ahmed.

'Good morning Harry.'

'Yes Ahmed.'

'I think you and I are past playing games, so I will be brief. I have a good idea of your activities, and you probably mine.

However, I think you are holding one of my colleagues, for what reason I do not know.

Coincidentally, I am holding one of your colleagues, who has been spying on me, once again for what reason I do not know.

Let me be clear Harry.

I think you and I should exchange our respective colleagues as soon as possible, certainly for your man's safety.'

'Any threats Ahmed, and you can forget a trade. Plus, if I find my man has been injured in any way, I will personally ensure that ultimately you will suffer a similar fate. Is that clear?

You should also understand that that your man has been singing to us for the last 24 hours, with significant amounts of vital information as to what you have planned, and what you are trying to do.

I would imagine that as a result of that you will want to question him closely yourself.

Now if you want to trade, where and when?'

'We understand each other Harry. That is good.

Time; 5.00/5.15am, tomorrow morning.

Place; Whitehall, going south from Trafalgar Square, just between Whitehall Place and Horseguards Avenue. My vehicle will be a Toyota Land Cruiser.

Yours will be?'

'Don't be completely stupid Ahmed. Whitehall, for an exchange?'

'Not at all Harry. Would you try and play tricks with me right in the middle of Whitehall? I don't think so.
Your car will be?
'A Volvo estate.'
See you tomorrow morning.'
Click and the phone went dead.
Harry's mind was racing.
He telephoned the Duty Officer to advise GCHQ that Ahmed's mobile was now on and to try and establish coordinates.
Should he call the Deputy for guidance or approval for laying on SO19 detachments?   Put them on Standby anyway.
He showered and dressed quickly, before calling Alain Dubois.
Harry had decided that with someone like Ahmed one should provide for the unexpected. So a discussion with Alain would be a good idea to formulate something from their side.
The Duty Officer then called back to say that Ahmed's mobile was off, so no trace was possible.

1100hrs High Street Kensington London

Alain was already seated at the back when Harry walked in Caffé Concerto.
They ordered coffee and croissant and conducted their conversation in a low tone.
Harry explained what had happened over the last two days and where the projected exchange would be taking place.
Alain listened attentively, then said,
'My friend, this Ahmed is a slippery fish. Do not assume for one minute that he will play straight with you. He will wriggle and try to get an advantage. What car will you be driving?'
Harry explained it would be a Volvo estate, one from the car pool that he normally drove.

Alain suggested he could provide Harry with a surprise back up, but he and one of his engineers would need to be able to work on the car for about half an hour that evening.

Harry thought that would be no problem, and they arranged to meet at a garage behind Victoria at about 1800hrs.

Alain stressed to Harry that he would continue to be his 'shadow' and would be there, in the background, on Sunday morning. He would have Harry on visual at all times, and would provide back up, at his discretion, at any time.

Harry smiled to himself, thinking that DGSE operatives certainly had operational independence, both in decision making and actions.

Alain then explained, so that Harry was completely in the picture, that they had an excellent friendly source within Mossad that kept them in the loop in those areas of common interest.

Intel had been passed to them concerning Ahmed, so he was already known to them.

He smiled knowingly at this point, saying,

'Yes Harry, we also know of your close relationship with one of their embedded operatives, but,' adding hastily,

'We have not spied on you at all. That relationship is your private business.'

'I should bloody well hope not', replied Harry testily.

'I will see you at 1800hrs at the garage.'

1800hrs Mews Garage behind Victoria Station

Harry drove the Volvo into the garage where he was waved by an engineer to park towards the rear.

Alain greeted him and said,

'Let the engineers do their bit, we can sit in the office and wait, it shouldn't take more than half an hour.'

About 40 minutes later an engineer stuck his head round the office door and said the car was ready.

'Usual operation?' Alain queried.

'Absolutely. Boot button.'

The engineer left, leaving Alain to explain, to a slightly bemused and astonished Harry, what been done and how it worked.

'Jesus Christ,' Harry exclaimed when Alain finished, 'I can't see me using this, but I suppose it's good to know it's there if I need it.'

Harry left the garage and drove back to West Square.

He needed to have one last conversation with Fayez before he handed him over.

2100hrs SIS(MI6) Safe House West Square London SE.

Fayez was sitting in the dark when the light came on and Harry entered.

'Stand up,' Harry said.

Fayez stood, not knowing what would happen next.

'You are going to be exchanged tomorrow morning at about 5 for one of our men, seized by your organisation.

You should be aware and prepare yourself because your 'brothers' have been told by us that you have provided significant intelligence as to your operations and what is currently planned.

I want it to be clear to you and your 'brothers' that if any harm has come to our operative then we will pursue each and everyone of you to administer similar punishment, even assassination.

My feeling is that your 'brothers' are very unhappy with your conduct so you will have some significant explaining to do.'

We will leave at 0415hrs, until then, reflect in the dark.'

With that Harry turned on his heel and walked out of the room, the door clanging behind him, and the light being extinguished.

Fayez collapsed on the floor in a heap, his whole body trembling, his legs not having the strength to support him. Fear had taken over as he imagined the retribution that could follow from Ahmed, or the Committee.

This time he cried; then wet himself.

Sunday 12th March 2006 Whitehall. 0445hrs.

Harry drove the Volvo estate carefully down the Strand and turned into Whitehall as the traffic lights turned green.

He had spotted the Toyota Land Cruiser in his wing mirror as he had turned left, and slowed to let it catch up as they drove down Whitehall.

There is a turning on the left hand side, Whitehall Place, about 50 yards before Horseguards Avenue where he saw the parked, unmarked, black Renault Laguna, facing towards Whitehall.

Suddenly the Land Cruiser accelerated past and slowed in front of him. He braked and stopped.

Ahmed climbed down from the Toyota, leaving his colleague Atif in the 4x4, and walked slowly back towards Harry, as he lowered his window.

Whitehall was very quiet at this time on a Sunday morning, so little curiosity had been aroused by the two car manoeuvre.

Ahmed smiled at him grimly, and said, 'Do you have the package?'

'Yes', said Harry, 'It's in the back under a blanket.'

Ahmed walked to the back of the car, opened the rear hatch, and lifted the corner of the blanket so he could see the look of panic in the trussed and gagged man's eyes. He glared at the man, uttered no sound, and came back to the window.

Harry spoke first.

'Now Ahmed, do you have my package?'

Yes, in the back.'

Harry walked over to the Land Cruiser and opened the back door to see Tom bound and gagged lying on the floor. Tom looked at him questioningly, whilst Harry risked a quick wink of encouragement.

Turning to Ahmed, Harry said, 'Release him.'

Ahmed leaned over and ripped the tape from Tom's mouth, then quickly undid the tapes binding Tom's wrists.

Tom clambered down and started to walk towards the Volvo as Harry spoke,

'You can take your package now.'

'Correct' said Ahmed, 'But change of plan Harry. We're taking the package and the car. Just in case people are looking for the Toyota.'

'What the hell…' Harry protested.

'Move over,' was the instruction, 'unless you………..'

The bulge in his coat pocket served as an incentive.

Harry got out slowly, and watched as Ahmed and Atif started to get into his vehicle.

'Harry, here are the keys of the Toyota, you won't have to walk,' Ahmed joked, as he tossed the keys to Harry.

Then Ahmed started the Volvo, and pulled gently away.

Harry watched the Volvo go down Whitehall and stop at the traffic lights at the bottom. As it waited for the red lights to turn green Harry dialled his mobile with the number Ahmed had given to him.

It was answered by Ahmed, as the lights changed green, and the Volvo turned left onto Westminster Bridge.

'Yes Harry.'

'After all of what has happened I just wanted to say good bye. Goodbye.'

As he said 'Goodbye', and *holding his spare Volvo electronic key fob close to his mobile*, he pressed the boot opening button.

A millisecond later the Volvo blew up in the middle of Westminster Bridge. The car and its occupants were spread over the bridge, and parts, both metal and human, landed in the Thames.

Harry tossed the Toyota keys onto the front seat of the Land Cruiser, closed the door, and walked up Whitehall towards Trafalgar Square.

He looked across to where the French registered Renault was parked in Horseguards Avenue and saw the headlights flash once before its engine started, and it pulled out into Whitehall.

He smiled grimly to himself as he thought of the reports that he and others would have to write and submit.

A few minutes later the quiet of a Sunday morning was broken for a second time; this time by the wail of police car sirens, descending on Westminster Bridge.

Note:

*[This explosive trigger is a modification/use of the remote keyless system contained in an electronic key fob.

If you lock your keys in the car and the spare keys are at home, call someone at home on their mobile from your mobile. Hold your mobile about a foot from your car door and have the person at your home press the unlock button, holding it near the mobile phone at their end. Your car will unlock.] *

1300hrs Near the RAC Club Pall Mall London

The Water Company lorry pulled up in the one way system of Pall Mall short of the RAC Club, and quickly put up barriers around their area of working.

Two engineers lifted the heavy rectangular manhole covers and placed them to one side, one immediately descending down the small step rungs set in the side of the wall.

A doorman from the club had seen the arrival of the team, and wandered out to enquire what was happening.

'What's up then mate?' he asked of the remaining engineer.

'Big leak on the main water delivery system. We've got to get some fairly large kit down there to sort it out.'

'Oh well, as long as it doesn't affect the club, that's OK then,' he joked.

'No risk of that we think, it's further East of you, so you should be alright.'

The doorman wandered away, now disinterested. He wondered what the story was on the explosion near the House of Commons early that morning.

No doubt the evening TV news would tell him. Things like that don't normally happen on a Sunday!

The two water engineers worked as quickly as they could. The self propelled crawler pig comprised several pieces and components, and which would be reassembled in the pipe.

The package to sit on the pig comprised two components to be coupled once underground. This was Saif's responsibility alone.

The third engineer was the crane operator. The truck had a small crane fitted on the rear deck for moving components from the bed onto, or into location for the engineers.

Transfer of the components was done quickly and effectively attracting no more that passing interest from pedestrians. There were few at this time; The Mall, leading to Buckingham Palace, is closed to vehicles on a Sunday, and is a magnet for walkers and tourists alike.

By 1530hrs the engineers had completed their work, packed up their lorry, and disappeared up St James's Street, turning left into Piccadilly, and making their way back to their depot in West London.

Not one foot policeman had passed down Pall Mall, in either direction, during their activity; the only occasion for concern was when a marked police car, with siren wailing, passed their operation without a glance, travelling in a westerly direction. Probably late for a tea break, or somebody was parking on Piccadilly, they joked between themselves.

XIV

Monday 13th March 2006 0900hrs -1700hrs Whitehall and No 10 Downing Street

Throughout the day Ministers came and went from their Ministries to Downing Street, all wearing the concerned, but gritty, pragmatic facial expression, when they know the world's media glare is upon them.

Some paused to make a cryptic comment to camera, or in response to a challenging question from a journalist.

However the standard line was, 'We've contained the threat, controls are in place, a full announcement will be made within 24 hours.'

It was obvious to all that a few heads would roll, lateral moves or demotions would follow. Such events often gave the PM and his closest colleagues the opportunity to repay a few scores, and elevate some junior Minsters who would be grateful for the promotion, and happy to toe the desired line for the foreseeable future. Or, certainly until their hubris and arrogance condemned them to a similar fate in time.

1000-1200hrs Room C10 SIS(MI6) London

Harry had spent this time debriefing Tom on his enforced detention by Ahmed, and the treatment he had experienced.

What came out was little in the way of new Intel; no attempt had been made to discover any information that Tom might be privy to, just some physical abuse, and the knowledge that he would be used as barter.

Tuesday 14th March 2006 1400hrs Ministers Office

That afternoon the Minister sat at his desk writing his resignation letter to the Prime Minister. He hadn't seen Anna that morning; she'd called in sick and said she might be back tomorrow. He smiled bitterly to himself; she would be very surprised he had resigned.

He had been called in by the Prime Minister on Monday afternoon and asked to 'step aside' in a Ministerial reshuffle. The recent events fell within his remit, and therefore he must carry responsibility.

The PM said that a fresh approach, and a younger face, was probably the answer, hence his request. There was no negotiation.

It was the usual letter; 'after having had the privilege of serving' etc, 'the time has come to spend more time with my family' etc, 'May I thank you, Prime Minister, for your constant support and encouragement'; the trite, lying phrases that litter every final letter from a Government Minister to the Prime Minister, only matched by the similar false sentiments contained in the reply.

He idly wondered what he would do with his time. Perhaps call in a few markers from those he had helped into public positions, collect two or three non-executive Directorships, yes, with those, his MP's salary, expenses and pension in due course, he would keep the wolf from the door.

He smiled, which suddenly drained from his face as a massive pain swept through his body. He clutched at his chest and felt himself losing consciousness. He tried to stand but fell, sliding partially under the desk. The last thing he saw was the red dispatch box standing near his chair as a red curtain fell over his eyes.

*

1315hrs London Heathrow Airport

At 1.15pm, London Heathrow, Terminal 1, strict security arrangements were being carried out on passengers for the El Al flight to Tel Aviv leaving at 2.20 pm.

The woman carrying her ticket and an Israeli passport stood patiently in the queue that was moving slowly forward as documents were checked.

She arrived in front of the El Al security man having already deposited her bag at the El Al check-in desk in the main departure hall.

He glanced at her ticket and passport.

'One way, Miss...Sayar, Miss Adina Sayar; you are not returning to London?'

'No I'm not planning to. I've spent many years working in London, but now I'm going home.'

'Family ties in Israel?'

'Yes, my family. My father Amnon Sayar died in the 6 Day War.'

'I'm very sorry to hear that. Have a good flight.'

He handed back her documents and she took the short walk into the departure lounge where they were already starting the pre-board announcements.

*

Office C10 SIS(MI6) London

At the same time, in office C10, Harry paused typing out his report and thought of Anna. He wondered how their relationship would progress or otherwise in the future. A lot of water had passed under the bridge since they had first met, but recent days together had made for some happy times.

No matter, he thought. Deal with it as it comes. No point in useless speculation.

He leant forward and continued typing his report. He would have to add a lot of verbal detail when discussing it with the Deputy.

*

Houses of Parliament Westmister London

At 1500hrs, Tuesday 14th March 2006, the Speaker called for the Prime Minister.

He stood up to a packed and muted House.

He cleared his throat, delaying his start for maximum theatrical effect.

'Yesterday, a great many of you will have seen and heard in the media details of the thwarted attack on Sunday on this House, which, if it had been successful, would have resulted in a major loss of life, both of the public and of members of this Chamber. Let me pay tribute to the members of the Security Services who have prevented a major terrorist assault on the heart of British democracy.

After months of observation and liaison work with our overseas partners the terrorist's plan was determined and the network infiltrated.

An attempt was made to penetrate the Palace of Westminster in broad daylight and thankfully, due to the quick-witted, trained response by CO19 of the Metropolitan Police, a major tragedy has been avoided. Regretfully, the vehicle exploded when hit, preventing us bringing the perpetrators to trial. At the same time two pedestrians were slightly injured, but I can report they are recovering well, and their injuries are not described as serious.

I ask this House to bear such facts in mind when considering the very necessary extensions to the current Terrorism Bill before Parliament, which I am sure will enable us to combat, more effectively, the very real threats that face us today.'

A general murmur of approval ran round the House as the Prime Minister sat down and the Leader of Her Majesty's Opposition rose to concur with the tribute and the proposal.

*

Over in Essex, at Buncefield, industry engineers and H & S inspectors were just starting to sift through the remains of the Oil Terminal to try and uncover what had caused the conflagration.

This would take months of investigation before cause and responsibility were determined. A slow laborious task faced them, with constant pressure from the media, Government departments, and insurance companies.

*

[Note: The Pall Mall sewer is part of the London water main system, extending from Pall Mall, down Whitehall, past the Palace of Westminster to link with piping running alongside the Thames.]

*

Below London, at a depth between 10 -15 feet, the self-propelled pig travelled slowly and silently along the pipe at about 50 yards per hour. It had been calculated that it should arrive close to the Houses of Parliament at about 1515hrs.

A Press Release, contained in a sealed envelope, sat on a junior editor's desk at the London Evening Standard.

The envelope had a large label on the front stating, 'Not to be opened until 1530hrs Tuesday the 14th March 2006'.

The 'dirty' bomb would cause considerable damage both physical, and by contamination. Public fear would be contagious.

Inside the slowly moving pig the timing device glowed in the dark.

0 hours, 6 minutes, 59 seconds...58...57...56...55...54...

END